LAVENDER AND BROWN - THE CASTLE HOWARD CHRISTMAS MYSTERIES

J.S. Neely

Copyright © 2023 J.S. Neely

This novel is entirely a work of fiction. The names, characters and incidents portrayed in it are the work of the author's imagination. Any resemblance to actual persons, living or dead, events or localities is entirely coincidental.

All rights reserved. No part of this book may be reproduced or used in any manner without written permission of the copyright owner.

Cover design by Ejp Covers

Paperback ISBN: 9798376235980
Hardback ISBN: ISBN: 9798396441705

Imprint: Independently published

For more information on the series, see the Lavender and Brown website: lavenderandbrown.com

Please rate and/or review on Amazon.

For those who hate parties.

*'Will all great Neptune's ocean wash this blood
Clean from my hand?'*
"Macbeth", Macbeth, Act 2, Scene 2.

> WILLIAM SHAKESPEARE

CHAPTER ONE

*Tuesday 11th
December 1888*

'None for you,' I said, sliding the plate of heavenly apple tarts further along my desk, away from the greedy grasp of Sydney's chubby fingers. 'I'm sorry, but...you need to go on a diet.' I shrugged my shoulders, disappointed that I was the one to have to tell him such devastating news. 'Facts are facts.'

'But...I'm not exactly fa–'

'Doesn't exactly look good, does it?' I remonstrated with my finger. 'With all the new clients and everything.' I picked up another of the perfect little tarts and popped it into my mouth, closing my eyes as the softness of the light fluffy pastry gave way to the tang of fresh apple and cream. 'Shame, as these are rather tasty,' I mumbled. 'Adam is a genius.'

'Wait, but–'

'Read the paper and pour me another tea. Make

yourself useful.'

'Me? But–'

'Tea!'

Sydney shook his head, muttering under his breath. A bad habit of his, but he poured the tea carefully through the strainer, for once not knocking the tea things about in a ramshackle manner. I licked the cream off my lips, trying to ignore Mrs Wilkins' attempts at ramming a rhinoceros through the ceiling. I had absolutely no idea why she thought this was a necessary requisite to cleaning up my room, but it was a conversation I would let go, for now.

The plate on my desk held three more of the tarts. They were fast becoming a cornerstone of my morning routine and a necessary complement to Mrs Wilkins' very slightly strong tea. It was a big help that Adam was now bringing them over in a sealed box too. This vastly reduced the risk of prying fingers.

'Are you going to read the paper any time today?' I said, unable to keep the frustration out of my voice.

'I'm pouring the tea,' Sydney whined.

'Well, hurry up, I want to see what they said.'

'You could always do it.'

'Too busy.'

He shot me that petulant look of his. 'Too lazy, you mean?'

'I'm thinking! Musing.'

'*Musing.*' Sydney shook his head.

I leaned back in my special new chair. An essential purchase. One that I had made thanks to the proceeds of our recent flood of new cases. My new chair allowed me to lean back effortlessly into a perfect musing position. Of course, I didn't replace Sydney's chair for three very strong reasons. One, it wouldn't be good for his diet. Two, it would encourage him to foster further bad habits. And three, excessive slouching wouldn't be a good look for Sydney and would quite put the new clients off.

I picked up my tea and sipped appreciatively. Then I gestured that Sydney should stop prevaricating and get on with the reading.

He gave me a stern look and then cleared his throat. '"*James Lavender Brown strikes again. The ingenious–*"'

'Still getting my name wrong.'

'I know.'

I'd sent the *York Herald* a frantic letter telling them not to mix my name up with Sydney's. Obviously, they'd not got around to dealing with my request, despite me labelling the letter as 'extremely urgent'.

I rolled my finger at him. 'Carry on then.'

'"*The ingenious detective, along with his team of sidekicks–*" that's charming that is.'

'Oh, do be quiet.' I took another nibble on a tart and washed it down with a sip of tea as Sydney continued:

'"*…have once again restored peace and order to*

the streets of York. Lady Huntington can now sleep easy in her be–'"

'It's hardly restoring peace and order, is it?'

Sydney lowered the paper. 'Are you going to let me finish?'

'Go on then. Get on with it!'

"'…sleep easy in her bed now that her ruby earrings have been recovered. This is the third case in December in which the magnificent James Lavender Brown and his team have wrestled with evil and–'"

'Wrestled with evil? Hardly.'

'Shush. *"…wrestled with evil and brought justice to the upper-class members of York society. The thirty-three-year ol–'"*

'I'm not thirty-bloody-three!' I slammed my fist down on my desk, which jerked the remaining tarts on the plate beside me. Sydney raised a mischievous eyebrow but continued:

"'…thirty-three-year old's detective agency can be found on High Petergate, York." There you go.' Sydney folded the paper over roughly and threw it on my desk.

'Thirty-three! I'm twenty-eight.' I stood up and sat back down again. This was something else I'd frantically scrawled in my important letter to the *Herald*. Sydney gulped his tea, eyes still on my tarts. I ignored his silent begging. 'Do you want to open the letters?'

'You mean, you want me to open the letters?' he said.

'That's very kind of you, Sydney.' I leaned back and stretched my hand towards the fire beside me. Newspaper articles aside, life was rather splendid. Short cases were bringing success and fame. Some of them even presented minor theoretical challenges. Nothing could go wrong from here.

'Oh. This one's for you. It's from the earl, George Howard,' Sydney said, having ripped open the first envelope.

'What does he want?'

'Why does he call you "Mr James"?'

'Oh, he's quite an old eccentric; perfectly harmless, mind. Does he want us to look into something? Has his favourite paintbrush gone missing or something?'

'No.' Sydney looked up from the letter but didn't elucidate.

'Go on then. What does he want?'

'It's an invite for Christmas. A party!'

'No chance.' A shiver ran through me at the horrific prospect of a party, especially one of the earl's making. I stood and warmed myself by the fire.

'Why not? I've not even read you the letter yet.' Sydney scratched at his yellow chequered trousers.

'Not a chance. The earl is tolerable when alone, but at a gathering...' I couldn't suppress a further shudder. 'What a nightmare. I told you about them, remember? Lord Talbot? More like

Lord Byron especially when it comes to cards. And then Mr Landley? Oh, Lord. He doesn't leave me alone and he doesn't stop talking about farming, not for one moment. And he's alway scratching…himself. And then the earl? He doesn't give you five bloody minutes of peace. He has you up and down, up and down. My God.' I turned my back on Sydney and felt a flicker of warmth from the fire.

'But it doesn't say who else will be there. He's inviting you and Rose, and it says "associates", so I wonder if me, Stella and Emma could go as well!'

'Not a chance in hell.'

'Why not? It sounds grand! The plan is to arrive on Christmas Eve. Enjoy a great Christmas feast. Return Boxing Day. All expenses paid. He says it's just a "little thank you."'

I spun around. 'Stay over? Are you *completely* insane? You go if you want. I'm not going.'

'Well, I can't go without you obviously, can I? You're the one who's invited. Sounds marvellous. I'm sure my Stella and Emma would love it.'

'No. Read the next letter.'

'But–'

'No.'

Sydney slapped the letter down on my desk and scooped up the next one. He took out his great temper upon the poor envelope, ripping it open like an angry child. 'It's from some acting manager of a hotel in Leeds.'

'I'm not going to Leeds.'

'What? Why not?'

'It's a dirty, miserable place. I've told you that before.'

'But…I've not even read you the letter yet.'

'Next.'

The outside door swung open which brought in a terrible, bitter draught. It was Mr Walrus, our new part-time driver. He called in every morning, with his silly moustache, to let in the cold.

'Do you need me today?' he asked.

'No. Close the door. Goodbye.'

He narrowed his eyes at me.

'No, thank you, Bob,' Sydney said, craning around in his chair. 'We won't be needing you today. Thank you.'

'Right.' He gave one last glare and then shut the door in his own time, finally removing himself and his moustache.

'It's bloody freezing,' I said. 'Chuck another coal on, will you?'

'Why don't you? You're standing next to the coal bucket!'

'I've never met anyone as idle as you, Sydney.'

'You're stood next to it!'

'Yes, but do you want me to dirty my fingers?'

He sat unmoved and then turned to look out of the window at the York Minster.

'Very well.' I tutted at him as I bent down and scooped up some coal from the bucket beside me and flicked it into the fire, watching the coals fall into the flames and the dustings of ash swirl into the air. 'Happy now that I'm probably going to die of coal dust contamination?'

'What? Why are you mean to Bob, anyway?'

'Who's Bob?'

'Bob. The driver.'

'Walrus? I don't like him. Of all the drivers you could have hired, you go and hire him.'

'What's wrong with Bob?'

'Got an attitude problem and he lets in the cold.' I motioned that Sydney should open the next letter.

'What about this hotel manager in Leeds? Says he's getting warning letters, says–'

'I'm not going to Leeds. I've told you. It's a dirty place. Next.'

Sydney opened another letter, and I shouted Mrs Wilkins down for more tea. I had to shout more than once as there were no signs of any immediate movement.

'It's from a Mr Harding about his daughter. He says she's getting expelled from school but she didn't steal–'

The door sprung open yet again. It was Constable Matthews. He stood in the doorway like a beanpole, and, as usual, he was out of breath. 'Mr Lavender…Sydney,' he barely managed.

'Come in and close the damn door. What do you want?' I said.

He stepped forward allowing the door to close behind him. I'd got rid of the bell above the door. It used to annoy the hell out of me. I'd endured it for half a year, and it only took Sydney five minutes to unscrew.

'A couple of things. Inspector Moss wants an urgent word with…one of you. Perhaps Sydney.'

'What did the inspector say, exactly?' I said because the constable wasn't fully telling the truth. His aura was a light shade of orange at the moment, an indication of a slight lie.

'Just that…he wanted a word…that Sydney would do.' He scratched at his ear.

'What did he say, exactly?'

'Well, that it was urgent. A missing person's case. That I should run round and fetch either of you, probably Sydney.'

'What did he say, *exactly*?'

'Well…'

'Go on, what did Moss say?' I pressed.

'Well, he said something like it was too early in the morning for bloody Lavender, er, sir, told me to get Sydney.'

Sydney found this amusing. I was about to offer a constructive comment but the damn door swung open yet again and almost hit the constable. It was Rose, our fully-fledged apprentice detective. She apologised to the constable as I quickly covered the tarts with the newspaper and stood up in front of my desk. If Rose saw the tarts she'd want one.

'Morning miserable. Morning Sydney.' She held the door. 'I'm just popping out to get a new hat. I'll be ten minutes.'

Sydney returned her greeting.

'Ten minutes? I doubt it,' I said.

'Oh, do be quiet. You know what I mean.' Her tone dropped ever so slightly. 'Did you, er, get the letter from the earl?'

Sydney leapt up from his chair behind me, and shuffled over to the hatstand. 'I'll go around with the constable and see what Inspector Moss wants.'

But my eyes were fixed firmly on Rose. 'We're not going.'

'I'm going to post the reply now. I bet you'd like to go, wouldn't you, Sydney?'

'Oh, yes. It looks grand!' Sydney replied, but he wasn't really looking at her, being too busy with his hat and coat.

'We're not going. Forget it,' I told them.

Rose shifted her smile to me, but this time it didn't reach her eyes. 'Yes, we are.'

'I'm not going on a two-day party, not for all the money in York, especially with that lot. I'd rather die first.'

The constable was about to leave with Sydney, but I stopped him. 'Before you go, constable, you said you had a couple of things. What was the other thing you wanted?'

'Oh, it's Sarah. Her sister's worried. Works in that big hotel in Leeds.'

Sarah was the constable's wife. God help her.

'No.' I shook my head and shooed the whole lot of them out of the door, reminding Rose not to post the letter upon pain of death. She shot me a funny look with those sharp green eyes of hers. It was a look I'd seen before. It's a look I imagine a tiger would give just before it's about to pounce. I shuddered at the thought, but I jerked out of my short trance, forgetting the tiger completely, suddenly aware of the presence of something much more sinister standing behind me. Mrs Wilkins.

'Why are you letting all the cold air in? It's freezing in here.'

'It's not me!' I protested.

'Don't take that tone with me. It's you standing there with the door open, nobody else. I can't see anybody else, can you?'

'Yes, but it–'

'Standing there, holding the door, letting all that draught in. It's cold upstairs, you know? That draught blows right up the stairs and...'

'Mrs Wilkins.'

'...goes right into my back. You would have thought you'd show someone my age more consideration, but no.'

She continued to ramble on as I carefully arched my way around her towards the fire.

'No consideration. No consideration at all. When you get to my age you...'

'On the subject of consideration, Mrs Wilkins.'

'…need to keep away from draughts, you…'

'A rhinoceros.'

'…can catch a chill…'

'Through the ceiling.'

'…and even die.'

'That would be terrible.'

She froze. 'Are you being funny again?'

'Wouldn't dream of it. Now, how about that tea?'

I sat down again and leaned back in my chair with a deep sigh. I'd have another tea and finish the remaining tarts with the paper. Then I'd turn my perpetual labours towards the rest of the letters. A bit of peace at last, aside from Mrs Wilkins. I wondered what Inspector Moss wanted. He hadn't called on us for a while, so it must be a serious missing person case. Someone very important. Royalty perhaps. I reached over and took up my paper. The apple tarts were gone.

CHAPTER TWO

'Do you like my new hat?'
I shot awake, rubbing at my eyes. I tried to sneakily dab a spot of drool from the corner of my mouth as Rose approached. Maybe I should put the damn bell back up? The green hat she was flashing at me looked exactly the same as the one she always wore, not that I ever took any notice of such trivial matters. Underneath it, her hair was a flow of silky red down to her shoulders. Her green eyes sparkled as usual, half out of mischief, half of their own natural accord.

'Yes, it's nice.'

I'd come to learn that when women asked such questions they weren't interested in a fair evaluative assessment of the new hat, the clothes, a pointless handbag – that's far too small to fit a book in, no – no, they were interested in receiving complimentary adjectives and positive affirmation. I wasn't going to be a party to it. Not at all.

'Nice? Is that it?' Rose took off her coat and hung it on the hatstand by the door, then joined me around the table, placing a hatbox beside her on the floor. '*Nice?*'

I'd also learnt that the quality of the adjectives counted, too. On this, I also wasn't prepared to budge. 'Nice' is a perfectly acceptable adjective. I wasn't going to usher-forth a descriptive narrative every time someone wore a new dress, combed their hair or put a new hat on their head. I'd meet the game halfway. They should be thankful for that.

'Yes, it's nice. Tell me you didn't post the letter?'

'Do you like the ribbons around the side?' She turned the hat around. I could still tell absolutely no difference whatsoever.

'Lovely. Tell me you didn't post the letter?'

She sighed and reached out for the teapot. 'Any tea left?'

'It'll be cold by now. I'll shout Mrs Wilkins down; she's still trying to ram a rhinoceros through the ceiling.'

'No need. I'll make it.' Rose reached for the tea things.

'Don't bother. I'll shout Mrs Wilkins down. That's what I pay her for.'

'Oh, James, don't be so selfish. I'll do it.'

'Selfish? Why is that selfish?'

'Making her run around after you.'

'That's what I pay her for!'

'She's not a slave, and she's old.'

'Completely irrelevant.' I shook my head, sighing. 'Did you post the bloody letter then, or what?'

But she didn't answer, gone as she had into the kitchen. I snatched up another letter and slid my nail down the edge carefully. It was from the *Herald*:

Dear Mr Brown,

Thank you for your letter dated 5 December.

Firstly, all of us here at the Herald *would like to offer our sincerest congratulations on your superb run of successful cases. As you know, we have always been keen supporters of your exploits.* (Well, that was not strictly true.)

In regards to your preferred nickname of 'James Lavender', dropping the 'Brown' (bloody nickname), *we feel somewhat that this would confuse our readership, and the editor has therefore decided to stick with your <u>actual</u> name.*

Furthermore, the editor perfectly understands your desire to appeal to a younger demographic (demographic?) *and to knock five years from your actual age. However, integrity and honesty are at the heart of everything we do here at the* Herald*, so we feel that we cannot 'bend the truth' for you* *in this matter. We will, however, endeavour not to mention your age in future articles, if this is somewhat of a sensitive issue.*

Sincerely yours,
Malcolm Wegwipe
(York Herald, *Journalist and Public Relations Correspondent.*)

'You've got to be bloody joking.' I threw the letter down in disgust.

'What are you complaining about now?' Rose shouted from the kitchen.

'Malcolm bloody Wegwipe and the *Herald*. Utter nonsense.'

Rose popped her head around the kitchen door. 'Who's Malcolm Wegwipe?'

'He's the Public Relations Correspondent for the *Herald*.'

'What's he want?'

'Nothing. It doesn't matter. Tell me you didn't post the letter back to the earl?'

'Tea's nearly ready.' She disappeared back into the kitchen.

Five minutes later, so not 'nearly ready', Rose came in with the tea. 'Here, lovely cup for you.'

I took the tea. It was a tad weak but better than waht Mrs Wilkins usually made. 'Well, tell me you didn't post the letter to the earl.'

'Thanks for the tea.'

'What?'

She sighed again, sitting down.

'What?' I repeated.

She shook her head.

I expect she wanted praise. I didn't understand this at all.

'You were making the tea for yourself, mine was just a by-product of that process, but... thank-you-for-the-tea, it's very *nice*. Did you post the letter?'

I could sense her tense, ready to stick her talons into me. 'Yes. Yes, I did.'

'And, what did you say?'

'I accepted, of course.' She turned away, then back as if ready for a fight.

'Wonderful, just wonderful.' I put my tea down and stood up by the fire, momentarily turning my back on her. 'I like my own space at Christmas. You know what the earl is like, you never get five minutes' rest. He'll have us bobbing up and down playing charades and God knows what, every other second. Not to mention the guests!'

'Well, it's not always about you, is it?'

I turned around to face her. 'I'm not saying it is. You can do what you like. Oh God, they'll be dancing, and the bloody Landleys, I just can't face them.'

'You don't know that the Landleys will be there, and if they are, they might not be sat with you. Why are you always so pessimistic?' She picked up her tea and took a big drink.

'I'm not pessimistic. I'm realistic. The Landleys will be there. They help run the estate, don't they? I'm not going. It will be a nightmare.'

She looked up at me. Her eyes seemed to soften, as did her tone. 'What about Stella and Emma? Wouldn't you think they'd like to go? It'll be a special Christmas for them.'

Sydney's wife and daughter. I picked up the poker and stabbed at the coals.

Rose continued:

'Think of poor Stella doing nothing but boiling Sydney's potatoes, watching them bob about in the pan for three hundred and odd days a year.'

'But Sydney *likes* potatoes.'

'I'm sure he does, but that doesn't make life exciting for Stella, does it?'

'No, but...' I poked at the fire some more, stabbing at the coals.

Rose remained quiet and then continued:

'And Emma – Emma who calls you her uncle – stitching dresses for hours on end, every day. Don't you think she deserves a treat? Just think how beautiful Castle Howard will be at Christmas, with a big tree all done up in lights. Just think how excited Emma would be. How Stella would feel. But no, they can't go because you might have to play charades. Well, that's fair, isn't it?'

'It's not as straightforward as that.'

'But it is!'

I put the poker back. 'Right, fine.'

'You mean, you'll go?' Rose came over to me, trying to touch my shoulder, but I turned away again.

'Yes, but I'm not happy about it.'

Rose placed her hand on my arm as the door came crashing through. Sydney.

'Not interrupting anything, am I?'

'Certainly not.' I snapped at him. 'What did Inspector Moss want?'

'Wants us to look into a missing person case urgently. Up at Sheriff Hutton.'

'*Sheriff Hutton*? What, right now?'

'Yes.' Sydney was still standing in the doorway, his cheeks red with the cold.

'But…we've sent the Walrus man away…and it's too short notice.'

'You sent him away, but Bob's waiting outside.' Sydney smiled. 'I fetched him back. The inspector says it's a mystery that's right up your street. A farm worker just disappeared, absolutely no trace of him.'

'A *farm* worker?'

'Yes.'

'Not royalty?'

'Royalty? No.'

'A farm worker?'

'Yes.'

Rose was playing about with her hat again with that damn sparkle back in her eyes. She turned to me. 'What's wrong? You weren't doing anything today, were you?'

Boaters. Cake. Papers.

'No, I…'

'Well, then.' She smiled and turned to Sydney. 'Sydney, what do you think of my new hat?'

'It's lovely. Absolutely grand. Love the ribbons.'

'Thank you, Sydney.' Rose turned to me. 'Go on then, James, off you go.'

'But…but, it's going to take about two hours to get to Sheriff Hutton.'

'Best be on your way, then,' she said.

'But…Sheriff Hutton… and a *farm* of all places.'

'Oh, I don't know. I'm sure it will be very… what's the word? *Nice*.'

CHAPTER THREE

'Details. Give me details. What did Moss say?' I said to Sydney, gesturing that he should shift his great carcass further along so that I had some space in the cab. I held my father's silver walking cane in one hand, the top of it resting against my knee. I'd asked Rose if she could handle things while we were gone. She said she was more than capable of handling things, which is exactly what I was worried about.

We were rolling along, having just turned onto Haxby Road, heading north to Sheriff Hutton. The great trees on either side had long since lost their leaves to the bleakness of winter.

'Go on then,' I urged Sydney, 'what did Moss say?'

'Not much. Moss said that Mr Swaledale had gone missing from a locked room, said that Mrs Wobble wa–'

'Wobble? What sort of name is that?' I was unable to hide a smirk, despite being annoyed at having to leave the house on such short notice.

'I know, Inspector Mos–'

'First, Malcolm Wegwipe, and now, Mrs Wobble.'

'Who's Malcolm Wegwipe?'

'Never mind, just get on with the story.'

'Well, Inspector Moss said that Mrs Wobble was…what are you laughing at?'

'Is that seriously her name? Mrs *Wobble*?'

Sydney joined in laughing too, and I ended up having to wipe the tears from my eyes. Sydney had to do likewise before he could continue:

'Anyway, like I was saying, Inspector Moss didn't give me any details, he just said that… she–'

'Mrs Wobble?'

'Mrs Wobble, yes, was in a terrible state because Mr Swalesdale's gone missing.'

'And he's a farm worker?'

'That's what Inspector Moss said.'

'He went missing from the farmhouse?'

'Well,' Sydney scratched his nose. 'He didn't say farmhouse, he said building.'

'Hmm.'

The journey into Sheriff Hutton was quite a tedious affair. I'd forgotten to take a book or paper, Sydney's fault, but somehow Walrus managed to get us there in under two hours. He pulled us close to the farmhouse property and then left us, as he went to tend to the horses at the nearby Castle Inn.

Sydney grasped the iron gate tightly, eyes bulging at the huge bull in the field beyond, held in only by a small, rickety wooden fence.

'What's the matter with you?' I said.

'I don't like bulls.'

'So, it might not like you. Get moving.'

Sydney hesitated, still behind the iron gate. 'I...I feel a bit sick-like – look at the size of his horns.'

'Sydney, it's freezing. Get your backside moving!'

'Keep your voice down. I don't like bulls. He's looking at me.'

'Well, yes, you're a big lump in yellow trousers. Of course he's looking at you. Go on, open the gate.'

He looked back at the bull and then at me. 'You go first.'

'For God's sake.' I sighed, pushing past Sydney. I swung the gate, which opened after a small protest and a squeak.

Sydney was still behind the gate, quivering. 'Be quiet, you'll scare him.'

'Scare him?'

'Yes, he might charge.'

'He doesn't look like he handles money.'

'What?'

'Never mind.'

I turned my back on him and pressed on down

the muddy path, towards the distant farmhouse, ignoring both the bull and Sydney. This was not my idea of how the day would have worked out. I had figured by this time, I would just be finishing my second portion of cake in Boaters, the papers fully read, winding down for the day after solving some little puzzle or other. Instead, I was trudging on a now-thinning path that was becoming increasingly precarious. I plodded further down with the help of my cane but stopped as I heard Sydney panting behind me.

'James, James, he's moving. He's coming!'

I turned around slowly. Sydney was ambling up the path, half-running, half-afraid to do so, his little legs striding forward unceremoniously. The bull was slowly moving at the side of the little fence, eyes on Sydney all the way.

'Oh yes, I think he likes you.'

'Don't say that. I'm scared.'

Sydney ran behind me, holding onto my shoulder, cowering.

I shrugged his hands away. 'Get off me. Get off, you daft fool!'

'Don't shout! He'll charge.'

'I've already told you, he has no monetary interest.'

'He's looking at me.'

'Oh, do be quiet.'

I continued striding down the muddy path with Sydney ambling sideways, unable to take his eyes off the bull, unable to keep from shrieking every time it calmly strolled forward in the field beyond.

I tapped on the farmhouse door with the end of my cane, disturbing some nearby chickens who clucked away around to the other side of the building. Sydney was still trying to hide behind me. I heard a dog yapping inside and the door opened. A thickset woman with a weather-beaten face and untidy brown hair opened the door. She had her sleeves rolled up and flour on her hands. Her arms were flabby yet muscular in an outdoorsy sort of way. She looked every part the farmer's wife.

'Mrs Wobble?' I asked, unable to keep the smirk off my face as I passed her my card.

'Can't read. Who's asking?' She turned her suspicious gaze from me to Sydney, who was still hovering behind me.

'We're private police consultants. We've been sent about…Mr Swaledale.'

At the mention of Mr Swaledale, her manner completely transformed, and she happily invited us inside. Sydney barged through the door and I followed after. A great sheepdog jumped up, barking wildly.

'Don't mind Killer. She's perfectly harmless.'

Dog owners always say that. I'm sure she was (even with such a colourful name), but I already had slaver on my hands and dog hairs on my trousers, and I'd not even sat down yet. Sydney fussed the dog, taking most of the damage, but he didn't seem to notice or mind; he just seemed extremely grateful to be inside out of harm's way.

'I'll put the kettle on,' Mrs Wobble said, waddling through into the kitchen. 'Take a seat.'

It was a large, stone-floored farmhouse, bare apart from a few old chairs scattered around the hearth and a few copper pots and pans on the walls. The fireplace glowed, not giving much warmth for a room of its size, but it was better than nothing. I sat on a threadbare chair, flicking the thick, white dog hairs from my trousers. The air hung with a strange mixture of freshly baked bread and wet dog.

Mrs Wobble bobbed her head around the door. 'I expect you'll be wanting cake.'

'Oh, yes please,' Sydney said.

I nodded suspiciously.

With the tea now before us and the dog shut safely away in the kitchen, I picked up the brown thing masquerading as cake. I had no idea what it was, but it was food, and I suddenly felt very hungry. I inspected it with some trepidation but took a bite, or tried to, as the damn thing was rock hard. I tried to bite at it again but to no avail. I took a large gulp of the ink-like tea and cradled it in my mouth, trying to use the heat to melt the rock.

'Very nice cake,' Sydney said, already halfway through his.

Mrs Wobble smiled at him. 'That's my very

own Albert Cake. Glad you like it.'

Albert Cake? What the hell was Albert Cake?

The tea started to do its job of dissolving the rock, and some of it broke away in my mouth. It tasted like ginger without the ginger, just a sort of fusty reminiscence of what could have been ginger a very long time ago. It was the equivalent of what tea tastes like if you use the same leaves, over and over again. This investigation had better be worth it.

'So, Mrs Wobble,' Sydney began, 'tell us what happened to Mr Swaledale.'

'It's terrible business. He's just gone, vanished into thin air.'

'Nobody just vanishes into thin air or otherwise,' I said. 'Tell us what happened, exactly.'

'Well, after I locked him in his room for the nig–'

'You locked him in his room?'

What sort of place had we come to?

Mrs Wobble remained undaunted. 'Why, yes, so he can get on with his business.'

I looked at Sydney, who shook his head.

'You lock your workers in a room?' I said.

'Why, yes.' She took a mouthful of tea. 'What's wrong with that? It's normal practice around here.'

Oh, dear lord, where had we come to? But then I'd suddenly got a terrible, terrible feeling that I knew what was going on, and if I was right,

Inspector Moss was for it. Some sort of joke. I held my head in my hand and let Sydney take over.

'What room did you lock him in?' Sydney asked, not a hint of suspicion in his voice.

'Why, in the barn, where else? Mr Wobble will be turning in his grave at what's happened. He's just vanished, like the others.'

Sydney got out a pen and paper. 'So, that was last night, I take it?'

'Yes.'

'Doesn't Mr Swaledale have his own key? Can't he–'

'His own key? Of course not.'

Sydney paused, but then nodded and continued writing. 'So, he was gone this morning?'

'Yes, that's what I keep saying.' Mrs Wobble shook her head and placed her cup and saucer on the little table in front of her.

I sniffed loudly and they both looked at me. 'This Mr, er…Swaledale.'

'Yes?'

'Does he have four legs?'

Sydney dropped his pen on the floor and bent down to retrieve it. Mrs Wobble looked at me strangely. 'Why, of course he does. How many legs should he have?'

'This Mr Swaledale's a damn sheep, isn't he?'

'Why, of course he is. He's a prize ram at that.'

'We've come all this way for a sodding sheep.' I

shook my head at Sydney. He was in for it as well. 'Swaledale's a breed of sheep, isn't it?'

'Why, yes of course.'

'I don't bloody believe it.'

'I know. He's just vanished.'

I sighed, shaking my head and stood up from the chair by the fireplace. I glared at Sydney, who turned away.

'We might as well examine the barn now, while we're here,' Sydney said, putting his notebook away.

'Yes,' Mrs Wobble added. 'You don't want to have to come back again, do you?'

'Come back again? Come back again?' I shouted.

'No, you'd be wasting your time in that case then, wouldn't you?'

I sighed and counted to five.

We plodded on round to the barn, my new shoes covered in soft mud and filth, and God knows what else. Mrs Wobble commented that my shoes were not very practical for farming, and I told her in no uncertain terms that I was not a farmer.

'Is this the barn where he went missing?' Sydney asked.

I jumped in, still frustrated by the whole episode. 'No, Sydney, I imagine she's taking us to another barn, a completely unrelated barn, just for the fun of it. What do you think?'

He smiled. 'Dunno.'

'This is the barn, yes,' Mrs Wobble said. 'Course, I've let the sheep out now, but it was locked at night with this padlock.' She took it off the barn door and handed it to me.

I knew a bit about locks and I poked about with it, playing with it in my hands, testing the locking chamber. This was a very tough lock to pick. I didn't think I could pick it myself, without great difficulty at least. I handed it to Sydney and went into the barn, carefully watching where I was treading. I examined the perimeter first, inspecting the walls for any defects. For an old-looking barn, the walls were very sturdy, and I could see no attempts of a break-in at all or anything else out of the ordinary.

'Padlock's good.' Sydney handed it back to Mrs Wobble, who was standing in the barn entrance, her cheeks bright red.

I had already finished my examination of the barn. There were no footprints other than Mrs Wobble's. I'd observed her footprints during our fascinating footwear conversation. Her boots had an extra thick tread around the outside, but aside from those, there were no other prints or other clues in the barn. It was just a damn barn and it smelt like one too.

I turned to address Mrs Wobble, who had her hands in her pockets, appearing completely immune to the cold and the smell. 'And the...Mr Swaledale, was definitely in the barn?'

'Definitely. I locked him in there myself.'

'Where do you keep the key to the padlock?' I asked her.

'In the kitchen.'

'Where does the dog sleep?'

'What?'

'Where does the dog sleep?'

'Killer sleeps in the kitchen, why?'

'Is there a spare key for the padlock? Does a neighbour have one, for example?'

She shook her head. 'No spare key. I'm friendly with Mr Tucker, but I wouldn't give him a spare key.'

A sort of lie. Why would she lie about a spare key?

I pressed again. 'There's no spare key?'

'No, not that I know of.'

'Are you sure?'

'Well...' She looked briefly behind her up at the sky, as if the dark clouds circling above held the answer to life's great mystery of the padlock's spare key. She turned back my way. 'I suppose there might be one. I don't really know.'

I rubbed at my head in frustration. Today had definitely not gone as planned. I would never have expected, when I got up this morning, to be standing in a barn, my shoes covered in muck, talking to a Mrs Wobble about a missing sheep. I thought I was supposed to be coming up in the world. 'Is there a spare key or not?'

'There might be.'

Give me strength.

'Is there a spare key, or isn't there?' I looked over at Sydney, who shrugged but seemed to be preoccupied with something, probably looking out for the bull.

'Well, you see,' she began, 'this farm, like most of the ones around here, belongs to the estate, so there may be a spare key. I don't know.'

'The estate? What do you mean?'

'The estate – Castle Howard, of course.'

'Castle Howard?' Sydney said.

'Yes, so if there is a spare key, then the earl has it. George Howard.'

Thankfully, the bull had wandered off somewhere, so I was able to walk back unmolested for the most part, with Sydney striding beside me rather than tugging at my shoulder.

'So, what do you think? Bit of a mystery, isn't it?' His eyes were still scanning the field in search of the bull, but it remained nowhere to be seen.

'Yes, it's a bloody mystery alright.'

'How do you think the shee–'

'Forget the damn sheep.' I pulled at the squeaky gate. 'That's not the mystery.'

'What do you mean?'

We closed the gate behind us and walked over to the driver, who was waiting for us on the other side of the lane. 'The mystery is why we were sent out here in the first place.'

'Back home is it?' Mr Walrus asked, opening up the cab doors for us with a scowl.

'No, take us to Silver Street,' I said.

'Silver Street?'

'Yes. I want to speak to Inspector Moss. Right now.'

CHAPTER FOUR

'Good evening, Mr Lavender, you're looking even more miserable than usual,' Staff Sergeant Daniels said, from behind his little booth. 'I wouldn't have thought that was even possible.'

'Where's Inspector Moss?'

'He's in Baaarnsley.'

'What'?'

'Baaarnsley.'

'Have you gone quite mad?'

Sergeant Daniels tapped his pen on the desk. 'Well, I was perfectly sane until I saw you.'

'Where's Inspector Moss?'

'He's upstairs, where do you think he is?'

I shook my head and told Sydney to follow. I'd dismissed Walrus, telling him that we definitely wouldn't be needing him tomorrow. I planned on spending a good deal of the day in Boaters.

I strode into the station to undisguised sniggers. There was nothing new in that, the officers were a strange bunch, but the sniggers seemed louder today. I started up the stairs to Inspector Moss' office, but behind me, the huge one, who looked like a gorilla, shouted out:

'Hey, Lavender, did you get more than you baaargained for?'

I spun around. 'What are you talking about?'

His face was lined with his usual mischievous smirk. 'Hey, you've got a new chair, haven't you?'

'Yes, yes, I have – what of it?'

'I'm thinking of getting a new chair myself.'

'Oh, yes.'

I didn't want a new chair conversation with Sydney present.

'Yes,' continued Gorilla. 'I'm thinking of getting myself a new baaar stool.' He laughed and they all laughed along with him.

'Come on, Sydney, they've all gone quite mad.' I continued up the steps towards Inspector Moss' office.

The inspector had a strange look on his face. 'Oh, Mr Lavender just got back from Sheriff Hutton, I gather?'

'Don't "oh, Mr Lavender" me. Yes, I've got back. Bloody missing sheep? What's all that about? Some sort of joke?'

Sydney followed in behind me, looking like this was the last place he'd like to be other than a bull field, that is.

The inspector looked up at me, hands raised in submission looking happier than usual. 'No, not at all. If you'd take a seat, I'll explain.'

'Bloody missing sheep. You told the constable and Sydney it was a missing person case.'

He shook his head. 'I never said missing persons. I said that Mr Swaledale was missing. If the constable or Sydney, or you for that matter, got the wrong end of the stick then....' He shrugged. 'I'm sorry about that.'

'No, you're not.'

'Take a seat.' He looked up at me.

'I have better things to do than swanning around fields all day looking for sheep. I had plans for today.'

'We didn't have any plans for today, did we?' Sydney said, puzzled.

I cast him a stern look and he turned away, hands in his pockets.

'Look, Lavender, take a seat.' The inspector added a 'please' in a softer tone, which was highly unusual for him. In fact, I don't think I'd ever heard him say the word before, and certainly not to me.

I sighed deeply but sat down in one of the two chairs behind the desk. Sydney sat in the other.

'What we're looking at here, Lavender, is a larger series of strange incidents.' The inspector laid a map on the desk and smoothed it out with his hands. He pointed to a few areas, but I didn't look closely.

'What sort of incidents?' I said.

'Similar to what I imagine you saw today. Cases of missing livestock, all vanishing in strange circumstances. Not like your regular rustling. A racehorse goes missing from a stable, with no signs of any break-in at all; cows disappearing in the middle of the night; then a prize ram goes missing from a locked barn, and other unusual thefts. I mean how does a cow go missing in the middle of the night? A sheep from a locked barn? And all of these thefts have one thing in common too.'

I sat up slightly. 'What's that?'

'They're all connected, in some way, to the Castle Howard estate.'

'I admit, inspector, that the nature of these incidents is unusual and possess a certain theoretical challenge, which arouses my curiosity, but at the end of the day, they're just animals we're talking about. Livestock. I don't see why you're concerned.'

The inspector sighed slightly and his huge moustache bobbled in agitation. 'These are expensive animals we're talking about in many of the cases. Would it be any different to you if they were ruby earrings?' He raised his eyebrows at that, no doubt in reference to the article in the *Herald* this morning. 'Or do you only work for rich old ladies now?'

I shifted slightly in my seat. The inspector's chair was not comfortable at all. He probably hand-selected chairs for this very reason, choosing the most uncomfortable ones personally. 'I see what you mean, but still...'

I could sense his agitation creeping up a notch. 'I've enough on my plate dealing with issues closer to home, trying to keep the local crime rate under control. I just don't have the resources to be sending my constables out on day trips to farms to search for missing sheep.'

'But you just said they were valuable.'

'They are. But while my officers are dodging cowpats, or not dodging cowpats for that matter, people are getting robbed and beaten in the streets. And then there's these.' He picked up a pile of letters and slapped them down in the middle of the desk.

'What are those?' Sydney asked.

'Letters. What do they look like?' The inspector picked one up. 'This one from Mr Eastwell, what am I going to do about his missing racehorse, blah, blah, blah.' He turned it over, slamming it down, starting a new pile like a game of cards. 'This one from Mrs Brigstock, bloody cow's vanished into thin air – how can a cow vanish into thin air? I sent Constable Matthews – he came back clueless, treading cow shit all over the place.' He slammed it down on the new pile. 'This one from a concerned party, a Mr Landley–'

'Mr Landley!' I nearly fell out of my chair.

'Yes, do you know him?'

'Do I know him?'

'That's what I asked.'

I shuddered and took a deep breath. Mr

Landley was the most boring man on earth.

'His damn letter goes on and on and on. Six and a half pages of it. I had to read it five times just to follow it; my mind kept drifting off.'

'He has that effect,' I said.

He turned it over, slapping it down on the desk with the others, and picked up another. 'Mrs Wobble from today.' He slammed that one down. 'Another one from Mr Eastwell, threatening to go to the commissioner this time.' That one got slapped down the hardest of all, and he picked up another. 'Mr-bloody-Landley again, six pages this one – you want to read it – you have trouble sleeping?' he shouted, holding out the letter and shaking it violently. He slammed it back down and picked up another.

'I see the picture, inspector,' I said, holding my hands up before he broke his desk in two.

'They're obviously all connected, and if I could get all of this off my back, I'd be a happy man.'

I very much doubted that. Something always came along to agitate his great moustache. In this case, I expected it was the note threatening to contact the commissioner that had brought on the final wobble.

'Will you take the case, Lavender?' He was almost pleading with me now. 'It's right up your street, after all.'

I turned to Sydney, who shrugged. 'I suppose,' I said.

'Wonderful!' He stood up, shaking my hand

and Sydney's, though it was not as if he had done anything. 'You must start with Mr Eastwell first thing tomorrow. Let me fill you in on the details.' He moved the letters off the map, and I got out my notebook.

◆ ◆ ◆

Later, as we were walking back towards High Petergate under the glow of the gas lights, I asked Sydney what he thought.

He strode along thinking before answering. 'It's unusual, isn't it? I mean, how are they all going missing? It's not as if you can carry a cow off by yourself, is it?'

'That is very true, Sydney.'

He was on a roll now. 'Also, in my experience, thieves force their way into properties, yet, in all of these cases, it seems, there were no signs of forced entry.'

'Quite correct.'

We stumbled upon a street seller, by the York Minster. He was selling pies to tourists, not always the safest bet, but my stomach rumbled heavily. I turned to Sydney. 'Do you fancy a pie?'

A stupid question.

'Me? Yes, I'll have a pie.'

Of course, he would.

'What pies do you sell?' I asked the seller after he'd just finished serving a large pie to an equally large man. The pie seller was a funny-looking chap with a bent nose. Never trust a man with a bent nose.

'Meat,' he said.

'What sort of meat?'

'Just meat.'

'Yes, but what meat?' I asked.

'Meat's meat, isn't it?'

I rubbed at the bridge of my nose and muttered a 'Christ' under my breath. 'Yes, but what sort of meat – beef, pork, chicken, horse, dog?'

'Lovely pie crust, thick and crispy. Family recipe.'

'Never mind the crust. What's the meat?'

'The crust is made from my family's secret recipe, passed down through the generations.'

'That sounds good,' Sydney said.

I shook my head at Sydney and turned back to the man. 'Never mind the crust. What's the meat?'

'It's meat, fella. Take it or leave it.'

'Forget it then.' I turned and started to walk away.

Sydney pulled on my sleeve. 'Hey, what about the pie?'

I shrugged him off. 'Well, he doesn't know what's in it, does he? You just heard the man.'

'Yes, but…they smell nice and the crust…'

'Christ in a barrel.' I fished in my pocket for a few coins and bought one, and then we turned the corner towards home. I glanced at Sydney, his face immediately full of pie. 'Did you spot the odd thing with the letters?'

He mumbled something back, bits of unidentified meat dribbling down his chin. I think he said 'what odd thing?' as 'what dog thing?' didn't make sense, unless he was referring to the pie.

'Mrs Wobble.'

He shook his head.

There would be absolutely no chance of an intelligent conversation now that Sydney had got his face in a pie.

I paused, standing in the centre of the courtyard outside the minster. I wondered if he'd noticed or not. 'Mrs Wobble's letter.' I gestured to the bunch of letters which I now held in my hand.

'What about it?'

'Well,' I paused for effect. 'When we met her this morning, she said she couldn't read, but yet she sent the inspector a letter.'

Lights seemed to come on behind Sydney's eyes. He muttered, 'Oh, yes.'

'And also, if the theft only occurred this morning. Then how had the letter already arrived on the inspector's desk? Strange, don't you think?'

❖ ❖ ❖

Rose was sitting in my chair writing a letter

when I got in. I'd sent Sydney home.

'You've been gone a long time.'

'Yes, I bloody well have.' I relieved myself of my hat and coat and started taking off my still-muddy shoes. At least I hoped it was mud.

'Had fun?'

'Not exactly.' I succinctly explained the most relevant particulars, though she called it moaning.

'And you haven't eaten, apart from Mrs Wobble's Albert Cake?'

I shook my head, wondering when she was going to get out of my chair.

'Do you want me to fix you something?'

Mrs Wilkins would have gone home by now.

'If you wouldn't mind?'

She smiled and climbed out of my chair as I ambled over to it, crashing down, my tired body sinking with aching pleasure after the great exertions of the day.

She made her way into the kitchen. 'Anything, in particular, you'd fancy?'

'Anything, as long as it's not tripe.'

I was joking, of course. I don't allow tripe on the premises.

She smiled and I sank further into my wonderful chair, letting out a deep sigh as I did so, closing my eyes for a brief moment.

I handed her the letters as I sipped the tea she'd made and picked my way over the bread, cold beef and cheese. As ever, she was attentive to every detail, eager to get to grips with the new problems I'd presented.

'Wait, so this Mrs Wobble said she couldn't read, but there's a letter right here.' She picked it up and started to examine it more carefully.

I nodded, pleased that she'd picked up on this detail straightaway, just as I had, naturally. 'Absolutely. Odd, don't you think?'

'Yes.' She read it over. It didn't seem to contain anything out of the ordinary, it simply outlined the missing ram situation and requested the inspector's help. She put it back down and picked up one of the others. It was the one from Mr Eastwell. 'Sounds threatening.'

'Yes, the inspector seemed fairly keen I visit him pretty soon.' I reached for the ledger. 'I'll fit him in Friday.' I turned over the pages of the ledger which is where we keep details of all our ongoing cases. 'What's this?'

Rose blushed. 'What?'

'It says, "Friday-Saturday, Leeds, Grand Hotel".' I turned to Rose waving the ledger at her. 'What the hell's this?'

'You told me to take care of things, so I did. I've booked us in.'

'You did *what*?'

'I read over the letter he sent, replied and booked us in. We're free, I checked.'

'I don't want to go to Leeds.' I slammed shut the ledger. 'Bloody Leeds, overnight?'

'The manager's getting all sorts of threatening

notes, says he's worried, but the police won't take it seriously. He's heard your–'

'Overnight? Leeds, of all places.'

She dropped her voice. 'Look, Sarah passed on your details when her sister got in contact recently. She recommended you, and he's paying handsomely, and we get an overnight stay, all expenses paid, *and*,' she emphasised, 'it sounds interesting.'

'I don't bloody believe it. It's too short notice. You'll have to cancel it.'

I'd made my decision and that was final.

'We can't cancel it now. Here, let me read you the letter, while you eat your supper.'

I held my head in my hands, while Rose read out the letter:

'"Dear Mr Lavender, I can imagine that you're a very busy man, but I am writing to you as a last resort. I am the acting manager of the Grand Hotel in Leeds. I have been receiving threatening notes and letters regarding a forthcoming conference. I have contacted the local constabulary, but they're not interested at all and won't take it seriously, even though I'm very concerned. The letters are instructing me to cancel a psychics conference".'

'A psychics conference?'

'Yes.' Rose continued:

'"The conference takes place on the weekend of the Friday-Saturday, 14-15 of December. If it's cancelled then the hotel will lose a vast amount of money and the hotel's reputation will suffer in the process. I've been unable to contact the owner of the hotel, despite sending several letters. He's currently on the continent on holiday and"–'

'Holiday, at this time of the year?' I picked up a cube of cheese. You can always rely on cheese.

'I don't know. He doesn't say much more, just begs you to reply, which I've already done, on your behalf. He encloses one of the threatening notes.'

'Let me look.'

She handed me the note.

Mr Westford. Cancel the devil's conference. Psychics are in a pact with Satan. Take heed of my warning, otherwise there will be blood on your hands.

'Intriguing.'

'I'd thought you'd say that. Apparently, all the notes are pretty much the same. I expect that you're glad I booked it in now, aren't you?'

I didn't want to give her the satisfaction of an affirmative so I just shrugged. 'Well, I'll book in Mr Eastwell about this racehorse for Thursday then, and we'll have a rest day tomorrow – well, I've got some, er, personal matters to attend to.' I glanced at Rose to judge her reaction, but there was an odd expression on her face. 'What, now?'

'You'll have to cancel your afternoon in Boaters, tomorrow, I'm afraid.'

'What are you talking about? What the bloody hell, now?'

She smiled sweetly. 'Tomorrow, we're school inspectors!'

'What on God's green earth are you talking about? You won't find me within five miles of a bloody school.'

CHAPTER FIVE

'Anybody?'
Nothing.
'Come on, does anybody know anything about the theft?'
Still nothing.

I could see I was getting absolutely nowhere, but I had to say something.

I was standing at the front of the class in St Catherine's School for Girls, with fifty sets of eyes staring back at me. The girls were all aged ten to fourteen, though some looked younger. I didn't know what to say or do. 'So, then...' But I'd long since forgotten how to teach arithmetic, simple or otherwise, as their teacher had told me to do for five minutes. Rose was for it when we got out of this place.

The eyes continued to stare at me expectantly, some of them blinking, but most of them not. One of the students coughed, the noise of which reverberated around the whole room. I would rather face street muggers and murderers than this lot. I'd even rather be at a party. It was also painfully hot in the class. I adjusted my tie and strolled to take up a more central position at the front, all eyes still on me.

'Well, then...imagine there's a dead body swinging from a rope.'

There were a couple of loud gasps, but I continued:

'You're in a locked cell. You're a police investigator, called out to solve a mystery. It's the body of a young man. The rope is attached to a large hook on the ceiling. Now, I know what you're all thinking, all of the checks, which I'm sure you're all very familar with, have been carried out. It's a corpse we are dealing with here. Now, here's the thing.' I was feeling much more confident now, as I always was when dealing with concepts of a theoretical nature. 'There's nothing in the room, no stool upon which to stand. No tables. Nothing like that. There's a pool of water on the floor but nothing on the walls and the body is hanging high up on the rope. So, how did he hang himself?'

I was met with a few mumblings as some of the girls looked at each other and then back to me, then silence once again. I heard one wasp faced girl mumble that my exercise was 'silly', but I just rose above it and ignored her.

'Come on. Theorise. How did the body get on the rope?' I encouraged.

A blonde girl at the back of the room put her hand up.

'Yes, you.'

'Sir, are you sure he couldn't jump up into the noose?'

'Ah, interesting. Yes, we must question what we are told. If we are told the body is too high up, we must test the theory, eh? I like your thinking. We'll try that in a moment. It's not an easy thing to do as you can't jump up as far as you think you can. Any other theories?'

A very young girl with a gap-tooth, dark hair and glasses, shyly half-raised her hand at the front. She was probably the smallest in the room.

'Yes, you. What's your name?'

'Jane, sir.'

'Well, Jane, let's hear it. Don't be shy, it doesn't matter if you're wrong. The trick is to throw out ideas, yes?'

'Sir, do we know that he hanged himself? What if someone hung him on the rope on purpose? Murder!'

There were a few excited murmurs at that.

'Ah, good thinking, well done.' I was beginning to enjoy myself. 'A very intelligent question.' She smiled back at me. 'A curious mind, I see. So, you need to examine the body for tell-tale signs of a struggle. What are you looking for?' I asked her specifically.

'Maybe marks on the body, sir? Signs that they'd fought back.'

'Exactly.' I turned to face the rest of the class once again. 'So, what do you do? You fetch a stool, climb up and look at the hands first, always the hands. Remember that. Specifically the fingernails. So, after a careful examination of the dead person's hands, you find nothing – no bruising, no fabric under the fingernails, nothing. Conclusion, Jane?'

'The man has most likely hanged himself.'

'Precisely.' I turned to face the class once again. Someone else had their hand raised. 'Notice what Jane said there too, "most-likely". It's important to always keep an open mind. Just because there are no signs of a struggle, it doesn't mean that there wasn't one, though this would indeed be a rare circumstance. It still has to be a consideration.'

'They could have been drugged perhaps?' volunteered another girl at the side of the room.

'Correct. But for now, take it that they've committed suicide. Yes, you at the back. You've been waiting patiently. What's your theory?'

'Sir, is there a ledge on the wall which they could have jumped off?'

'No, there's nothing on the walls. Good try though. All the walls are perfectly flat.'

The girl at the back, who had first raised her hand, did so again.

'Yes?' I pointed.

'Sir, what about the window, did they jump from the window?'

'Ha, ha, the window. Rooms have windows, yes? Good try but no, the window is too far away to jump from. Besides, there's no ledge.'

I could see Jane at the front was thinking again, unsure whether or not she should contribute. I encouraged her to continue.

'Sir, you mentioned that there was water on the floor.'

'I did, go on.'

'I don't think you would mention that if it wasn't important. I think that's got something to do with it.'

'Ah, Jane, I can see you've got a sharp mind. Well spotted.'

She smiled back at me again, showing off the gap in her front teeth.

'Sir,' a girl a few places behind Jane shouted excitedly.

'Don't shout out, raise your hands, but go on.'

'Was the water high up, did they swim through it and now the water has gone?'

'Another very good idea. I can see this is not the dunce class, but no the water is very slight, and the walls are perfectly dry.'

The blonde girl at the back of the room, who had spoken first, did so again.

'Ah, you again. A third try. What's your name?'

'Claire, sir.'

'Go on, Claire.'

'Are you sure they didn't jump, sir? Maybe if they ran and jumped.'

'No, I've told you it's too high and you can't jump as far as you think. Shall we all give it a try?'

A few unsure nods greeted my words.

'Right, everyone on their feet. Come on.' I waved them up.

A few half-stood, but many seemed reluctant to do so. Jane at the front did and a few around her.

'Go on, stand up, behind your desk. Give yourself some space, if you can.'

'Please, sir,' one girl at the front said, 'but miss doesn't allow us to stand in class. We get shouted at if we stand during a lesson.'

'What? Good God! What is it, prison? Well, I'm in charge now, and I say you can stand. We all need to conduct the jumping experiment, don't we? We can't do that sitting down.'

She nodded, still unsure, but got to her feet, as did the others.

'Now, make space if you can. So, I want you to imagine there's a noose approximately three feet above your head, yes?'

They nodded, faces now eager.

'Now obviously, you should never, ever try this with a real rope, just use your imagination. What I want you to do is jump up, on the spot, to see how far you can jump. Go on. Shall I show you what I mean? Like this.' I jumped up on the spot as if heading a football. 'Now, you try as best you can. Give it a go.'

One or two started to jump and then the

others followed, and soon all fifty or so of them were jumping up and down on the spot, trying to loop their heads through an imaginary noose.

'There, that's it, well done. You can't jump as far as you thought, can you?'

They continued to jump, one or two of them trying to take a small run up to jump higher.

'That's it, be careful, but try to get as high as you can. It's not very high, is it?'

The door to my left flew open. Rose stood next to their usual class teacher, a stern-looking woman with dark glasses. She was open-mouthed and looked rather distressed. 'GIRLS!' she screamed, but they ignored her, or couldn't hear her.

'What in God's name is going on? I can hear it at the other end of the corridor.' This was the headmaster, appearing behind her, stunned into silence when he saw all girls jumping on the spot behind their desks, trying to hang themselves on an imaginary rope.

'Don't worry,' I told the teachers, 'we're conducting a theoretical experiment.'

'Good God,' he muttered.

'GIRLS!' the teacher shouted again, and the girls stopped jumping, one by one, looking disappointed and ashamed.

Rose shook her head, smiling.

'Never in my life have I seen such behaviour. I told you to do simple arithmetic with them, for five minutes. Fve minutes!' the teacher said to me, shaking her head.

'Look, I'm not good with all of that. We've been conducting a theoretical locked room sit–'

'It's not a zoo. It's a school,' she interrupted, rather rudely I thought.

'I know, you've got some very bright students here and–'

'It's not a zoo.'

'I know, you've already said that.'

'Mr Johnson. Mr Johnson,' the headmaster said.

I suddenly realised he was referring to me and the undercover name Rose had provided.

'Yes?'

'You're not school inspectors, are you? I want you out of the school right now, before I send for the police. I take it you're press or something. I want you out, right now.'

I took that as a sign that the lesson was over.

'Get out of my classroom,' the angry teacher snapped at me again. 'And girls, the rest of you, sit down!'

'Sorry girls. Got to go. Well done, today, you're all very smart, keep it up.' I turned to walk away with Rose.

'Sir.'

I turned. It was Jane.

'Yes?'

'Ice, sir. He was standing on ice, but the ice melted…'

'Jane, you've got it – well done! You'd make a

wonderful investigator.'

She smiled back at me, even wider than before.

The blonde girl at the back of the room raised her hand.

'What is it, Claire?' their teacher snapped.

'Can we have sir back again, Miss McCallan?'

Their teacher looked at me sternly. 'No, you cannot.'

'Aw, miss, his lessons are right good.'

'NO!'

It was probably time to leave.

◆ ◆ ◆

Earlier in the day, Rose had made me visit Mr Harding, whose daughter was threatened with permanent expulsion, following the theft of the headmaster's gold watch. It was found in her bag after a search and she was suspended pending further investigation, an investigation which had seemed to come to a standstill. She was definitely innocent, as she wasn't lying when I had questioned her about it this morning. Her father was terrified that the expulsion was going to be carrried out, but thought any action on his behalf would sway the decision against his daughter, Tilly. So, Rose thought it would be a good plan to pose as school inspectors.

'You looked like you were enjoying yourself,' Rose said, as we were just leaving the school gates, the headmaster bolting them behind us with a clang.

'Yes, well, I didn't really have much choice, did I? Not surprisingly, they wouldn't speak out about the theft. Did you find anything out with the teacher?'

'Miss McCallan? Nothing at all. She wouldn't open up.'

'Not surprising; she didn't seem very forthcoming.'

'How about the headmaster?'

'Nothing.'

'Where do we go from here with the case then?' she asked, preparing to cross over the road to the waiting Walrus.

'I don't know.

❖ ❖ ❖

Sydney sprang up to stoke the fire upon our return. 'Ah, James, I wasn't expecting you back so soon.'

'Yes, well, here we are.'

Sydney continued to stoke the fire. 'Enjoyed the school?'

'He did.'

'Oh, shut up. What you been doing anyway, you lazy lump?'

'Who me?'

'Of course, *you*, who the bloody hell else? Mrs Wilkins?'

My coat found a companion next to Rose's on

the stand.

Sydney stammered. 'I've taken a statement from Constable Matthews – about his farm trip. I've left it on the desk for you to read.'

'I bet that's a fascinating read.'

I desperately needed to sit, but Sydney was still in my way, messing about with the fire. I shoved him to one side and slumped into my chair. 'Ah, that's better.' But, the seat felt warm. I stared at Sydney, seeing a spot of colour rising in his cheeks. 'Have you been sitting in my chair?'

He looked down at me. 'Er, I've got to go now, unless you need me for something?'

'I've told you not to sit in my chair. I's mine. You've got your own. This one is not good for your diet. It encourages you to slouch.' I stretched my legs out some more.

'I don't need to go on a diet.'

I softened my voice. 'Sydney, the first stage is acceptance. You won't succeed in your goals if you don't have acceptance.'

'I don't want acceptance. I don't have any goals.'

'My point exactly.'

He shook his head and sulked in silence until Rose joined in the fray:

'Stop being mean to Sydney.'

'I'm not being mean to Sydney, quite the opposite in fact. I'm encouraging him to meet his goals.'

'Sydney doesn't need to go on a diet. He's

perfect as he is.' She slapped his belly, and Sydney grinned, standing taller.

'Anyway, we should all go to the pub to discuss things, get everyone together. All these cases are terribly confusing,' he said.

'We'll go tomorrow, after we've been to Mr Eastwell's. I'm not moving a muscle now. I'm drained.'

Sydney's bottom lip quivered. 'Please.'

'No, I'm too tired.'

'Please.'

'No.'

'You can do that summing up thing.'

'What summing up thing?' I asked.

'You know, that thing that makes you feel important?'

'I'm not going to the pub.'

Sydney's lips quivered some more, and Rose brushed his shoulder soothingly. 'Why don't you ask Constable Matthews?'

Sydney's spirits lifted. 'Do you think I should?'

'Yes. Here, take this.' I flipped him Matthews' missing cow statement. 'Ask him about that in more detail. It could be *very* important.'

He caught it. 'Really?'

'Yes, really vital to the case.'

'Alright, I will.' He quickly said his goodbyes.

'I'm not reading that tripe,' I said. 'Can you imagine? Constable Matthews' report on a missing cow.'

She laughed lightly and joined me at the table.

'So, what are we going to do about this school case?'

I told her that I had no idea but that I would sleep on it. She started telling me about the finer details of the Leeds Hotel case until there was a short tap at the door. It was Emma, Sydney's daughter.

'Uncle James. Rose!' she enthused, running over to the desk. 'I've managed to get away for a moment. I just wanted to thank you.' She made as if to hug me, but then seemed to remember I'm not one for embracing, and she smiled sweetly instead.

'Hello, Emma,' I said. 'Thank you…for what exactly?'

'For Christmas! Castle Howard, of course, silly.'

'Oh, yes. I thought it would be a nice treat for you.'

Rose at the side of me shook her head, but then her expression changed into something more thoughtful. 'How old are you?'

'I'm fifteen, why?'

Rose stood up, touching Emma's hair, close to her left ear. 'I think you could easily pass for thirteen, fourteen.' She turned to me. 'Especially, if we make some small adjustments.'

'What do you mean?' Emma asked, smiling.

I looked at Rose harshly, uttering just one word, but a resounding one: 'No!'

CHAPTER SIX

'Did you pick up the essentials?' I asked Sydney, as we made our way into Walrus' cab.

'Yes.'

'Adam's Tarts to Go?'

'Yes, they're in here.' He indicated the box on his lap, shaking it slightly, but not enough to disturb the treasure within. He knew better.

Walrus urged the horses on, and we were on our way to Howsham, a small village just south of Castle Howard. We were about to visit Mr Eastwell – a Mr Eastwell who was getting ever more hostile in regards to his missing racehorse.

'Inspector Moss seems keen we create a good impression.' I laughed, handing Sydney the note from my jacket pocket that he'd sent with Constable Matthews this morning. Sydney read it out loud with one hand still on the box:

'"Lavender, <u>why</u> haven't you visited Mr Eastwell yet? I told you to go the <u>very</u> next day. Don't be a pain in the behind. <u>DO NOT</u> annoy Mr Eastwell. He's *very, very* important!!!'" He handed me the note back. 'What do you think it means?'

'Well, what do *you* think it means? It's hardly cryptic, is it?'

'Why didn't you go the very next day?'

'I had planned to, more or less, but Rose had me messing about at the school, didn't she? That's her doing.'

'I suppose, but you could have gone afterwards.'

I turned to him sharply. 'Not really though, could I?'

'Why?'

I folded Inspector Moss' note away in my jacket pocket, thinking of Adam's fudge cake. 'What's this Mr Eastwell like?'

Sydney pondered his response as we clattered north, over the cobbles in the bitter air. 'He's well known in racehorse circles, knows his stuff, but…'

'But, what?'

'He's not an easy man to get on with. Got a nasty temper.'

'I see.'

'Very nasty.'

Sydney had lived in York much longer than I had, so he often knew the finer details.

'And he's good friends with the police commissioner. You… you won't get us in trouble, will you?'

'Trouble? When do I ever do that? Pass me a

tart.'

He gripped the box tightly. 'Let me tell you about last night, first.'

'Last night? Why, what happened last night?'

Sydney rubbed his chin. 'Constable Matthews has got a theory.'

'Oh no.' I considered jumping out of the window. 'Spare me, please.'

'No, listen. Constable Matthews thinks that the cow is either invisible, or it's jus–'

'Stop! Spare me the pain.' I rattled the latch on the window.

'No, listen. He thinks that it's either invisible or, it could have disappeared in a–'

'Sydney, stop!'

'What?'

'It sounds fascinating, but why don't we leave it for later? Something to look forward to. Pass me a tart.'

I was hungry. I'd meant to grab one with a cup of tea first thing, but I found myself short on time through no fault of my own. Mrs Wilkins had thrown some shoes at me for no reason and I'd had to take shelter in the kitchen.

Sydney seemed reluctant. 'Oh, that was kind of you, about Emma.'

'You mean about the Christmas thing? I know, it's going to be horrific.'

We turned right, past the Dalton household in Bootham, and I couldn't help but gaze out of the window with a shudder. The run-in with that horrible family was still fresh in my mind, but it had all worked out well in the end.

'Christmas thing?'

'Castle bloody Howard! Pass me a tart and stop being a fool.'

'Oh, no, not Castle Howard. I meant about the school.'

'School? What do you mean, about the school?'

Sydney looked out of the window as we were about to leave Grosvenor Terrace towards Haxby Road. I seemed to spend half of my life trotting down Haxby bloody Road.

'What do you mean about the school?' I repeated.

Sydney turned around. 'For giving the go-ahead.'

'What are you talking about?'

Sydney shook his head. 'Doesn't matter.'

'Course it bloody matters. Pass me a tart.'

Sydney wafted my hand away from the box. 'For going undercover-like.'

I scratched my forehead. 'Sydney, if you don't start talking sense there's going to be trouble.' I reached out for Adam's box, but he pulled it away again.

'Well, Rose said it was perfectly fine.'

I took a deep breath to stop myself from going insane. 'Are you talking about Rose sending Emma undercover at that damn school?'

'Yep.' He smacked his lips as he said it.

'She never listens to a word I say. Sometimes

I think she's running the damn agency, not me. Just pass me a bloody tart.'

Reluctantly, he put his grubby hands in the box and fished out a tart. I took it from him, wiped it down from all of his potential diseases, and placed the whole thing in my mouth. I needed it, and it was absolutely divine. Thankfully, I've got these tarts to keep me sane in a world populated by fools.

We trotted on and on, with the bite of the cold intensifying with every surge forward. Winter really was a time of permanent misery: the bitter cold, the bleakness of the early nights, the dangers of ice on the paths (this morning I'd nearly slipped getting into the cab, Walrus' fault), and in many respects, worst of all, the enforced gaiety of the Christmas period.

I pulled my coat around myself and took to the habit of regularly checking my pocket watch. The plan was to take a tart on the hour and then another with half an hour to go, load up on something at the Eastwell property, a cake perhaps, then leave a tart for the journey home. This should be sufficient until I got back home and crossed to Boaters.

Sydney was clearly struggling with the box on his lap. I'd told him earlier that struggling was part of the journey to a 'new you', that nothing which came easily was worthwhile. He hadn't thanked me for my words; he'd simply gripped the box more tightly, and avoided the conversation entirely, so I'd let the matter drop.

'Tell you what,' I said, being kind. 'I'll let you sniff the box, just a bit. That way you get the pleasure of the scent but not the sin of the bite.'

'Rose is really bad letting Emma go undercover if you didn't give the go-ahead. Not my fault that.'

'I know it isn't. Pass me a tart.'

It was now upon the hour.

Sydney looked terrified all of a sudden. 'You should be really mad at Rose.'

'I am, Sydney, but...' I froze. A cold fever ran down my spine and this one wasn't from the season. 'Sydney. Pass. Me. The box.'

Sydney wiped his forehead, then shouted forward. 'Bob! Stop the cab!'

The cab jerked to a halt as the horses were suddenly stopped. My head went crashing forward and while the cab was still in motion, Sydney jumped out of the door and ran back down the track.

'What in the hell just happened?'

I only just saved the precious box from falling to the floor. I hugged it to myself and flipped off the lip.

Empty!

Sydney was a dead man.

I leapt out of the cab and ran around the other side. Sydney was running back along the track in the direction we had just come, his chubby legs all at odds with the speed he was trying for.

'Sydney, you bloody thief!'

I gave chase, and he looked back at me, eyes wide with fright.

I ran after him, gaining ground. 'You're a dead man!'

He tried to pick up speed, but then his foot scuffed over a dent in the road, and he toppled over, head first into the ditch on his right, straight into some prickly, winter bush. 'Aww, help!'

I ran up behind him. 'Serves you bloody right!'

'Help, James! Help, I've stung myself. It hurts.'

'Good.'

I peered over the ditch. I could just make out some little legs kicking up from the depths of the shrubbery, some type of holly bush by the looks of it.

'Ouch. I've sat on something sharp.'

'You won't be stealing my tarts again then, will you? That's what happens when you break the law.'

'Help me, please. I'm sorry.'

'Oh, for God's sake.'

I stumbled down the ditch carefully, grabbed a flailing hand and pulled Sydney up out of the damn bush.

❖ ❖ ❖

My first impression of Mr Eastwell was not a favourable one.

We were standing in his stabled area, his little dark eyes staring out at me behind his stern, aggressive little face as he marched towards us, riding crop in hand. 'It's about time.' He stopped before us like a drill sergeant, staring at me, but I held his gaze.

'Mr Eastwell.'

'Don't "Mr Eastwell" me. Do you know how long I've been waiting?'

'I don't really care.'

'Excuse me?' He switched his riding crop from one hand and placed it under his other arm.

'I said, I don't really care.'

His horrible little face didn't look happy at that, but good. I didn't like him.

Sydney tugged on my sleeve with his left hand. He still held a bedraggled rag in the other. He'd been rubbing his backside and legs for the remainder of our journey here, but it hadn't seemed to have done any good. He told me his Mam had said that water on a rag cured all types of bush prickles. I'd told him this was complete nonsense, but he wouldn't have any of it, as once again his faith in his Mam's old wives' tales belied any sense of logic.

Mr Eastwell moved closer to me, his stern little eyes unmoving. 'Do you know who I am?'

Sydney tugged on my sleeve again and said in my ear, 'Remember what Inspector Moss said?'

I'm not one for being threatened, especially by little men.

'Do you know how much this racehorse cost me?'

I could feel his spittle land on my upper lip.

I wiped it off. 'I don't really care.'

Mr Eastwell whirled, but Sydney jumped in. 'Why don't you show us the stable?'

Mr Eastwell was unmoved.

'So we can help,' Sydney added.

Mr Eastwell broke his gaze, for now, and led the way.

We followed him into the stable. It was clean and modern and looked very secure. A bucket of fresh hay sprouted from an empty stall.

As with Mrs Wobble's barn, I examined the perimeter, looking for any clues or weaknesses. The floor was cushioned with straw so there was not even a chance of a footprint. It was also immediately obvious that there was no way this horse had got out any other way than the main door.

I could feel Mr Eastwell breathing heavily close behind me. 'Well, man, what do you make of it?'

I walked past him and examined the lock. This one was no padlock, but a secure keylock as good as any main door. I poked my finger through it to try to find any evidence of tampering, but there were no signs of anything untoward.

'Excuse me. I'm not used to being ignored.'

'Did you hear anything in the night?' I asked.

'What?'

I turned to face him. 'The day the horse went

missing, did you hear anything in the night?'

His house wasn't too far from the stables.

'No, of course I didn't. If I had, I would have said in my letter to Inspector Moss, wouldn't I?'

I looked over to Sydney, who was shoving the remainder of the rag under his belt at the back of his trousers. I turned back to Mr Eastwell. 'There's nothing to see here.' And I started to make my way out, past the horrible little man, but he blocked my exit with his riding crop, resting it firmly against my chest.

'You better find him,' he said.

I grabbed hold of the crop with one hand and pulled it away. 'Do not do that again.'

Sydney bounced over, dropping the now disintegrated rag. 'What does this horse look like?'

Mr Eastwell sniffed. 'He's a big black stallion, sixteen hands high.'

'Has he got any white marks?' Sydney asked. 'Like on his nose?'

Mr Eastwell smirked. 'No, but he's got two training marks on his flanks.'

'Training marks?' I said.

'Yes, training marks.'

'What's a training mark?' Sydney asked.

Mr Eastwell's lip curled. 'A training mark is where you break them in. He was a wild one, was old Wellington. But that's what whips are for.'

I stiffened. 'Mr Eastwell, a man who harms a beast is no man.'

He smiled at that. 'Mr Lavender, for the price I pay for these racehorses, I can burn them if I like. Discipline, that's the way to raise man and beast. Now, are you going to find my racehorse, or not?'

I walked back into the stable yard.

He stopped behind me. '*You*...are trying my patience.'

I didn't respond. Then I felt his finger jabbing against my back. I spun around and stared at him squarely. Then I poked him in the eye.

He reeled back at once, hand covering his face, and kneeled to a crouch. He cried out in pain. 'Just what in the Lord's name? Idiot! What have you done?'

He rubbed at his eye again and stood up, hand still covering it. He whipped his riding crop back, but his arm paused mid-strike.

'No, you don't.'

Sydney.

'Let go of me.'

Mr Eastwell shook against Sydney, but there was no way he was going to get the crop out of Sydney's hands. 'I'll see you pay for this, Mr Lavender, just you mark my words.'

'I think not.' And then I strolled away down the lane towards a waiting Mr Walrus. I suspected cake was out of the question.

◆ ◆ ◆

'So, that's why he thinks the cow's vanished.'

Sydney gave me a knowing wink and leaned back in his chair. He picked up one of his two beers and swallowed a huge gulp of it. Smacking his lips in satisfaction, he took up another urgent guzzle and wiped his mouth with the back of his sleeve, his thirst momentarily quenched.

We were sitting in our usual corner of the Punch Bowl, in the quiet room, huddled around the open fire. It was one of those nights of bitterest cold which seemed to invade no matter how many layers one wore. My fingers were still stiff as I reached out and took a sip of my beer, watching the flicker of the flames as they cast their shadows on the oak panelling behind me.

'Completely vanished,' Sydney said. 'Just disappeared into thin air.'

'Cows can't just vanish into the air, thin or otherwise.'

Sydney shook his head. 'Well, that's the constable's theory.'

I pulled at my ear in frustration. Maybe I should yank the thing off, and the other one too, then I wouldn't have to listen to this drivel. 'Oh, well then, if the constable says so it must be true.'

Sydney nodded happily. I thought in regard to the wise constable's theories, but he was gesturing to an older gentleman who had just come in from the cold.

'Evening, Sydney, evening…Mr Lavender.' He hunched his way towards us.

I had no idea who he was.

'Evening, Bill,' Sydney said, 'come and get yourself warm by the fire.'

I hoped he wasn't inviting him to our table.

He stepped by me and warmed his mittened hands by the fire, his fingers bent with age and cold. The flames illuminated the man's white whiskers and the lines around his eyes, though I still couldn't work out who he was, but then Rose arrived with Constable Matthews.

'Ah, Rose, Matthews. Come and join us by the fire.' I indicated the warm seats beside us, the seats that the old man was currently encroaching upon, and he retreated to the table behind us. Rose and the constable joined us.

'So, how was Mr Eastwell?' Rose asked.

A large smile spread across Sydney's face. 'James poked him in the eye.'

'You did what? Tell me you didn't poke a client in the eye.'

'Well, not at first.'

Rose didn't look too happy. 'Not at first? James, how could you?'

'He was a horrible little man. Anyway, you've got something to answer for, haven't you?'

Rose adjusted her hat. 'You mean with Emma?'

'Yes, with Emma.'

'I'm sure she will be fine.' Rose tapped Sydney on the arm, encouraging him to order food.

'Don't go changing the subject. I know Emma's bright, but I'm not sure dragging her into undercover detection is the wisest move.'

'She'll be fine, now tell me about Mr Eastwell, and how you came to poke him in the eye.'

Sydney relayed the story as we sat by the fire and ate stew, which had been brought in, as usual, by Millie, who was looking heavy these days despite being only five months pregnant. This was most unfortunate as the child would grow up without a father. Rose had organised a church charity fund for Millie and cases like hers, but take-up had been piteously low. Sydney always tipped Millie handsomely, but tips would only go so far.

I had let several of Sydney's grunts and splutters go, but I could no longer contain my irritation.

'Do you have to slurp like that?'

'What?'

I indicated the dribbled gravy that was currently all over the table.

'I'm enjoying my food,' Sydney said. 'Anyway, why don't you theorise?' He winked at Rose. 'Keep you happy-like.'

'Good idea, Sydney,' Constable Matthews said, 'I'd love to hear your thoughts; it's always interesting to see how your mind works.'

Naturally.

Rose started to choke on something, and the constable offered her a drink, but she said she was quite well.

'Right.' I'd had enough of my meal, so I pushed the remainder towards Sydney, and he tipped the lot onto his plate. I sat up a little straighter. 'So, let's start with the main case.'

'The animals?' Sydney dabbed at the new flood of gravy with a large chunk of bread.

'Of course. What we have is a series of missing livestock, all going missing in mysterious circumstances.'

'Like Mrs Wobble's sheep?' Sydney said.

The constable put down his knife. 'And Mr Brigstock's cow?'

'But, how did Mrs Wobble write the letter?' Sydney asked, still dabbing at the gravy. 'She couldn't write.'

'That's obvious.'

'Someone else wrote it for her, but how did it get there?' Rose asked. 'There was a stamp on the letter, but it wouldn't get to Inspector Moss within a few hours the very same day.'

'I worked that out the same night. It's hardly challenging.' I took a drink of my beer, enjoying the frustration forming on her face.

'How?'

I smiled at her but continued my theorising. 'All of the missing livestock are connected to the Castle Howard estate. Not one single case involves farms that are not connected to Castle Howard estate, therefore...'

'Therefore...what?' Sydney looked up, but then winked. 'Just joking.'

'We need to visit Castle Howard as soon as we can,' Rose said. 'Another reason to thank me.'

Constable Matthews shrugged. 'Could be a coincidence.'

'Hardly,' I said. 'Most of the farms in the wider area are not connected to the Castle Howard estate. I checked. I read about it in my library and calculated the odds. Therefore, the overwhelming statistical probability arises that the thefts are directly connected to the Castle Howard estate, but there's no way the earl would be behind it. So, who's trying to sabotage the earl's reputation? And, for what reason? And how, of course, are they doing it?' I gave the constable a quick look. 'Cows don't vanish into thin air.'

Rose took a sip of her beer. 'There's something more I don't understand too.'

'What's that?'

'Why would someone at Castle Howard have a spare key to a padlock? I mean, house keys I can understand if they own the property, but keys to a padlock? Seems strange.'

'Yes, that's something which occurred to me as well, naturally. I don't know. It's something I will muse upon.'

'What should we do when you're in Leeds tomorrow?' Sydney asked as he dealt with Rose's leftovers. The constable was still picking over his small plate.

'I don't want you sitting around. Go back to Mrs Wobble's to confirm what I already know.'

Rose sighed. 'Isn't that a waste of their time, if

you claim to already know it?'

'A bit, but they can go and find out anyway. It keeps Walrus on his toes too.'

'Oh, James, you're such a pain.'

'I'm not being a pain. Even if you suspect your theories are correct, and let's face it, I'm not often wrong, you still have to put the donkey-work in and Sydney is exceptional on that front, aren't you, Sydney?'

Sydney looked up from my question. 'What's that?' He tackled a rather large potato in one go. 'What do you make of this Leeds thing?'

'Oh, I don't think this will be a difficult one to solve.'

'Why do you say that?' Rose asked.

I half shrugged. 'It's Leeds, it's hardly the capital of theoretical crime.'

Rose looked uneasy, but with a creeping smile at the corner of her mouth. 'Anyway, about Leeds, I've got a little surprise for you.'

'What?'

'Tomorrow, at the psychics' conference.'

'Yes?'

She leaned closer to me, whispering. 'We're going undercover.'

'What the Jesus?' I nearly spilt my drink as it was on its way to my mouth. 'Why are you obsessed with going undercover?'

The old man in the corner looked up, already intrigued.

'You're not going as James Lavender.'

'I do hope you're joking?'

'I'm not.'

I was worried now.

'What are you talking about?'

'You're going as a psychic. You're going as… The Great Edmundo!'

'WHAT?'

CHAPTER SEVEN

So it was that I found myself in a train carriage on my way to Leeds (of all places), dressed as The Great Ed-bloody-mundo. Absolutely unbelievable. It had taken a lot of persuasion on Rose's behalf, but here I was, dressed in a long-flowing cloak, shining top hat and fake pencil moustache. My father's walking cane completed the outfit. I was staring at advertisements in the Herald, doing my best to avoid eye contact with Rose, who was seated opposite. For the last few minutes, she'd been trying to capture my attention. Not a chance.

'I've got something for you,' she said, at last.

I flicked over the page.

'I think you might like it.'

I rustled the paper and pretended to read.

'Oh, never mind. Gone off Adam's cakes, have you?' She brought out a small box from her bag and held it in her lap. 'These are specials. New recipe. I might have both of them myself, then.'

I let down the paper on my knee. 'What are they?'

'Oh, no, it doesn't matter.'

I licked my lips. I'd only managed to get two tarts in this morning, as we were running late to the station. Sydney's fault. 'What's in the box?'

She lifted the lid and peered inside, then looked up. 'Oh, nice.'

'What are they?'

'Oh, just two raspberry and cream cinnamon swirls – with custard.'

I couldn't help but lick my lips again. 'Pass me one, then.'

She smiled, scooped one out of the box and passed it to me gently, cinnamon swirl laid out flat on the palm of her hand.

The bloody thing was delicious.

'Why don't you share your idea about Mrs Wobble?' she said when we'd both finished the delightful swirls, still licking our fingers. 'Share your theory.'

I shook my head.

'Go on then, how did Mrs Wobble write the letter, even though she couldn't read? I gather someone else wrote it for her, but how did it get to Inspector Moss' office the same day?'

We rushed through a tunnel and the world went dark for a moment, and then we were just as soon back out of it again. A cloud of steam and smoke billowed by.

'It's so obvious.' I touched my fake moustache. It felt so awkward; never in my life had I sported any facial hair as I found it extremely irritating.

The fake moustache was bad enough. 'I don't really feel like talking.'

She rubbed at her mouth with her finger and thumb. 'Oh, go on. Share your clever theory. She mentioned a Mr Tucker. Did he write it for her? But how did it get there?'

I tweaked the moustache until Rose told me to leave it alone. 'Yes, I suspect Mr Tucker wrote the note for her. What must have happened is that he wrote the note, but then he must have hand-delivered it, on his way to market.'

'How do you know?'

'She mentioned a Mr Tucker, but he wasn't there with her when myself and Sydney visited the farm. I suspected he'd come into town to the market place or for some other such reason. That's what must have happened. Sydney and the constable can check the facts just to make sure there are no loose ends.'

She leaned in closer. 'You are smart, aren't you?'

'Of course.'

We left the fascinating conversation behind and discussed the upcoming psychics' conference. We were to first meet with Mr Westford, the acting manager, then attend the conference after checking into our rooms. I couldn't take the threats against the psychics seriously. Surely nobody would go to such extreme lengths as murder, just because they objected to these people?

I stroked the cloak Rose had procured for me from God knows where, but the material was growing on me, and I did feel rather dashing. The hat, and certainly that ridiculous moustache, I could still do well without.

We arrived at Leeds New Station, and we alighted onto the busy platform as ever into the middle of a hostile crowd. We found our way to the exit, pushing through the throngs of people. Outside, I was immediately struck by the huge clouds of smoke that hung oppressively in the air.

'Look,' I pointed. 'I told you Leeds was a dirty place.'

'Oh, stop being miserable, come on.' We pushed on to The Grand just around the corner.

It was immediately apparent, however, that there was trouble brewing outside the hotel, with seven protesters and two police constables in an obvious altercation. One of the protesters held a large placard with the message, 'psychics are the devil'. One of the constables was trying to wrestle it from him, but a stout fellow was tugging it back.

I strolled over. 'What seems to be the problem, constables?'

'Who are you? Keep your nose out of it,' one of the constables said, the one struggling with the placard. A blunt fellow, if ever there was one.

Then it dawned on me that I wasn't here as myself.

'I'm The Great Edmundo, psychic.' I bowed before them, sweeping my top hat. 'At your service.'

I thought that was a nice touch, and I was getting used to the hat.

The protesters stopped wrestling with the constables and turned their aggression my way.

'Devil worshipper!' one shouted.

'Spawn of Satan!' another spat, pushing his way towards me. The other constable stopped him.

'What's your problem?' I said.

Rose ran up and joined me, hastily tugging at my sleeve, doing an adequate impression of Sydney.

The other officer blew his whistle and shouted at the protesters to get back.

'Devil worshipper!' another shouted.

'He already said that. He was lying too.'

The scuffle continued for a while, with insults being traded back and forth, but it was broken up by a cavalry of reserve officers responding to the police whistle, and they dragged the protesters away.

I turned to Rose. 'Well, I did try to warn you about Leeds.'

❖ ❖ ❖

We were seated in the hotel manager's office, which was surprisingly pokey, considering the size of the hotel, but it felt even more cramped as Mr Westford had drawn up a chair just in front of the desk. The actual manager, Mr Thompson, was currently on holiday with the hotel owner, Mr Clement.

'I can't thank you enough for coming, Mr Lavender; it's been such a troubling couple of weeks.' He had small wire glasses on that he kept adjusting as he spoke. 'Very stressful.'

I nodded slightly, probably looking quite ridiculous in the cloak I was wearing, but he didn't seem to mind. If anything, he was clearly relieved that help was at hand, regardless of dress. 'Tell me, have you had any more warning notes?'

He nodded nervously and went over to the desk, retrieving a piece of paper from the top drawer. 'Here.'

I took the note. It was in different handwriting to the first. A poor hand with terrible grammar, which threatened his life should the conference go ahead. I passed it to Rose. 'I wouldn't worry. It's an empty threat.'

Rose looked at me quickly and studied the note.

The man looked only partially relieved. 'How can you be so sure?'

But I had spotted something of interest behind him on the shelf. A familiar name on the spine of a book lodged in between some dull-looking files. I sprung up out of the chair, walked past him and took it in my hands, skimming the pages.

He was still talking behind me. 'How can you be sure?'

'I just know,' I said, not bothering to turn around, still skimming over the book.

'And you have written to the hotel manager and the owner about the threats?' Rose said.

'Yes, yes. I have.'

'And you've had no reply?'

'Hey, look, Rose,' I said. 'Macbeth.' I showed her the bookmarked page. 'Have you ever played Lady Macbeth? I bet you'd make a good one.' I laughed, but she didn't seem too impressed.

She repeated her question to Mr Westford.

No, Mr Westford still hadn't had a reply to his letters.

'What's the full outline for the conference?' Rose asked.

I laughed. 'Doubl, double, toil and trouble.' I put the collected works back on the shelf.

'James!'

Mr Westford looked terrified. Clearly not a fan of fine humour. He took a few moments to compose himself (which involved lots of adjustments of his glasses), before he could relay today's events. The whole thing started at one. There was to be a drinks reception, which (thankfully) included light snacks. Then it was the conference, followed by an evening meal. It sounded pleasant enough if you liked socialising with a bunch of misfits. I was neither a fan of socialising, nor misfits, so I was far from thrilled by the combination of the two. Regardless, I would just get on with it now that I was here, like the professional I was.

Mr Westford rang for the porter, who was quickly on the scene, a small stout fellow with a flat nose. 'Ah, Tom. Can you show Mr Lavender and er, Rose to their rooms, please?'

Rose always insisted on being addressed by her Christian name. I had no idea if this was an Irish thing or a Rose thing.

The man nodded and picked up our bags. 'If you'd like to follow me?'

Rose reassured Mr Westford, telling him not to worry, though her words hardly seemed to have any effect at all.

Our new friend, Tom, took us back through the main hotel reception, along the red and cream carpet, back towards the hotel entrance. They'd posted the blunt-looking police constable on the door, due to the earlier trouble outside. He still didn't look very impressed.

Some misfits were now arriving, streaming through the double doors. There was a tall, thin man in a long blue coat, with the most ridiculous pointed, curly moustache that I had ever seen in my life. I had to stop to take it in. I couldn't help but laugh. It looked like he'd stuck two hungover caterpillars on the side of his face. I touched my own fake one, quite happy with it now. 'Rose, look at him,' I found myself saying, pointing.

The man jerked his head my way, his face creased in anger.

Rose jabbed my arm, and we continued to follow the porter up to our second-floor rooms, 211 and 212. The porter dropped our bags and wished us a pleasant stay. He was lying, so he didn't get any tip. Not that I would have tipped anyway. Tipping people for the job that they do doesn't make logical sense.

I entered my room. Always a surprise. Like opening a present. The room was small but adequate. I dropped my bag by the door and went to the window. Something I always did when entering a hotel room. The view was not as horrific as I'd imagined – a quiet side street. There was still the oppressive air of smog in the distance, which blocked out the majority of light, but its darkness didn't quite seem to reach the side of the hotel itself. A group of workmen guided a packhorse and cart down the road, towards the distant arch of a bridge. They looked much like ordinary workers, not thuggish at all. On the nearside pavement, a young mother held the hand of her small boy as he struggled along in the cold. They too looked almost civilised. Other than that, it was relatively quiet on the side street, which meant I would probably be able to sleep tonight, as long as the bed wasn't too soft. I went over to it and knocked it with my fist. Rock hard. Perfect.

Surprisingly, it didn't take Rose long to get

prepared. She was dressed in a black and green dress that shimmered slightly in the light, but we were still running a little late for the welcome drinks (her fault, as I suspected she'd take longer so I was in the middle of polishing my shoes when she knocked upon my door).

Constable Blunt was still standing by the door and he eyed me suspiciously as we walked through the hotel reception to the 'welcome room', as it had been called, on the stand outside the entrance.

There were around thirty people altogether, most of them walking around with drinks in their hands, quietly chatting, eyes on everyone else. Those who knew each other hung around in little groups. I heard one of them say, 'Oh, my, that's Hilda Broomwell.' Naturally, I had no idea who Hilda Broomwell was, and nor did I care, but I got the impression that I was about to find out.

Not all of the misfits were dressed like wizards. In fact, I felt somewhat overdressed. There were a few dressed like me, not as dashing, obviously, but of similar descript, but there were also many more ordinary-looking people, who you might have thought were simple businessmen or bankers on a business trip if you weren't standing in the middle of a bunch of so-called psychics.

The high ceiling had been decorated well, with wide swirls in gold and cream, but Rose nudged me along.

Mr Westford was hovering around in the centre of the room, welcoming the guests. He still looked terrified, shaking his glasses around all the time. He really shouldn't let death threats get to him so easily. He spotted us and made his way over.

'Ah, Mr...The Great Edmundo. Can I get you and your *assistant* a drink?'

His lips were positively trembling.

'Not for me.'

I wanted to keep my mind sharp, but Rose took a glass of wine.

'Rose, look. The caterpillar man is over there, talking to that huge woman.'

'James!'

A few people turned their heads, and I heard someone tut.

'Ah, that's Geoffrey Bellington and Madam Devereux,' Mr Westford explained.

I shuddered at the sight of Madam Devereux. She reminded me of an unfortunate encounter I'd had with a similar-looking gypsy creature in a pub in York. A painful experience.

He invited them over, including Hilda Broomwell, who had been hidden behind Madam Devereux. Apparently, Hilda was the lead speaker. She was a thin streak of a woman, with wispy dark hair going off in all directions. She had an annoying habit of asking a question, then answering it herself. 'How are you? Looking forward to the conference, I expect,' was her opening gambit, but my attention was taken by a young, blonde-haired maid in the corner of the room. She was serving cake, and no one was around her. The Hilda Broomface woman was still talking, answering her own questions, but I wasn't interested. I was interested in the cake; more specifically, the woman serving the cake. She bore an uncanny resemblance to Constable Matthew's wife.

'Excuse me,' I said, walking over to the suspected Miss Anderson, weaving through the crowd. Rose followed.

'That was a bit rude, walking away like that. After cake again?' Rose said, still behind me. 'It's you who should go on a diet.'

'Not at all, I have the perfect body weight, but I'll have to have a portion…to keep my cover.'

'What do you mean?'

I went up to the young woman. She looked a few years younger than the constable's wife, maybe early 20s, but she had the similar nose and jawline as that of her sister.

'Cake, sir?'

She picked up a knife and hovered it over the delicious-looking chocolate cake.

'Er, yes please, large slice.'

She was about to cut me a small piece.

'Bit more.'

She edged the knife to the left. 'Here?'

'Bit more.'

'Here?'

'Bit more.' I indicated with my finger. 'Left a bit.'

'Here?'

'Keep going.'

She smiled. Her sister's smile. 'Tell me when.'

'Left a bit.'

'Now?'

'Bit more.'

'Here?'

'Yes, that will do, for now.'

She cut through the cake. Cream and chocolate sauce oozed onto the plate, and she passed it to me.

'Great. 'Have you noticed anything suspicious?' I asked as I scooped up a spoonful. It was beautiful, a thing to rival even one of Adam's holy creations, almost.

'Suspicious, sir?'

She seemed confused. She asked if Rose wanted cake.

'Please. About one-fifth the size of his will do.'

'Don't be greedy,' I said. 'Suspicious, you know, anything odd? Strange comings and goings?'

My last comment was directed at Miss Anderson.

She looked around the room at the gathering of psychics. 'Odd, sir? Comings and goings in a hotel?'

Then it dawned on me. She didn't know who I was. I scooped in another mouthful of cake, and then I leaned forward, conspiratorially. 'I'm not The Great Edmundo. I'm James Lavender, the great detective, and you're Miss Anderson, I expect?'

A bright light came to her blue eyes. 'Oh, I see. Yes, sir. Jane Anderson.' She seemed excited. I liked her. 'Kevin talks about you all the time. Says that you have a brilliant mind.'

Yes, I really liked her.

'Does he indeed? Who's Kevin?'

'Kevin. Kevin Matthews.'

I still wasn't following.

'Constable Matthews,' Rose said, with a sigh.

'Oh, of course.'

I never really associated Constable Matthews with having a Christian name. And I hadn't been paying much attention at the wedding. Tedious affairs, weddings.

I heard Rose sighing again. She must be enjoying the chocolate cake. I was spooning in mine quickly as Mr Westford was about to open the door to the conference.

'Suspicious?' Jane said after I reminded her of the question. 'No, nothing I can think of. It's such a shame though, Mr Lavender; Mr Westford is so nice. Much nicer than Mr Thompson. Even the owner likes Mr Westford better, I can tell.'

'But there haven't been any odd comings and goings?' I dabbed at my mouth as some of the chocolate sauce had tried in vain to escape. 'No break-ins, anything like that?'

'No, Mr Lavender. Not that I'm aware of.'

I put my fingers to my lips. 'The Great Edmundo.' But nobody was within earshot anyway, as they were all gathering around the door, eager to go into the conference room.

'Have there been many protests?' Rose asked.

I noticed she'd nearly finished her cake. Unbelievably greedy.

'Nothing like today's one. A few od–'

But someone screamed. A woman. The sound was coming from the entrance of the conference room. I grabbed my cake and ran.

'Make way, make way.' I parted some people with my cane while balancing my cake in my left hand. Mr Westford was by the door, eyes wide with fright.

'Mr Lavender,' he said, trembling.

So much for the cover, but I'm not sure anybody heard.

'What's wrong? Move out of the way.' I tapped several people with my cane. They seemed annoyed. 'Shift out.'

The woman screamed again.

'Let us through, please,' Rose said, managing to clear a few people.

I got to the door where Mr Westford was trembling, but then someone's hand hit mine and my bloody cake fell on the floor and some great fool stepped back in it, squashing the chocolate goodness into the cream carpet.

I turned to face the person who had knocked my hand in the melee. It was the caterpillar man.

'You great idiot.'

The woman screamed again.

'I know, I was enjoying that!' I said to her, but she wasn't listening or screaming at the squashed cake. Her gaze held fast towards the far end of the room, towards the raised stage, as, on the wall were written the words, 'your going to die,' in dripping red, and below that, a body was hanging from a rope.

CHAPTER EIGHT

The body was a dummy. A crude one at that. Rose had been first to act, springing into action and clearing the room of Hilda Broomface, the cake stamper and a few of her ilk So, it was just me, Rose, Mr Westford and Constable Blunt examining the scene. Jane Anderson was currently trying to pacify the guests in the 'welcome room' but, by the sound of the shouts and general confusion, she was struggling.

'So, Rose, let's look at what we've got.' We were before the stage, staring up at the hastily constructed dummy. 'First, the writing on the wall above – not the world's greatest grammar.'

'You're referring to the "your" part of the message?'

'Yes.'

It was the same as in the note we'd just read in the manager's office.

'Mr Lavender, I hardly think grammar is the most pressing point, right now,' Mr Westford said, lips still trembling.

'Oh, I disagree. It's very important.'

'But, by the sound of things, we should act quickly.' Rose referred to the steadily raised voices in the so-called welcome room.

'Fine.' I hopped up on to the stage and reached up to the message, smearing some of the red onto my finger. 'Paint, not blood, of course, and it's still slightly wet.' I bent down to show Rose. 'When did you last check this room, Mr Westford?'

'About half-past eleven.'

I glanced around the room. 'Are there any other doors, any other entrances to this room? A trapdoor, even?'

'No, no. The entrance behind is the only one.'

'And was it locked?'

'Yes.'

'Are you sure?'

'Quite sure, Mr Lavender.'

'Where is the key?'

'In my pocket.'

'Any spare keys?'

'Spare keys? Yes, in the office.'

I took out my pocket watch. It was one thirty-five. 'So, someone had to have done this between half-past eleven and one-thirty? But realistically from half-past eleven to one, as the drinks reception started then?'

'It would appear so, Mr Lavender, but look here, shouldn't we call the whole thing off? It's too risky. I can't risk the safety of my guests.'

'Make my life easier if you did,' Constable Blunt muttered, arms folded.

'No, Mr Westford. There's no need for that,' I said.

Mr Westford's mouth creased at the edges. 'Are you *absolutely* sure?'

'Of course I'm sure,' I said, brightly. 'I'm never wrong.'

He turned to Rose. 'What do you think?'

She looked at me briefly. 'You can trust Mr Lavender.'

I heard her whisper, 'I think,' but he didn't hear her.

There was a bang from the door and Jane Anderson appeared. 'Sir, I can't hold them back for much longer. They're panicking.'

'Mr Westford,' I said. 'Go out there and tell them that The Leeds Psychic and Medium Conference, 1888, will go ahead as planned, or my name's not James Lavender!'

Or was it The Great Edmundo in this context?

Jane Anderson was about to go back into the reception room with Mr Westford and the constable, but I called her over. 'Did you see anybody coming into the room when you were setting up the cake stall?'

'I don't think so, I–'

'Try to think.'

'No, Mr Lavender, no one that I saw, but I was busy going back and forth from the kitchen.'

'I understand, thank you.' I jumped back onto

the stage and started hunting around. Rose asked me what I was looking for.

'The paint tin. I'm guessing whoever wrote that didn't want to be seen walking through the hotel with a tin of red paint. Help me look.'

We searched and it didn't take long to find the paint. It was in a large cardboard box in the corner of the room, behind the stage. Rose found it.

'Ah, a large cardboard box,' I said. 'Interesting.'

'What could possibly be interesting about a large cardboard box?' Rose asked.

'Dummy.'

'Excuse me?'

'They needed space to fit the dummy in.'

'Oh, I see.'

'I picked up the paint pot. The lid hadn't been fully closed. Do you keep this paint on the premises?' I asked Jane.

'I couldn't be certain, sir, but I expect so.'

I spun around letting the cloak swirl behind me. Rather fetching. 'Let's summarise.'

Rose craned her head around at the banging on the door. 'Quickly...'

'Fine.' I listed the significant points on my fingers. 'Poorly written message, still damp with red paint. A dummy hanging from a rope, poorly constructed. A large cardboard box. A room with only one door, locked. Mr Westford had the key in his pocket but there's a spare in the office. Short time frame for the message to be written. How's that?'

'Perfect.'

I pointed to the dummy and the message above. 'Now, what the hell do we do with all of this?'

◆ ◆ ◆

Hilda Broomface stood behind the lectern, preparing to address the room. She swept several strands of hair away from her face before she could see all the eager faces (minus mine) staring back at her. She looked both nervous and confident at the same time, if that was even possible. 'Are you all looking forward to the conference?'

Lots of affirmative noises.

'No,' I shouted.

Broomface continued:

'I bet you are all looking forward to it.'

The crowd clapped her pointless question cum-statement. I was sitting behind caterpillar man of all people, in the second row.

'Welcome all, sorry about the… misunderstanding earlier. Now, I hope you are all comfortably seated? I trust you are all comfortably seated. Welcome, to The Leeds Psychic and Medium Conference, 1888.'

There was a further round of applause. Caterpillar face shouted 'bravo' for some bizarre reason.

Hilda let the crowd die down before speaking. 'Mediums, psychics...'

'Fakes,' I said to Rose.

'...fortune tellers...'

'Frauds.'

'James!'

Somebody rudely hushed me.

'...seers of the other side. How ever you prefer to be addressed, welcome.'

Another round of applause. I wondered if she was going to do anything other than ask and answer her questions and continually welcome people.

She held her arms out wide, and the crowd clapped again. 'Welcome.'

A no, then.

Earlier, we had taken the dummy down and placed it in the cardboard box, then hidden it in the corner of the room. We didn't have time to wash the paint away, so we covered it with a large screen that we had found by the side of the hall. Then Jane had gone to tell Mr Westford to let the misfits in.

'For the next two hours...'

I stood up. 'Not a chance.'

Rose hissed at me. 'What are you doing? Sit down.'

Caterpillar turned around. 'Do you mind?'

'No.' I grabbed Rose's hand. 'Come on, we're not needed here anyway now, and if I'm not mistaken, there will be another little incident brewing.'

❖ ❖ ❖

'Did you all enjoy the conference? I'm sure you did,' Hilda Broomwell said, raising a glass of sherry. We were seated around an eight-seater table situated in the centre of the large room for the evening meal. Myself and Rose were seated together alongside Caterpillar, Madam Devereux, Hilda Broomface and a few others I didn't bother to learn the names of. I could see right through the open door into the hotel reception. Caterpillar had wanted the door closed, due to a draught, but I had insisted on it remaining open. I had a strong feeling he didn't like me, and I suspected he'd knocked the cake out of my hand on purpose. I'd mentioned this to Rose earlier, but she'd said we had other things to concern ourselves with.

'So, The *Great* Edmundo? I must say, I've never heard of you,' Caterpillar said, picking up a knife and fork and tackling his beef.

'Well, I've never heard of you either.'

He laughed. Falsely.

'You've never heard of Geoffrey Bellingham? I must say, that's a good one.'

I picked up my own knife and examined the handle to see if it was made in Sheffield. I always did this. It was. My father had once co-owned a cutlery factory, but that felt like a long time ago now.

I cut my beef.

'No, never heard of you.'

Rose tapped my foot under the table.

'You must be new to this business, then?' He smiled at me irritatingly, his stuck-on caterpillars dangling to one side.

I finished chewing the beef. 'Business? You call it business, going around parting people from their money for nonsense. I don't call that business myself. I call it fraud.'

Hilda Broomface dropped her fork. Madam Devereux sucked in air as if she'd been drowning and a few of the others tutted. I popped another square of beef into my mouth. Not bad.

Mr Westford swooped over. 'Is everything to your satisfaction?'

'The food's excellent,' Geoffrey Caterpillar muttered, looking my way. 'Just some of the company could be better, though I suppose such things can't always be helped.'

I put my knife and fork down and addressed the table. 'Look, I'm not saying all psychics, mediums, misfits whatever you want to call yourselves, are all bad, but exploiting people's fears, I can do without, and that's what the majority of them...*us* do.'

'Like insurance salesmen?' Madam Devereux said.

I had to admit, she had a point there.

She continued. 'True, there are a lot of frauds

in our business, but you shouldn't be dismissive of the arts. I can tell that you're special.'

'He's definitely special,' Rose said, but nobody heard her. Nobody listens to 'assistants'.

'How do you mean?' I asked Madam Devereux.

She looked troubled, but comfortable with it. She picked up a small carrot and ate it delicately, looking at me all the time. When she had finished, she said:

'You are different from all the rest of us.' She then turned to Rose. 'And for you, I see a golden dove.'

Total nonsense. I sprung out of my chair, scooping up my cane that had been resting against my left leg. It was now time. Jane had captured my attention through the door as planned, anxiety etched on her pleasant face. I dashed to the side of the room and hid by the side of the door. A man with a hood, gun in hand, came crashing into the conference room to a chorus of screams. I brought the end of my father's cane down as swiftly as I could on the back of the man's wrist. It went with a crack, and the gun dropped to the floor.

'Ow,' the hooded man shouted.

Then I whacked him over the head for good measure and he fell to the floor.

People froze and looked up in a general state of terror and confusion. Some people stood. A glass smashed on a far table.

Constable Blunt barged through the door, took

one look at the man and placed him in handcuffs.

'Fear not,' I said, 'everything is well.' People were still trying to make out what was going on, and their confusion made quite an amusing picture, but gradually they returned to their seats and I addressed them all. 'I came today to the conference as The Great Edmundo with my assistant over there.' Some people looked around at Rose, but then just as quickly their eyes were back on me. 'But I am not The Great Edmundo.'

There were a few cries of shock and a gasp from the caterpillar man.

I took off the fake moustache, followed by my top hat and cloak, which I placed on a nearby chair. The cane, I kept. 'No, I am not The Great Edmundo. I am The Great James Lavender, private detective!'

There were a few more cries and a few claps, but most people didn't know what to do.

I pointed at the man held by Sergeant Blunt. 'This man here was trying to ruin your little conference, but myself and my associate over there have put a stop to it. So now your conference can go ahead as planned.'

There were a few mutters, then Mr Westford started clapping from the back of the room and soon everyone followed suit. I motioned that Rose should come up and join me, but she declined. I bowed, taking in the applause. It was good to be appreciated.

◆ ◆ ◆

Later, back in the manager's office with Mr Westford, I went over everything.

'So, how did you know it was the porter, Tom Ward?' Mr Westford asked, his lips no longer trembling.

Rose looked at me in the funny, knowing sort of way, a smile still on her face.

'Well, first thing's first. The crowd outside did not believe what they were saying.'

'You mean, about the psychics being the work of the devil and all of that?'

'Yes, they were all lying.'

'How do you know?'

Rose intervened. 'He's good with body language.'

That seemed to satisfy him.

I continued. 'They didn't believe what they were saying. I purposefully addressed them all when we saw them protesting outside the hotel. I could tell that all of them were lying.' I turned to Rose. 'Conclusion?'

'They were paid.'

'Correct.'

Mr Westford grinned.

I proceeded. 'That meant that the death threats were fake. They weren't religious maniacs.'

'Yes, but how did you know it was Tom? How

did you work it all out?'

I stood up and walked past him, rescuing the collected works of Shakespeare from between the dull files once again. I turned to the bookmarked page. 'Macbeth.'

'What?'

'The first note. About blood on your hands. An obvious reference to Macbeth. The hotel manager, Mr Thompson, had been reading Macbeth as he wrote the note he left behind with Tom, prior to his holiday with the hotel owner. The initial note was in a much neater hand.'

'But why?'

'Jane Anderson provided the clue. She said that Mr Thompson was not a kind man, and even the hotel owner preferred you. Mr Thompson was worried that you would take over his job, so he manufactured the whole charade. Using Tom to help. He probably paid him handsomely.'

'Good God.'

'My guess is that he intercepted the letters you sent Mr Clement. And Tom probably did the same on this side. Mr Thompson wanted you to fail with the psychic conference, losing the hotel money and causing the owner embarrassment. Mr Thompson wanted to eliminate his rival.' I closed the book and placed it back on the shelf, then I sat back down.

'I can't believe it,' he said.

'You shouldn't be surprised what people will do in order to maintain their social standing.'

'But what about the other note? The dummy?'

I shook my head. 'That was crudely done. Tom was desperate that the little plan wasn't working, so he took upon all of that by himself.'

'The painted message?'

'Yes, he knew that I was a detective as you addressed me by my name when you sent him for our bags. It was probably then that he also picked up the spare keys.'

'I see.'

'When he saw us to our rooms, he then had a window of opportunity to grab the pre-prepared box and sneak into the conference room. He only had to linger to watch Jane slip into the kitchen then he made his way in. Who'd notice a porter carrying a cardboard box through a hotel, anyway?'

'That was quite clever,' Rose said. 'But what about when he came out of the conference room? What if Miss Anderson saw him? He was taking a risk there, wasn't he?'

I shrugged. 'Perhaps, but then again, he could have passed it off as last-minute preparations. We couldn't prove he had anything to do with it. He could have claimed he was checking the lighting or something like that. As it happened, Jane Anderson was still in the kitchen. It only took a few minutes to write the message, put up the dummy and slip out again.'

'Well, I think it is quite remarkable, Mr Lavender.'

'Think nothing of it.'

Tom Ward had immediately confessed the whole thing to the entire room. Constable Blunt had examined his revolver and had found the barrel empty, so there had been no real threat to life, as I expected, but his bursting in on the scene with a weapon would have sent the whole room into chaos.

I had expected that he would strike at the start of the meal, as soon as possible, which is why I had positioned Jane Anderson in such a way that she would see him walking through the hotel lobby and could alert me to his presence. I'd chosen the exact seat so I could see her face through the door which I had insisted remained open. Easy.

I'd first suspected him when he was lying about wishing us an enjoyable stay. Genuine porters might not care much either way, but they wouldn't positively lie about wishing someone a happy stay. Of course *he* would, as he wanted us to fail in our mission.

'Well, you have been simply amazing, Mr Lavender.' He turned to Rose. 'You both have.' He shook our hands. 'Jane told me about you, Mr Lavender, said you wouldn't let me down, that you were quite brilliant, and it turned out to be true.'

'Of course. As soon as I got your letter, Mr Westford, I sprang into action. You can always trust James Lavender.'

Rose coughed. I hoped she wasn't coming down with something.

He stood to shake my hand. 'If there is anything I can ever do, Mr Lavender, anything at all, just name it.'

I thought for a second. 'Well, there is one thing.'

'What's that?' he immediately shot back.

'Have you got any more of that delicious chocolate cake?'

CHAPTER NINE

'Yep, a pig's gone missing,' Sydney said. 'Fancy that.'

'I know. You keep on saying.'

I was sitting in my chair, having only just returned from Leeds. And Sydney was going on and on about a missing pig.

'Yep, just disappeared from Mrs Dibbs' farm. Another one connected to the Castle Howard estate.'

I rubbed at the bridge of my nose.

'I know. Terrible, isn't it?'

I picked up the ledger. Rose had called in to see Sydney, but I'd sent her home. I was not going to move out of my chair for the rest of the day. I thought sending Rose home was the best way to ensure this success. I added the payment from the Leeds trip to the ledger, ignoring Sydney's continued waffle about the missing pig. He'd paid a visit to the farm with Constable Matthews, and apparently, the missing pig fit right into their 'vanishing into thin air' theory.

Sydney cracked his knuckles. 'Anyway, tell me more about Leeds.'

Good God. Not usually a statement I'd relish. I told him briefly about my brilliant deductions and a few other vital incidents.

'She trod in your cake?'

'I know, stupid woman.'

'But it was the caterpillar man's fault?'

I was about to answer, but I was deafened by a huge bang from upstairs. This one sounded like an elephant.

'Mrs Wilkins!' I shouted. 'What the hell is going on up there?'

The only reply was another falling elephant.

'Mrs Wilkins!'

There was a pause. Silence, followed by footsteps on the stairs. Footsteps which were getting louder.

Sydney chuckled to himself. 'Ho, ho, ho, you've done it now.'

Mrs Wilkins burst into the room. 'What are you complaining about, now? Can't you go back to Leeds? I was able to get on with my jobs without complaints when you weren't here.'

'It's just the–'

'I came in. Got on with my tasks with no complaints. Mr Brown was happy with my tea. Thankful even.'

'Mrs Wilkins, it's just that–'

'You've been in five minutes and already you're shouting. What's your problem?'

'Stop shooting elephants.' I flicked my wrist, dismissing her, but yet she stood there motionless, hands on hips like some housekeeper from hell, guarding the underworld.

'What funny remark is that?'

I put the ledger back down. 'The African animals. Through the ceiling. I can't think straight.'

'I'm cleaning. Don't you want me to clean?'

'But why does cleaning involve ramming things through the ceiling?'

Sydney was watching the conversation, a stupid grin still on his face, going back and forth like he was in the front seat of a lawn tennis match.

Mrs Wilkins was unmoved. 'I have to move the bed. The other things, the table and chairs. Do you want me to clean under your bed, or not?'

'You *clean* under my bed?'

'Of course, I clean under your bed!'

'Oh, I never noticed.'

Mrs Wilkins' face flamed. 'You ungrateful so and so.'

'Just stop ramming things through the ceiling. Go on now.' I shooed her away. This didn't seem to impress her. I grabbed hold of the ledger in case she should throw something at me again. But, luckily, she just turned around and bounded back up the stairs.

Sydney raised a mocking eyebrow with every

bang on the stairs, alternating between his left and right eye, wincing dramatically each time.

'You can shut up as well. Put another bloody coal on the fire.'

It had turned bitter cold now, and the dark outside obscured the pleasing view of the minster. Every so often, the chimes still pulsed their regular heartbeat into the room.

For once I could hear the chatter of drinkers across the road in the York Arms, almost within touching distance. It was such a shame that this small public house was frequented by navvy types; otherwise, the practicalities of a small public house just across the way was not lost on me. Maybe I should get a petition going to clean up the place? 'So, no other news?'

'No, nothing.'

'Good.' I put my pen away and leaned back in my chair. It was good to be home in front of the warmth and crackle of the fire. I could feel my eyes starting to close already.

'Oh, there is one other thing.'

'What?'

'Nothing much, just that Inspector Moss wants to see you, urgently-like.'

'I thought you said there was nothing. He can wait until tomorrow.'

'Hmm.'

'What do you mean, hmm?'

Sydney looked uncertain. 'Says you should go over as soon as you get back. Immediately-like.'

I scratched the back of my hand. 'Am I ever going to get a moment's peace? Just one?'

'He did sound quite angry.'

'He's always angry, but *you* just said there was nothing else. Now there's this bloody thing. He can wait until tomorrow.'

'I forgot, but he was very, very angry.'

'He can wait until tomorrow.' I closed my eyes and leaned back in my musing chair.

'Well, if I were you…'

I opened one eye. 'What?'

'I'd go around pretty sharpish. Now-like.'

'Oh, for God's sake.' I slammed a fist on my desk. 'Never a moment's peace, not one. What's he want, anyway?'

'He didn't say, but I think it was about…' Sydney leaned forward, doing his wise old gnome impression. 'That man.'

'What man?'

'You know, the eye thing?'

'Sydney, if you don't tell me what "the eye thing" is, I'm going to pick that poker up an–'

'That man.'

I reached for the poker.

Sydney quickly found his voice. 'You know, about you poking Mr Eastwell in the eye?'

'Oh, that?'

Sydney nodded. 'Yes, I expect so. Shouldn't you go then?'

I sighed. I hated getting up in the warmth to go out into the cold. It was completely uncivilized.

'Fine, let's see what Moss has to say for himself, and then I'm not moving for the bloody Pope.'

◆ ◆ ◆

Sergeant Daniels was the staff sergeant on duty. He always seemed to be on duty whenever I called in. He sat behind his little booth in the police station with a sour expression on his face. Despite this, I didn't much mind him. Annoying Sergeant Daniels was always a joy.

'Ah, Lavender, delighted to see you.' (His face said otherwise.) 'I've heard that you've been a very busy man. Merlin, the Wizard, wasn't it?' He put his pen down and gave me his full attention. Very unusual.

'What?'

'Show us a magic trick.'

'I haven't a clue what you're talking about.'

His eyes narrowed slightly. 'No rabbits?'

'Where's Inspector Moss?'

That question always annoyed him.

He sighed. 'Oh, not asking about my health today, then?'

'How are you? How's your Auntie Maggie?'

He tapped a pen on his desk. 'Aunt *Maureen* is doing fine. Wonderful. She loves being sick in the morning.'

His Aunt Maureen was having a baby, despite her being almost forty.

'That is indeed wonderful. Good to hear. Send

Margaret my regards.'

'Maureen. Her name is Maureen.' He let go of the pen, which rattled around on his desk.

'Right, yes. Where's Inspector Moss?'

He sniffed. 'Oh, you're here to see Moss, then? Not to enquire about my Auntie Maureen's morning sickness.'

'Where is he?'

He shook his head dramatically. 'Bad news. He's out, having tea with the Queen.'

'Really?'

'No, of course not! Why would he be having tea with the Queen?'

'Where is he then?'

'He's upstairs in his office, where do you think he is, you great fool?'

'Great, thanks.' I turned and walked away.

Yes, annoying Sergeant Daniels was one of life's little joys.

Making my way inside the busy station, I was met with the usual nonsense, the chief culprit again being the huge officer, Gorilla.

'Ah, Mr Lavender's here, lads!' he shouted, standing up and giving me a round of applause. 'We can all sleep soundly in our beds tonight.'

This comment was met with several jeers and sniggers, his beady-eyed friend being one of the leading protagonists.

I made my way to the stairs.

'Hey, Mr Lavender?' Gorilla shouted when I was half way up.

I turned. 'What?'

'You found the missing pig yet? Is it under your hat?'

I shook my head and proceeded up the stairs towards the good inspector's office. Gorilla never made much sense.

I peered through the little window, spying on Inspector Moss, trying to work out which type of angry mood I would find him in. He didn't notice me so I continued to peer, nose pressed against the glass until he turned his head and jumped with a start. 'Jesus Christ, Lavender! What the *hell* are you doing?'

I took this as a signal to enter. Inspector Moss was still shaking his head. 'Care to explain *this*?' He produced a letter, slapping it down on his desk.

'It's a letter.'

'I know that!' His large moustache bobbled, never a good sign. 'Would you care to explain the contents?'

I briefly skimmed it over. 'It's from Mr Eastwell. He doesn't seem that happy.' I cast it back on his desk.

'Yes, and why would that be?'

I shrugged. 'Don't know.'

He pulled at his hair. He didn't have much to work with. 'You don't bloody know?'

I shrugged again.

'Let me help. I told you to go easy on him. He's a difficult man, but he's rich and powerful. Has a lot of connections. The commissioner for one. I gave you the note. I *told* you.'

'Yes.'

'Don't "yes" me.'

'No.'

'No? Good God. I told you to go easy and what did you do?'

He was shouting now. I could handle his shouting.

'I don't know.'

'YOU DON'T KNOW?' He picked up the plant pot from his desk and threw it at the back wall. It smashed into several pieces, spraying water into the air and scattering soil everywhere. 'You poked him in the EYE!'

'Oh, yes, I remember now.'

He would calm down in a bit.

'Oh yes. Oh, bloody yes!'

'Yep.'

He seethed back in his chair, gripping his hair again. I counted to three. 'So, was there anything else? I've had a busy week.'

He stopped pulling his hair and glared at me. 'Oh, I'm so sorry, so sorry to take up your precious time. Been too busy dressing up as a wizard, have you?'

It took me a moment to realise what he was on about. 'I wasn't a wizard. I was the Great Edm–'

'I don't care!'

'Oh.'

'What did you poke him in the eye for?'

'He was annoying.'

'You're annoying. I don't poke *you* in the eye, do I?'

'No.'

He scratched his neck and seemed to calm down a notch. 'Have you made any progress on the damn case? Any sign of his racehorse?'

'No, no, not just yet.' I tried to lean back in his chair, but there really was no give in it.

'When are you going to do something? Have you spoken to Mr Landley yet?'

I woke up at this. 'What? No, dear God, no.'

'What are you waiting for? Go speak to him tomorrow, first thing.'

'It's Sunday tomorrow and I'll probably be seeing him at Christmas for the part–'

'Lavender.' He was quiet now, controlled.

'Yes?'

'First thing tomorrow, Sunday or not, I want you to go and speak to Mr Landley. Find out what the hell is going on. You understand? First thing tomorrow.'

'I understand what you are saying, yes.'

'Good. Now get the hell out of my sight.'

❖ ❖ ❖

Four days later, we were on our way to see Mr Landley. I had wanted to go Sunday, as the inspector had suggested, but I felt that it was best to send him a letter first informing him of our visit. He replied by return of post. 'A quick note, just to let you know...', which went on for seven pages. It took me a day to skim-read it.

Then Adam, across at Boaters, didn't look very well. He'd gone awfully pale. I had said as much to Sydney and Rose and that I felt obliged to keep an eye on him, with me being such a close, personal friend. So I had spent the vast majority of yesterday sat in Boaters eating and reading, ensuring that he came to no harm. He seemed well in the end, probably just a passing thing.

Then there was the business with the school. Emma had called in to see me. I'd given her some helpful advice and encouraged her to team up with the little gap-toothed girl, Jane. I told her that she was a bright one, and Emma went away happy enough. After that, I'd needed a little nap.

So, it was that on Wednesday afternoon, myself and Sydney found ourselves in the Landley drawing room. His country house was exactly as I'd pictured it would be, seated on the edge of Castle Howard, offering excellent views, but with old and fusty décor and crammed to the brim with junk. Sydney's eyes were wide with charm when we'd first arrived; now they were frozen with fright as Mr Landley continued his non-stop farming diatribes:

'I told you, didn't I, Margaret? Didn't I, Margaret? When I saw Mr Lavender, I said, there's a man who wants to run a farm. Didn't I, Margaret? Got farming blood in him.'

'It's not that I want to run a far–'

'I knew it. I could sense it. I could tell you were listening and taking in my knowledge. There's no point in having knowledge if you don't share it, is there? Is there, Margaret? Margaret?'

The poor suffering woman nodded, but Mr Landley didn't notice.

'I told you, didn't I? Time. Time is the secret of crop rotation.' He wagged his thick finger at me. 'Time, Mr Lavender. Time. Let nature take its course. Ha ha.'

Good God, not this again.

His eldest son, Anthony, started creeping past his father, using our presence as a means of escape. I bet the poor lad never got any peace. He'd be constantly lectured about manure. Just five minutes and I was already going insane. I had to fight through the jungle of nonsense before I could get to the point of our visit.

'Ah, yes, terrible business. I've never heard anything like it. I said as much, didn't I Margaret? Margaret? Didn't I? Margaret, didn't I say as much?'

Margaret sat in the corner, a slight twitch of her face indicting an affirmative.

'Have you not got any theories on it?' I managed to get in.

'Theories? Such exciting words, eh Margaret? No, no. Never seen anything like it. Cows going missing. Sheep. Horses and pigs. The whole thing is quite mysterious, Mr Lavender. I said as much to my friend, Mr Parsons. He's been in the farming business almost as long as I have and he's never seen anything like it either.' He shook his head and scratched at his huge bushy sideburns, showering the carpet with dead skin. 'Not in all my years have I seen anything like it, I–'

'Have you visited the places recently?'

I looked over at Sydney, who was still frozen in shock.

'The places, Mr Lavender?'

'The, er, scenes of the crimes, as it were.'

'Visited? Yes, I went to see Mr Eastwell, the very next day after his horse went missing. Took Anthony with me. And I spoke to Mrs Wobble just last week, didn't I, Margaret? Margaret, didn't I go to speak to Mrs Wobble just last week? Margaret? Margaret?'

Jesus. I would have to lie down for a week after this.

I had to cut through several more 'Margaret, Margarets' before I could ask him about the key situation.

'Keys to the properties are kept at Castle Howard, but they're never used nowadays.' He scratched at his chin, his white stubble protesting against his rough fingers. 'Have I told you the secret of manure, Mr Lavender?'

'What about spare keys? Do you keep padlock keys?'

'Paddock keys?'

'Padlock keys.'

'Oh, I thought you said paddock keys. Ha, ha. Imagine that, paddock and padlock, sound the same, don't they? Don't they, Margaret? Margaret? Padlock and paddock. I mean paddock and padlock, sound the same.'

'Padlock keys!' Sydney said, struggling. The only time he'd spoken a word.

'Yes, yes. Paddock and padlock, ha, ha.'

'We have to go now.' Sydney stood up and ran out of the room.

'Oh, is your little friend quite well, Mr Lavender? Upset stomach. I'll tell you a secret about the upset stoma–'

'Mr Landley! *Please*. Do they keep padlock keys at Castle Howard?'

'Ho, ho, I imagine you could get all the keys you want at Castle Howard. It's a huge place, Mr Lavender, isn't it, Margaret? Margaret?'

'No, I meant about–'

'You know, Mr Lavender, if you're serious about starting in farm management, you should come over more often. Shouldn't he, Margaret? Margaret? Margaret?'

I stood up quickly and ran out of the house.

We had more luck with Simon, the Castle House steward. Simon was an oasis of sanity in an insane world. Perfectly organised, he answered questions quickly and efficiently. Keys to the properties were kept in a storage cupboard. No, they didn't have keys to all the padlocks, but yes, they had all the keys to the properties they owned. Yes, he could show me the cupboard. Yes, they were all there and accounted for. No, they didn't have a padlock key for Mrs Wobble's barn.

I had just asked Simon for a list of people who were to attend the Christmas party. I wanted to know, but then again, I didn't. But in the end, I'd rather know the suffering I'd be up against. Thankfully, the earl wasn't up from London yet. So, we were waiting in the long corridor, while Simon was off writing out my list, and then we could get off home. I was sitting cross-legged observing Sydney walking up and down pretending to be lord of the manor, hands behind his back.

'Mr Laven-dah,' he said, in a ridiculous voice. 'I say dear chap. Do you want to stroll around my gardens?'

I got something in my eye, so I dabbed at them with my thumb and forefinger.

'Tired, Mr Laven-dah?'

'Enjoying yourself?'

'Yas, enjoyed a nice morning stroll through my estate.' He glanced at a portrait. Some snooty Queen. 'Ah, don't you find art so restoring, Mr Laven-dah?'

'Oh, do be quiet.'

It didn't take long for Simon to come back with the list. I thanked him and quickly glanced at it. Mr Landley was on it, naturally. It was absolutely certain that I was going to get seated next to him at Christmas, absolutely certain. I also noticed Lord and Lady Talbot – they were out for revenge, so that would be fun. Thomas Parsons? 'Sydney, didn't Mr Landley mention a Mr Parsons?'

Sydney stared at me blankly, but I noticed Simon start.

'Is this Parsons friends with Mr Landley?' I asked him.

'Well, sort of, but…'

'But, what?'

'Well, I'd say they were more like rivals, really.'

'Rivals, eh? That's interesting. That's very interesting indeed.'

CHAPTER TEN

The minster courtyard was awash with clumsy Christmas folk, the majority of whom were crammed around the giant Christmas tree which lit up the whole square. Two people had already trodden on my toes and I'd lost count of the number of times I'd been jostled around. Mulled wine was the predominant aroma, not unpleasant upon the first hint of its spicy fragrance, but it soon became sickly-sweet and over-powering. Sydney was circling around with two cups of the stuff, not generally a fan of wine, but he couldn't find anything else.

Rose came and clutched at my arm, pointing at something high up I couldn't make out, perhaps the yellow candle lantern lights, which hung high upon tree branches and nearby lampposts, flooding the icy ground with flickering miniature snowflakes. The market stalls were thronged with people in search of Christmas clutter. The worst was the repulsive candle stall which fought with the spiced aroma of the mulled wine and made me sneeze repeatedly. This attracted a few hostile stares as if I carried with me the third coming of the plague.

The choir over in the minster were warming up their voices, ready for the torturous Christmas carol service that I was being forced to attend.

'This is lovely, isn't it?' Rose said, standing beside me once again, having momentarily abandoned me during my sneezing fit.

'What is?'

'The tree, the square, everything.'

'If you say so.'

She was about to bite but then spotted something on a stall and dashed off to carry out a detailed investigation. Her space was filled by Emma, grinning up at me, and her new friend, Jane, the little gap-toothed girl from school.

'Enjoying yourself, Uncle James?' Emma asked.

She knew I hated crowds.

'How's the investigation going?' I asked them.

'That's what we wanted to speak to you about,' Emma said, looking around as if someone might overhear.

I leaned in a little, taking care not to spill my largely untouched mulled wine on the top of her head. 'Go on.'

She looked at Jane before speaking. 'We think we've worked out who's done it. There's a girl. Laura!'

'She's a bully,' Jane added. 'The girl who was rude to you when you taught us.'

I vaguely remembered an ugly wasp-faced girl when I was teaching them.

'Yes, we think Laura stole and planted the gold watch to get Tilly in trouble. She's horrible like that,' Jane said.

'How do you know?'

'We think we heard her bragging about it,' Emma said. 'To her friends.'

'Well, they're not really her friends.'

Emma agreed. 'But how do we prove it?'

I rubbed my eyes with my left hand, no doubt still suffering from the scented candles. 'A bragger, eh?' I noticed them casting an eye over to a sweet stall. 'Hey, do you want some sweets?'

Emma hesitated. 'No, thank you, Uncle James.'

A lie of course.

'Come on, let me get you some sweets. It'll give me time to think of a solution to your little problem.' I walked with them up to the stall. An old woman with an incredibly pink nose was weighing out sweets from a jar and then handed them over to a little urchin boy who grasped at them greedily and ran off. I told the girls to choose what they wanted.

Emma took her time. 'Can I have a small bag of those please?' she said finally, pointing at some red and yellow boiled sweets. Her friend nodded, still unsure.

'A small bag? Get more than that. Take the

whole jar,' I told them.

The pink-nosed woman jerked her head at me.

'What else would you like? Do you like the rhubarbs?' I pointed at another jar.

'A whole jar, uncle? Don't be silly.'

'Of course! Why not?'

She laughed. 'That's far too much.'

They still looked unsure. 'Look, we're all going to be dead at some point, so you might as well enjoy the little things in life, hadn't you? Both those jars and that one.' I instructed the pink-nosed woman, who looked at me strangely.

'I don't sell them by the whole jar, sir, just by the bag.'

'Then fill them into bags until you've used the whole jar.'

She nodded wearily and began counting out the sweets which piled up in front of her. Emma and Jane both laughed as the bags of sweets grew higher and higher. While the woman was weighing out the sweets, I thought of an idea that might work. I whispered in Emma's ear my plan, which I hoped for their sake would work. They were quite animated by the prospect. I always knew it was a good plan to get Emma involved.

'Hello.' Sydney bobbed at the side of me from out of nowhere, smacking his lips. 'It's growing on me, this mulled wine.' He pulled a face and tilted the cup to look at its disappearing contents. 'Do you like it?'

'Yes, as much as you do.' I showed him my cup which was still more or less full.

'Oh, can I have it then?'

'But you don't even like it! Unbelievable.' I shook my head but handed it over. He grinned as he took it, stopping to flick out something that was floating on top.

'A little twig. You know what that means, don't you?' he said.

'What do you mean?'

'What my Mam always said about twigs floating in mulled wine?'

I shook my head in disbelief. 'Did your mother have sayings for every damn thing? Go on then, what?'

'A twig in the brew means that heavy snow is due.'

'Utter nonsense.'

◆ ◆ ◆

We were seated in York Minster, in the third row from the front for the Christmas carol service. I was dazzled by the amount of (thankfully, non-scented) candles which flanked the choir on either side. Watching their reflected light distracted me through the early vocalisations. I followed the flickers as they illuminated the great stained-glass windows on both wings and the statues of the Kings of England frozen in time.

It felt like the incessant choir flooded the whole of the minster, reaching out to every crevice and vaulted ceiling, into every dark inch, lighting even the deathly tombs below. It was relatively endurable, but then the inevitable happened.

I leaned into Rose who was on my left. 'How long's it going to go on for?'

'Isn't it beautiful?'

'Indeed. When does it finish?' I asked.

'Sorry? What?'

'When can we leave?'

But the carol had finished and I couldn't hear her for the sound of applause. I never really understood applause. A quick clap to show appreciation is acceptable, but prolonged applause shows some want of wit in my book. Most people were continually clapping because everybody else was, which made no practical sense at all.

'When does it finish?' I repeated, but she just smiled back, lost in the new carol that the choir had begun. Another one referencing baby Jesus.

I occupied myself throughout the noise by thinking of the new block of cheese I had at home. One success from the Christmas stalls at least. I'd cut myself a few thick wedges before bed and take up a glass of claret. Something to look forward to at least.

I tried not to think about the upcoming Christmas stay at Castle Howard. I had one more day of peace before that crazy nonsense began, but I felt the list burning in my inside jacket pocket and so I took it out again. It was written in Simon's neat hand.

George Howard, the 9th Earl of Carlisle, will be entertaining the following guests over the Christmas period this year:

Lord Charles Talbot
Lady Isabella Talbot
Mr John Eastwell
Mrs Gertrude Eastwell
Mast David Eastwell (son, 17 years old)
Mr Geoffrey Landley (estate manager)
Mrs Margaret Landley
Master Anthony Landley (eldest son, 17 years old)
Master Frederick Landley (youngest son, 12 years old)
Mr Thomas Parsons (estate advisor and bailiff)
Mrs Jane Parsons
Miss Louise Parsons (daughter, 18 years old)
Mr Malcolm Wegwipe ("York Herald" correspondent)
Mr William Brookes
Miss Rose McCarthy
Mr James Lavender
Mr Sydney Brown
Mrs Stella Brown
Miss Emma Brown (daughter, 15 years old)

Yes, this was going to be fun. Lord Talbot

and Mr Eastwell couldn't stand me. Lady Talbot did seem to like me, which was even worse, especially when she and Rose were constantly at each other's throats. Then Mr Landley! Holy Jesus. Malcolm Wegwipe was going to get a piece of my mind though. I don't know why I agreed to this. Nothing good would come of it.

The choir finished another carol and everyone clapped like maniacs. I didn't clap at all, as I had clapped previously, acknowledging my appreciation sensibly. The applause dragged on until they started up another damn carol. This one was about a shepherd watching a sheep. This reminded me of Mrs Wobble. I needed to get out.

I nudged Sydney; he was singing along, his cheeks flushed red with pleasure. 'What time's this thing finish?'

'WHEN SHEPHERDS WATCHED...What, eh? Oh, nine.'

'*Nine?*'

There was no way in hell I could endure another hour and odd of this noise. I tapped my fingers on my chair. I wouldn't have any problems getting up and walking out. I considered it a valid option. However, I knew it would result in a lot of unnecessary earache. I leaned in towards Sydney, who was still singing along. 'Do you fancy a beer?'

He broke out of his singing. 'Yes, after the show.'

Show?

I licked at my lips and leaned in again. 'Are you sure you don't fancy a lovely beer, right now? A fat pork pie? Lovely and plump.'

He stopped singing and looked shocked. 'What about the sing-song?'

'There'll be other Christmas concerts, but pork pies might sell out fast.'

'Oh, I don't know.'

'Wouldn't you prefer a nice beer? A crispy pork pie on the side?' I nodded. 'Dip it in a bit of mustard.' I smiled at his reaction. The prospect of a pie with a blob of mustard on the side, washed down with a beer was clear on his face, but then he looked troubled, casting a glance towards his wife and the choir up ahead.

'Why don't you get up and I'll follow.' I prompted him out of his chair. 'Go on, the others won't mind.'

He licked his lips. 'Go on then.' He stood up and said something to Stella before excusing himself hastily. He bumbled past me and Rose (choosing the longest way out), and squeezed all the way down the line, banging the chairs of those in front in the process. Indignant murmurs came from the row behind as he momentarily blocked their view.

'Where's he going?' Rose whispered to me.

'I don't know. The pub probably, you know what he's like. I'll go and find out.'

'But you'll miss the carol service.'

'I know. I was enjoying it as well, but...' I

shrugged, 'I need to make sure he's well.'

Rose rubbed my arm briefly, whispering. 'Sorry if you miss it.'

I sighed and flashed her a morose expression. 'Me too.'

I stood up, following him down the line causing the same chaos Sydney had just caused with yet more indignant murmurs. A small fight broke out behind me, but I didn't care. I was getting out of the service and was heading to the quiet of the pub – a much better prospect. Poor Sydney though was in for a hell of a lot of trouble later on from his wife, but then again, one has to take some personal responsibility. He was, after all, the one who had walked out right in the middle of the Christmas carol service. He could be unbelievably rude at times.

◆ ◆ ◆

Another sheep had gone missing at Mrs Wobble's farm. I'd sent out the deadly duo, Sydney and the constable, to investigate as I was far too busy with bookwork which I couldn't get out of. It was the same story; missing sheep from a locked barn, no witnesses. Thankfully for Mrs Wobble, not a particularly expensive ram this time, but that in itself struck me as very suggestive. Very suggestive indeed. Sydney had returned to confirm the story. Well, more accurately, the constable had, as Sydney had refused to leave the protection of the gate. Apparently, the bull was looking particularly fearsome, so it was the constable who had to gather the details and suffer more of the rock-hard Albert cake. After relaying the exciting events of their mission, Sydney had to return home immediately, as Stella had banned him from the pub. Luckily for him, we were soon to depart for Castle Howard.

'But just to walk out like that, what got into him?' Rose asked me, as she sat in Sydney's chair. 'I'm not surprised Stella's banned him from the pub.'

I shrugged. 'Sydney's like that.'

There was a gentle tap on the door, and in walked Emma and Jane both sporting wide smiles. I encouraged them to shut the door quickly. It was icy cold outside, but they didn't seem to mind; young bones don't feel the cold.

'Cat got the cream?' I said.

'It worked!' Emma blurted.

'Just as you said,' Jane added.

'Bravo!'

'What worked?' Rose asked.

There was a thud from upstairs. Another elephant had fallen victim to Mrs Wilkins.

'We caught her,' Emma said.

'Laura,' Jane added. 'We trapped her. Tilly can go back to school.'

'We solved the case, Uncle James!'

'I never doubted you for a moment.'

'Perfect! Tell us what happened,' Rose said,

standing up to hug them both. Something of an overreaction in my view, though I was glad for them, naturally.

It had worked just as I'd hoped. Jane had gone to fetch the headmaster and she'd kept him in the corridor just behind the door, while Emma had asked the wasp-faced girl about the missing watch, feigning wonder. A bragger likes to brag, and she confessed the whole thing to the 'new girl', not knowing the headmaster was just through the door listening to every word. The wasp-faced girl was immediately expelled from the school and a letter of apology was on its way to Mr Harding. His daughter, Tilly, was to be reinstated in the New Year. Case solved. It was to be arranged that both girls would receive a healthy payment as Mr Harding was paying well.

Rose was still hugging the girls. 'Brilliant, well done. I told you it would work, didn't I, James?'

'What? It was my idea.'

Rose bit her lip. '*Your* idea?'

I crossed my legs, leaning back. 'Obviously.'

'Oh James, do you *actually* practise being infuriating?'

I frowned. 'What do you mean? You might have fixed Emma's hair a bit, but the initial idea was mine, clearly.'

She shook her head and turned back to the girls and fussed them some more, before seeing them off. Emma had to help her mum prepare for tomorrow, as Sydney was refusing to help pack. Apparently, he was just sitting in his room staring out of the window. I'd told her that I was well used to his bone-idle nature, but that I'd see her in the morning.

'Well?' Rose said after they'd gone.

'Well, what?'

Rose was still talking at me, but I'd drifted off the last few minutes.

She sighed. 'I hope you've got us all a nice gift, especially Emma.'

'*Gift?*'

'Yes, a gift – gift for Christmas Day, of course.'

'Oh, right, yes. You expect a gift on Christmas Day? Wait, what, for everybody?'

She laughed, thinking I was joking. 'Of course, silly.'

Rose stood up, wishing me a good night, and reminding me to be up early in the morning. As if I could ever forget. She closed the door quickly behind her, but she'd still let in a spell of cold.

'Mrs Wilkins! Mrs Wilkins!' I shouted.

A thud acknowledged my shout, and she eventually stomped into the room. 'What?'

'How do you fancy doing a spot of Christmas shopping?'

There was no way in hell I was leaving the comfort of the fire, for it was turning colder than ever outside as if a storm was brewing. Mrs Wilkins could do it.

CHAPTER ELEVEN

The following day we all set out for Castle Howard under the worst snowstorm I'd ever seen. The thick and threatening grey clouds that hung above us promised no let up. If anything, it looked set to get worse. If that was even possible.

The bad omens had been there from the start, as the day had begun in a frantic rush, and we'd only just made the train. This was thanks to Mrs Wilkins and our not so friendly driver.

Mrs Wilkins had been late handing over my wrapped presents and went off in a huff after I'd tapped my pocket watch. She'd stated that I could 'stuff my stinking Christmas' and had made obscene suggestions of what I could do with the gifts. Daily abuse for no reason. I'd come to learn that York really had a terrible slew of housekeepers.

Then, there was Walrus. His attitude was even

worse. He'd complained all the way to the station about the lack of time, even though I'd explained more than once that it was Mrs Wilkins' fault. But still, he'd huffed and puffed, especially when lifting down the huge trunks that Rose and Stella had brought. (Clearly, both of them thought we were stopping for a year.) He'd even rudely barked at me when I'd stood behind him providing helpful lifting critiques. Some people were clearly beyond teaching. Fortunately for us, Sydney had been on hand for the second drop, and he'd helped with the trunk removal under my watchful eye.

I was still, of course, dreading the whole affair, and I had scowled at Rose as we'd climbed into the carriage to register my protest, but I'm not sure she'd noticed.

Now, Rose and Emma were chatting side-by-side next to me in our first-class carriage, as paid for by the earl. The earl was completely batty, but you couldn't fault his generosity.

Across from us, Stella was clearly still a little annoyed with Sydney. Rose had told me, in a quick whisper, they'd been arguing about something else this morning, his green trousers most probably. I expected their moods would lift when we got there. Should we do so. For the snow was settling quickly, and the fields beyond were already covered in thick blankets of deadly white. It might be difficult, if not impossible, to manoeuvre the small lanes to Castle Howard in the journey from the train platform. There existed the very real possibility of getting trapped and dying of exposure. On second thoughts, maybe this was a better alternative to making it to the party and enduring the torture there.

'Do you really think this is a good idea?' I said, as the snow battered the train.

Rose looked a little unsure, glancing at the clouds. 'Well, we can't turn back now, can we?'

'Yes. Just get the train back at the other end. No party, no gathering – a brilliant idea.'

Emma looked crestfallen. 'Oh, Uncle James, don't say that.'

Stella reassured her. 'It'll be well, dear,' she said, looking up at me and thus ending the discussion. She looked smartly dressed today for one who spent most of the time in the kitchen, but not as glamorous as Rose and Emma. Of course, I wore my usual black suit. I didn't own any other colours. Besides, I always looked dashing, so why change?

It was a truly horrendous experience getting off the train. The open platform offered little in the way of protection from the relentless snowstorm. Fortunately, the earl's carriages were waiting for us at the other side, and I'd managed to jump inside one quickly, before much of the snow could really penetrate. Rose helped Emma into our carriage, climbing in after me, but Sydney was still messing about with the luggage.

'Oh, it's cold,' I said to Rose, rubbing my knees, as she came and sat beside me.

'I know, but it won't take us long to get there, hopefully,' she added, looking at the road ahead.

'Well, I did say, but...'

'Why do old people always complain about the weather?' Emma said.

'Old people? I'm twenty-eight, you little–'

'James!' Rose knocked me on the shoulder and Emma smiled.

Sydney was lifting a trunk onto the carriage in front with the help of a footman. His coat was already covered in snow and he'd only been out there a few minutes. The heavy trunk squashed against his nose as he lifted it up even further to be tied on top. I tapped on the window. 'Sydney, you great lump, get a move on. It's cold in here!' I turned around to Emma. 'You know, your dad's a good fellow deep down, but he's bloody bone idle. He should have got that trunk up by now.'

The journey along the lanes was as hard going as I'd predicted. Twice we had been stuck. Twice the footmen and Sydney had struggled to free a wheel, but they'd managed to get us going again under my expert advice. It wasn't long before the outline of Castle Howard became visible through the dense air. As we got nearer and nearer, it did look like some magical palace and I waited for the inevitable gushing of adjectives.

'Oh, James, isn't it beautiful?' Rose said.

Emma was equally taken. 'It's wonderful!' She

squeezed Rose's arm. 'Thank you. Isn't it just stunning, Uncle?'

'Yes, it's very nice.'

I heard the rumble of a third carriage behind ours as we pulled up. I strained around. I prayed it wasn't the Landleys; I needed a few moments of sanity. The carriage door flew open, and a man stumbled out. I recognised the trousers at first, bright yellow, like Sydney's favourite pair. It was William Brookes, a harmless, vacant fellow. I was safe, for now.

I jumped out of the cab into the heart of the storm and hurriedly trampled over to the main entrance. My left foot slipped in the snow, but I managed to right myself thanks to my walking cane, and I hopped up the steps into the house. Rose and Emma followed on behind, holding their hoods tightly against the elements. Sydney helped Stella out of the cab, and they joined us. The trunks were left for the footmen to collect. Sydney had got away without helping once again. The efficient Simon ticked us off on a list inside, as William Brookes, friend of the earl, followed on behind, saying a 'good morning' to us. I wondered if he'd realised if it was even snowing? It was also gone twelve, so it wasn't even morning.

'He's got yellow trousers.' I heard Sydney grumble to Stella. 'Told you I could have come in mine.'

'Your green ones are more suitable, Sydney.'

'Yes, but I pre–'

But even Sydney stopped bickering when he caught sight of how the Great Hall had been decorated. A huge, majestic Christmas tree, cast in red and gold, towered at the far end. And the candles. There must have been hundreds. They bathed the whole room in golden light, right up to Antonio Pellegrini's stunning painted cupola above. Emma gasped when she saw it, and gripped Rose's arm. 'I've never seen anything so amazing.' But there was little time at the moment for admiring things. The first port of call was to get out of our wet outer clothing in front of a roaring fire. We'd arrived at Castle Howard alive, through the worst snow I'd ever seen, and there was no going back.

◆ ◆ ◆

Having left the opulence of the Great Hall behind, Simon had led us to the turquoise drawing room where I'd immediately gazed up at the walls and the ceiling. It had lost none of its Georgian period charm, but that was not my primary concern. For, seated in the centre of the room was Mr Landley! He immediately broke off his conversation with another disagreeable looking chap and stood up to greet me. I dashed to the fireplace and quickly removed my slightly damp outer clothing. I shoved Sydney, who was standing in the way, along. I was afforded half a minute warming time, before I was assaulted by the great bore, who all but yanked my arm from its socket.

'Ah, Mr Lavender. Glad you could make it. I did wonder if you would, considering the weather, eh? I said as much, didn't I, Margaret? Margaret, didn't I say as much? About the weather. Margaret? Didn't I say that about the weather?'

Poor afflicted Margaret. No wonder the woman was dull and grey. She was seated further behind, by a small table, talking to the wife of the man Mr Landley had been lecturing when we walked in.

Mr Landley was still shaking my hand enthusiastically, but he finally broke off to introduce me to his friend. 'Mr Parsons, this here is Mr Lavender. He's great fun! He wants to be a farmer!'

Mr Parsons stood up and shook my hand just as vigorously. He was a short, square-faced, kindly-looking chap with round wire-framed spectacles and tidy hair. Yet he still grasped my wrist like a man twice his size. 'Pleased to meet you. Did it take you by surprise?' He spoke in a quiet little voice, straightening out his smart, grey jacket as he conversed.

'Did what take me by surprise?'

'THE WEATHER!' he shouted.

What the hell? I nearly fell over in fright.

'Calm down.'

'Obviously I meant the WEATHER!' He shook

his head and twisted away from me in disgust towards Sydney.

'You know, you'll have a heart attack if you carry on like that,' I said.

Mr Landley stepped in. 'Don't you mind Mr Parsons. He's a passionate fellow.'

I took glass of champagne from a waiting footman. 'Yes, well. I think he's got issues.'

'Afternoon,' Sydney said, shaking Mr Parsons' hand nervously and casting a weary glance at Mr Landley.

'Ah, got over the runs, have you?' Mr Landley asked him, remembering the last time Sydney and myself had called round, when Sydney had run out of the house to escape him. He was about to enter into one of his 'Margaret, Margaret,' episodes, no doubt a pearl of wisdom about the runs, when Rose rescued us, asking to be introduced to the rest of the party. There was a brief interlude of introductions, which I took advantage of by turning my back on everyone and warming myself by the fire.

Sitting just behind the torturous Landley, at the side of Margaret, were their two boys. The elder one, Anthony, was mooning across at the Parsons' table, clearly bored by his younger brother's attempts at mischief. Mrs Parsons had possibly once been attractive, especially if her daughter was anything to go by, but now her toad-like eyes and hungry expression made her slightly repulsive. Rose, Stella and Emma mingled with the party, leaving me at the mercy of Mr Landley and Mr Parsons. William Brookes joined with another fellow at the far side of the room. He was writing something down in a little book, his foppish hair half-covering his face. This was probably Malcolm Wegwipe. If it was, he was going to get a stern talking to later.

Mr Parsons had recovered his composure and he addressed me again, in a quiet, polite manner. 'So, you're a detective?'

I observed him carefully. No signs of aggression. 'Yes.'

'And you're the one looking into the missing animals?'

'I am.'

Mr Parsons took off his glasses and wiped them with a little cloth he had in this pocket. 'Intriguing.' He put his glasses back on. 'And shocking.'

'Indeed,' I said.

'Utterly shocking. One of the worst things to happen since the nag's mate.'

I looked at Sydney, who shrugged. 'What's the nag's mate?' I asked.

'OH MY GOD!' He gripped his face as if he wanted to rip it off. 'The NAG'S MATE!'

I shook my head.

Mr Parsons was still gripping his face. 'The rabies incident of 1838!'

'What rabies incident of 1838?' I asked, fascinated by the little man before me.

'You don't know about the Nag's Mate incident of *1838*?' he shouted. 'When a rabid dog bit a sheep, then the sheep bit a horse, then the horse knocked over a cart load of apples.'

'No.'

'Oh, my GOD!' He started pulling at his hair again. Sydney leaned away from him, eyes wide both in amusement and fright.

Mr Landley stepped over, hands on Mr Parsons' arm, laughing. 'Now, don't you mind our Mr Lavender here. He's such a humourist. He's only having you on.'

I looked over at Rose who suppressed a laugh.

Mr Landley continued. 'Everybody knows about the Nag's Mate incident. Hey, we'll have to tell Mr Lavender the cow story later, eh? What do say, Mr Lavender? Mr Lavender? Do you want to hear how the cow got stuck in the snow? Mr Lavender?'

I shot Rose an icy glance, but she wasn't looking now, or was pretending not to. Christmas with the lunatics had begun.

Sydney finished his champagne and grabbed another two off a silver tray. Not a bad plan in the current circumstances. I took another one myself and sat down in a wide armchair. Mr Landley slapped a heavy hand down on my arm, thick hairs curling on his hand. It was more like an ape's hand. 'So, how is the investigation going?'

I was just about to answer, as it was for once

a sane question, when an unwelcome voice from the doorway prevented my reply.

'That's an excellent question, Geoffrey. Have you located my racehorse yet, Lavender?'

Mr Eastwell.

Landley and Parsons visibly shrank back, sitting down in their chairs.

'It's an ongoing investigation,' I replied stiffly.

I had actually given Constable Matthews the Christmas job of trying to trace any potential avenues of sale, but I wasn't going to tell him that. Sydney had also put the feelers out, amongst his less scrupulous contacts. The less I asked on that point, the better.

Mr Eastwell strode towards me, his pointed nose leading the way. He was followed by a younger woman, clearly his wife, and his equally pointed-nosed son. A little spoilt Lord in the making if ever there was one.

Mr Eastwell came closer still, pointing a finger directly at me. 'I want to know what you're doing about my racehorse, *Lavender*,' he said. Sydney inched from his chair instinctively. The little chatters of noise puffed out one by one, into near total silence. I could only hear the little scratchings of pen across paper in the far corner of the room. Wegwipe.

I would have ignored Mr Eastwell anyway, but the earl strode into the room immediately breaking the tension. 'More guests!' he shouted, genuinely excited. 'Champagne! More champagne!'

The footmen, who already had champagne on standby, looked at each other, then just hovered around a bit more. The earl took one himself, and I knew what was coming. 'But...don't tell the wife!'

Mrs Parsons laughed, and there were a few polite guffaws elsewhere.

Mr Eastwell slithered to one side, joining his wife and son around a table at the far end of the room, his aggression waylaid, for now.

Rose stood up to meet the earl, and embraced him fondly.

'Rose, my dear!' He clasped her shoulders and stared into her fierce green eyes, then down to her matching dress. 'You look lovely, just lovely.'

'Thank you.' She gestured for the others to stand and they went over to meet him too. Sydney first, followed by Stella, then Emma with a curtsy and a smile. As was usual, he insisted they address him simply as George.

Mr Eastwell sat still, his dark eyes silently staring into space, and I could not shake my growing sense of unease. I could feel it nagging, deep down inside me. I'd felt this presence before, and I was certain, certain, that I was not just in the presence of a horrible little man. I could feel it – I was in the presence of evil.

CHAPTER TWELVE

Most of us were allocated rooms in the west wing. Rose had been given a room next to mine. Sydney, Stella and Emma's room was just opposite, close to William Brookes', the vacant fellow. I was relieved to have escaped the clutches of Messrs Landley and Parsons to retreat to my room for a brief period of sanity.

Naturally, the first thing I did was to go to the window and cast open the heavy curtains. Well, it was certainly still snowing! I couldn't see much through the thick swirls of white which blew violently against the pane.

I tried the bed. It was too soft and luxurious for my tastes, just like the room – too distracting. I prefer my bedrooms plain. Whereas, here, rich tapestries hung on the walls depicting Greek and Roman chaps in various athletic poses. All very well in a museum, but far too crowded for a bedroom.

I wandered next door to Rose. 'What's yours like?' I said as I pushed the door open widely.

She gasped as she was in a half-state of undress, and I immediately averted my eyes.

'Don't you knock?'

She didn't sound very pleased.

'What are you getting changed again for? We've only just got here.'

She sighed heavily. 'That was just for travelling in. It's not my day dress.'

'No wonder the trunks had looked heavy. Tut, tut. No thoughts for Walrus.'

I left her to it and went over to Sydney, knocking on the door this time. There was no way I wanted to catch Sydney in a half state of undress!

Stella opened the door and invited me in.

Their room was much larger, having to accommodate more beds, but it was as equally grand as mine, if not more so. Sydney was laying back on the huge four poster bed, hands behind his head, gold swirls interwoven in a rich tapestry around him. 'Ah, Mr Laven-dah,' he said, in his ridiculous, mock aristocratic voice, rolling a hand towards a chair. 'Pray, be seated.'

But before I could dismiss his nonsense, Emma attacked me in a crushing embrace. 'Oh, Uncle James, this is wonderful! Sorry,' she added, pulling away from me. 'I know you're funny with all of that, but this place is like nothing I've ever seen before or imagined. It's magical!' She laughed, as if aware she sounded over-excited but still didn't care. 'I feel like a countess!'

I recovered my posture, brushing down my jacket, which had become a little creased under her assault. 'Yes, it's not bad,' I replied.

◆ ◆ ◆

I headed towards the stairs with Rose beside me. She was dressed in purple this time. I don't know why she had to dress again. I told her as much, and she was about to moan at me, claiming that she'd already explained, when she stopped abruptly. As on the stairs we came face to face with a familiar couple – Lord and Lady Talbot! We had the misfortune to encounter this unsavoury pair during our last visit to Castle Howard. Lord Talbot had vowed to take revenge after losing money to me at cards. It was safe to say that Rose and Lady Talbot were not exactly on the best of terms either. I had no idea why.

'Mr Lavender,' Lord Talbot said, smiling with hostile self-confidence. I still saw him as a Lord Byron figure – certainly the dangerous to know part.

I returned his cold greeting.

'James,' Lady Talbot said, purring as she moved towards me, thrusting her hand into mine, expecting me to kiss it, but I just left it there and she withdrew it. She still smiled, then she glanced dismissively at Rose. 'Still with Miss McCarthy, I see. Why, she must be talented.'

Rose stiffened. 'Lady Talbot, still as obnoxious as ever, I see.'

Lady Talbot smirked. 'Ah, *Miss* McCarthy, jealousy is such a bitter condition, don't you think? Then again, the Irish as a race are quite a jealous lot, are they not?'

'Oh, I don't think you could call the Irish jealous, Lady Talbot. You could call the Irish a lot of things, but being jealous of spoilt privilege is not one of them.' She nudged me towards the steps.

Lady Talbot flicked her fan into life. 'Goodbye, James, *Miss* McCarthy. No doubt we can continue our fascinating conversation into the faults of the Irish at a later time, being that it is such a large topic.'

'Goodbye, Lady Talbot.' Rose went down a step before turning back towards her. 'These steps are really steep, be careful not to trip and fall all the way down.'

Striding back into the drawing room, the first thing I noticed was the earl immediately jumping up like a maniac. 'Rose! Mr James. Hurry up, it's treasure hunt time!'

Oh no.

I turned around to be met with a grinning Sydney, with Stella and Emma beside him.

'Gather round! Gather round!' the earl shouted.

Here we go.

We all had to cram around the fireplace. 'I've organised a Christmas treasure hunt for you. Simon, here, will go through the rules.'

We had to wait for everyone, with Lord and Lady Talbot being the last ones to re-emerge before Simon could explain the rules.

'Ladies and gentlemen, here's how it's going to work,' Simon began, when everyone was ready. 'You're all going to get into teams of three and read through a series of clues.'

Clues, I could handle.

People started chatting, craning around, already working out potential groupings. I thought myself, Rose and Emma would form a formidable team, but maybe Emma would want to join with Sydney. Simon had to raise his voice over the murmurs around him. 'The first team back here with the treasure wins.'

'How exciting. What do we win?' Mrs Parsons asked.

'Ah!' the earl said, 'that would spoil the surprise, but there is a final twist. The teams will be drawn at random. Team building. Good fun!'

Holy Jesus.

'No way,' I said, but my voice was lost in the hectic jostling of people eager to squeeze to the front.

A little wooden box had already been organised, which Simon now held for the earl to pick out names. There were eighteen of us in total, after Stella had somehow got out of playing the game, so there would be six groups of three.

'I bloody hate this stuff,' I said to Sydney, who wasn't listening to me as usual.

'Good this, isn't it?' he said. 'Exciting. Who do you think you'll get?'

'I dread to think.'

I glanced around the room, lingering on Mr Eastwell and Lord Talbot. Probably that pair. They were staring at each other. They couldn't stand me, but by the looks of it, they couldn't stand each other either. Too similar, perhaps?

Simon held the box out as the earl popped a hand in and excitedly rummaged. 'Here goes.' He removed a piece of paper and looked at it obscurely, then twisted it the correct way around. 'And the first person is...young master Landley.'

The little boy, Frederick, smiled and got a clap on the back from his father which nearly knocked him over.

The earl continued. 'And he'll be joined by...Mr Brown.'

Sydney took a bow and went to stand by the young man, shaking his hand.

'And the third in the group will be...Lady Talbot.'

There was a polite round of applause, but Lady Talbot did not look impressed with being stuck with a young boy and Sydney. She still cut an attractive figure, with her blonde hair and her sharp blue eyes. She moved some way towards them but kept her distance, sulking at the prospect of the next hour or so with Sydney and the young boy. The young fellow looked pleased enough though, as did Sydney for that matter. I shook my head at him, warning him to keep well away from her.

The earl got our attention again and continued, clearly excited by the prospect of drawing out bits of paper with our names on and causing chaos in the process. He was a little quicker this time. 'Group two. Mrs Eastwell, Rose McCarthy and Master Eastwell.'

There was another small round of applause for some strange reason. The rest of us looked at each other in anticipation.

'Group three,' boomed the earl. 'Mrs Parsons, Miss Parsons…'

Someone shouted 'fix.'

'…and, let's have a look.' The earl felt blindly until he found a piece of paper. 'Mr Wegwipe.'

Oh, hell. There was still Mr Eastwell, Lord Talbot and Mr Landley left.

'Group four. Mr Brookes. Lord Talbot and…Mr Eastwell.'

There were several very noticeable 'oohs and ahhs' and both men unsuccessfully tried to hide their displeasure. I was getting better at reading body language, now that I had to work harder around Rose. I still had no idea why my condition didn't work around her.

The earl hastily proceeded. 'Group five. Master Landley, Mrs Landley and...' He paused for dramatic effect, which switched some eyes away from Lord Talbot and Mr Eastwell, '...young Miss Brown.'

Oh no.

The earl surveyed the room. 'That leaves, Mr James, Mr Parsons and Mr Landley.'

Dear Lord. I'd landed myself with Mr Parsons and Mr Landley. It couldn't have been much worse.

◆ ◆ ◆

Mr Landley had elected me as team captain, and he stood right beside me, his hairy hand on my shoulder. Mr Parsons was close as well, the little man having just shaken my hand again. I opened the first envelope that we had just been given:

> *Oh, what a Dickens it be,*
> *To not quite finish me.*
> *Hunt me and you'll find,*
> *More clues of my kind.*

'The kitchen!' Mr Landley shouted, right in my ear.

'Jesus.' I reeled away, knocking into Mr Parsons' chin, though he didn't seem to mind.

'The kitchen!' Mr Landley shouted again. Completely unaware of the pain he'd just caused.

I rubbed at my ear. 'What are you talking about, the kitchen?'

The earl was peering at us. A large grin on his face.

'The kitchen, Mr Lavender.' Mr Landley tapped his nose, knowingly. Two groups had already left the room. Rose's and Emma's.

'Why the kitchen?'

Mr Landley was still tapping his nose. 'Why, leftover food of course. "Not quite finish me." Leftover food. What do you think, Thomas?'

Mr Parsons scratched his chin. 'Quite a quandary, I'd say.'

'I'm telling you, it's the kitchen bins,' Mr Landley said. 'Leftover food.' Mr Landley started to dash away, until I held him back.

'What's Dickens got to do with the kitchen and leftover food?'

He shook his head at me, disapprovingly. 'I thought you were supposed to be a detective? Dickens *ate* food.'

'Well, of course he *ate* food, everyone does!'

Mr Landley nodded wisely, clearly not getting my point. I tried again.

'Dickens is clearly a specific clue. There has to be more to it than that.'

'Yes, Mr Lavender. Dickens really liked food. To the bins!'

I shook my head. 'It's not the kitchens. I know what it means.'

Mr Landley looked unsure. As did Mr Parsons.

Two more groups left the room, one to the right, the other to the left. There were just ours and the Wegwipe group left in the drawing room, with the earl still watching, clearly enthralled by our discussions.

'It's Edwin Drood,' I said.

'Who's Edwin Drood? A farmer?' Mr Parsons asked.

'*The Mystery of Edwin Drood*,' I said, more loudly. 'Dickens' unfinished novel.'

Mr Landley shook his head, smiling. 'No, I don't think it is.

'It is. Look, I'm pretty sure Dickens only finished six instalments, and there are six groups of us, so that would fit neatly. The next clue must be in the library.'

Mr Landley still looked unconvinced, holding his hands aloft. 'Well, well, Mr Lavender. I still think it's in the kitchen bins myself, but we can try the library first. You're the team captain, after all. I said to Margaret, didn't I, M–' But he turned around looking lost, as there was no Margaret to confirm the nonsense he was about to utter.

We were the third group to find the next clue, which was lodged in between the pages of June's instalment of *The Mystery of Edwin Drood*. It had been left out on a small table in the centre of the library for convenience. I held the next clue in my hands.

Mr Landley shook his head. 'Well, well, Mr Lavender, I dare say you were quite correct.'

'Quite correct. Good show,' Mr Parsons said, adjusting his small spectacles.

'Go on then, open the second clue,' Mr Landley said, pointing his thick finger at the envelope in my hand.

I opened it carefully and slid out the note:

> *Think longingly, um, and rest on me,*
> *From Yorkshire was I originally be.*
> *With heart of stone, cold man am I,*
> *This is where your precious clue lie.*

'The bathroom would be my suggestion.' Mr Parsons said, not really looking convinced.

Mr Landley scratched his sideburns, releasing a cloud of dead skin. 'Oh, I don't know. That's a tough one, isn't it, Mr Lavender?'

'Yes, it's certainly more interesting,' I conceded. 'I've got the top line, obviously, but the others are more challenging.'

I couldn't quite get the cold man from Yorkshire clue; there were a lot of cold men in Yorkshire, in more ways than one. 'No, it's in the museum, but I don't know where exactly.'

Mr Landley sounded surprised. 'How do you know it's in the museum?'

'Think longingly – muse, then at the um part. Museum. But what's a cold man from Yorkshire that you rest on? A chair?' I turned to Mr Parsons. 'A stool?'

He scratched his chin. 'The bathroom?'

'I don't think it's in the bathroom, do you, Mr

Lavender?'

Mr Parsons seethed, throwing his head back. 'IT'S THE BATHROOM!'

I jumped back, colliding with Mr Landley.

'It's obviously the bathroom. Oh my GOD! You think and rest in the BATHROOM!' He made as if to pull his hair out again.

I stepped back to give him space. He was still raging away.

'He's got a point, Mr Lavender.' Mr Landley said. 'The clue is in the bathroom! You rest upon the toilet. Well done, Thomas.'

'JEsus Chrissst.'

I grabbed Mr Landley's arm as he was about to run off again. 'It's not. It's in the museum. What about instead of resting on something yourself, is it something you can rest *things* on?'

'The BATHROOM!'

I rubbed my ear again. 'A table?' I said.

Mr Landley appeared to jump up on the spot. 'The Blue John table!'

Mr Parsons froze.

I turned back to Mr Landley. 'There's a Blue John table? Cold man – blue John, and Blue John is a precious stone from Yorkshire, so that would fit! Let's go!'

I dashed to the doorway, not seeing the person coming the other way – Mr Eastwell.

'You bloody fool!' he yelled, as I collided into him, banging against his shoulder. 'You incompetent, damn fool.'

'Oops.'

'Don't you "oops" me.'

I pushed past him, onwards to the museum.

'Damn fool,' he repeated at my retreating back.

Approaching the museum, I almost collided again, this time into Rose.

'Steady on.'

'Sorry,' I said.

She bit her lip in smugness. 'Bit slow with the clues, aren't you?'

I paused briefly. I could hear Landley and Parsons, panting from the other side of the corridor. 'I got the museum, but the last part about the Blue John took a little teasing.'

'Oh, I didn't get that. Museum was enough. Then we found them on the table.'

'Oh.'

'Bye.' She waved and headed back the way we'd come, crossing the paths of Parsons and Landley. I considered just following her, but she'd probably gone wrong on this one. I headed on into the museum and almost collided again into another Eastwell, this time the little snotty one. People really should be more careful.

'Watch where you're going,' he snapped, before walking slowly in the direction that Rose had taken. His mother followed him, still lingering in the museum. She was definitely younger than Mr Eastwell, mid-thirties, perhaps not unattractive in a rich, high-cheek-boned, horsey sort of way, but hardly likeable.

We searched for the Blue John table, which was not hard to find, having been placed near the centre of the room next to a statue of a Greek youth eating grapes. There were five unopened envelopes upon the little antique table. That meant we were currently second behind Rose's team. Good, but not good enough. I snatched an envelope up and slid my nail down the side, taking out the note:

> *Feel their eyes upon you,*
> *As you search for your third clue.*
> *For good luck you will need,*
> *If your tune is to succeed.*

'The music room!' Mr Landley shouted, full in my face this time.

'Is there a music room?'

Mr Landley looked puzzled. 'Well, not really, no.'

'Then it's not in the music room then, is it?'

'Ha, ha, sharp mind, Mr Lavender! Amazing stuff!'

'Well, not really. If there's no music room, then–'

'Wait 'till I tell Margaret; she will be very, very excited. Very excited. I said to Margaret, wait until we play the treasure hunt game. I bet Mr Lavender will be a genius at that one.'

Mr Parsons was breathing heavily, though I didn't know if from his little outburst or the running. 'The piano in...the drawing room?'

Mr Landley nodded. 'Yes, yes, the piano in the drawing room. Let's get moving.'

This didn't sound likely. 'Why would this involve luck?' I glanced around, but nobody else was entering the museum just yet, though it would probably be just a matter of time.

Mr Parsons suggested the drawing room again, in a dignified manner. To save another explosion, I agreed, and we jogged down there.

The earl was where we left him, and he waved his arms around in the air excitedly when he saw us. We were the only ones in the room, aside from Stella, who was nursing a hot drink. The earl continued to wave his arms. He was never still. 'Ah, Mr James, Mr James, enjoying the treasure hunt?'

I gave him some non-committal reply which he seemed to appreciate. Mr Landley responded in his usual drawn-out way, but Mr Parsons was too busy hunting around in the piano for our next clue. Judging by his face, he wasn't having much luck.

Then it came to me. Good luck and tune. Fortune. 'The statue of Fortuna. With the other statues looking on. Come on! That's where the clue is.'

The earl smacked his lips 'Ha, ha, Mr James Remarkable, quite remarkable. I'll never forget that time when you found the missing...'

We left him to his reminiscences regarding his missing sketch as we ran from the drawing room. Mr Parsons clattered over the floor as we dashed towards the Antique Passage, but we froze as a deathly scream rang around the corridor – a woman's. We looked at each other then I ran towards it, a flash of red coming towards us. Lady Talbot.

'Help, help!' She ran towards me. 'I've been assaulted.'

'What?'

'Help, James.' She grasped hold of me. 'That great oaf attacked me.'

'Who?'

Mr Landley and Mr Parsons continued up the corridor, so that it was just me and Lady Talbot. Alone. She continued to press against me, wriggling as she did so. 'It was horrible.'

Sydney stumbled into the corridor, his cheeks flushed. Lady Talbot screamed again, grabbing hold of me so tightly that I could hardly breathe.

'Help, help! He's going to attack me again.'

'What the…that's Sydney.'

Sydney approached further, mumbling something, dazed and confused.

Lady Talbot screamed again and twisted me around, interposing myself between herself and Sydney.

Sydney stuttered. 'She…fell into me.'

'No, no, he attacked me – he *groped* me.'

The earl came running behind us. 'What's the problem, folks?'

I spun around with Lady Talbot still attached

about my person. 'No problem, just some misunderstanding.'

I heard footsteps coming in the opposition direction. 'I heard screaming, what...*James*?'

Rose.

She narrowed her eyes at Lady Talbot who was still squashing herself against me.

'What's going on?' Rose said.

Lady Talbot turned around to Rose, smiling at her. 'That oaf attacked me, but James here rescued me. I'm safe now.' She dug her nails into my wrist.

Rose stared at her darkly. She was about to say something, but then we heard the smash beyond, followed by another scream. We looked at each other, then ran towards the bottom staircase where the sound had come from, Lady Talbot momentarily forgetting the 'assault'.

'He's dead!' someone shouted, just out of sight, just around the corridor on the right.

Another scream. Spinning around the corner, we were met with a man lying on his side. He was surrounded by broken pottery and blood. It was Mr Eastwell, with Mrs Parsons standing over him screaming. Rose was the first to react, crouching down and feeling Mr Eastwell's neck, then reaching for his wrist which she held in her hand gently. 'There's a pulse.'

I knelt down next to her, careful not to cut myself on the pottery, or whatever it was. He had a large graze on the side of his head that was still bleeding, but it didn't look serious. It looked like he'd just been stunned. A near escape perhaps.

'He's dead! He's dead!' Mrs Parsons shouted. The earl was trying to comfort her, but she was in such a state she didn't notice. 'He's dead!'

'He's not dead, you daft bat,' I said, but she continued to shout anyway, bringing almost everyone to the scene.

Malcolm Wegwipe peered over us, writing something in his notebook.

'Give him some space,' Rose said, and again more violently when Wegwipe continued to scribble away unmoving.

'Someone fetch a drink of water,' Rose said, but nobody moved. Emma was last on the scene yet was first to respond to Rose's request.

There was a great deal of commotion, but I insisted that the majority of the party leave and they did so reluctantly, at least forming a wide enough circle around us.

'Now, George,' I said, when enough space had been cleared and Mr Eastwell was sat up, drinking the water. 'Where was the pot?' I pointed to the shards still around Mr Eastwell, when he looked confused.

'Why, Mr James, that's not a pot. It's an eighteenth-century vase. It was going to be the prize for the treasure hunt…I suppose we'll have to abandon that now.' He sounded crest-fallen.

'Yes, yes, but where was it?'

'On the top of the stairs. On the little table."

'Show me.'

I followed the earl, Sydney followed me, and Wegwipe followed him. He was like a shadow, that man. The earl stopped us at the small mahogany table at the top of the stairs. 'That's the one, Mr James. An accident, you think?'

I looked at Sydney, who still looked troubled. 'Hmm, I'm not so sure,' I said.

'But, the vase was on the table. It could have fallen off. Don't you think, Mr James?'

Wegwipe pointed with his pen under the table. 'What's that? A button?'

I bent down to retrieve it, holding it in the palm of my hand for all the others to see. 'It's a button, yes, and I recognise it.'

'You do?' the earl said.

'Yes. I do. It's mine.'

CHAPTER THIRTEEN

'Time's incessant seasons bring their wreck and ruin, do they not?' I said to Sydney, letting the thick curtains fall back into place with a sway.

'Yeh, what?'

'It's still snowing. Heavily.'

'I told you it would. My Mam's rhymes never fail. But why didn't you just say that, then?'

'I did.' I turned to face him. He was standing in my doorway ready to go down, to what I suspected would be yet another round of chaos and disaster.

'No, you didn't.'

'Well, I did. *Clearly*. Otherwise what was I looking out of the window for?'

'Yes, but you said it in that funny voice – about Time's winged chariot and all of that,' he said.

'I didn't mention Time's winged chariot. I said

that the incessant seasons bring their wreck and ruin. I never once mentioned Time's winged chariot, you're the one who brought that up.'

'Yes, but you–'

Stella appeared behind Sydney. 'Have you two quite finished?'

'Yes, have you?' Rose added, behind her.

I was just waiting for Emma to chime in now.

Rose opened the door wider. 'Come on. I'm starving, time for food.'

'You're always starving. You're worse than him.' I pointed to Sydney. 'Maybe that explains his bad mood? He gets more argumentative when he's hungry.'

Rose grinned. 'What's your excuse, then?'

Then I noticed Rose's dress. 'By God, you've got dressed again, how many times?'

'Uncle James!' Emma said, sternly, appearing between them. I thought it was just a matter of time. 'You're supposed to say how lovely she looks and not complain all the time.'

'I'm not complaining. Who's complaining? Why are you all ganging up on me? And if I were to compliment her on her ability to get dressed, I'd be constantly complimenting her on how she looks, several times a day.'

Emma smiled. 'Ah, you're finally getting it.'

'Look,' Stella said. 'Let's just head down.'

The voice of finality had spoken.

❖ ❖ ❖

'Groper!' Lady Talbot shouted, as we descended into the drawing room, which was already awash with noise and accusation. 'He attacked me!'

Sydney's cheeks flushed as they do easily. 'I… she fell into me, on the stairs.'

'Don't worry, Sydney,' I said. 'Lady Talbot, stop spreading nonsense.'

Sydney was of course telling the truth.

She stood up pointing at Sydney with everyone else looking on. 'He attacked me!'

'He did no such thing. You fell into him,' I replied.

She turned on me. 'How do you know? You weren't there.'

All eyes came back my way, including Lord Talbot's who was currently coldly calculating the scene with distaste. Behind me, the others took their seats with Sydney taking the furthest one away from Lady Talbot. He hunched down in his seat quivering slightly.

'I just know,' I said, somewhat feebly.

I felt a shadow hovering behind me. It was Wegwipe and his foppish hair. He was standing, as always with his notebook and pen in hand. 'Excuse me, but can you explain how your button appeared at the crime scene? Mr Brown?'

'Mr bloody Brown? I told you. It's James *Lavender*.'

'Oh, yes.' He smirked. 'Your little letter and, ahem, the age thing. Regardless, how did your button appear at the crime scene, care to explain?'

Crime scene? But maybe he wasn't far off the mark. I wasn't buying for one moment that the vase had toppled of its own accord, but had it been meant to startle or to kill?

'Mr Brown?'

'I will find out. I am a great detective, after all – the best.'

Wegwipe licked his lips, turning the pages of his notebook. 'You're not exactly on the best of terms with Mr Eastwell, are you?'

He never missed anything, this man. He was always poking his nose into things.

'Was anyone?'

Not a bad little riposte, if I do say so myself.

He nodded very slightly, then scribbled something down in his little book. He seemed somewhat satisfied, if still thoughtful.

'What I plan to do,' I added, 'with the earl's permission, is to conduct an inquiry.'

'Ah, excellent, of course, of course, Mr James. That will be fun. Brandy. Let's have brandy to calm the nerves.' The earl clapped his hands at the footmen, but he didn't need to as they were already on the case.

'All I need is a room,' I said to the earl.

It might get me out of some of the Christmas nonsense too.

'How do we know you can be trusted?' Mrs Eastwell said. 'It was your button under the table after all. How do we know you didn't try to kill my husband to get out of finding his racehorse?'

'What? Excuse me, but that's the most ridiculous thing I've ever heard in my life. Who would commit murder to get out of searching for a racehorse? It's utterly stupid.' I took the offered brandy. Christ how I needed it.

There was a sharp intake of breath.

'How dare you call Mother stupid?' the Eastwell boy said.

'I didn't call her stupid, but it was an utterly stupid statement.' I swirled the brandy, taking a large sip. 'Obviously it's acceptable to accuse someone of murder, but not acceptable to call them into question for doing so. That's stupid.'

'I have excellent faith in Mr James,' the earl said. 'He's a remarkable fellow. Did I not tell you how he once magicked a missing sketch from thin air?'

Mrs Eastwell seemed half-satisfied but was about to say something else, when Rose interrupted her. 'And where were you, might I add? You weren't with me at the time, having had an argument with your son. You went your separate ways.'

'Yes, well.' Mrs Eastwell licked her lips and returned to her seat, placing her hands on her knees. Lord Snooty hovered by her. Lady Talbot also seemed satisfied, for now.

'Guests! Let's have more brandy!' the earl boomed.

'I thought you were supposed to have brandy

after the meal?' I said to Sydney.

Sydney shrugged, evidently still a little uncomfortable and grateful for the offered brandy.

'Just…don't tell the wife!' the earl added.

There was a smattering of strained laughter, and the brandy was passed around swiftly by the footmen. I thanked the one who brought me a top-up. I turned to the earl. 'I'll need a private room, tomorrow. To conduct the inquiry,' I added, when the earl looked back at me blankly, clearly having already forgotten the whole thing.

Some of the guests did not look happy about this, not one bit. Just what had they to hide I wonder?

◆ ◆ ◆

There were sharp gasps from several of our party when we came into the dining room. Red and gold swirling decorations covered the rich mahogany table, combining with the natural greenery of wild holly branches, ivy and even roses from the earl's own gardens. Roses in December! The scent was one of Christmas pine and warm berry from the tall, scented candles seated in golden candlesticks. A large tree sat in the corner completing the scene, with matching red and gold decorations adorning its draping branches.

I once again cast my eyes over the rich

artwork that hung from the wall. A Rembrandt. I momentarily got lost in the warm, fuzzy glow of the character he was depicting, some merchant or other, by the looks of it. He was hunched over in a thick, woolly coat – perfect for the season.

'Oh, Uncle James, it's magical,' Emma said to me, yet again, a phrase that was fast becoming irritating.

'Yes, it's really nice,' I said, as I searched through the table settings, looking for our name tags. I prayed to God that I wasn't sat next to Mr Landley again.

Mr Eastwell had returned, saying that he felt much better after his rest. He hadn't remembered anything about the 'accident' when we'd briefly questioned him upon his recovery. His wife had demanded that he be taken up to his room, to which there had been no objections.

'Here we are,' Rose said, finding her place at the long table, just left of centre. She pointed at the seat opposite, which was indeed mine. I immediately picked up the one next to me, 'Mr Brown' it read, thank goodness. Then I checked the seat on my left, and my heart sank.

'Ah, Mr Lavender, I see we've been seated together again.' Mr Landley patted my arm with his greasy hand. 'I've got some interesting things to tell you about farm management during the winter periods.'

'Good God.'

'I know. I told Margaret that you'd be excited

about it.'

I sat down, removing the napkin that had been left on our seats in the shape of a frog. Quite why they put them on the seats I've no idea. It just gave you an additional job to do.

'What's with the frog napkin?' I said to Rose.

'It's a swan, silly.'

'Looks like a frog.'

I pulled it apart and sat myself up to the table, tucking the dead frog over my knees as Mr Landley rattled in my ear.

Sydney nearly knocked the table as he sat down beside me, only just catching the empty wine glass that he'd almost toppled over. He was always smashing glasses. He looked up embarrassed. 'When are they pouring the drinks?'

'In a minute, I expect.'

As soon as I said it, the footmen and maids were swiftly on the scene. White wine to go with the first course.

'Have you got any ale?' Sydney asked the young maid who'd approached him.

'Jesus, Sydney. You're not in a tavern now,' I said.

The young maid didn't look troubled by the question. 'I don't think we have ale, sir. I will ask.'

'We can't take you anywhere,' I said.

'What are you complaining about now?' Rose said, though she seemed to be joking and quite excited.

'Just this big lump wants ale.'

'I was only asking,' Sydney said.

'So, Mr Lavender,' Mr Landley continued in my left ear. 'The secret of the winter period is…'

I looked around at everybody; most of them were seated now except for the earl who was still on his feet at the head of the table, waving everyone into their chairs in his usual jubilant manner, even though everyone was already seated.

Lord and Lady Talbot were closest to him. Lady Talbot cast a glance in our direction. I couldn't work out if she was looking at myself or Sydney. It was an open stare, hoping for some sort of reaction. Trouble. I knew she hadn't finished with her drama around Sydney.

'…so, you see it is far from a time that should be neglected. It can actually be quite a productive period. I always say this, don't I, Margaret? Margaret…'

'Sorry, sir. There's no ale.' The maid had returned.

'Oh, never mind. Can I have two glasses of that white stuff, then?'

'White stuff?' I said. 'I think he means the wine.'

The maid blinked but poured some of the quality hock then retreated back into the kitchens to fetch another glass.

Sydney faced me, puzzled. 'I never can understand this posh way of drinking.'

'What do you mean?' I said, fully expecting some little pearls of wisdom.

'Why not fill the glass right up to the top, like a nice, frothy pint of ale?'

Rose's green eyes glowed with inner mischief. 'It's to give the wine room to breathe, Sydney,' she explained, taking a small sip and rolling it around her mouth.

'...didn't I, Margaret? Margaret? Didn't I say that...'

Sydney shook his head. 'I don't understand it.' He picked up the glass, peering through it as if trying to find something inside other than the wine, then gulped the whole thing in one go. 'Hmm, not bad. I still don't understand why they don't fill it to the top though. I don't get the breathing thing. If they only half-filled glasses in the taverns they'd have a riot on their hands.'

'What do you think, Mr Lavender?' Mr Landley asked.

'Er, indeed.'

He patted me on the shoulder laughing. 'I knew you would agree. I said he had farming blood in him, didn't I, Margaret? Margaret...'

The maid returned, with a slight flinch upon seeing Sydney's glass completely empty, but then neutrally poured him out two glasses, smiling. She turned to leave, but Sydney stopped her. 'Er, excuse me, love. But if you're only going to pour in half, like in that posh way, can I have two more glasses, please?'

Her eyes widened for an instant, but she nodded politely and went to fetch two more glasses from the kitchen.

'Jesus, Sydney, you don't have to guzzle it down like that! Wine's a sipping drink,' I said. 'You're supposed to actually *taste* it.'

The earl was now seated and was helping himself to the wine, a few of the others laughing falsely at something he said. I didn't need to be Newton to work out the joke he'd just told.

Sydney looked like a big child before a great mathematical sum. 'I don't understand all this sipping business.'

'Go on,' I said. 'I think this is going to be enlightening.'

'Well,' Sydney began, 'I don't see the point. If you like it, then drink it. If you don't, then drink something else.'

'Pure genius.' I raised my own glass. 'The point, Sydney, my old friend, is to actually taste the drink, swill it around like this, release its aroma. Smell the bouquet. Like this.' I took an exaggerated sniff. 'What can I smell?'

'Wine?' Sydney offered.

'What can one detect, *within* the wine?' I took a little sip. 'Subtle hints of jasmine and vanilla, I perceive. Yes, they do a little dance upon one's palate.'

'Eh?'

I put my glass down with a sigh. 'You try it.'

He put his big snout in his own glass, gave it

a quick sniff and then finished the whole thing. 'Tastes like wine to me.'

'And what did you detect within it?'

He twitched his nose. 'Grapes.'

The maid came back carrying two more glasses, then stopped again when she noticed one on the table was already empty. She put the two glasses down, then filled them both from a fresh bottle. She then smiled and was about to walk away, when Sydney stopped her. 'Excuse me again, love.'

'Yes?'

'You might as well fill the other, save you coming back-like.'

I shook my head at him.

The oily fish course had been and gone, and the conversation turned to the missing animals.

'Terrible business, Mr Lavender, eh?' Mr Landley announced. 'The whole episode is quite shocking. Mrs Wobble is quite out of her mind with worry. It's the worst thing to happen around here in fifty years, I said to Margar–'

'Really?' I said. 'Fifty years?'

'Quite so, Mr Lavender, quite so. After the Nag's Mate affair.'

Mr Eastwell slammed a fist down on the table, clanking some cutlery in the process. 'Never mind Mrs Wobble. My racehorse is the chief concern here. When are you getting him back?'

'Ah, the joys of Christmas,' I said to Rose, raising my glass in mock celebration.

This didn't seem to go down well with Mr Eastwell. 'Don't you play silly with me.'

Mr Parsons cleaned his glasses. A regular habit, I'd noted. 'I think it's a damn shame.'

'Guests!' shouted the earl, waking up Margaret who had just nodded off. 'Let's have champagne!'

The footmen, like little ants, began to scatter.

'But…'

I was waiting for it, and so was Emma, with a smirk. Sydney gulped down another glass of wine.

'Don't…'

I looked over at Rose, who was also smiling and looking quite nice in her pale lilac dress.

'Tell…'

The young miss Parsons was looking over at Anthony Landley, a suggestive smile touching her lips.

'The…'

Lady Talbot sat upright, casting dangerous glances around the table, but returned her eyes to the earl.

'W–'

But there was a crash through the door from the right. A large snowman stomped his way towards the table! Lady Talbot screamed. Margaret Landley seemed to jump up out of her chair. Mr Eastwell stood up, squarely like a boxer.

The snowman turned to the earl. 'My lord, I'm so sorry. It's your wife, the countess, sh–'

The earl jumped up out of his chair. 'My wife?

My wife is here? HIDE THE DRINKS! REMOVE THE DRINKS! Quick! REMOVE THE DRINKS!'

The footmen dashed in, clearing the table of wine. Sydney grabbed hold of his glasses, resulting in a mini tug of war which ended in a large spillage on the table.

'HIDE THE WINE!'

The snowman took his breath, the snow falling from his coat. Underneath, I could see a thin trace of red and gold. 'It's the countess... she's trapped. Trapped in the snow...outside.'

Mr Parsons stood up. 'Oh, dearly me.'

Mr Landley agreed. 'Stuck? Out there?'

Relief and fright took joint custody of the earl's features. 'My wife? Trapped in the snow?'

'Please, help. You must come quickly,' the snowman said to the table, slowly beginning to turn into a footman once again. 'She's stuck and Aurea's with her.'

'Aurea! Gather the footmen!' the earl shouted. Then he addressed the table. 'Men, can you help?'

The men on the table sprang up. I went to get my hat and coat too. There was frantic dashing and panic all around, until eventually, most of us were equipped to join the rescue party. Sydney beside me, with the others and the footmen, made our way towards the main entrance, lanterns in hands.

I immediately reeled under the force of the snowstorm as I clambered onto the steps outside. There had been absolutely no let up in the weather. It was obvious there was no way in hell that we would be leaving the day after tomorrow, even if the snow abruptly stopped, which didn't look likely. The footmen, and most of the party, journeyed through the snow, struggling towards the distant carriage. I took a courageous step forward too, and the icy blanket swallowed my shoe, riding right up the bottom of my trouser leg. I immediately jerked it back, shaking it. I took a further step backwards and encouraged Sydney to follow the others. It was probably best to direct the proceedings from the afar. It would seem the best use of my intellectual faculties.

'That's it. Keep it up!' I shouted. 'Don't stop, keep trudging through it. Bit more. A little bit more. Go on.'

It was slow progress, but they were carving their way forwards, stumbling on and on towards the sunken carriage. Sydney stumbled and fell in the snow, then he got up and righted himself. 'Sydney, you great lump!'

I was beginning to lose sight of them as individuals, as they blended into the distance; little drunken sticks of black against a sea of white. Their lantern lights, little fireflies in the night, but they were almost upon the carriage now. 'That's it, carry her out!' I shouted, but my expert direction got lost in the storm, dying amongst the clouds of snow which hurtled frantically by in the hellish wind.

With the countess and her young daughter safely rescued, we made our way to the warmth of the fire in the drawing room (which had been stoked up with extra logs). The orange glow was a most welcome friend indeed. A flock of maids surrounded the countess and her young daughter, removing their sodden outer clothing.

Then the maids then turned on us, her rescue party, and I handed over my damp hat. The other rescuers crammed around the fire before me.

'Make way, make way,' I said, pushing through them. 'My foot's wet.'

I squeezed through the Landleys to the front, sticking my foot out, gratefully enjoying the immediate warmth which circulated through my toes, rising up my trouser leg. Someone behind me tutted, oblivious to just how wet my foot and trouser leg had become. The flames continued to lick away at the logs, as the heat fought its way against the frostbite in my toes. Thankfully, the danger had now passed, though I still stood, circulating my toes, just to be on the safe side. Nature was, after all, an unforgiving beast.

CHAPTER FOURTEEN

'Have I told you about my little bottom problem?' Mr Landley said, seated at the side of me in the drawing room.

The pork pie I was about to eat hovered in the air, then was put back down again on the table in front of me. Undeterred, Sydney on my right picked it up and threw it in his mouth, and chewed on it contentedly.

There had been no attempt to restart the meal in the dining room after the interruption. Instead, food was being brought to us by footmen on rotation. Little plates of chicken, pies, parcels of fish, mince pies, spices, but no alcohol, absolutely no alcohol. Apparently, according to the earl, they didn't have any of the devil's brew on the premises.

'Yes, I've got a really bad itch.' Mr Landley circulated his backside on the chaise longue, causing it to rock from side-to-side.

'Right.'

'It's really bad, Mr Lavender.'

'Is it?'

Mr Parsons stood in front of us. 'Would that be a dose of the dreaded piles, Geoffrey?'

'Yes, the doctor gave me some ointment for it.' Mr Landley started leaning over and scratching under his belt from behind, his elbow knocking my back.

The countess had despatched the young girl to bed. She had been clearly exhausted by the whole 'surprise' affair. The earl was thrilled to see his daughter Aurea, but not so thrilled, it seemed, to see his wife. The countess was now sitting in front of us, hogging the fire, holding a glass of warm milk in her long and delicate hand. A thick dark jewel hung on her finger, reflecting the rays of firelight.

The chaise longue was still rocking under Mr Landley's frantic scratching.

'Music, let's have music,' the earl said, a little less enthusiastically than normal, I observed. 'Miss Parsons, would you?'

'Certainly,' she said, standing. She looked pleased with herself as she spun around in her lacy, white dress. She glanced over at the Eastwell table before moving over to the piano, but they weren't looking her way. She made a show of preparing to play, adjusting the seat, and then flexing her fingers. Anthony Landley looked on adoringly. She smiled shyly at him out of the corner of her eye, touching her expensive-looking diamond earring before focusing her attention fully on the piano. She played a Chopin nocturne, delicately, with skill and charm. I was grateful for the soft, moonlight music (as I often thought of it), which relaxed my mind and body after such an exhausting rescue. I still felt a spot of cold on the tip of my toe, but at least any remaining threats of frostbite had passed.

Sydney leaned into my ear. 'Why can't we have a drink?'

I pointed at the countess, who was still holding the glass of warm milk. 'You can have milk.'

'But it's Christmas. We should be allowed a drink at Christmas.'

The earl could sense his pain. 'Would you like a *special* milk, Mr Brown?'

Sydney didn't realise he'd been overheard. 'No, milk gives me nightmares and terrible wind and worse stuff.'

The earl winked. 'Ah, but this is *special* milk.'

The countess frowned but didn't comment. Sydney looked at me, then back to the earl. 'No, thanks.'

'Sydney shouldn't drink a lot of milk,' Stella said, a note of warning in her voice.

'Are you sure, Mr Brown? We can *warm* it up for you.' He winked at Sydney again, but Sydney just gave him a blank stare.

Rose leaned over and whispered something in Sydney's ear, to which Sydney's whole expression changed. 'Oh, yes please, a nice milk, *extra* warm.' He winked back at the earl. A waiting footman sprang into action again and vanished from the room. He returned quickly with a tray full of *special* milk. Stella did not look happy. The earl picked one up, and Sydney picked up three, having gone without a drink for what had been a little over an hour.

'Oh, that's lovely,' Sydney said, a line of milk-foam around his lips after he'd gulped the first glass immediately. 'Nice little *kick*,' he added.

The earl tipped his head, taking a sip of his brandy-infused milk.

Stella motioned with her finger at the top of her lip, that Sydney should wipe his mouth, but he didn't notice as he was too busy polishing off the second, followed by the third glass. A footman was on hand to provide him with top-ups keeping a smile on Sydney's face and a frown on his wife's.

The latest nocturne had come to an end and we clapped politely, but none of us more enthusiastically than Mr Landley's eldest son, Anthony. The youngest of the Landley brood said something suggestive to his brother, which resulted in a heavy kick in return. Miss Parsons switched into Listz's, Liebestraum No. 3, which always reminded me of the rain. Chance would be a fine thing.

'We're going to be stuck here, aren't we?' I said to Rose.

'What's that?' Her attention was on the music.

'We're going to be stuck here, in this house.'

'What?'

'The bloody snow outside.'

I was hushed by several people, and I folded my arms in protest. Gradually, I turned my attention back to the music. Little, golden notes like tiny droplets of rain, calming my annoyances. That was until Sydney broke my trance with a little music of his own. A most unfortunate reaction to milk

◆ ◆ ◆

With the last of my brandy nothing but a distant memory, I lay twisting and turning, over and over in the squashy bed as I knew I would. Although reduced in ferocity, the snowstorm still kept up a persistent flurry against the window. But worst of all was the procession of Greek and Roman figures on the walls and fabric around me. I was particularly occupied with one tall fellow, who had funny hair and was carrying a large, bent stick. Just what on earth it was, I couldn't conclude. A strange weapon or a farming implement were the chief suspects, but neither seemed to fit. I knew it would trouble my mind. My thoughts should really be turning to other matters. I would probably wake up with the solution to the man with the bent stick, instead of figuring out who had tried to harm Mr Eastwell and who had tried to set me up for it.

Last night had not ended so badly. Miss Parsons had kept up with her piano for a while, and Sydney's flatulence had eventually died down. The Eastwells and the Talbots were amongst the first to leave for bed, which had considerably improved the mood. Then, when the countess also left, and the special milk could be legitimately replaced with special brandy, the mood improved even further. We spent the remainder of the night content to stare into the fire, listening to the soft trills of the piano until, one by one, eyelids gradually began to close.

◆ ◆ ◆

I'd almost started to drift off when I thought I heard something just outside my door. I froze to listen. A slight creak, or was it just the wind finding its way through the house? No. It was there again. A clear footstep, with a shadow momentarily flickering under the door as if from a candle's reflection. I rose silently, throwing on my dressing gown, and crept towards the door with my walking cane. A footstep again and then a slight knock upon my door, as if from one finger of a knuckle. Hesitant, but clear. Who the hell was it at this time of night?

I twisted the handle and slowly pulled the

door open. Lady Talbot. She was standing there, candle in hand, dressed in her undergarments.

'Oh, James, I…think I've got the wrong room.'

'What is it you want, Lady Talbot? It must be two in the morning.'

She flicked her long eyelashes at me. 'It's just, well…I'm terribly scared. The incident this afternoon and the snow outside.'

'I'm sure you'll be fine, Lady Talbot, now if you'll exc–'

She held out her hand, preventing me from closing the door. 'No, don't. I need to speak with you. It's urgent.'

'What is it?'

'Aren't you going to invite me in?'

'WHAT?'

'Let me into your room, I need to speak with you.' She had a desperation in her eyes that I'd not quite seen before.

'Well, I hardly think it's proper! Maybe in the morning I coul–'

She put her hand on my shoulder. 'I think there's going to be a murder, I–'

The door next to mine opened swiftly. Rose.

'James, what's going…?' She caught sight of Lady Talbot, whose hand still lingered on my shoulder, a finger brushing against my collarbone.

But none of us answered as a wild shriek rang out at the far end of the corridor.

'What was that?' Rose said.

The shriek grew into a wail.

Lady Talbot dropped her hand, and the three of us made our way down the corridor as swiftly as we could with only the aid of her lone candle.

The hellish shriek still rang out, and then a man's voice tremored above it. 'GOOD GOD!'

'Whose room is that?' I said, following the bobble of the candle that was in danger of going out.

Rose pointed ahead. 'I think it's the Eastwells.'

'HELP! HELP!' another voice, possibly the wailer from inside.

I was the first to get to the door and I flung it open.

I was met with the most terrifying sight. A sight that will stay with me for a very long time – Sydney urinating, right over the bed of Mr and Mrs Eastwell! And, by the looks of things, Mr Eastwell was drenched. Sydney's eyes remained closed

'God. Good God!' he shouted, trying to unsuccessfully shuffle out of bed backwards, prevented by the headboard, the array of fluffed-up pillows, and Mrs Eastwell beside him screaming.

'I knew the milk was a bad idea,' I said to Rose.

'Get him away! Get him away!' Mr Eastwell was still struggling to avoid the stream of hot liquid, the steam of which rose from the bed like something from a nightmare.

I heard a clatter behind me.

'What's going on?'

It was Stella.

'Sydney's sleepwalk again,' I said.

'I knew it. I said no milk, but he wouldn't listen.'

Stella turned as someone touched her shoulder. Bloody Wegwipe. Pen in hand once again. 'Ahem. What's going on?'

Stella weaved through myself, Lady Talbot and Rose towards Sydney. His eyes held that far-off daze, but at least he was finished. He put the offending article (which had been thankfully shrouded in shadow) away, as Stella tried to lead him from the foot of the bed.

'He's a dead man! A dead man,' Mr Eastwell shouted.

More people arrived in the corridor. The Eastwell boy, who had his own room. Then Emma. 'What's going on?' she asked.

'Your dad's sleepwalking,' I said, leaving the bit about the urinating out, but she wasn't stupid.

'You. Are a dead man!' Mr Eastwell roared. 'I challenge you to a duel.'

'He can't hear you. He's sleepwalking,' I said. 'It's because of the milk.'

'I don't care. He's a red man.'

'Excuse me, Mr Eastwell,' Malcolm Wegwipe said, his little rat face poking through. 'Did you say he's a "red" man or a "dead" man? It's just…we aim for accuracy here at the *Herald*.'

'I don't think so! I'm twenty-bloody-eight.'

'Now, Mr Brown, I already–'

'What is all the noise about?' Lord Talbot said.

Malcolm Wegwipe withdrew, as Lady Talbot began to fill her husband in. 'Well, I was with James outside his room, when–'

'What were you doing there?' he shot back.

More people in the corridor. The Landley brood!

'We were just chatting, weren't we, James? He was about to invite me into his room when–'

'Are you trying to take advantage of my wife again, Mr Lavender? Do we need to make it two Christmas duels?' Lord Talbot said.

'Now, look here,' I began, but Stella pushed past me, guiding a stumbling Sydney down the corridor, preventing my immediate reply.

Mr Landley's head craned around the door, a thick smile spreading on his rugged face. 'What's going on here?'

Mr Parsons was at the side of him trying to poke his head through the door in the limited space.

'Oh, nothing, Mr Landley.' I tried to shoo him back. 'Why don't we all go back to bed, eh?'

Mr Landley sniffed loudly. 'Urine! Ha, ha. Urine has many practical uses around the farm. Great stuff urine. Margaret, doesn't urine have many practical uses around the farm? Margaret, Margaret, doesn't urine have many practical uses around the farm? Margaret? Margaret?'

'Mr Landley, it's past two o'clock in the mor–'

'Aha.' He wagged his great finger at me. 'In farm management circles time is–'

'We're not farming!' I shouted.

'He's a dead man! A dead man,' Mr Eastwell was raging now. He stepped out of bed, past his wife, and hurled the top sheet to the floor. 'Do you hear me? That man is dead.'

Mr Parsons shook his head. 'He's not a very happy man, I can tell. Reminds me of the Avery Market affair.'

'What's the Avery Market affair?' I found myself saying.

Oh, no…

'GOOD GOD! The AVERY MARKET affair!'

'Forget it. Forget I spoke,' I said.

'Margaret, Margaret. What do we say about time in farming circles? Hee, hee, Mr Lavender wants to go into land management and…'

'Who in HELL, doesn't know, of the AVERY MARKET affair? Mr Parsons tried to rip off his own face in frustration.

'STOP!' I shouted. 'For Christ's sake stop! Everybody go back to bed. Right now!' I flapped my dressing gown closer, suddenly feeling the bitter cold. 'This is utter madness.'

Silence. Then eyes followed Mr Eastwell as he made a slow walk towards me. I gripped my cane tightly. Face-to-face he stood, not ten inches from my nose. 'First, you poke me in the eye. Then you nearly knock me over in the corridor. Then someone dropped a vase on me from the top of the stairs.'

'Yes, you're not having a good week,' I said.

'Then there's this utterly disgusting insult. I'm telling you, Lavender, tomorrow, Christmas Day or not, someone is going to pay for this. Someone's going to die.'

There were not many things in the world that I think I would agree with Mr Eastwell on, but on this matter, we were in total agreement. Tomorrow, someone would die.

CHAPTER FIFTEEN

I'd fallen asleep immediately after returning to my room. I felt like I'd quickly grabbed an unbroken four or five hours when I shot awake. I'd worked it out. The room was in near-total darkness, with only a faint sliver of moonlight coming through the tiny gap in the heavy curtains. The Greek chap was carrying an adze. A wood-working tool. I remembered reading about it in an old history book as a child. With that problem out of my mind, I could now fully focus on the Eastwell business. I turned around and dozed off again in a flicker, only to be awoken what felt like seconds later by a loud knock.

'Go away,' I shouted.

'Uncle James. Get up, it's Christmas Day! We're waiting for you. It's nine.'

I groaned. Never a moment's peace. 'Give me a minute, will you?'

'But, we're waiting for you so we can open our

presents. Everyone's ready.'

I groaned again. 'Oh, alright. Give me five minutes – wait, make it ten. Fifteen. I'll be out in fifteen, or maybe twenty. Call it twenty.'

Half an hour later, I stumbled over to Sydney's room. Rose was there too, seated and waiting patiently, dressed in light green today – another new outfit no doubt. She wished me a 'good afternoon'.

'What took you so long?' Emma said.

'You look terrible,' Sydney said. 'Had a bad night's sleep, m'lord?'

'Well, yes. No thanks to you!' I twisted the chair around next to Rose and crashed down upon it.

'Me? What's it got to do with me?'

I stopped rubbing my eyes. Sydney was lying on his grand bed, hands behind his head, and looking perfectly rested.

'It has everything to do with you!'

'He doesn't remember,' Emma said. 'We've already been through this. Can we open our presents now?'

'Sleepwalking, was I?'

'Don't bloody grin. You caused chaos,' I shouted.

'Not my fault. If they'd have let me have ale instead of the posh stuff, like special milk, I wouldn't have sleepwalked.'

'Yes, well, Mr Eastwell's now threatening a duel. His wife looked like she wanted to kill you as well.'

'Can we stop all the talk about killing, please?' Stella said. The final word on the matter as usual.

Emma tossed me a package, neatly wrapped in brown parcel paper, tied with string. 'Here, Uncle James, open yours first.'

'What's this?'

'It's your gift, of course. Open it.'

I did as she bade, having had a little trouble with the string at first, but then opened the thing to reveal a little jewellery box. 'What is it?'

'Open it up.' Emma sat on her bed, a pile of her own unopened presents beside her.

I lifted the lid. Two silver cufflinks. I pulled them out of the casing and examined them in the light. They had 'JL' engraved, with a decorative swirl around the edges.

'Do you like them? Try them on,' Emma said.

I did so.

'We thought the silver would match your cane. Do you like them?'

I popped them into place, feeling the weight and smoothing the surface. 'Yes, actually, they're not bad.'

Stella frowned.

'Thanks,' I added.

Emma grinned happily.

I hoped the opening process wouldn't take all day. I was desperately in need of tea and eager to start the inquiry. I took up the bag with the gifts I had instructed Mrs Wilkins to fetch and passed them around in haste.

Emma opened hers first, struggling with the expert wrapping that they were impressed with (I told them I had many talents), before tearing it open. 'What is it?' she said, examining the pack I'd given her.

'It's a detective kit: notepad and pen, magnifying glass and part of my very own special fingerprint kit, consisting of black and white powders and special papers.'

'Oh, thank you, Uncle. I love it.' She made as if to hug me then ended up tapping my shoulder.

'Well, you did seem interested when I'd brought it round that time.'

'Of course, I was!'

Stella opened hers – a pinafore with a picture of the York Minster on the front. I couldn't tell whether she liked it or not. Her face was not exactly animated.

'It's the York Minster,' I told her. 'When you're boiling Sydney's potatoes, you can look down and see it. Good, eh?'

Sydney was more excited by his – a hipflask full of whisky with his initials on. Rose likewise was pleased with a special edition of Shakespeare's sonnets. I had to sit through more painful opening of gifts, my stomach rumbling for tea, before I could get away from the whole business and down to breakfast. I just wondered what sort of reception we'd receive.

❖ ❖ ❖

The earl had allocated one of the other drawing rooms to be taken over for the important purpose of breakfast. I imagined the main dining room was already being prepared for the Christmas Day feast. Another opportunity for us all to gather together again with Mr Landley in my ear.

The blue drawing room was as spectacular as the turquoise room, only there was no piano in this one and it felt a little colder. Little circular tables had been set up so that families and groups could sit apart. An excellent idea. Probably Simon's. I immediately scanned the room, half expecting Mr Eastwell to spring up and challenge Sydney like he had last night, but there was no sign of him or any of the Eastwells. Nor Mr Landley, thank the heavens. Only Anthony Landley, who was chatting to Miss Parsons at a large table in the centre of the room. She held her hand over her mouth, and she looked away when we walked in. I noted Lord and Lady Talbot in the back corner, eating smoked salmon if my nose was not mistaken. Fish in the morning, I will never understand. Fish at pretty much any time for that matter. Wegwipe sat with William Brookes, finishing an egg, his notepad not far away from him on the table. I pointed to the other corner. Sydney shrugged and Stella gave a nod, so that is where we encamped.

The excellent footmen were there to tend on me immediately, and I did not have to wait for my much-needed tea. I asked for scones with jam and cream.

'Oh, that sounds lovely,' Emma said. 'Can I have those, too?'

'Cake for me, thanks,' Rose said.

Stella ordered toast with butter.

'Can I have some potatoes please, boiled?' Sydney said.

I shook my head. 'Potatoes? For breakfast?'

'Yes, what's wrong with that? Not posh enough for you?'

'It's not that, is it? You don't have potatoes for breakfast.'

Sydney looked hurt. 'I just fancy some potatoes with a nice knob of butter, or is that not allowed now, either?'

'Let him have potatoes,' Rose said.

Our breakfast was promptly delivered. Scones, cake, toast and boiled potatoes. I was first to the jam pot, smearing my freshly baked scone with thick, strawberry goodness. The cream was heavenly thick too, and I couldn't help but be liberal with it; it would be rude not to. I took a large bite, and the delicious sweetness flooded my mouth. Smacking my lips, I washed it down with the hot tea. Decent. I should send Mrs Wilkins here for training.

'Oh, by the way,' I said, briefly pausing on the eating front. 'I worked it out.'

Emma leaned forward eagerly. 'Who was it?'

'I finished my current mouthful. '*Who* was it? You mean, *what* was it? It was an adze. A woodworking tool.'

'What?' Emma shook her head. 'I meant the attack on Mr Eastwell.'

'Oh, that? Well, I...' I was about to explain when Mr and Mrs Landley strolled into the room. Their younger son was trailing behind, holding his ears back like a monkey and sticking out his tongue. Mr Landley immediately spotted me and dashed over to our table.

'Ah, Mr Lavender, my bum is much better this morning.'

I put my scone down again. 'Wonderful.'

'Yes, no itch at all.'

'Great.'

He turned to Sydney, who had a large boiled potato in his mouth. 'Ho, ho, Mr Brown, all that was exciting last night, yes? I said to Margaret...'

'I'm not sure exciting is the correct word,' I said.

'Well, we wondered what all the fuss was about. Nothing like a bit of fun in the middle of the night, eh?'

Mr and Mrs Parsons came into the room and joined their daughter and Anthony Landley at their table.

'Ah, Thomas, good morning.' Mr Landley

waved, still standing at our side. 'I was just saying to Mr Lavender here that my bottom problem is much better this morning and that there's nothing like a bit of fun in the night. Didn't I say that, Margaret? Margaret, didn't I say that there's nothing...'

'Don't let us keep you from your breakfast,' Stella said, but Mr Landley didn't hear her and continued his nonsense.

Mr Parsons seated himself and placed a napkin over his knees. 'Did you say you got the cream from the doctors or the vets?'

'Oh, yes, from the doctor. What you have to do is rub the ointment right in.' Mr Landley turned back to me, his thick finger in front of my nose, his other hand a balled fist, demonstrating the correct application. 'Right in, Mr Lavender, right in. You see, Mr Lavender, a less experienced chap might not apply ointment in the correct manner, but you have to go right in. Like this.' He demonstrated enthusiastically. 'Right in, Mr Lavender, right in.'

Rose put her tea back on her saucer. 'I think your wife is ready for breakfast now.'

'What's that, dear?'

'She means go away,' I said.

'Ho, ho, Mr Lavender. Very funny.'

'I wasn't joking.'

'Ho, ho, wonderful, very witty. Isn't he witty Margaret? Margaret, Margaret, isn't Mr Lavender, witty?'

Margaret half-nodded and joined the Parsons table, and eventually so did Mr Landley. With them out of the way, I finished my scone (not letting Mr Landley's posterior problems upset me this time), still on the lookout for the Eastwells.

◆ ◆ ◆

'Morning guests!' shouted the earl, as he hobbled into the room, his little daughter laughing merrily on his back, her bright blonde hair flowing behind her. He ran around the room, weaving his way around the tables as people were finishing their breakfasts. 'Piggy monster! Piggy monster!' he chanted, his daughter laughing each time he said it. 'Piggy monster! Piggy monster!' He dashed beside Sydney, and Aurea's trailing foot smacked him on the side of the head. A potato popped out of his mouth and landed in the sugar bowl.

I'd already finished my scones and had helped myself to a second portion. There was still no sign of the Eastwells. Whether they had already breakfasted early or were just late coming down, I didn't know. Everyone else was here, apart from them and the countess.

The earl stopped in front of us, clearly exhausted. He dropped his little daughter to the floor upside down, then spun her onto her feet at the last moment. This elicited more cries of laughter. 'Build a snowman! Build a snowman!'

she giggled.

'Later, later.' The earl slapped her playfully on her behind, and she ran out of the room laughing.

'Guests!' the earl shouted. 'Let's play little balls!'

'Little balls?' I said.

'Great game is little balls,' the earl said almost gravely.

Mr Landley turned around. 'We call it ball in the hole. Don't we Margaret? Margaret, don't we call little balls, ball in the hole? Margaret? Margaret?'

'But, what about the inquiry into Mr Eastwell's accident? We don't really have time for games,' I said.

'Nonsense, Mr James, nonsense. Everyone has time for little balls.'

'Yes, but the inqui–'

'Later, later. You can do all that *later*. Let's play little balls. FIVE POUNDS to the winner!'

Mr Landley got to his feet, cheering. Mr Parsons stood, clapping.

'I say, capital,' William Brookes said, in what was practically the first thing he'd said since his 'good morning' monologue yesterday.

Malcolm Wegwipe stood. Permanent notebook in hand. 'What about the Eastwells?'

'Ah, yes, unfortunately, they're indisposed, Mr Wegwipe,' the earl said.

Malcolm Wegwipe scratched something in

his book. 'And the inquiry into the attempted murder of Mr Eastwell? Mr Lavender Brown, care to comment?'

'We're playing little balls, Mr Wegwipe,' the earl said, sounding hurt before I could reply.

'Ah, well that's fine.' He scribbled in his notebook, reading out what he was writing. 'Ahem. "Mr Lavender Brown refuses to conduct a murder inquiry as he's too busy playing little balls." I'm sure our readers will be most interested.' He put his notebook away in an inside pocket. 'All set.'

'Now look here,' I began, but Wegwipe cut me off.

'That's fine. You don't have to explain. You're a busy man. I understand that.'

I rose to my feet. 'But I want to conduct the inquiry. And it's not a *murder* inquiry.'

'Hmm, if you say so.'

But our conversation got drowned out in the nonsense as the earl started to chant. 'Little balls. Little balls. Little balls.' And encouraged others to get to their feet.

The Landley bunch did so, the youngest son banging on the table. 'Ball in the hole. Ball in the hole.'

'Little balls,' continued the earl. 'Little balls. Little balls.'

'Ball in the hole. Ball in the hole.' The little Landley imp kept banging on the table, causing a knife or a fork to clatter to the floor. Margaret

Landley clipped him round the ear.

I went up to the earl to try to talk some sense into him, but to little avail.

'Mr James, the game won't take long. You don't want to disappoint the children, do you? On Christmas Day? Come, now.'

'No, but...'

'That's settled then. Just twenty minutes or so, then you can come back and have some more fun with the inquiry.'

❖ ❖ ❖

We were taken to the Antique Gallery, the long corridor with the disapproving statues. Little balls (or ball in the hole, depending upon which loony one asked) turned out to be a marble game. The earl could barely contain his excitement as he gave us five marbles each. Simon had explained the rules. The rules that were hardly difficult to comprehend – land one marble in the hole in the wooden block to go through to the next round. As a child, I didn't have any friends, so books and games were familiar companions. This meant I would be good at the game. An expert, one could argue.

Unfortunately, I was the only one in our party who could make such a claim. Emma put up a fair fight, and Rose bettered Lady Talbot, but Stella was pretty damn poor and Sydney was terrible. All of his marbles scattered everywhere. Lost at the end of the corridor, hidden in shadow.

The Landley brood on the other hand were crack shots. Apparently, they played 'ball in the hole' at least five times a week. Such fun it must be living out in the country. Mr Landley kept offering me advice, and as usual, trying to confirm his nonsense through a barely-functioning Margaret. But it was bloody Wegwipe who was even more annoying. In the first round, we went in age order. I was about to go when the pesky fop stood in my way:

'You're thirty-three, aren't you, Mr Lavender Brown? 'I'm thirty, so shall I go first?'

'I'm twenty-bloody-eight! I keep telling you this.'

'Ah yes, the letter. I remember. Still, aiming for a younger demographic? Ahem, shall I just go?'

I didn't have the strength with which to argue.

It was my turn in the later rounds, but I paused as the countess came strolling down the corridor.

'What's all the noise?' she asked, in a quiet voice. She stepped forward gracefully. Her black dress looked too thin for the season, but she showed no signs of discomfort.

'Be careful, dear,' the earl said. 'We're playing little balls. Don't step on the wooden block.'

She glanced down and stepped to one side. 'Where's Aurea?'

'Oh, she's running around somewhere.'

The countess blinked. She then passed me,

searching for her daughter, a worried look on her face.

'Come on, Mr James. Your turn,' the earl urged.

In the end, it came down to myself, Lord Talbot and the Landleys. Lord Talbot tried to take advantage of this by adding to the stakes. I tried to put an end to it. 'Lord Talbot, I'm not throwing in five pounds on a game of little balls. Are you quite mad?'

Lord Talbot smirked. 'Well, if you're not brave enough. What do you say, Mr Landley? An extra five between me and the whole of your family. That gives you a four to one advantage.'

Mr Landley held out a shaking hand. 'Deal.'

'Excellent.' Lord Talbot turned to the little Landley boy. 'Well, child, you can go now. Five pounds of your father's money resting on your shoulders.'

Frederick missed the first two by a long way but steadied himself, improving on the next and slotting the ball home on his fourth. He stood up to a loud cheer.

His brother Anthony was up next. Long and thin, like Constable Matthews. Lord Talbot drew in a sharp, exaggerated breath when Anthony's first shot missed. This seemed to put him off and he went out of the competition.

Margaret followed, but she had her husband in her ear talking about manure again. She also rolled all of her balls quickly and went out in a matter of seconds. Lord Talbot couldn't suppress a laugh.

Mr Landley stepped up, looking ill and for once short of words. So I wasn't surprised to see him crumble and go out too.

'Oh dear,' Lord Talbot said, smiling. 'Interesting what the weight of money adds, is it not? Your turn, Mr Lavender.'

Both of us went through into the next round, leaving only myself and Frederick Landley against Lord Talbot. The block was moved back three more feet.

The crowd gathered around, tense and excited.

'Three ball final,' Lord Talbot said, just as Frederick was about to roll.

'What?' Mr Landley said. 'Ball in the hole always has five balls.'

'Yes, but, we're playing little balls, not ball in the hole, are we not? Three ball final.'

'But, Margaret…'

But neither Margaret nor the earl could prevent Lord Talbot from insisting on a three-ball final.

Two marbles were taken from young Frederick's hand. This seemed to zap his confidence. His sure-fire approach crumbled and he followed the fate of the others.

'Never mind, Mr Landley,' Lord Talbot said. 'It's only money.'

'But you have to beat Mr Lavender first,' Mr Landley said. 'Come on, Mr Lavender!' He banged on my shoulder, and I almost fell over.

I rubbed my new cufflinks then bent down to try. My first shot hit the wood, close but still inches from the hole.

My second shot went closer still, being but an inch from the hole. I felt that with three more shots I could make it but with just one attempt it was a tall order. I rubbed at the marble in my hand, feeling its glassy smoothness over my fingers, before rolling straight towards the wooden block. It looked in, but then it zigzagged and rolled to one side. I'd lost.

'Such a shame,' Lord Talbot said, moving to take my place.

'Ha, we are back in if you miss,' Frederick said, sticking his tongue out and blowing a raspberry at Lord Talbot.

'Yes, but I won't.'

Lord Talbot's first ball looked in, but it veered off towards the end, only missing by half an inch. He shrugged and confidently rolled his second shot straight towards the hole. This was, however, at the same time as Mr Eastwell strode towards us.

'I say, what's going on here? Where is that clown? He's dead.'

It happened so quickly. Lord Talbot's ball rolled straight into the hole just as Mr Eastwell slipped and went flying into the air. He fell backwards, and his foot crashed on the little wooden block, smashing it to pieces. At the same time, his head went with a crack against the base of a statue. A solitary marble rolled back towards Lord Talbot's hand.

'I'd won!' Lord Talbot shouted. 'My marble went in the hole.'

Mr Eastwell rubbed the back of his head. 'My head. I've cut the back of my head.' He removed a hand covered in blood. 'I stood on a damn marble. Whose marble was that?'

Sydney went bright red.

Mrs Parsons dashed over to Mr Eastwell.

Lord Talbot looked at us all. 'My marble went in the hole. Did you see it?'

Strangely, no one had.

Mrs Parsons instructed her daughter to fetch a towel for Mr Eastwell's wound. As she was moving reluctantly behind us, the countess passed her, running towards us, looking extremely flustered and out of sorts. 'I can't find Aurea. I can't find her anywhere.'

The earl answered. 'She'll just be playing around somewhere. No need to worry.'

'She's not! I...I think she might be outside... outside in the snow.'

'She won't be outside in this, surely?' the earl returned.

The countess started to panic. 'I don't know... I. She wanted to build a snowman.'

I remembered the little girl's words at breakfast. She did mention building a snowman, but if conditions were anything like yesterday, she couldn't last more than five minutes. In a fraction of the time it'd taken us to play the game, the snow could have entirely swallowed her. The little girl could be dead.

CHAPTER SIXTEEN

There was panic and chaos from all quarters and shouting – a great deal of shouting. The urge to get outside as quickly as possible was obvious. Even a moment's delay could be a matter of life and death, but I grabbed Sydney's arm as he was about to dash off like everyone else. 'Footprints. We must check for footprints.'

'What's that?'

'We need to stop people from disturbing the steps.'

I set off towards the main entrance with Sydney following behind. We got to the Great Hall, but people were already scrambling in front of us.

'Stop!' I shouted. 'Hold on.'

The outside doors were already wide open. A blistering snowstorm was painfully evident. People continued to stream through the door.

'The steps. Keep off the steps!'

I stopped at the doorway, with Sydney behind me. 'Get off the steps! The footprints.'

Beyond, people were frantically calling for the girl, scattering away in random directions. The snowstorm clawed at my face with icy fingers. I dreaded to think of the girl lost out here. I quickly turned, crouching down to the steps. 'Just look at this now.'

'What are you looking for?' Sydney asked.

'The girl's footprints, of course. If we could trace the footprints, it would give us an indication of where she went, but now...' I held my arms aloft. Still, I scanned the steps as best I could.

I'd not been at it a minute when a shadow obscured my view.

'What are you doing?' Wegwipe said, hunched over, notebook and pen in hand as usual. 'Shouldn't you be helping look for the girl?'

'I am.'

He sniffed. 'Ahem, I don't think she's on the steps.'

I glanced up at him, then back down, continuing my search.

'Any joy?' Wegwipe said, after a minute or two.

'Not yet.'

'I still don't think she's on the steps.'

I sighed. 'Look, why don't you go and run around in the snow like everyone else? Walk down on the right.' There was virgin snow on that side and he couldn't do any damage there.

He jotted something down in his book and put it away in his inner jacket pocket. 'Right. I'll leave you two playing on the steps then.'

He took himself off down the side and disappeared into the distance.

'Should I join the search?' Sydney asked.

'No, there are already plenty of people out there. We're best suited to looking for the prints. In fact, go back inside and find Simon, or a footman who looks like he knows what day it is, and bring him back here. Hurry.'

Sydney dashed off.

With Sydney gone, I continued my search. It turned out the steps weren't as bad as they first appeared. I used the whole length of the steps to work out, to ninety-eight per cent of accuracy, that she had not taken this route out into the snow. And, given that she had not yet been found out front, it was all but safe to say that she hadn't come out this way at all. I'd reached this conclusion just as Sydney returned with Simon, the house steward, who had been taking care of the countess.

'How can I help, Mr Lavender?'

I insisted that he take us to every external door in the building, whether it was locked or not, and we ran off in search of little footprints in the snow.

❖ ❖ ❖

'Take me to the countess immediately,' I told Simon, having thoroughly conducted our search.

He guided us through the rear of the house to where we had breakfast that morning. Mrs Landley, along with Miss Parsons, were seated by the countess who sat in the centre of the room. An untouched glass of milk stood before her on the table. She looked deathly pale but there were no signs she had been crying. Her face was fixed and determined. Lady Talbot was also there, head resting on a hand, looking bored by it all. They all looked up sharply as we approached.

'Any news?' the countess asked.

'She's not outside,' I said, sitting in the chair I sat in this morning. Sydney joined me.

'How can you be sure?' she asked.

'Footprints, or lack of them.'

I waved a solitary maid forward, who had been hovering around the countess and asked her for a glass of hot chocolate.

'Footprints?' the countess said.

'Yes, there are no footprints in the snow. So, she must be in the house.'

'Oh, thank the heavens.' The countess touched her heart. 'We must search the house again.'

Miss Parsons placed a bold hand upon her arm. 'Hold on a minute. How can you be so sure, Mr Lavender?'

'I calculated it.'

Her face was the picture of distaste. 'You *calculated* it?'

'Indeed, I did. She's in the house, trust me. Countess, you've checked her room, I take it?'

Miss Parsons spoke for her. 'Of *course* she has.'

I still addressed the countess. 'Are there any other rooms she usually plays in?'

'We've searched everywhere, Mr Lavender,' the countess replied. 'Everywhere.'

'Still, it is a rather large house.'

Mrs Parsons came in and sat beside her daughter. 'Mr Eastwell is resting. He's with his wife. Any sign of the child?'

They drifted into a conversation and I switched out of it. Instead, I turned to Sydney and sipped the excellent hot chocolate that had just arrived. 'We have to trace the girl's metaphorical footprints.'

'Yeh, what?' Sydney said, looking at my drink.

'We need to trace where the girl went. Now she ran off in that direction, remember?' I took another sip. It was delicious.

'But that was a while ago now.'

'True, but, it's a starting point. Where's Rose and the gang, anyway?'

'Don't know.'

'Not helping, obviously,' Lady Talbot said, from the other table.

I looked up but turned back to Sydney. 'We need to try and trace where the girl went if we can.'

But I looked up to the sound of heavy footsteps. Anthony Landley panting.

'They've...they've found something. Outside.'

The countess stood up, pushing Miss Parsons to one side, who was still on her arm. 'What is it?'

Anthony was unable to meet her desperate gaze.

'What is it?' she repeated, not loud but her natural authority made it sound so.

'It's out in the snow.'

Her eyes darkened. 'What is?'

'It's a glove. A...a little red glove.'

'Oh, my God. Oh, my God. Oh, my God.'

Miss Parsons turned away from the countess and addressed me bitterly. 'This is all *your* fault.'

'Mine? How is it *my* fault?'

'You're supposed to be a detective, aren't you? Yet you're sat there drinking hot chocolate, while all the real men are out looking for her.'

The countess' sharp intake of breath cut through the room. It chilled straight to the heart, or the brain rather, as the heart really was just a muscle that pumped blood around the body. She seemed to look straight through Anthony Landley, who was now shivering. She questioned him further as Miss Parsons continued to turn her wrath my way.

'I call it disgusting,' Miss Parsons continued. 'You're doing nothing.'

I took a heavy gulp of the hot chocolate, then clattered it down on the saucer. 'I *am* looking for her.'

'Really? It doesn't look like it.'

Stella came in, taking in what was going on, and came and sat with us without speaking.

'Disgusting,' Miss Parsons repeated.

'Just because I'm not running around in the snow, it doesn't mea–'

But the earl came crashing into the fray. 'They've found her glove. Thomas has found my Aurea's glove.' He looked utterly dejected and almost hugged his wife. He turned to me pleadingly, passing the glove to the countess, who snatched it from him. 'Mr James, can you help?'

'Oh, he's too busy drinking hot chocolate,' Miss Parsons said, but the earl hadn't heard her, being too lost in his own grief.

I stood and briefly placed my hands on the earl's shoulders trying to capture his attention. 'Where did they find the glove? Is it definitely Aurea's?'

'It's hers,' the countess said, holding it desperately. She twisted it over in her fingers and clutched it to her chest.

'Where was it found?' I asked the earl, who was struggling to focus, even more than he normally does.

'It was in the snow.'

'I know that! Where exactly?'

'Outside.'

Christ. 'I gathered that, but how far down?'

'Deep down, deep in the snow.'

The countess shuddered at that phrase. Miss

Parsons followed suit.

'How deep?' I said.

'Oh, does it matter?' Miss Parsons snapped.

'How deep?' I repeated, still trying to get some sense out of the earl.

'Very deep, a foot at least. Thomas found it when he fell over in the snow.'

'About a foot down, you say?'

'Yes, Mr James. About that.'

I tried to get the countess' attention. 'Don't worry, there's nothing to worry about. Trust me,' I told her.

'Nothing to worry about?' Miss Parsons snapped again. 'How can you say that?'

Wegwipe came in alongside Mr Landley. Which was all I needed.

'Have you found her?' the countess asked them in desperation.

'Er, no,' Mr Landley said. 'Not yet, I was looking for Mr Lavender. I said he would be able to help. He's an incredible detective. Didn't I say that, Malcolm? That Mr Lavender would be able to help? Malcolm? Didn't I say that?'

'Oh, he's in here drinking hot chocolate,' Miss Parsons said. 'He's too busy, I'm afraid.'

'Hot chocolate?' Malcolm Wegwipe licked his lips and reached inside his jacket pocket, withdrawing his notebook. 'Hot chocolate, was it?'

'Look, I...'

He started reading what he was writing.

'"Finished playing in the snow. Now partaking of hot chocolate. Girl still missing." Could I bother you for a quote? I'm sure our readers would be most interested.'

'Yes, I'll give you a bloody quote. Can everyone calm down and listen to me?' I strode forward, ensuring I had everyone's attention. 'I can assure you, beyond the bounds of reasonable doubt, that the girl is *not* outside. I found absolutely no trace of any footprints anywhere.'

'But it's snowing outside,' Miss Parsons said.

'Is it really? I hadn't noticed. Yes, it's snowing outside, but the steps are partially covered. I must admit the step condition looked hopeless at first, but on further investigation, I was able to conclude, following a mathematical formula, that she hadn't been out front.'

Sydney smiled, nodding, as did Mr Landley, who'd started to sport his usual smile again. I continued. 'Then, as opposed to continually running around shouting, like a mad chicken in the snow, I used my *brain*. It's the thing that's in your head. It's often neglected, I find. With the help of Simon, I discovered no trace of any footprint from any of the exits which are also covered, meaning – she's *not* outside. That is, unless she can fly. Can she fly, Miss Parsons?'

Miss Parsons turned her head.

'But what about the glove?' the countess said. 'The glove is definitely hers.'

'It is of no consequence.'

'No consequence, Mr Lavender?' Wegwipe said, still writing everything down.

'No consequence,' I repeated.

'How can that be?' the earl asked.

'It was buried in a *foot* of snow?'

'Yes,' the earl nodded.

'Then she hasn't only just lost it then, has she? It must have come off yesterday, after the rescue. I turned to the countess. 'Did she have both gloves yesterday by the fire?'

'I…I don't know.'

'She will have lost it yesterday.'

'Ah, I see, Mr James,' the earl said. 'I think I see.'

The countess turned to a maid behind her. 'Send for Mary.'

The maid curtsied and started to walk away.

'And brandy. We need brandy,' the earl added.

The countess eyed her husband but did not object on this occasion.

'If she's not outside,' Miss Parsons said, fire now back in her eyes. 'Then *where* is she?'

'Well, that's what I was trying to work out before I had to explain myself over and over. So, do you want me to go into the mathematical formula I used to calculate against the probability of her going out of the front door, or should I continue looking for the girl?'

Miss Parsons crossed her arms.

'Thought so.' I returned to Sydney and sat back down. My hot chocolate had gone. I hadn't realised I'd drunk it all. 'Come on, Sydney. We'll start to track the girl.'

I stood up again and started to walk towards the exit where little Aurea had walked earlier this morning, as Sydney lingered briefly to speak to Stella. Apparently, Stella had got drawn into helping Mrs Parsons take Mr Eastwell up to his room. Personally, I'd have left him to it. No, she'd not seen Emma or Rose.

'Come on, Sydney, let's – hey, what's that on your lip?'

Sydney quickly wiped his face. 'Nothing, nothing.'

'Bloody thief.'

We walked towards the rear door, but I stopped to observe the maid as she returned with a tray of brandy. I was just listening to confirm what I already suspected.

The countess immediately turned on her, asking her if she had found both of Aurea's gloves yesterday when she had been undressing her by the fire.

'No, countess, now that you mention it, there was only one glove. Sorry, I didn't think it was important.' Her eyes darted to one side.

The countess thanked her reassuring her, that all was well. She turned my way, thanking me also, as did the earl.

The earl handed the countess a brandy from the table and she took it up reluctantly. She moved it towards her lips. For the first time, I noticed that her hand was shaking ever so slightly.

I walked towards her, trying to make eye contact, but she wouldn't look at me. She wouldn't look at anyone. 'She's in the house. Trust me.'

She nodded slowly.

'You can always trust Mr Lavender,' I said brightly, trying to lift the mood.

A solemn silence descended, broken only by a harsh crack of a log on the fire.

Then we all started as a figure crashed into the room. It was the Eastwell boy. 'I've found her. I've found her.'

The countess sprang up, touching the earl's shoulder.

'I've found her.'

'Yes?' the countess whispered.

'I've found her and…she's dead.'

The countess screamed and dropped the brandy glass which smashed on the floor.

'She's dead and she's been murdered,' the Eastwell boy stammered.

CHAPTER SEVENTEEN

The death of a child is a crime against nature. If hell exists, it is a place where all those who do harm to a child should burn for all eternity, and I for one would light the pyre.

The countess had collapsed, only prevented from doing herself harm by those around her, who caught her before she hit her head on the table. The earl could only repeat his daughter's name with lips that wouldn't cease their trembling. And in the shouts and cries of those around him, nothing but shared horror and pain existed.

The countess refused to be seated or deterred in any way from seeing her child. The earl's protestations quickly relented when he saw, reflected in her eyes, the sheer force of a mother in the throes of eternal grief.

We followed the incoherent Master Eastwell

through the halls and winding corridors, up the stairs, strangely, towards the west wing. I'd thrown some questions at him but quickly realised it was pointless in his state of shock. He couldn't speak and there was nothing in his eyes. Behind us, the earl kept repeatedly mumbling his daughter's name, but no sound could be heard over the countess' wailing cries.

I grabbed Sydney's arm as we approached the top of the stairs. 'You must help me to keep the countess away from the child.'

Sydney looked back at her with some trepidation. Such a task would not be easy, even for him, but we had no time to linger, as we continued to follow David Eastwell past our room towards the far end of the corridor.

My mind had little time to question who could possibly have killed the girl and for what ungodly reason. Yesterday, I had felt the sense of danger in the air, but never for one moment did I think it was going to result in the death of the child.

'Where are we heading?' I asked him. 'Where's the girl?'

But I wasn't even sure he recognised the fact that I was speaking. Instead, he stumbled down the corridor and we followed him towards the Eastwell rooms. What on earth had she been doing there?

David Eastwell stopped outside of his father's room, pointing at the door, then held back. 'She's in there.' Was all he managed, refusing to even look in that direction.

I positioned myself in front of the door, hardly daring to twist the handle myself, but I knew I had to. I had to keep my revulsion at bay and lead the way professionally for the countess and the earl. With a slight tremble I hoped was detected only by myself, I pushed the handle down and entered the dark bedroom.

Mr Eastwell sat on the bed in a state of frozen shock, his hands covered in blood.

'Where is she?' I asked, rather pointlessly, as the only place she could be was round the other side of the bed on the floor.

Behind me, the countess was still wailing, with Sydney doing his best to hold her back.

I inched around the bed, hardly daring to look.

Mrs Eastwell lay on her back in a pool of blood. Her eyes were dead to this world.

I addressed Mr Eastwell. 'Where is she? Where is the girl?'

But he was still in a state of shock, just like his son.

The countess broke through Sydney's grasp, having seen that something wasn't quite right. She dashed to my side, then reeled at the sight of Mrs Eastwell's corpse, only to look around in confusion. 'Where's Aurea?'

I shook my head.

The countess turned and fled from the room. I followed. She clasped Master Eastwell by the shoulder, shaking him violently. 'Where's Aurea?' Again and again, she shook him until he broke out of his daze.

'I…I, she's dead. Mother's dead.'

'Where is the girl?' I said, firmly.

'Girl? What girl?'

There was a collective sigh. Could it be that the girl was still alive after all? But if so, where was she?

◆ ◆ ◆

Mrs Eastwell had been stabbed, the wound gaping and grotesque, but there were no immediate signs of the murder weapon. If Mr Eastwell had gone mad and stabbed her, what had he done with it? The top priority though, of course, was to locate the missing girl. All staff had been instructed to continue the search, leaving myself, Sydney and the earl with the body and Mr Eastwell, whose hands were thick with blood. Still, he wouldn't speak, and I soon grew tired of trying to get through to him.

'Sydney, move Mr Eastwell into the other room. And make sure it's locked, so we can continue the search for the girl.'

'Right.'

'Where's Rose, anyway? Trying on a new dress?'

'I dunno.'

Sydney caught Mr Eastwell by the crook of his

arm and led him down the corridor without any protest from him.

The earl looked uncomfortable. 'Mr James, will you be needing anything else?'

'No, you can go down. Oh, actually, can you send me Simon?'

'Of course.' He couldn't meet my eyes. 'Mr James, what do you think has happened to my little girl?'

'I don't know exactly, but I'm sure she's safe.'

He nodded solemnly and left.

I returned my attention to the body. It looked like the dagger, or whatever had been used, had gone into her heart. There was a lot of blood. An awful lot of blood. I instinctively examined her hands and wrists but found no defensive marks, nor any signs of a struggle aside from the crumpled bedsheets, which had been half-dragged on the floor.

Without disturbing the corpse, I felt around the body for the weapon. Nothing.

There was blood on the bed sheets. Long, dark smears on the left-hand side, where the body had been found. Nothing along the foot of the bed but dampness. 'Feel that,' I told Sydney, who was just returning from his little task.

'It's soaked.'

'Yes. Did you secure Mr Eastwell in the room?'

'I did.'

'Where is the key?'

Sydney patted his backside pocket.

'Good,' I said. 'Nobody's going to try stealing that. You stay here. Make sure nobody gets in or out.'

Sydney glanced over at the body. 'Well, I don't think anybody is getting out.'

'You know what I mean. Do a quick fingerprint search as well, but that's rather pointless with all the people that have already been in this room, especially last night.' I sniffed. It was still rather pungent.

I strode past Sydney, down the hall heading towards the sudden shouting at the bottom of the stairs. A footman was lingering around. I leaned over the banister. 'What is it?'

'In the breakfast room, sir.' He pointed the way.

'What is?'

'I don't know, sir.'

'Well, that's useful.'

I made my way down hastily, careful not to trip as the steps were indeed steep. When I got into the breakfast room, the first thing I noticed was Rose. She was standing in the middle of the room close to the countess, Emma not far away, smiling. The countess turned around as she heard me approach, the young girl in her arms. 'They've found her. They found my Aurea.'

The earl was there, crouched beside her, stroking her hand. He was also crying.

I turned to Rose. 'Oh, so you weren't trying dresses on, then?'

'Dresses?'

'Never mind. Where was she?'

'Emma found her first.'

I indicated that we should retreat to our breakfast table, joining Stella, who'd stood up to greet her daughter. I waved the maid over, who was fussing around the little girl. She came reluctantly.

'Yes, sir?'

'Hot chocolate for me.'

'Sir?'

'One of those delicious hot chocolates I had earlier, if you don't mind? And some food, I'm starving. It's gone one.'

'Oh, I'm seeing to the girl. I can fetch Mary.'

'Yes, fetch Mary – for the stomach…it doth a rumble.'

It turns out that Emma and Stella had done exactly what myself and Sydney were about to do, which was to track the girl's metaphorical footprints. Apparently, Aurea had played a game of hide and seek with one of the cook's sons, and they had tracked her down to one of the disused bedrooms. She was asleep in an old wardrobe with a blanket over her head.

'Yes,' Emma explained. 'She'd had honey cakes for breakfast, so I knew that if I looked halfway down on the doors, I might be able to track her finger marks. I used this to help.' She put down the magnifying glass on the table that I'd given her this morning. 'We managed to follow the trail most of the way.'

'Excellent work,' I said, genuinely impressed.

She beamed at me as I took another generous sip of the hot chocolate and ate some cake. Both the cake and the hot drink were absolutely divine. Hot chocolate could replace coffee as my afternoon beverage of choice. I wondered if Adam did a hot chocolate as delicious as this back home. I rolled it around my mouth and thought of home for just a moment, already missing the solitude.

'Isn't she wonderful?' Rose said.

I smudged a bit of chocolate away from my upper lip. 'Who?'

'Emma, of course!'

'Oh yes, but we've got bigger problems.'

'What bigger problems?'

But the earl came over to our table, just as word had got around to those outside and several of them came streaming into the room, cheering loudly. The earl turned back to them briefly and gave a wave, but returned his full attention on Emma and Rose, shaking their hands vigorously. 'I cannot thank you two enough. And also you, Mr James. I'm forever grateful. Forever grateful.'

Rose and Emma were naturally modest at the earl's praise, though he eagerly returned to his daughter and wife, but not before I'd asked for a space in an outhouse for the body. He immediately sent a footman away to organise it.

'What body?' Rose asked.

'I was just about to say. Mrs Eastwell's.'

Rose narrowed those sharp eyes of hers. 'What? What's happened?'

'She's upstairs. Dead. Stabbed in the chest, blood everywhere.'

'James!' Stella said, looking over at Emma, though Emma didn't seem to mind.

Rose was shocked. 'She's been murdered?' A few people paused in their coat unravelling and the rumour soon got around the jubilant crowd, hushing it once again.

'Yes. One large stab wound to the chest. We've got Mr Eastwell locked in a room. Sydney's up there currently. We need to go and sort it all out, I expect. It *appears* to be a straightforward case of husband gone mad, though there are one or two odd things.'

'Odd things?' Rose asked, taking the same question away from Emma's lips.

I put my spoon down, my cake being finished. 'A missing weapon but blood upon the hands...hardly an apt partnership.'

'Let's go then,' Rose said, standing, as did Emma.

Stella reached for Emma's hand. 'You can sit down, young lady.'

Emma looked crestfallen.

'It's well.' I told her. 'I need you here.' She looked up at me. 'I need you to use these.' I pulled my ear. 'And those.' Pointed to my eyes and then thumbed to the crazy lot behind me. 'Eyes and ears, understand?'

Emma nodded, but still looked glum.

'Come on then,' Rose said, preparing to leave.

'Just a moment.'

'Why?'

'Just one more of these,' I said, shaking my empty hot chocolate cup in the air.

❖ ❖ ❖

'What took you so long?' Sydney asked, wandering from side to side, a sulk brewing, I could tell.

'Busy. A lot to consider.'

Sydney didn't look like he believed me. I could tell with his eyes. Natural petulance. 'Busy, how?'

'Hot chocolate,' Rose said. 'And cake.'

'Hot chocolate? Where's mine? I'm starving.'

'Oh, Sydney. Stop being greedy. You stole mine, so I had to wait for a replacement. That's on you. Anyway, we have got a dead body on the floor, a prisoner locked in the other room, and you're whining about filling your face with cake. Come on.'

Sydney puffed out his cheeks and took out his new hipflask. He took a hasty drink then put it back in his jacket pocket. 'Sorry, just I–'

'Never mind about that, you've wasted enough time already.' I turned to Rose, who was looking apprehensive about the body on the floor, sort of half-looking, half not wanting to. 'So, what do you make of the scene?'

She paused, blinking a few times.

'Go on. She's dead. She won't bite.'

Rose nodded, moving closer to the body. 'Oh my, there's an awful lot of blood.'

'There is. Have a quick look at the body and the scene. What do you make of it?'

She quickly got down to work, not shy anymore around the body, though she didn't touch it. She examined it closely and took in the condition of the bed. She took a step back when she'd finished. 'Lots of blood but no weapon as you said. Have you searched for it?'

'I didn't have the time for a thorough search, but it's clearly been taken out of the body.'

She opened a few drawers without success, then went to the window and threw it wide open, letting in the biting cold. 'Can't see properly.'

I rubbed at my arms. 'We'll send Sydney down.'

Sydney huffed. 'Why do I always have to be the one to do the running about?'

'Because…you're good at it. You're a natural. Off you go now, shoo.'

Sydney groaned but dashed off and I continued searching for the missing weapon. I looked under the bed again, in the wardrobe, and down the sides. I then turned my attention to the smaller items of furniture, like the chest of drawers and the small table. I examined everything carefully, but there was no sign of any weapon. There was, however, a rag covered in blood in the table drawer. 'Look at this.' I handed her the rag aloft with my finger and thumb, careful not to touch the blood.

'Hmm, what's that for?' she asked.

'I don't know.'

She handed it back and I placed it by the body, then returned to the window. I could just make out Sydney struggling along in the snow in the far distance. 'Hurry up, it's cold with the window open!' I shouted, but I don't think he heard me as his little legs still bobbled along at exactly the same pace. He shuffled further along and stopped several windows away, examining the ground by his feet. 'Over here, you daft fool!' I shouted, waving at him.

He looked up and stumbled along. 'Look on the floor. There, right there, anything?'

'What?'

I sighed. 'Any signs of a bloody weapon?'

'A weapon with blood on it?'

I yanked my head back in frustration, hitting the top of it on the window pane. 'Jesus. Just look for a knife or a dagger, and be quick about it!'

I waited a few moments, almost catching frostbite again. Sydney shouted up. 'I can't see anything.'

'Just keep looking around a bit and then come up.' I closed the window with a thump, rubbing at my head.

'What do you make of it?' Rose asked, startling

me.

I continued to rub at my injury. 'It still doesn't quite add up. Mr Eastwell was covered in blood, but the weapon is nowhere to be seen.'

'It has to be somewhere.'

'True. That's not all that's bothering me.'

Rose glanced at the dead body again, shuddering. 'It isn't?'

I sat down in a chair. 'No. Mr Eastwell.'

'What about him?'

I explained that the psychology around him didn't seem to fit. That he didn't strike me as one prone to shock. That he could be faking the whole thing, making a mess of the crime scene, struck me as a distinct possibility.

Rose had suddenly gone quite pale. 'What next?'

'We can get the body removed, and then we question Mr Eastwell.'

When Sydney finally decided to make an appearance, puffing and half-covered in snow, he flipped me the key from his back pocket and we continued down the hall, our shadows looming in front of us. 'Let me do the talking,' I said, knocking on the door. 'Mr Eastwell, we're coming in. Stand back.' I didn't expect him to run at us, but it paid to be on the safe side. Sydney prepared to face any sudden surge, fist clenched. Rose stood behind him.

He didn't answer, so I pushed in the key and opened the lock. 'Ready?' I swung the door wide open. 'Mr Eastwell?' I stepped into the room with Sydney at my back. 'Mr Eastwell?' But Mr Eastwell was not there. The room was empty.

CHAPTER EIGHTEEN

'I don't bloody believe it,' I said, surveying the empty room. Rose by instinct swung back the wardrobe door to reveal nothing but a small cloud of dust. 'Sydney, did you hold on to the key at all times?'

Sydney patted his backside pocket. 'Yep.'

'Damn. There must be a spare.'

'Hey, do you think he's vanished, just like those sheep?' Sydney asked.

'What are you talking about?' I moved round to the sides of the bed, checking for anything out of the ordinary, but there was nothing amiss. I went to the window, opened it and looked outside. I couldn't see anything but snow and ice.

'You know, the farm pets? Mrs Wobble's sheep and all the rest of those animals.'

'Farm pets?' I slammed the window shut. 'Oh, do be quiet.'

Rose shook her head. 'What are we going to

do?'

'About what? The dead body, the missing weapon, or the missing deranged murderer?' I said.

'I propose we start with locating Mr Eastwell,' Rose said, dryly.

'So what's the plan?' Sydney asked.

Ever the man of action, when he's not being lazy.

'I want you two to do a quick search up here. Grab a footman or two to help so you have the numbers. Search along the corridors on the upper floor, call into any open room, and then join me downstairs. Make sure you stay together at all times, you understand? Do not go wandering off alone.' I looked over sternly at Rose, who met my stare blankly. 'It could be dangerous.'

'What are you going to do?' Sydney said.

'I'm going to go down and address the crowd. People need to know what's happening so they can stay safe.'

'Right, let's get moving,' Rose said, and they left the room. I followed into the corridor, pausing only to quickly examine the lock. It was a fairly standard affair but there was no evidence of tampering. I closed the door and went the other way. Almost immediately, however, I stumbled into Malcolm Wegwipe, who was standing in the corridor leaning against the wall, his little black notebook in hand. 'Deranged murderer on the loose? Make a good story, that.'

'You shouldn't listen at doors.'

'Was she brutally stabbed? Will Mr Eastwell strike again? Is it just a matter of time?'

'I want you downstairs, now. In no way do I–'

'The Christmas Day Massacre – Deranged Murderer on the Loose. Yes, a good one that, don't you think?'

'Downstairs.'

'Was she having an affair, Mr Brown?'

'It's Lavender! And downstairs.' I pulled him back and marched him back down the corridor.

'Or, was he the one having the affair and she found out?'

I stopped. 'Look, just what are you getting at?'

He rubbed his finger and thumb on his chin. 'Well, if you let me on in the details, I have a pretty good clue what's been going on.'

'If you have information, you tell me about it, do you hear?'

'Certainly, anything to help the law. If you let me in on the investigation, I'd be more than happy to help.'

I grabbed him by the collar, pulling him to one side. 'You tell me right now, regardless. What are you blabbering about?'

'It pertains to a certain...young lady...well, not so young and Mr Eastwell. I happened to be lingering upstairs yesterday, quite by chance you understand, when–'

'Get on with it.'

'Right. I have reason to believe that Mr Eastwell and Mrs Parsons, were, ahem, more than mere acquaintances.'

'So, what are you saying?'

'I'm saying that it is possible Mrs Eastwell found out, challenged her husband over it, an argument broke out...' Malcolm Wegwipe shrugged. 'These things happen. I've seen it all before, but the deranged murderer bit, well, that's great news. A fantastic new angle!'

'Great news? Are you kidding?' I was shouting now.

'Oh, well, of course. It's terrible. Shocking even, but that's what readers want. I'm merely doing my job and you're doing yours. We are the same, you and I, profiting from crime.'

'We are far from the same.'

'You can argue all you want, but it's true. You're happy enough to rise with the sensation and milk it along the way. Not done you badly, the Astonbury affair, has it?'

I ignored his jibe. 'Do you have any evidence of what you are implying, regarding Mr Eastwell?'

'I have my own eyes and ears, Mr Lavender Brown. As I say, I was admiring the plant pot outside Mr Eastwell's room yesterday (lovely decorative pattern), when I heard voices. A woman's, and not Mrs Eastwell's, that's for sure. I saw the door handle turn, and I stepped into the shadows. I didn't want to cause embarrassment, you understand? And then I saw Mrs Parsons come out of the room, and well...'

'Well, what?'

'Her hair was a little untidy, and she looked flushed.'

'Wegwipe, I don't have time for tittle-tattle.' I continued down the corridor, dragging him by the arm.

'I know an awful lot of things, Mr Br... Lavender. I'm a good source to have onside.'

'I'm sick of your snivelling.' I dragged him for so long, and then he picked up the pace, and then he followed on behind into the breakfast room, which was awash with excited chatter.

'What's going on, Mr Lavender?' the countess asked. She had one arm around her daughter, who seemed amused by all the fuss around her.

'Yes, what's going on? There are rumours that Mrs Eastwell is dead,' Mr Landley said. 'Very, very shocking. I said to Margaret, that can't be true as we were talking to her just this morning. Weren't we, Margaret? Margaret? Tell Mr Lavender that we were talking to her just this morning. Margaret?'

'Mr Lavender?' Mr Parsons said, seated next to Mr Landley. 'Are you sure? I saw her this morning as well.'

Everyone else was looking on.

I licked my lips. 'I'm afraid it's true. Regardless of any morning interactions you might all have had. She is, now, I'm afraid, quite dead.'

Miss Parsons gasped and there were other

cries of disbelief.

'Oh, I say,' Mr Parsons said. 'Are you sure?'

'Of course, I'm sure.'

I raised my hands to ward off any further scrutiny and then surveyed the room. Everyone seemed accounted for apart from Mrs Parsons. Miss Parsons was trying to comfort Master Eastwell but he was hunched away from her in a corner silently weeping. Wegwipe was scribbling away, pen in hand. The Talbots were still. The Landleys all seemed to take up the same wide-eyed expression. Even William Brookes seemed to take stock of the news.

'I say,' he said. 'Mrs Eastwell is dead?'

'Yes.' I glanced at Emma, who had been looking at me all the time. 'She's been murdered.' This set the crowd off again into more fits and starts, although Lady Talbot seemed to perk up.

'A murder, how delicious,' she said.

'Murdered, how?' Miss Parsons asked.

'That's not all,' I added. 'Our chief suspect, Mr Eastwell, is missing.'

'Missing, Mr James?' the earl seemed surprised. 'How can he be missing? He was locked in a spare room, wasn't he?'

There were a few more murmurs at that.

'He was, but now he's gone.'

'Missing from a locked room?' William Brookes said.

People turned towards him as if surprised that he'd spoken twice in quick succession.

'Correct,' I confirmed.

The countess cut through the noise with her natural authority. 'What now?'

I sat down on the nearest empty chair. 'First, we search the house.' I wagged my finger at them. 'Methodically.'

'I'll help, Mr Lavender,' Mr Landley shouted, standing up to attention.

'You can count me in,' Mr Parsons added, standing beside him.

'Listen to me.' I told them. 'This is not going to be like the search for the girl, which was absolute chaos. It's going to be a logical search conducted by myself and my team, but yes, I will take advantage of an extra pair of hands or two.'

'Excellent, excellent, Mr James,' the earl said also standing.

I cut off further conversation. 'When I conduct the search, I want everyone else to remain here and not to leave this room under in circumstances. Is that clear?'

There were a few agreements, but Lord Talbot was not one of them. 'Oh, so who put you in charge?' He was seated at the far corner table, a glass of something rolling around in his hands.

'I did.'

'Quite right,' the earl added, which had the effect of silencing the dissent. It was also pointed out that Sydney had over twenty years of experience with the police. So, with the weather cutting off outside access to the local constabulary, the earl pressed the case that we should be responsible for leading the investigation.

'Now,' I continued. 'I will need to interview people after the search, but for the moment the main priority is finding Mr Eastwell and Mrs Parsons. Now, does anybody know the whereabouts of either of them?'

Several people turned to look at each other, but faces, on the whole, were blank aside from Master Eastwell who had gone quite pale.

'Mr Parsons, do you know where your wife is?'

He shook his head.

Miss Parsons sighed. 'He doesn't know where Mother is. Nobody does.'

'So, we have two missing people.'

'Fantastic,' Malcolm Wegwipe said, licking his lips.

I turned on him. 'Excuse me?'

'Oh, nothing, Mr Brown.' He scribbled furiously. 'Nothing at all. Terrible, it's terrible. What a horrible Christmas it's turning out to be...'

Yes, well, I agreed with him on that front.

❖ ❖ ❖

It didn't take long for the reliable and efficient Simon to appear at my side. He bowed his head politely. 'Mr Lavender?'

'Simon, is there a skeleton key for the rooms

upstairs?'

'Not one key in particular but there are several spares.'

'Can you bring them to me?'

'Of course.' He bowed again and left.

Mr Eastwell had to be somewhere, as surely he wasn't outside. 'What's the weather like out?' I said to the crowd.

'The weather, Mr Lavender?' Miss Parsons said.

'That's what I asked, yes.'

'Planning on going for a little walk in the garden?' Wegwipe said. 'Or to build a little snowman, perhaps?'

Miss Parsons sniggered, as did Anthony Landley.

'What's the weather like out?' I repeated, a little more forcefully this time.

'It's currently stopped snowing, Mr Lavender; why do you ask?' the countess answered. Her eyes were always serious I noticed.

'Thank you.'

'Can I go and look for footprints as well?' Emma said, suddenly by my side, understanding the nature of my questioning.

'No,' Stella said.

'Not by yourself,' I added. 'But you can join the search with me.'

'Thank you.'

'She's not going anywhere,' Stella said.

'Oh, she'll be fine. I don't think Mr Eastwell is that deranged anyway, and she'll be with me and the earl. I could do with her young eyes,' I told Stella.

Stella wavered but then agreed, somewhat reluctantly.

Simon reappeared after just a few minutes, at my elbow again, with a bunch of keys. I handed them to Stella, telling her to pass them to Sydney and Rose to check the locked upstairs rooms. I asked Simon to check the rear exits and then turned to Emma. 'Ready?'

She beamed at me in her usual way. 'Let's go.'

The earl walked beside us and we proceeded towards the Great Hall with Mr Landley and Parsons following on behind.

'I say, this is all rather exciting,' the earl said, as we made our way towards the entrance. 'Terribly exciting.'

'Exciting? What, catching a deranged killer?' I asked, momentarily stopping, but quickly picking up pace again.

'Yes. Like a treasure hunt.'

We stopped outside of the entrance to the Great Hall. The doors were firmly closed.

'When we're on the farm, we have many, *many* exciting moments,' Mr Landley said. 'For one thing, there's the lambing season. Always a most exciting time…'

'Mr Landley. Do you think we could leave the lambing talk until after we have found Mr Eastwell?'

'Well, the lambing is of course the highlight of

the sea–'

'Mr Landley!'

'What?'

'Concentrate and be quiet.'

During the lambing conversation, the earl had carefully opened the doors and Emma was already poised on her knees as the door swung open, immediately exposing us to the elements.

'Bit chilly out,' Mr Landley observed.

'What did you expect?' I said.

Mr Parsons pulled his jacket closer.

'Move out,' I said, but Emma was already standing up.

'There's nothing there,' she said.

I glanced at the steps, but she was quite correct.

We then turned to our laborious mission of searching the ground floor. I let the earl lead us through the most productive routes, always on the lookout for Mr Eastwell, straining for footsteps that may be ahead of us or around any corridor. The task soon felt overwhelming, as the vastness of the place made the search rather hopeless. It didn't help that the earl and Mr Landley slapped the ground when they ran, alerting the possible murderer in waiting. Still, there was nothing that could be done to prevent this, as the alternative of creeping around slowly didn't strike me as that productive either.

'Stop,' I told them, as we entered the turquoise drawing room, having been unsuccessful for too long. The drawing room looked like it was in a state of trepidation between post-Christmas activity and abandonment. 'Let's sit down a bit. We need to think.'

'Well, my back is rather aching,' Mr Parson added.

The fire had already been lit and I thought sitting in front of it would help me to think, so I spun a chair around and crashed down upon it. 'Emma, come sit with me.'

Emma did as instructed. 'What are you thinking, Uncle?' she asked.

'Well, for a start, all of this running around searching for Mr Eastwell is just not working. There are too many rooms.' I warmed my hands by the fire. 'I need to get into the mind of what's happened. I don't just run around like a loony. I'm James Lavender.'

'James *Lavender*?' the earl said. 'I thought James was your surname. I thought Lavender was a nickname?'

I turned around, my mouth, I'm sure, half hanging open. 'No. My name is James Lavender. It's not difficult to comprehend.'

'Ho, ho. Mr James likes to have his little jokes, doesn't he? Even at times like these. He's got a great sense of humour!' The earl stood up and slapped my back. 'Mr James is also a *wonderful* detective. He'll soon sort all this business out, ho, ho. Don't you worry,' he said to Mr Landley and Mr Parsons, who nodded along eagerly. He then motioned over a solitary footman who just happened to be walking past with a blanket in his hand. Most of the others were involved in the search. 'Shall we get a little drink? Keep the spirits up, eh?'

Mr Landley and Mr Parsons agreed.

'Drinks! Bring drinks!' the earl instructed. 'What shall we have, a little sherry, eh?'

'I'm fine,' I said.

'Nonsense. Nonsense. Bring five glasses,' he told the footman. 'Make it ten glasses of sherry! It is Christmas after all. Just don't–'

'Tell the wife,' I finished.

'Exactly, Mr James, exactly!' He slapped me on the back again. 'Now you're in the spirit of things.'

I sighed but didn't protest. I had more important matters to contend with. Emma let me think, but the crazies tried to talk to me once or twice. It looked likely that Mr Eastwell had killed his wife and had, somehow, escaped from a locked room. But things still didn't fully add up. For a start, why would he go to the trouble of hiding the weapon but do nothing about the blood on his hands?

The sherry arrived and I drank without really thinking, even though sherry was not a tipple of choice. It was something to occupy my hands at least.

'Go on, get that sherry down you! The wife is in the other room, hee, hee,' the earl encouraged.

'She thinks we are looking for a murderer as well! Such fun.'

I sipped on the sickly sweetness, my eyes lost in the smoking fire. I had felt there was evil in the air and the distinct possibility of murder, but I wouldn't have guessed Mrs Eastwell as the victim. Perhaps Mrs Eastwell had confronted her husband when she'd discovered the affair? Or, maybe she'd confronted Mrs Parsons and Mrs Parsons had killed her?

'Drinking sherry, I see.'

I turned around. Malcom bloody Wegwipe. 'What do you want?'

'Oh, I thought I'd help.' He took up his pen once again.

'Go away.'

'No need to be like that, Mr...Lavender.'

'Mr Wegwipe, come and join us. We're just having a little sherry.' The earl pulled a chair back.

'Yes, I can see.'

'Go on dear,' he said to Emma. 'Drink up.'

Emma did so reluctantly, though she seemed to enjoy it greatly, her cheeks flushing.

'So, Mr Lavender, given up searching for Mr Eastwell, have you?' Wegwipe sat down and took up the offered glass of sherry which was teeming to the brim as per the earl's instructions. Sydney would approve at least.

'Another bottle! Another bottle,' the earl said. 'Go on, it's Christmas.'

'George,' I said. 'There's a murderer on the loose, trapped within these very walls.'

'Oh, I like that,' Malcolm Wegwipe said, licking his finger. 'You should be a writer. If your, ahem, detective thing fails, there's a place for you at the *Herald*. Just seek me out.'

'I'd rather starve.'

'Hee, hee, isn't Mr James such a humourist?' The earl was having his third glass re-filled. 'Merry Christmas, everyone!'

'Merry Christmas!' Mr Landley said, knocking glasses with the earl. 'To the Castle Howard estate and future farming prospects!'

Mr Parsons raised his sherry, then took a little sip. Mr Landley picked at his ear and some of the contents fell on my trousers. I frantically swept them away.

I'm sure there was a time when I thought my intellectual pursuits would get me somewhere in life. I have never been one for ambition, for that is the pursuit of the unwise, or one for making lots of money, for that is worse; but somewhere, something that fits a happy medium in some existence must be possible. Avoiding Mr Landley's ear dirt, while fending off the earl's sherry was not part of that ideal. Neither was running around a house, however beautiful, in search of a deranged lunatic at Christmas. Yet, this was the sort of thing I'd come to expect from my time as a so-called detective.

'Enough of the nonsense. I've thought of a…'

But I had to drop my words as another scream echoed through the room. A woman's.

'Who was that?' Emma said.

'I don't know. Come on.' I jumped up, nearly knocking over the bottle of sherry in the process.

The earl followed me, running towards the direction of the scream, sherry glass in hand, his other hand covering the top. 'Run, Mr James! I'm behind you.'

Emma was fast and I struggled to keep up, but I wasn't far behind. We made our way to the bottom of the staircase. A body of a woman. Mrs Parsons, if I wasn't mistaken.

Mr Parsons threw his hands up to his face. 'Oh, Jane, dead!'

We ran to the body at the bottom of the staircase. It was Mrs Parsons, face down on the marble floor, blood running around in little streams at the side of her head.

Suddenly, she arched herself upwards. 'I've been pushed!' she screamed. 'I felt the devil's hand upon my back.' She crashed back down again as if from exhaustion.

Her cries alerted the arrival of some others, Anthony Landley, the Talbots, and some staff amongst them. Mrs Parsons screamed again. 'I felt him on my back. Mr Eastwell, he…tried to kill me.' Then she collapsed into unconsciousness, her cries cut off in the empty hall.

It was true then. We had a deranged murderer on the loose and his name was Mr Eastwell.

CHAPTER NINETEEN

I cupped my chin in my hand, my elbow propped up on the table in the room the earl had provided, and closed one eye for a short moment of repose. I'm not sure what the space was used for in normal circumstances, but it was a much-needed breakaway to think and digest the recent unsavoury events that had taken place at Castle Howard.

Behind me, the one arched window, like a solitary eye peering out at the dying snowstorm, cast fading moonlight onto the table (and the large plate of tarts and biscuits in front of me). I reached for the mug of hot chocolate beside them. The flickers of gas lights around the wall panels reflected on Sydney's greedy face, with his little sticking-out tongue, as well as Rose's magnificent eyes which were currently studying the notepaper on her lap. Her tongue licked out at her lips. A habit she has when thinking –

unless it was a throwback to the jam tart she'd taken from me earlier.

Sydney and Rose had found nothing in their quick search through the rooms upstairs; no obvious signs of Mr Eastwell at least. Simon had the same ill luck in his search for new footprints. We had learnt from Stella that people hadn't obeyed my instructions to keep together in the breakfast room either. She said they had sat occupied for a while, but when boredom struck, several people wandered. Under strict instructions to inform me immediately should anything arise, the earl had sent search parties of reliable staff in groups of twos and threes. But as of yet, there were absolutely no signs of Mr Eastwell. This provided us with the space to take stock of events and to partake of the excellent tarts and biscuits.

'Hands off.' I slapped Sydney's greedy paw as he reached over, his great bulk all but tipping over the little wooden table.

'I haven't eaten since the potatoes at breakfast. It's nearly four!' His big brown eyes were sullenly pleading.

'Don't get aggressive. One, you can have one.' I held up a finger to emphasise that one meant one, not three.

He snatched at the largest jam tart on the plate and whipped it back into his great cavern of a mouth. I don't think it touched the sides.

'Unbelievable. Anybody would think you'd

never eaten.' I picked up a choice biscuit and dipped it into the steaming hot chocolate, then let it melt away in my mouth.

Rose was still fiddling with the paper in front of her. 'Are we ready to interview yet?'

I'd told her that she could take the notes as she was a faster writer than myself, and Sydney's big childish scribble was too much for anybody to contend with.

'Shortly. I want to toss a few more theories around first. Where's Emma?'

'Still being told off by her mother, I expect.'

'Why?'

Rose tutted. 'You know, the whole coming back half-drunk thing after tracking down a crazed murderer with you?'

'Oh, that?'

'Yes, *that*.'

'Is that all?'

Rose shook her head. 'Is that all?'

'That's what I just said. I don't understand why people repeat questions. It's just so tiresome.' I noticed Sydney eyeing the plate in front of me. 'No.'

'One more, please. I'm starving.'

'Let him have one,' Rose said. 'Stop being cruel.'

Cruel? Helping a friend achieve a diet goal was not cruel. Even in times of crisis, but I didn't bite. Instead, I held a biscuit out before him. 'Tell us your theory and then you can have one. If it's a good one, that is.'

'Eh?'

'Do I have to repeat myself constantly? Tell me your theory of what is happening in the house. You know, this big place we're in, and if it's half... no, a *quarter* intelligent, you can have one. Deal?'

He opened his mouth and closed it again.

'No disappearing into thin air theories, mind,' I said, wagging the biscuit before him.

'Well, Mrs Eastwell is dead–'

'Well done. Pray continue.'

He nodded. 'She's been stabbed by her husband, maybe because she was...No, *he* was having an affair with Mrs Parsons.'

'That's just what I told you Wegwipe said, but...' I broke the biscuit in half, and then one of the halves into a half and gave him the quarter, which he gobbled up. 'Go on, tell me more.' I waved the remaining half and a quarter at him.

He licked his lips at the vanished quarter portion, then began again. 'This is why Mr Eastwell pushed her down the stairs just now.'

I threw him the other quarter. 'That fits, but what about yesterday?'

'Yesterday?' A completely blank expression stared back at me as if yesterday hadn't existed at all.

'You're referring to the attempt on Mr Eastwell's life?' Rose said.

'Oh, I'd forgotten about that,' Sydney said, eyes fixed on the remaining biscuit half, which was fast melting in my hand.

'Give him the biscuit and stop being cruel.'

'I'm not being cruel; it's excellent training.'

The door in front of me opened and we turned. Emma, her face downcast.

'Where's your mother?' I asked her.

'Don't worry. She's still in the breakfast room.'

'Good. I could do without another earache.'

Emma pulled up a chair beside Rose.

'We're just discussing what we think happened,' Rose told her.

'Maybe Mrs Eastwell tried to kill her husband, but her husband got there first,' Emma said, more cheerful now, discussing matters of murder.

'Sounds like a typical marriage,' I said.

Rose gave me that tiger look.

'Sydney?' I waved the remaining biscuit half his way.

Rose snatched it from me and gave it to him. 'Stop teasing.'

'What have you done that for?' I said.

'It's cruel. I told you.'

'It's not cruel. Go on then, Sydney. Earn the biscuit half.'

He chewed on it contentedly, savouring it in front of me. 'I think Mrs Eastwell tried to kill her husband-like, but her husband got there first.'

'Absolutely bloody genius.'

'What about Mrs Parsons?' Rose asked me. 'Surely, she has a motive?'

I took a long drag on the hot chocolate that Simon had provided, which was cooling down. I'd need to drink it before it got much cooler. Hot drinks should be taken hot; cold drinks taken cold. No in-between. 'Naturally, gets the wife out of the way nicely, doesn't it? Obviously, she's a main suspect in the crime, but anybody could have done it with the hunt for the girl going on and all the chaos that involved.'

'Well, go on then, Mr Brilliant,' Rose said. 'What's your theory?'

'Apt name, but no. I'm not theorising just yet, but there's something else.' Sydney nodded along as if he shared my thoughts. 'The button,' I offered him.

'What button?'

'The little button under the table. My button.'

'What? You tried to kill him?'

'No, of course not!'

Sydney grinned.

I shook my head at his childish attempt at humour. 'Something very odd is going on. Something very odd indeed.'

Rose agreed. 'The murder weapon missing. Mr Eastwell with blood on his hands...'

'Yes, there's something else as well,' I said, observing their faces closely.

'What's that?' Emma asked, in a faint whisper.

'Evil. I can feel it. Through all the nonsense – all the chatter, the ear dirt, games of little balls; we're in the presence of evil. Has anybody else felt it?'

The room went silent and it seemed to get darker, and colder, as if a shadow or a presence had invaded our little space.

Bang!

The four of us jumped up from out of our seats.

'Jesus Christ!' I exclaimed.

Rose inhaled sharply, hands over her heart.

Another fist banged on the door. 'Mr Eastwell?' I said to the group. 'Has Mr Eastwell been found?'

The door creaked inwards.

Stella.

'Emma, what are you doing in here? I told you, you're not to get involved.'

'All's well,' I said. 'There's no sherry knocking around.' I grinned, but then I quickly dropped it, in response to Stella's flash of unreasonable annoyance. No sense of humour that one. I tried to reassure her. 'We're just discussing the murder.'

Stella didn't appear to be very reassured. 'This is not a game. There's a madman running around. I won't have my daughter caught up in this. She's *fifteen*.'

'But Mum, please.'

'No.'

I felt sorry for her. She was clearly just as much a fan of theoretical puzzles as I was. 'We weren't discussing the brutal stabbing or the hunt for the lunatic, just–'

'No.'

Stella had such a poetic way with words. She could be a student of Mrs McCarthy's (my previous temporary housekeeper of few words and Rose's stepmother).

Emma stood up reluctantly and walked over to her mother.

'Emma.' I pointed to the relevant areas of my face. 'Eyes and ears still, yes?' I told her. 'It's very important to keep them on the crazies.'

She nodded, a slight tremble on her lip but reassured by my genuine request.

'Send in Mrs Parsons, will you?' I told them both. 'It's time we asked some questions.'

CHAPTER TWENTY

Miss Parsons helped her visibly-shaken mother to the chair before her. 'She shouldn't have to answer your questions. She's had a terrible shock. Mr Eastwell just tried to kill her or have you forgotten that?'

It had been a little over an hour since her fall so I don't know what she was talking about. I told her she could leave, yet she still stood there, tall and defiant.

'I think I'll stay if it's all the same to you?'

'It isn't. You need to leave,' I said.

After a dramatic little protest, chin at all angles and with Rose repeating the instruction icily, she parted our company.

'Now, Mrs Parsons,' I said. 'Tell us again what just happened on the stairs.'

'I was pushed. I felt the flat of a hand against my back.'

'Are you sure?'

'I think so.'

'You *think* so? What were you doing there in the first place?'

'I...er, I can't remember.'

'You're going to have to do better than that. Were you looking for Mr Eastwell?'

'Mr Eastwell? Why would I be looking for Mr Eastwell?' She looked at each of us.

'I don't know. You tell me,' I said.

There was a jutting of her chin, an expression Miss Parsons had just recently shown.

'Were you having an affair?' I asked.

Not a question that seemed to go down very well.

She stood up sharply. 'What sort of question is *that*?'

'Is that a yes?'

'Mr Lavender, I've just been attacked and you're asking me improper questions. I don't know who you think you are.'

She made as if to walk away, but she froze when I raised my voice: 'Mrs Parsons, this is a murder investigation.'

'Well, stop asking stupid questions then.'

Rose took up the questioning. 'Tell us about the room? What did you see in the room, just before Mrs Eastwell was killed?' she asked softly.

'Murdered,' I corrected.

Mrs Parsons mellowed very slightly, sitting back down after a brief glance in my direction. 'What do you want to know?'

Rose continued. 'Well, were they arguing when you left them? What were they doing?'

'No, they weren't arguing. Mr Eastwell had just received a bad blow to the head. He was dazed. Confused. His wife came in and took over.'

'Took over, how?' Sydney said.

'She was looking after him, *obviously*. She fussed around him on the bed and she told me to leave.'

I bet she did.

'You weren't particularly keen on Mrs Eastwell, were you?' I asked.

She gave me that look again. 'I didn't kill her if that's what you're suggesting.'

'What about the murder weapon? Did you see any weapon?' Sydney asked.

'There were no knives in the room that I could see.'

'How do you know the murder weapon was a knife?' I said, with a friendly smile.

'I've just been attacked! Why are you treating me like a criminal?'

I picked up my hot chocolate and put it back down again after a sip, as it had gone too cold. 'A bit of a temper there. Did Mrs Eastwell really annoy you?'

'*You're* really annoying me.'

'He tends to have that effect on people,' Sydney muttered.

'Do you actually have any sensible questions to ask me? Or, as a woman who's just been attacked, can I go and recover?'

'Do you know where Mr Eastwell is?' I asked.

'No, no I don't. Can I go now?'

I held my palm towards the door. 'Feel free.'

'Merry Christmas!' Sydney added, cheerily.

She shot him a look of utter contempt and left.

'Was she telling the truth?' Rose asked.

'Yes, for the most part, about not killing her at least, and the whereabouts of Mr Eastwell.'

I sent Sydney off to find David Eastwell. He brought him back, hand over his shoulder, and guided him to the chair that Mrs Parsons had just left.

'This won't take long,' I said.

Sydney strolled around back to his chair. 'That Miss Parsons, well…she's a one alright.'

'How do you mean?' Rose asked.

'She didn't want the young lad here to go anywhere.'

'Oh, really?' I turned towards young Eastwell. 'Now, when you saw your mother brutally stabbed, did you–'

Rose jumped in. 'What Mr Lavender here means is that we need to ask you some difficult questions. Is that going to be alright with you?'

David Eastwell nodded once.

Rose continued. 'Now, can you tell us your movements around the time the little girl went missing?'

I was about to repeat the question as he seemed like he hadn't heard it, staring off into space over Sydney's shoulder, but then he spoke slowly. How he had changed from the spoilt little Lord we'd seen upon arrival. 'I heard the shouts.'

'What shouts?' I asked.

'Of the footmen and people – everyone.'

'Where were you?'

'In Father's room.'

'All of you?'

'Yes, no. Father had just left. It was just Mother and me when we heard the shouting in the morning.'

'Little balls,' Sydney said.

'What?' David said.

Sydney quickly clarified. 'Mr Eastwell stepped on someone's marble, during our game of little balls. It…it could have belonged to anyone.'

David looked at him, still puzzled. I encouraged the young man to continue his narrative.

'I left the room to see what all the shouting was about and then I joined in the search for the girl.'

'I see. Then what happened?' I picked up my hot chocolate and then remembered it was cold so I put it back down again. Besides, I felt slightly sick with it. Maybe I'd overdone it. You can have too much of a good thing.

'I was outside and someone mentioned that my father had been hurt, that he'd cut his head badly. I came back to check on him and that's when…I saw her.'

Rose leaned towards him instinctively, motherly almost. 'Go on.'

'She was dead…It was horrible.' He crouched over as he'd been suddenly afflicted by terrible stomach pains. He was rocking slightly.

'Was she on the floor or on the bed?' I asked him.

He glanced at me from his crouched position. 'What?'

I repeated the question.

'On the floor.'

'And your father?'

'He wasn't there. He wasn't there at all.' He shifted away from us, crouching over once again.

'Then what?' Sydney asked.

'I came running for help.'

'Was there a knife?' I asked.

He looked puzzled. 'A knife?'

'You know…' I tried to think of a polite way of saying it. I turned to Sydney for help.

'Sticking out of your mother-like,' he said.

Rose sighed. Sydney has a terrible way with words.

'No. Oh, my God.' He covered his face and began crying.

'Well done, Sydney,' I said. 'You've done it again, bloody useless.'

'Sorry, I…'

Rose offered the young man some reassuring words, while I played with the cup in front of me, trying to claw some warmth out of it, as it was cold in the room. I couldn't wait to get out of it and get back in front of the fire.

I caught David's attention when he finally seemed to have recovered a little from his bout of depression. 'You didn't see your father at all? Not in the corridor or on the stairs?'

'No. I just ran downstairs for help. That's when I saw all of you.'

'You say that someone told you about your father, who was that?'

'I don't remember. Anthony, I think.'

'Do you know where your father is now?' Rose asked.

'No. No, I don't.'

Another blank. Rose again asked me if he was telling the truth when he departed, and indeed he was. We brought in Wegwipe. I wanted to know everything that he knew, but he was keeping his cards close to his chest.

'Naturally, I would be more than happy to tell you everything I know as a public servant. But, there exists such a thing as client confidentiality, you know?'

'This is a murder investigation,' I said.

'I know, but...all the same...are you feeling quite well, Mr *Lavender*? You look awfully pale.'

I had suddenly felt a rising wave of nausea. 'I'm...fine.'

'You don't look it.'

I stood up and turned my back on him, looking out of the window. It was completely dark now, yet I could just make out the thick snowflakes that were falling softly in the moonlight. I felt another wave of nausea. 'Can you two continue?'

'What's wrong?' Rose asked.

I ran past her, through the door and down to the long corridor towards the Great Hall. I tried to make it outside, but I managed only just as far as the huge Christmas tree. I bent over and retched, spraying the contents of my stomach all over it. I retched and retched, all over the tree again, until I had nothing more to give. Merry Christmas indeed.

CHAPTER TWENTY-ONE

'Wanton vandalism, that is,' Wegwipe said, behind me, as I was trying to get some fresh air on the steps outside. 'Being sick all over the Christmas tree. Spoiling the joy for the kids.'

'Oh, do be quiet.'

'Too much hot chocolate and not enough sharing biscuits,' Sydney added, at my side.

'You can be quiet as well. Where's Rose?'

'Questioning people. Anthony Landley, I think.'

I took another deep breath and rubbed my shoulders against the cold, my eyes automatically scanning the ground for invisible footprints. The drifting snow was dying in the air now, falling very slowly in the moon's glow. There would be no going home tomorrow. We were now trapped by the conditions and the investigation.

'Anthony,' piped up Wegwipe. 'What's she speaking to Anthony for?'

'Do me a favour,' I said.

'What's that?'

'Mind your own business and go away.'

'Not very polite, Mr Lavender Brown, I must say. Your attitude strikes me as...a little off.'

'A little off?' I turned and glared at the toad, and he eventually slinked away under a rock somewhere.

I took another icy lungful of fresh air. 'Come on, Sydney, let's get back inside. I think I'll be well enough now.'

We stepped around the maids who were trying their best to clean up the Christmas tree. I offered them a brief, shy apology before making my way towards the drawing room with Sydney lumbering on behind.

The immediate hot glow of the fire was a welcome one, and I walked gratefully over to it. Conversations between Miss Parsons and David Eastwell ceased as we strolled by them.

I gave Emma and Stella, who were seated in a far corner, a quick nod as I warmed my hands. Lord Talbot, seated in the other corner, gave me a distasteful glance.

I still felt a little queasy and I was now firmly put off hot chocolate. I'd not been sick like that since enduring so many lies at the Dalton household.

The ever-grinning earl came towards me with

Mr and Mrs Landley and their younger annoying little offspring, Frederick. The little imp threw something at his brother which missed, hitting Sydney on the back of the head. Whatever it was plopped to the floor. A wet piece of paper by the looks of it.

'Ho, ho, great fun!' the earl said, by my side. 'Mr James. I heard about your little accident. Brandy, you must have brandy!' He clapped his hands and a footman sprang into action as they usually do.

'Accident?' Mr Landley said, a wide smile parting his thick sideburns. 'Have you had an accident, Mr Lavender? There's nothing shameful in that. I often have little accidents, don't I, Margaret? Margaret, don't I often have little accidents? It's because of the ointment. But a quick change of underclothing is all it takes to make matters right again. Margaret, don't I...'

'I haven't had *that sort* of accident, Mr Landley, thank you very much. I was sick.'

'Nothing shameful about it, Mr Lavender. Nothing shameful at all. Remember, Margaret, just last week I had a little accident on the stairs at your mother's? Remember, Margaret? On the stairs. I had to borrow some of her underclothing, remember? It was all good fun in the end. It's the cream, Mr Lavender. It has that sort of effect. There's nothing wrong...'

'Mr Landley! I don't have a problem.'

'No, no. I can lend you some cream. When you shove it right up, the cream helps the spot, but it can cause little squirts.'

'Mr Landley.' I threw up my arms. 'I don't want the bloody cream.'

He bowed before me, a little wink in his eye. 'Of course, Mr Lavender. You don't want to tell the ladies about your little bum problem. I perfectly understand – they won't hear it from ME!' he shouted.

'I don't have a...' But I stopped at the sight of Mr Parsons' cheery face. 'Who's got a bum problem?'

'Mr Lavender here, but it's fine. I'm going to lend him my cream.'

'The one from the doctors or the vets?'

I rubbed at the bridge of my nose again and turned around to face the fire, wondering if I should jump into it and burn myself alive to end the suffering.

❖ ❖ ❖

I was seated next to Rose and Stella, sipping on the brandy the earl had provided, with him seated next to me trying to encourage me to drink more than I wanted. Rose had conducted further questioning and had given me her notes. I would look over them later when I was feeling better. She said that nothing struck her as immediately telling.

'Come on, Mr James! The wife is just upstairs. Let's have another one. It will help with your nerves.'

'I don't have any nerv–'

'I will,' Sydney said, taking three more from the tray and turning to his lovely wife. 'Just as long as there's no special milk.'

The earl nodded happily though, taking another brandy himself. 'You know, Mr James, this has been one of the best recent Christmases ever. All of us together in this amazing building, trying to–'

'One of the best Christmases ever?' I nearly spat out the brandy I'd decided to sip.

He looked affronted. 'Why yes, of course. Good company, some good games like the treasure hunt and little balls, a little–'

'You do know there's a murderer on the loose?' I said.

'Why, yes, but…'

'But what?'

'Weellll. You can't have everything, can you? We all have to be grateful for what we've got. For what God has given us.'

'Aye,' Mr Landley said, his hand around his own glass of brandy. 'We do that.'

'Yes, but…the stabbing,' I said. 'What's that got to do with God?'

'Ho, ho, Mr James. The Lord works in mysterious ways, does he not?' The earl took another sip of the brandy, his eyes darting towards the door every time he did so.

'Well, it could be argued that the Lord does

indeed work in mysterious ways,' Mr Parsons said.

Mr Landley concurred. 'Think of all the little children, Mr Lavender, eh?'

'What little children?'

Mr Landley continued. 'Why, all the little children who struggle at Christmas-time. Wouldn't they like the opportunity to be in this wonderful house, drinking this fine brandy and about to eat a huge feast? I'm sure they would.'

'Mr Landley,' I said, trying to remain composed. 'I am not disputing the suffering of the poor. I'm quite aware of that, and I'm quite affronted by their suffering myself, but it's hardly an apt comparison. It's a bit of a dead argument, and it doesn't change the fact that somewhere in this house a murderer lurks.'

There was a brief pause, then Miss Parsons said:

'There's just no pleasing some people.'

'What are you talking about?' I snapped.

'James. Why don't we all go upstairs to dress for dinner?' Rose said, getting out of her chair and placing a warm hand on my shoulder.

'That's just a ridiculous thing to say. Am I supposed to be happy that a woman has been murdered, and that I'm stuck here for longer than expected?'

Miss Parsons shrugged. 'You always seem to be complaining about something.'

'Yes, well, when there's a murderer in our

midst, then yes, I have a notion that our situation is not all good and jolly.'

Wegwipe sniffed. 'What's that, Mr *Lavender*, you said before? I didn't quite catch it. Something about the poor children? Something about not caring about their suffering.'

'I never said anything like that!'

'A quote then?'

'Go away.'

Rose grabbed at my arm. 'Come on, let's go up and change.'

I scratched the top of my head. 'I don't need to change.'

'You've got something on your trouser leg.'

I looked down. A little stain from the Christmas tree incident. 'Right, let's go up.'

'That's an early night,' Lady Talbot said to Rose as we neared the far end of the room. 'But I suppose servants do as they are told, do they not, Miss McCarthy?'

Rose spun around, her eyes ablaze. 'Do you have something to say, Lady Talbot?'

The whole room went silent.

Lady Talbot smiled. 'Ah, *Miss* McCarthy, I'm sure you'll be married one day, but until then…' She shrugged.

'Lady Talbot,' Rose said, calmly. 'I'm sure that one day you'll also get what you deserve.'

We left the room with Sydney, Stella and Emma.

'Why are we they still putting on a full

Christmas feast, anyway?' I said as I made my way up the staircase. 'I would have thought they'd have cancelled it.'

Sydney inhaled sharply. 'Cancel the food? We've still got to eat, haven't we?' he said. 'We're still having turkey, aren't we?'

'Don't worry, Sydney,' Rose said, 'I'm sure there's still turkey.'

'And wine?'

Rose pulled a face. 'I'm not sure about the wine.'

'What?'

'Can you two stop nattering? I'm trying to think.' We'd finally reached the top of the staircase, but something didn't feel quite right.

'What's wrong?' Rose asked.

I shook my head. 'Listen.'

I could hear a strange noise. A whistling. Like a calling, and it was cold, terribly cold. Even the flickering of candles felt different somehow.

'I can't hear anything,' Sydney said, shaking his head.

'Me neither,' Rose added.

'It sounded like a fox,' Emma said.

'Shhh. There. Did you hear it?' I asked. But the sound had gone.

'Well, very enlightening, Mr Lavendah,' Sydney said, in his ridiculous voice. 'Now can we get something to eat?'

'I think it was a fox,' Emma repeated.

'Don't be silly, dear,' Stella said. 'What would a

fox be doing in the house?'

I started on towards our rooms. 'Don't take forever getting changed again, Rose. I want to be downstairs.'

'I don't take forever getting changed!'

I had to laugh at that. 'I could grow a beard in the time it takes you to get ready.'

'Like a married couple,' Emma added, with a devilish little smile.

I shot her my coldest glare, to which she merely smirked.

I pondered if I should get changed, then lie on the bed for a while. Or, lie on the bed for a while then get changed. The latter option won me over. Just ten minutes repose, I decided, would be pleasant. But, a light would be a good precaution. I struck a match with a rasp, and lit the lamp, holding it close so that I could see what I was doing. I flicked my wrist to extinguish the flame as soon as the lamp fired to life. Immediately, I felt that something was not right. A sense. A feeling. Something not in place.

I stood unmoving as the lamp flickered and my eyes adjusted to the new light, the Greek and Roman figures toiling once again.

It was the chair! It wasn't straight against the dressing table. I would never leave a chair like that. Even in a hurry. Someone had been in my room. Surely, neither Sydney nor Rose, in their quick search for Mr Eastwell, would have had to come all the way inside, and the maids had been too preoccupied to clean. No, someone else had been in my room.

I broke from my standing repose and examined the flat of the chair, peering at the top of the backrest with the help of the lamp. I crouched down, my eye scanning the surface, but I didn't touch anything. I closely examined every inch of the backrest, until I spotted exactly what I was looking for, right on the corner of the chair on the wooden slat. A single, unbroken fingerprint.

I fished out a handkerchief from the drawers beside the bed and turned my attention to the dressing table, taking care not to disturb the chair. It was too late now, but first thing tomorrow morning I would lift the print. I put the lamp back down. I started to rub my eyes, but I hastily drew my hands back at the stickiness I'd pressed to my eyelids. My heart beat loudly as I flung open the drawer again, and there, glinting from the light of the lamp, was a knife covered in blood.

CHAPTER TWENTY-TWO

'Do you think it's the murder weapon?' Sydney asked.

I afforded him a brief glance. 'Yes, I think so. Seeing as it's a knife covered in blood.'

'But what's it doing in your room?'

I asked Emma to fetch the fingerprint materials and she responded swiftly, leaving myself, Rose and Sydney puzzling over the weapon.

Rose turned to me. 'It doesn't seem to add up. If it's Mr Eastwell why go to the trouble of planting the kitchen knife, but then not bother to wash his hands? And if it wasn't Mr Eastwell who planted the knife in your room, then who was it? And for what reason? Who would have it in for you like that?'

'Shouldn't they form a queue?' Sydney said.

'I don't know,' I admitted. 'First, the button,

and now, the knife. Who searched the room earlier?'

'I did,' Sydney said, proudly.

'Was the chair like this?'

He thought for a moment. 'The chair was definitely in the room.'

'I know that! Was it twisted like this?' I gestured towards the chair. 'I wouldn't normally leave a chair twisted like this.'

He shook his head. 'I don't know.'

'Useless.'

'We were dashing from room to room looking for Mr Eastwell. Why? What were you doing? Drinking hot chocolate?'

'Sherry,' Rose said, under her breath.

I wagged my finger at Sydney. 'Don't get aggressive.'

'I'm not being aggressive. I'm just saying.'

'Apology accepted.'

'I wasn't ap–'

'So, whoever planted the kn–'

'*Whomever.*'

'What?' I said.

'*Whomever* planted the knife, you mean?' Sydney folded his arms.

I gritted my teeth. 'It's is *whoever*, but stop getting aggressive and petulant! You always get like this before a face-stuffing.'

'I'm not being petulant and aggressive. I'm just saying.'

'Don't.'

'Shouldn't we keep on track?' Rose said as Emma arrived with the fingerprint materials heaped up in her hands.

'Right.' I took the kit from her. 'So, if we don't know whether the chair was moved then this could have been planted at any point after the murder. Was the door locked or unlocked, Sydney?'

'It was locked.'

'Are you sure?'

'Yes, no. I mean, it was unlocked.'

'Christ in a barrel. Was it locked or unlocked? Not that it seems to make much difference these days...'

'It was definitely unlocked. I remember because I got the key Simon had given me. I took it out of my pocket to unlock the door, but it was already locked.'

I looked up at him sharply.

'Unlocked, I mean,' he added hastily. 'The door was unlocked.'

'Right, finally. Well, I definitely locked it before coming down.'

'Are you sure?' Emma asked.

'I think so, yes.'

'Perfectly clear then, I must say.' Rose sat down on the edge of my bed. 'What are you going to do about the kitchen knife?'

'Nothing. I think it would be best to keep it to ourselves, for now at least. It might be easier to work out who is trying to set me up that way.'

Rose agreed.

'Right, Emma and Rose, come over here. I've got a little mission for the both of you that's right up your street. It involves being pretty sneaky and devious. I'm sure you'll manage it perfectly.

◆ ◆ ◆

The Christmas table had naturally lost its sparkle. Whereas yesterday there were little gasps of delight, today the orate decorations appeared out of place in light of recent events. The countess did her best to appear as inviting as possible, under the circumstances, but her words of welcome were uttered in a perfunctory manner. The seating arrangements were as before except the absence of Mrs Parsons, her daughter and David Eastwell (and naturally Mr and Mrs Eastwell...) Miss Parsons had volunteered to support David Eastwell in the drawing room. Fate decreed my eternal damnation next to Mr Landley, and he squeezed my hand as we sat down.

Lady Talbot had been grinning and staring in our direction for the last few minutes and I thought it was only going to be a matter of time before she said something. I was not wrong.

'Funny, isn't it?'

'What is, dear?' the earl asked her.

She smiled. 'All of us just sitting here waiting for soup when there's a crazed killer on the loose.'

She hunched her shoulders and smiled further.

Lord Talbot took up the reins. 'Yes, well these so-called investigators must not forgo their soup. Heaven forbid.'

Lady Talbot laughed, hand over her mouth.

There were still absolutely no signs of Mr Eastwell.

'It's like those missing animals, isn't it, Mr Lavender?' Mr Landley said, picking up on the Talbot conversation.

'Well, I...' I broke off as our soup arrived.

'What soup is it?' Sydney asked, craning his head forward.

'Ah, oyster soup. Marvellous!' the earl boomed. 'Guests, enjoy!' He raised his wine glass and looked over at his wife at the far side of the long table, who on this occasion had allowed us one glass each. An extremely rare event indeed.

The countess half-raised her glass of water, her daughter neatly dressed in black seated next to her, waiting patiently for the soup.

'I love oyster soup,' Sydney said.

'You love every soup. Anyway, you can have mine. I don't care for it.' I took a light sip at my white wine, which was fragrant and perfectly cold to the touch.

'Oh, grand.'

As soon as it landed in front of him, Sydney began slurping it. Emma told him to hush. I thanked the maid who gave me my soip but pushed it in Sydney's direction.

'Lovely. Do you want your bread?'

'What?'

'Your bread roll?' Sydney reached across my person but I slapped his hands away.

'Yes, I do.' I began tearing small chunks off it, letting it melt in my mouth. It was fresh and quite delicious.

'Are you just going to eat bread like that?' Rose asked.

'Yes, how else am I supposed to eat it? By sticking it up my nose?'

'No, I mean...why don't you dip it in your soup?'

'I don't like fish soup.'

'It's *oyster* soup.'

'I know; I don't want it. ydney's having it.'

Sydney put one hand around the dish, fearful I would take it back.

'It won't taste too fishy if you dip it in around the edges,' Rose said.

'Why are you still going on about the damn soup?'

She picked up a silver butter dish and tried to pass it over. 'Do you want the butter, then?'

'No, absolutely not. I rarely have butter on my bread unless the bread's hot out of the oven.'

She rubbed at her chin. 'Are you just going to eat it plain like that?'

'Yes, it's perfectly delicious.'

Emma whispered something to her mother and they both laughed.

I held the bread defiantly in my hand. 'I like plain bread. There's nothing wrong with that. What's wrong with that?'

Rose shook her head. 'No, no. It just looks a bit odd, that's all. Just plain bread?'

Sydney tutted, shaking his head dramatically. 'There's just no civilising him, is there? Can't take him anywhere.'

I ripped off a large piece of bread and glanced further up the table. Lady Talbot immediately caught my eye:

'James, have you got any idea where Mr Eastwell is? Do tell. It's terribly exciting, is it not?'

'That's not quite how I would phrase it, Lady Talbot.'

'Yes, but you're such a skilled detective. Surely you must know something?'

'That's true, of course, but...'

I paused as Mr Landley hooked a hairy hand over my left arm, squeezing it heavily. 'You know, Mr Lavender, there's a wise old saying we use in the farming world that I think would help here. Do you want me to tell it to you?'

'No.'

'It goes like this: don't start the harvest 'til Barnet Day is due. Wait 'til the morning until you have a few. If you take up the corn on Lamblet's Eve. Don't hold back water unless you want to grieve. Wise words, eh?'

He continued to usher forth his usual barrage of 'Margarets', to which she half-nodded wearily, sucking in her soup through her twisted lips.

Mr Parsons enthused. 'Oh, Barnet Day. What a fantastic rule! Do you have any Barnet Day memories you want to share, Mr Lavender?'

'I have absolutely no idea what you are talking about. What the hell is Barnet Day?'

Mr Parsons grabbed his ears. 'Aaarrrgghhhh!'

Mr Landley shook his head with a large grin. 'Ah, Mr Lavender, come, come. It's a very common saying. Very common one indeed and very wise. Very, very wise.'

I looked up at Rose, who bit her lip.

Mr Landley continued. 'Very wise saying indeed. Barnet Day, eh?'

'Well, thank you for that, Mr Landley. That was…very helpful. I'm sure,' I said.

Mr Parsons stuck his head in the soup, shouting into it, burning his face in the process. Everyone else just ignored him.

Mr Landley slapped me on the back with so great a force that I spat out a small chunk of undigested bread, which landed in the middle of the table, next to a salt and pepper pot. 'Barnet's Day rule, ha, ha. Wonderful! Glad to help, Mr Lavender. Glad to help. You can always count on me.'

The soup was taken away and a course of pheasant was in the process of being brought in. In the changeover, Emma slipped Lady Talbot's soup spoon under the table, giving me a small wink.

The small pheasant was delicious so there was no providing Sydney with an extra portion this time, much to his disappointment. The dish passed by without too much pain and I'd fallen into my usual rhythm of providing Mr Landley with a few mumbles now and then and the occasional 'indeed' which always pleased him. The maids quickly cleared away the small empty plates, minus Mr Parsons' fork, which found its way under the table, safely tucked away into Rose's bag.

'Any more wine?' Sydney asked the earl, tilting his long-since empty glass.

The earl's lips trembled as he shot his wife a brief look. 'Ah, er, Mr Brown–'

'One devil brew I allowed,' the countess said. 'No more.'

Sydney looked back at the earl, whose lips continued to tremble. 'Er, we have apple juice. Would you like *apple juice*, Mr Brown?' The earl winked.

'No, thank you very much.'

'Are you sure? It's *special* apple juice.' The earl smiled briefly, extinguished by the flicker of the countess' quick glance.

Sydney turned to me, his voice low. 'What is it with all these posh drinks? Why can't I just have a beer?'

I sniffed. 'I think you should try the special apple juice.'

'But I don't like apple juice.'

'You'll probably like this one.'

It wasn't long before a sea of maids and footmen brought in the main Christmas meal. Piles of vegetables, potatoes, stuffing, and several carved turkeys soon covered the table, leaving Sydney gasping mid-special apple juice. 'Look at all this lot.'

The earl stood up at the head of the table, his glass of special apple juice raised above his head. 'Guests, it's been a wonderful time!' He coughed. 'Give or take a few minor issues, but nevertheless, I wouldn't change it for the world.'

Minor issues? I looked towards Rose but she wasn't looking my way.

The earl continued:

'Most of the family couldn't make it this year due to...particular circumstances. But to have you lot here is wonderful! Absolutely wonderful. I'm sure Mr James and his team will solve the little hiccups we've had. So, I want you all to raise your glass in memory of Mrs Eastwell, and to wish you all a very merry, well...' He looked over at his wife. '*Happy* Christmas at least. Happy Christmas!'

A chorus of approval met the earl's words. I half-lifted my glass of wine in his direction. Sydney swallowed his whole and raised the empty glass to a maid who filled it again. 'Nice, this special apple juice,' he said. 'Tastes a bit like wine.'

'Ah, are we civilising *you* then?' I said.

'Eh?' Sydney scratched his head.

'Never mind.'

He covered his plate in everything. It was just a massive pile of meat, potatoes and veg. He then proceeded to cover the whole thing in thick gravy, most of which teemed over onto the table.

'Sydney, you pig.' I reached over for a side dish of carrots and carefully spooned a few on my plate next to the turkey.

'Lovely,' Sydney mumbled, a dessert spoon in his hand. He rapidly scooped up an unidentified plethora of gravy-covered food. Lady Talbot looked on, horrified.

'You just can't take him anywhere,' I said, picking up the salt, but I paused mid-salt shake. There was a folded piece of paper underneath the pot. I put the salt down and picked up the note, unfolding it. It read:

The devil sleeps consumed by guilt,
From his dead wife whose blood he spilt.
A calm repose his visage shows,
A place of worship his evil blows.

'What's that?' Rose asked, her nose twitching.

'George, is this note yours?' I waved the note in his direction as I passed it over to Rose. Emma craned her head to read it over Rose's shoulder.

'What's that, Mr James?' The earl looked up from his filled plate.

'The note. Did you write the note? A new treasure hunt, perhaps?'

'Note, Mr James?

'It doesn't matter. Did anybody else write the note?'

Blank faces.

Rose handed it back.

'Oh, do read it out, James,' Lady Talbot said.

I read the note out slowly, watching people's reactions as I did so.

'What's it mean?' Sydney asked, reluctantly pausing from his face-stuffing.

'Trouble.'

'Ho, ho, Mr James, another puzzle, eh?' the earl enthused.

Mr Parsons wiped his glasses and glanced at the note but shook his head.

I looked at everyone and all their eyes were on me. 'It's a note, supposedly from Mr Eastwell. And if I'm not mistaken, he's already dead.'

CHAPTER TWENTY-THREE

'Come on.' I stood up, turning to Sydney, but he held fast to his plate.

'What? Must we go right now? Can't I just finish this?'

'Come on!'

Sydney did so but only reluctantly, spooning in several last-minute mouthfuls before he stood. Rose was already on her feet.

'Ho, ho, where are we all going?' the earl said, effortlessly abandoning his meal. 'Exciting, another treasure hunt, eh?'

Mr Landley and Mr Parsons hovered around him, but Stella forced a disappointed Emma back to her seat.

'"A place of worship his evil blows,"' I repeated.

'The Temple of the Four Winds,' Rose said.

'Exactly.'

It was one of the many follies on the estate.

We gathered our garments and emerged onto the steps to find the air biting, but the snow no longer falling. We turned left and made our way in the direction of the stone monument.

Upon the corner of Castle Howard, however, I beat my head at my own stupidity; for there in the snow, lay a single trail of footprints leading from the bottom of a high downstairs window. I briefly crouched down to examine them. A man's. 'I've been a great buffoon.'

Rose joined me. 'Mr Eastwell's?'

'I can't believe how stupid I've been. From a bloody window.' The sound I'd heard when we trampled up the stairs to get ready for the Christmas meal had been the noises I could hear coming from the open window. Perhaps the cry of a fox or some other creature.

I shook my head, but led the trek like the Pied bloody Piper, tracing the footprints towards the Temple of the Four Winds.

On the way, we passed various half-hidden statues amongst trees laden with snow. I stumbled but steadied myself with the help of my cane and Rose.

The earl laughed. 'Ho, ho. Such fun, eh, Mr James?'

'What, nearly falling in the snow on the way to a dead body?' I replied.

The earl continued on in his usual manner as I corrected my footing.

Mr Landley piped up. 'I've got an amazing

story about getting stuck in the snow.'

'I thought you would have. Sounds fascinating,' I said. 'Tell me later just before bed.' I pointed out that he should stay with Sydney, whose job it was to hold back the loonies.

The Temple of the Four Winds was a large neoclassical structure, which loomed out of the ground like a mausoleum. Its feet were covered by the snowdrift as if, it too was struggling to stand in the conditions. I circled the base looking for footprints or any other clues, but there was nothing aside from the prints that trailed up the main entranceway. Rose followed me up the steps, past the severe life-like statues which seemed to gaze at me as if I'd walked into their bedroom while *they* were in a half-state of undress. The main door was ajar, with lantern light streaming out into the night.

'Something's not right,' I said, as I thrust my cane in the doorway and sprung open the door, and there, for all to see, was Mr Eastwell. His body slumped on the floor, unmistakably dead.

◆ ◆ ◆

There then followed the most ridiculous commotion as the crowd pushed past Sydney, who toppled backwards head-first into the snow. It was impossible to tell who had started the frenzy, but surge forward they did. First, the Landleys and the Parsons, then the young David

Eastwell, whose eyes locked in horror at his father's slumped body.

He ran towards him.

'Stop!' I tried to prevent him, but he leapt over my cane and crashed prostrate before the body. He was followed by Mr Landley and the whole Parson family and then Lord and Lady Talbot.

'Sydney, get up and get them away!' I flapped my cane at the herd, accidentally hitting Mr Landley on the backside in the process.

'Ouch – Margaret, was that you slapping me on my posterior?'

'Get up, get away!' I shouted, continuing to tap at them with my cane. 'Lunatics! This is a crime scene.'

Sydney, like a Greek hero, pulled them away from the body, but by that point any potential clues would probably have already been lost.

'Get back,' I shouted at Miss Parsons, who was still standing by the body.

'Really, Mr Lavender,' she said, twisting her head to one side. 'You're acting as if you own the place.'

'Sydney, escort them all back in the house, right now!'

'Come on, miss,' Sydney said, attempting to steer her by the elbow, but Miss Parsons jerked away.

'Get off me!'

'Oh, be careful,' Lady Talbot said, suddenly appearing as if from nowhere. 'He's a well-known groper that man. He attacked me yesterday. We haven't forgotten about that, don't you worry.'

Sydney's cheeks were already red but they now turned a brighter scarlet. 'I'm not, you...fell into me, on the stairs.'

'Never mind all that,' I said. 'Get rid of them.'

'Ho, ho, Mr James. You were right about Mr Eastwell, he certainly looks quite dead,' the earl said, peering at the corpse.

I rubbed my head. 'Can you help take everyone inside, please? Give them all a brandy if you want...for the shock.'

'For the shock! Excellent idea, Mr James, excellent!' He hobbled along, half-jumping, back towards the house with a new lease of energy. His journey was made easier as the snow had already been trampled by our approach. When they disappeared into the distance, all I could hear was a final dying shout above the wind. 'Brandy! We must have brandy! For the shock!'

With the eternal fools out of the way, we were free to conduct an initial examination of the scene. The air was now quiet and calm, with just the gentlest whistle of the wind on our backs as we observed the body. 'Tell me, what do you see?' I said.

Rose pressed a little closer to Mr Eastwell's body. His face was twisted in agony, and there were fresh vomit stains down his shirt. An empty cup lay overturned amongst a bag and other provisions by his feet.

'Poison,' Rose said, 'I would say poison.'

'It certainly looks that way.' I fished in his coat pockets and pulled out a folded piece of paper.

'What's that?'

I flicked it open. 'It's a suicide note, by the looks of it.' I passed it to Rose, who read it with a glance. The hand was printed like the note we'd just read, detailing his guilt at killing his wife. It was brief and to the point and signed at the bottom in a shaky hand. 'It's a bit strange, print-writing a suicide note, don't you think?' I said.

I poked open the black leather bag by his feet, careful not to touch the metal buckles, though any prints we might happen to find would most probably be useless now, thanks to the melee. Food, water and warm clothing made up its chief contents. As well as a map.

Rose handed me the note back, sniffing the unpleasant smells around the body. 'Arsenic poisoning, do you think?'

'Quite possibly.' I handed her the bag, while I looked around the body. Nothing but an array of cigar butts. I squeezed them and held them to my nose. 'Recent, but they don't tell us much. Apart from the fact that he's been here a while.'

She put the bag down by her feet. 'Why have a map, planning to run away, but then decide to kill yourself?'

'Exactly.'

'Could have been prepared beforehand?' she

suggested.

'I doubt it.' I took a breath, taking in the cold air in an attempt to ward off the scent of death. 'I'm not buying it, sorry. You don't pack a bag of provisions like this.' I tapped the bag with my cane. 'Food, water, map. Then prepare a suicide flask and note, you know, *just in case*? I'm sorry, but this is not suicide. This is murder. We still have a deranged murderer on the loose, and his name's *not* Mr Eastwell!'

◆ ◆ ◆

David Eastwell had collapsed on his way back to the house. He was a spoilt little lord but nobody deserved to have experienced such losses in such a manner. I'd insisted on a reliable footman to stand guard outside his room with a loaded pistol with instructions not to allow anyone near. If it was some rival trying to eliminate the Eastwells, for whatever reason, then clearly he'd be the next target. I was determined that this wasn't going to happen.

Arms folded, I stood before the rest in the drawing room, surveying them all. The bemused expression of the earl, the countess who still looked eternally broken – the rest a range of faces in-between. Unfolding my arms, and standing squarely, I began. 'All of this nonsense stops right now. Murder is not a game. It's not a treasure hunt. I cannot, will not go on with this lack of discipline from you all.' I paused a moment to allow my words to sink in. 'Many of you have just trampled over a crime scene. It's as if one of you were trying deliberately to destroy evidence!'

Several faces turned away, but Lady Talbot, close to me, whispered, 'Oh, I do like it when you're being stern.'

But her silly comment was not heard as the earl dropped a teaspoon on the table, after stirring his special hot chocolate. 'What about a nice game of blindfold tiddlywinks?'

'No more games,' I said.

'Oh, we play blindfold tiddlywinks every day. We've been looking forward to it,' Anthony Landley said.

The earl concurred. 'Great game is blindfold tiddlywinks.'

The annoying Parsons child turned to his mother and said loudly:

'Mum, why is the bad man not letting us play blindfold tiddlywinks?' He sniffed as if to fight back tears.

Miss Parsons looked up at me from her seat by the fire. '*Scrooge*.'

'I'm not talking about little games inside. I'm talking about what just happened out there.' I pointed in the direction we had just come from.

'Mr Eastwell killed himself,' Miss Parsons said.

I shook my head. 'He was murdered.'

There were a few cries of shock at that, and Malcolm Wegwipe shot up, notebook in hand.

'Murdered? How so?'

'I'm not at liberty to say. It's an ongoing investigation.'

'So, does a murderer still lurk amongst us?' He jotted something down in his book, his dark little eyes scanning the mumbling crowd. 'Is he, or she, still hungry for blood?'

'Can we stop this talk?' the countess said, her hands over her daughter's ears, even though her child was drawing in a book and not listening to those around her. The mumbling ceased, and for a moment the only sound was the crackling of the fire and the familiar scraping of Wegwipe's pen. 'I'm sure, Mr Lavender, that you will want to conduct your investigation more privately?'

'Indeed. I will be speaking with every one of you before we return to examine the body and the crime scene in further detail. Sydney will remain here to ensure nobody leaves in any circumstances. I do hope that's clear.'

I turned and walked out of the room.

CHAPTER TWENTY-FOUR

Rose followed me and we made our way into the so-called incident room.

'Who do you want to question first?' she asked, preparing the note paper.

'Bring in Mr Landley.'

'Really?'

'Well, we might as well get him out of the way.'

Mr Landley pulled up his chair with great enthusiasm. 'Mr Lavender, always wise, calling on me first, eh?'

'Yes, might as well get the pain over with.'

'I said to Margaret, I bet Mr Lavender calls on me first. I said that he'd need my advice, that…'

'Mr Landley, please be quiet.'

'…you'd call on me in times of need. Well, I'm here. What can I do for you?'

'Do you know anything about the deaths?'

'Deaths?'

I wanted to hit my head on the table in front of me. Hard. 'You know, the Eastwells – the stabbing and the poisoning?'

'Oh, right, yes. Of course, of course. I was thinking about the farm. Terrible, isn't it?'

'Do you have any theories on who's responsible?'

Mr Landley twisted his head and pulled his chair closer, conspiratorially. 'I said to Margaret that you'd ask me, that…'

'Mr Landley, please, we're short on time.'

'…you'd call on me first, well…' He moved even closer still, taking a peek at Rose, as if deciding if he could speak plainly in front of her. 'I won't forget to pass you the bum ointment.'

I sighed. 'Can we stick to the murder investigation?'

Mr Landley sniffed. 'Oh, yes. You know what I think? I think there's a madman on the loose. Living on the grounds.'

I paused a moment, looking at Rose who was writing his words down. 'Whereabouts on the grounds?'

'There's plenty of places to hide on the grounds, Mr Lavender. The mausoleum for one. Then there's plenty of sheds and outhouses on the estate.'

'So, you think the killer is living out on the grounds and coming in the house, leaving notes and committing murder?'

Mr Landley winked at me.

'But there are no footprints in the snow, and how are they managing to sneak in and out of the house unseen?'

Mr Landley's gazed on, smiling and scratching his thick sideburns.

I tapped my finger on the table distractedly and decided to change my approach. 'How would you describe your relationship with Mr and Mrs Eastwell?'

'Relationship, Mr Lavender?'

'What were they like? Did you get on with them?'

He shook his head. 'They were not the sort you got on with, they…they weren't like you.'

'How do you mean?'

'Well, they were too serious. Never played any games as a family. They had no sense of fun like you do.'

Rose started to snigger, which changed into a terrible coughing fit.

'Are you well, dear?' Mr Landley said, passing her the water jug from the middle of the table.

She covered her mouth with a fist. 'I'm fine, thank you.'

I looked at her but continued. 'Did you hold any grudge against the Eastwells? I imagine they made enemies pretty easily, especially Mr Eastwell.'

Mr Landley screwed up his already screwed up face. 'Do you want me to tell you that cow story yet?'

'The what?'

'The cow story. You know, you told me to tell it you later, when we were outside. You said to tell it you later. About how the cow got stuck in the snow.'

'Oh, that. Well, I sometimes have trouble sleeping, but just answer the question about Mr Eastwell.'

'It's a wonderful story, the cow got stuck in the snow and Mr Parsons...'

'Mr Landley.'

'...had to help to get it out. Well, I'll tell it to you, later. Mr Eastwell? Let me think. I didn't get on with Mr Eastwell. Very stern. No fun at all.'

'Mr Landley, theoretically speaking—'

'Ha, ha, that's what I like about you, all these fun words...'

'Mr Landley, please stop talking.'

'...I said to Margaret, I couldn't wait to be questioned. I said I'd...'

'Mr Landley!'

'...be in first, I said it. I did.' He stopped, looking up at me, smiling.

'*Theoretically* speaking...if you no longer ran the estate—'

'No longer ran the estate! What fun! I'm always going to run the estate until Anthony takes over. No longer run the estate, ho, ho. Wait until I tell Margaret that one. She won't be able to contain herself!'

I reached for some water. 'Mr Landley. Did the

Eastwells hold something over you? Did you kill them to stop them from spreading something that would ruin your position or that of your family?'

That got his attention. I felt his eyes on me as if he was going to shout, but then he burst out laughing. 'Mr Lavender, such fun!' He struggled to speak through his laughter, having to wipe his eyes with his crusty sleeve before he could continue. 'I said to Margaret. You can count on Mr Lavender for a fun time!' Then he started laughing again.

'Did you kill him?'

He continued to laugh. Rose, took over. 'Mr Landley, are you stating that you didn't kill Mr and Mrs Eastwell?'

I thought he hadn't heard her as he was still laughing, then he said:

'Oh no, dear. Such fun. Such fun.' Then he recovered himself.

Rose put her pen down. 'Well, thank you for your time. Can you give us five minutes then send in your wife please?'

He stood up and he shook my hand heartily. 'I most certainly will. Got to let Margaret have her share of the fun, eh? Well, I'll be seeing you later on…with that cow story, yes?' He winked at me again as he left the room, giving Rose a cursory wave.

'Jesus Christ. He's hard work,' I said, leaning back in the chair as far as it would allow. How I missed my new chair back home.

Rose nibbled the end of her pen. 'You don't think he's responsible in any way, do you?'

'Mr Landley? No.'

'And he was telling the truth on the last question?'

'Yes.'

If the colour grey could be represented by anyone on earth, it was Mrs Landley. She dripped and reeked of it. The pearls around her thick neck had even turned grey, worn down like the woman before us with the continual onslaught of Mr Landley's verbal diatribes. I couldn't stand more than five minutes of his nonsense, so how this woman had endured more than twenty-five years of it was beyond me. She sat before us without saying a word, her head twisted slightly to one side. When she spoke, which was a rare event, she made little rabbit-like jitters with her mouth, which seemed to run at odds with the rest of her plain features.

Rose began. 'Mrs Landley, thank you for seeing us. Can you shed any light on the deaths of Mr or Mrs Eastwell?'

She made a gesture with her head which could have been interpreted as both a nod and a shake.

'Mrs Landley, can you answer, please?' I said.

The shaking and nodding continued, then stopped just as soon as it began. Then there came from her lips a brief 'no'.

'Is that a "no", you can't answer, or a "no", you

can't shed any light on the murders?' I said.

Her face jittered around again, but no answer broke forth.

'Mrs Landley, I'll make this simple for you. Did you kill Mr Eastwell?' I asked her.

The jittering of the lips continued, but she uttered a 'no'.

'Did you poison Mr Eastwell?'

She circularly nodded and shook her head like before. I asked her to speak out loud, encouraged by our previous progress. 'No. Not me.'

'Mrs Landley there's no need to go on at length.' I smiled at Rose, who didn't seem to appreciate my joke. 'A simple "no" would have been sufficient. Do you have anything else you can add?'

Mrs Landley shook her head or nodded, depending upon one's interpretation. I turned to Rose to see if she had any questions but she shook her head, so I asked Mrs Landley to send in her eldest son.

Anthony Landley was a skinny bag full of nerves. He couldn't look either of us in the eye. He bit his lip and tapped his foot, then twisted in his chair.

'So, young man,' I began. 'What have you got to say for yourself?'

His eyes shifted to one side again and he scratched his freckly skin. 'What do you mean?'

'Come on? You've clearly got something to tell us. Get it off your chest,' I said.

'I...I don't know anything.'

'Did you kill Mr Eastwell?'

'What? No!'

'You better tell us what you know. This is very serious.'

He swallowed and nodded, then looked directly at me for the first time. 'I don't know anything for sure, just...I know Lord Talbot hates him.'

'Imaginings are not much use to us, are they?' I said. 'Do you have any facts on the matter?'

He shook his head. Rose picked up the questioning. 'Tell us about Miss Parsons.'

At the mention of her name, he immediately blushed. 'What? What do you mean?'

I jumped in. 'Is that why you wanted to get rid of David Eastwell? Only, his parents got in the way, did they?'

'What? Of course not. It's nothing like that.'

He scratched his chin and his cheeks grew even redder, but in so far as the murder, he was telling the truth, but he wouldn't part with the information. Rose tried a few more questions but he would only give us mutters and trembles. Without a doubt, Anthony Landley was hiding something, but what was it? What did he know?

CHAPTER TWENTY-FIVE

We questioned his younger brother afterwards, who had nothing to say, only to complain it was soon to be his turn at blindfold tiddlywinks as he swung on his chair. So Rose let him go as Sydney popped his head through the door.

'How are the interviews going?' he asked.

'Sydney, you're supposed to be watching the loonies,' I said.

'Everyone's there. They're all playing a game and Stella is watching, so can I join you?'

'Fine,' I said. 'Go fetch Mr Parsons.'

Sydney swallowed once, then left the room.

Mr Parsons sat before us, having taken an age to adjust his chair. He eventually settled and sat upright as if eagerly awaiting our questions. Rose had thanked him and he replied graciously, nodding his head in a courteous manner.

'So,' I began. 'Can you shed any light on the

murders?'

He clasped his hands together and sat up even straighter in his chair. 'You know, I have been thinking on it.'

'Good. Go on,' I encouraged.

'Well, it strikes me as two very different crimes. A stabbing and a poisoning – if that indeed is the case. So, do we have two murderers?'

Rose looked up from her note-taking. I stared back blankly, then turned back to Mr Parsons. 'What do *you* think?'

'I would say so, yes.'

'And your theories on the culprits?' I asked.

He frowned at that. 'I couldn't say. I have no idea.'

'No idea?'

'No.'

Rose asked him a few standard questions, some hinting at his own whereabouts which he answered without fuss.

We could no longer ignore the question of his wife's alleged affair.

'Could you...would you have had any *personal* grudge against Mr Eastwell?' I asked.

He twisted his head a little. 'Mr Eastwell?'

'That's what I asked.'

'Me? No. I mean, I didn't like him, but no one did.'

'Did, er, Mrs Parsons *like* him?' I hinted, fearing an explosion on his behalf.

He seemed to stiffen slightly. 'My wife?'

Sydney leaned over the table. 'Having an affair-like.'

'Jesus, Sydney,' I said.

Mr Parsons twitched his nose. 'Oh, I'm not one for rumour.'

'Wegwipe doesn't think it is rumour,' I said. 'Did it push you over the edge? And, you do have a bit of a temper, let's be honest.' I waited again for the explosion.

'Temper? Why, deary me, no.' He shook his head with a little chuckle. 'And as for Mr Wegwipe, well...I don't particularly follow what he has to say.'

Good man.

I left it a moment then leaned in. 'You didn't kill Mr Eastwell, then?'

I gripped the end of the table. Rose, I noticed, held her pen more tightly.

'Me? Oh, no. Deary me, no.'

Sydney puffed out his cheeks.

Mr Parsons looked thoughtful. 'You know, I was once at Mrs Wobble's. You know Mrs Wobble?'

I nodded.

'I was eating her delicious Albert Cake when I noticed Rufus staring at me through the window.'

'Rufus? Who's Rufus?' Sydney asked.

'RUFUS! Oh, my GOD, RUFUS!' Mr Parsons leapt up out of his chair. 'Rufus the bloody bull!

Everyone knows the bloody bull is called Rufus. JESUS!' He started screaming, then bent over, pulling at his ears.

'Well done, Sydney,' I said. 'You've done it again.'

'Rufus. It's the name of Mrs Wobble's bloody bull! Obviously!'

'Can't take you anywhere,' I said to Sydney as he tried hiding under the table.

Mr Parsons stood up on his chair, still trying to rip off his ears. 'What a STUPID question, aarrgghhh.'

I could now only see Sydney's chubby fingers gripping the edges of the table.

'Rufus' eyes. You bloody FOOLS!'

◆ ◆ ◆

It took us a while to recover from Mr Parsons. We simply sat in the quiet, enjoying the sound of rain falling on the window pane. Rose thought the two-killer theory sounded plausible but I hadn't the energy with which to reply.

Next up, came Miss Parsons. The little vixen immediately clashed with Rose. 'Are you quite qualified to ask me questions?' she said, after a few preliminary observations.

Rose flinched, but she held herself in reserve, then hit back after further remarks:

'Your little flirting not getting you anywhere with David?'

Miss Parsons looked uncomfortable for the first time, shifting a little away from Rose in her seat, and stroking a strand of blonde hair to one side. 'I don't know what you're talking about.'

Rose tapped her pen deliberately. 'Hmm, I think you do.'

'Besides, it's nothing to do with you.'

I sighed. 'Do you know who killed the Eastwells?' I asked her.

She snorted.

'Look,' I told her. 'We will get to the bottom of this, I can promise you that. All it takes is a wrong word here or there, a clue left behind somewhere. Take the body of Mr Eastwell out there. It's safe from the elements. It could be something as little as a mark under the fingernails, a shoe print, a stray button. Anything. Whatever it is, we'll find it, so you best just tell us anything you know, right now.'

She smiled back at us, but still didn't comment.

'We're not really getting anywhere,' I said, after her departure. I asked Rose if she had any theories.

'I've been thinking about Mrs Eastwell.'

'Yes?'

'Yes. I don't think she was the target. I think Mr Eastwell was the target and–'

'And she got in the way?'

'Exactly.'

'So who do you think has done it and why?' I

pressed.

She sat up a little straighter in her chair. 'From the very start, it was obvious that Lord Talbot and Mr Eastwell didn't get on. They've obviously got some longstanding feud.' I nodded and she continued. 'Lord Talbot had the opportunity when the girl went missing. He, like almost anyone, could have sneaked in and tried to attack Mr Eastwell, not counting on Mrs Eastwell being there.' She shrugged. 'Wrong place, wrong time?'

'Go on.'

'So, he kills his wife, then puts her blood on the sleeping Mr Eastwell. He then plants the knife in your room and returns to search for the girl.'

'Meanwhile?'

'Meanwhile, Mr Eastwell wakes up in shock, sees the blood on his hands and panics. He tries to clean it off but fails. Then young Eastwell comes in and sees the body. He comes back to tell us.'

'During which time…?'

'During which time, Mr Eastwell comes back and sits on the bed and that's when we find him.'

I nodded. 'What about the next one? The poisoning.'

'The poisoning? Well, Lord Talbot helps him escape , but plants arsenic in his flask.'

'Hmm.'

'What do you mean "hmm"?'

'Yes, no. It's not bad.'

'Not bad?' She didn't look terribly pleased.

'Just…?'

'Just, there are a few plot holes, but tell you what. Let's get Lord Talbot in. Let's see what he has to say for himself,' I said.

Lord Talbot sat crossed-legged, the permanent sneer on his lips badly dressed up as a thin smile. 'Why, to what do I owe this *pleasure*, Mr Lavender?'

'What can you tell us about the murders?' I said.

He sniffed as if stifling a laugh. 'Couldn't happen to a nicer man.'

'You had a history with Mr Eastwell, I take it?'

'Many people did. I, for one, cannot say I'm sorry to see him go.'

'Did you murder him, Lord Talbot?'

He smiled but didn't answer.

'You find murder amusing?'

'It's rather a pointless question, isn't it? Asking if I murdered him. If I did it, I'm hardly going to confess, but if I didn't and I say "no" then you're hardly going to believe me. So it's a rather pointless question, is it not?'

'All the same. We're conducting a double murder investigation. Just answer our questions and then you can leave.'

He looked at me, this thin smile creasing around the edges. 'I'm not going to be answering any questions.'

'Why not?'

'Because you don't have the authority and

I'm about to launch legal proceedings against that man.' He pointed at Sydney, who looked troubled. 'No need for vulgar duels. We're all civilized here, are we not?'

'I didn't do anything,' Sydney said.

Lord Talbot simply smiled.

'He's innocent and I think you know it, but if you don't answer our questions, you'll be considered our main suspect.' I was annoyed that he had annoyed me, which is what he had been trying to do.

'You won't get anything out of myself or my wife.'

Rose tried. 'Can't you just tell us what you know?'

He turned around as he was leaving, looking down at Rose. 'Why should I want to do that?'

'To bring justice to his killer and Mrs Eastwell's.'

He laughed. 'Justice.'

'What's so funny?' I said.

'Justice, Mr Lavender. A strange concept, don't you think?'

'Not really. It's perfectly simple.'

He sniffed and shook his head as if disappointed, his hand still on the door handle. 'Justice. Mr Eastwell got what he deserved. I'll tell you, that's justice. I would wish you success in your endeavours, but I hope he gets away with it.'

I smiled. 'So, you think it's a man?'

'Nice try, Mr Lavender. Nice try.' Then he left.

Lord Talbot had not eliminated himself from the crime. Was Lord Talbot guilty of murder or was he merely protecting the one who was?

CHAPTER TWENTY-SIX

'He's refusing to come in,' Sydney said, having returned at last from the main drawing room.

'He's what?'

'He's refusing to come in.'

I glanced at Rose and turned back to Sydney. 'Why?'

'He says he's "uncomfortable with the scenario".'

'He's uncomfortable with the bloody scenario?'

'That's what he said.'

I shook my head. 'Unbelievable.'

Lady Talbot had refused to be interviewed 'on grounds of safety' owing to Sydney's presence, and now Malcolm bloody Wegwipe was also refusing. Before that, we'd questioned the earl and countess but they could add little to our investigation. The same thing was true with William Brookes, whose presence in the house was still a complete mystery to me, as he didn't seem to do or say anything much at all. Why was he even here?

'What's he being awkward for?' I asked.

'Dunno.'

'Go back out and ask him again.'

'He's not going to come, is he?' Sydney said, arms folded.

I banged my fist against the table. 'Sydney, get out there and bring me Malcolm Wegwipe.'

'Well, fine. I'll ask again but I bet he refuses.'

As Sydney left, I stood up and opened the window. A flurry of rain blew in. 'Yes, it looks like it's still raining.'

'I can see,' Rose said.

I peered through the pane, lifting the latch and opening it wider. The rain splattered further inside, carried by the fierce wind, invading our little room.

'It still feels cold though,' I said, looking out into the night, but not seeing much. 'It's foggy. Really foggy and the rain's quite heavy.'

Rose wiped her sleeve. 'Yes, I can feel it. It's hitting my arm.'

'I know. Who would have thought I'd look forward to rain? You know what that means, don't you?'

Rose didn't seem to feel my enthusiasm. 'That I'm getting wet?'

'No, no. It means that we can go home soon.'

'Yes, but I'm still getting wet.'

'Yes, but it means that we're not going to get stuck here for much longer. If we find the murderers, that is.' I spun around fully, putting my hands behind my back, ignoring the flurry spitting over my shoulder. 'Just think, Rose. I can go back to my library room, sit with a book, head across to Boaters – to the Punch Bowl!'

'James, shu–'

'I can help myself to some more of that excellent cheese.'

'Shut the damn d–'

'Sleep in my hard bed. Take the papers, and read the latest theories. Sit down for five–'

'JAMES!'

I stopped, puzzled. 'What?'

'Close the damn window. I'm getting wet!'

'Oh, right. You should have said.' I shut the window with a bang as Sydney came back in. 'No Wegwipe?' I asked.

'No, he's still refusing to come in.'

'Right, I'll see what all this nonsense is about.' I stormed past him and out of the room. Wegwipe was wasting my time, interfering with a murder investigation, and more than getting on my bloody nerves.

❖ ❖ ❖

I came in in a rage but stopped as soon as the

room went silent. Mr Parsons was seated in the centre of the room, blindfolded. He was carefully flipping little wooden counters into a bowl with the Landley and Parsons broods seated around him.

The Landley brat looked up at me and then leaned towards his father. 'That bad man is here.'

Mr Landley looked up. 'Ah, Mr Lavender! Have you come to play blindfold tiddlywinks?'

'No.'

'Great game is blindfold tiddlywinks,' the earl said, standing behind him, eyes alert to every flip.

I sighed. 'No, I'm conducting a double murder investigation and trying to track down a killer.' I surveyed the room, happy that everyone seemed to be here at least.

'Ah, that's a shame,' the earl said.

Mr Landley waved. 'We play blindfold tiddlywinks every day. Don't we, Margaret?'

I waited while he consulted Margaret several more times before I found myself drawn into his nonsense.

'Seriously?' I said. 'You play it every day? *Every day*?'

'Absolutely, Mr Lavender. Absolutely.' He appeared to shudder at the hellish prospect of life without blindfold tiddlywinks. 'It's one of the very first things we do when myself and Anthony get back from the farms.'

'The very first thing?' I had better things to do

than question him about tiddlywinks, but I just couldn't let this one go.

'Oh yes, blindfold tiddlywinks is a must for our family, Mr Lavender. A must!'

'As well as little balls?'

'Ball in the hole!' shouted the young Landley boy.

'Never mind,' I said, making my way over to my victim. 'A word with you.'

Wegwipe was seated alone at a table in the corner of the room, a familiar smug smile on his face. 'Certainly.' He motioned that I should join him, but I remained standing.

'What's all this about refusing to be questioned?'

His smile remained. 'Oh, I'm not refusing to answer questions, Mr Lavender, just...' He looked around the room. 'I have nothing to hide.'

Rose and Sydney appeared behind me, having just fought off a game of blindfold tiddlywinks.

'Mr Wegwipe, we're cond–'

'Conducting a double murder enquiry, I know, but you've not been truthful with us, have you?' He brushed his hair to one side, and I felt the interest of the room grow around us. 'So, in those conditions...' He held his palms out towards me and shrugged his shoulders.

'What are you talking about?'

He eyeballed the room dramatically, then turned back to me. 'The murder weapon.'

'What murder weapon?'

'The one in your room.'

There were cries and shouts behind me. I heard Miss Parsons, and Lord Talbot in particular.

'Who told you about that?' I said.

Malcolm Wegwipe shook his head. 'I'm afraid a reporter never reveals his sources. You know that.'

'What's this about a murder weapon?' Miss Parsons asked.

Rose told her to be quiet

Lord Talbot strode over. 'It's an important question though, is it not?'

'Yes, the murder weapon was planted in my room,' I said.

Miss Parsons huffed. '*Planted?*'

'Yes, indeed, planted,' I repeated.

'Are we safe, Mr Lavender?' Mrs Parsons said, coming over to join her annoying daughter, having left the delight of blindfold tiddlywinks behind.

'No, probably not. Seeing as there's a murderer in this room.'

'How do we not know *you're* not the murderer?' Lord Talbot said.

Miss Parsons joined in. 'Yes, as the murder weapon seems to have appeared in your room, after all. Not to mention the button by the table yesterday.'

'Indeed,' Lord Talbot added.

'Utter nonsense,' I said, as Lady Talbot came

over, smiling.

'You can sit down,' Rose said.

'Ah, Miss McCarthy, caught between a brute and a murderer, are you?'

'Hey, I'm not a brute,' Sydney said. 'I've done nothing wrong.'

'We'll see about that,' Lord Talbot muttered.

The countess stood and walked over calmly, speaking with quiet authority. 'Can everyone be seated, please? Let Mr Lavender and his team sort out the...unpleasantness.'

Lady Talbot smiled at Rose but retreated, as did the others, but paused as Malcolm Wegwipe spoke:

'Ahem. You know, if the killer wanted to conduct a little interview...Let's say, for example, if I'd seen who'd planted the note on the table, and they wanted to come forward, then...' He shrugged his shoulders.

'Wegwipe, if you have important information then you tell me, right now,' I said, forcefully.

He held out a palm in that way of his. 'I was speaking strictly in theoretical terms.'

'No, you weren't. If you don't talk, you'll put yourself in danger.'

He looked taken aback for a moment, but then returned to his usual self. He picked up his little black book and tucked it carefully into his jacket pocket. 'I have nothing more to say.'

CHAPTER TWENTY-SEVEN

The night was drawing on and I'd been listening to conversations closely, trying to catch out any lies. However, the countess had banned talk of the 'unsavoury events' for fear of upsetting her daughter, so this heavily limited my chances. As usual, the earl had us up and down playing games. Cards and charades were the latest, but the games had at least been replaced with music with Miss Parsons currently playing something sedate.

'How long do you plan on keeping us here, James?' Lady Talbot said. 'You can't keep us here all night.'

Eyes shifted my way. It was a fair point. Master Eastwell had been allowed back into the room, now that we were all present, but we would all have to sleep at some point. Aurea was already asleep in the arms of the countess, and I got the impression the countess herself wanted to retreat to her quarters.

'Well, er, obviously we have to sleep, Lady Talbot,' I said.

Miss Parsons finished her piece and waved her hair back, drawing attention to her expensive diamond earring, something she had been doing all night.

'Capital!' Williams Brookes said, clapping enthusiastically.

Heads craned around to the far corner of the room for the rare event of William Brookes speaking. Sydney looked, then scratched at his trousers and gave his wife a not-too-pleasant glance. Green trousers suited him but he didn't see it that way. Miss Parsons continued to play, a fast-trilling piece this time which contrasted sharply with the current sombre mood around the fireplace.

'Well, Mr Lavender?' Mrs Parsons said, by Lady Talbot's side.

'Naturally, people need to sleep. We need to be on guard, ensure all doors are locked, and only go around in twos or more.'

'Well, I don't think that's good enough,' Mrs Parsons said, apparently taking over her daughter's role as the obnoxious one in the room.

'What else do you want him to do?' Rose said.

Suddenly, I was almost knocked to the floor by Mr Landley. His hairy hand still rocked my shoulder. 'Time for my cow story yet?' The chaise longue started rocking and I realised he was scratching his behind again. I shifted across in my seat away from him, closer to Rose, but there wasn't much space.

'It's a fantastic story, Mr Lavender, about how the cow got stuck in the snow. Isn't it a fantastic story, Margaret? Margaret, isn't it a fantastic story?'

Mr Parsons concurred.

'Storytime!' the earl boomed. He pulled up a chair closer with conversations regarding people's safety evidently to be replaced by Mr Landley's cow-stuck-in-the-snow story. Miss Parsons stopped playing, aware that attention had shifted from her to Mr Landley. She did not seem impressed.

'So, once, on the farm, Mr Lavender,' Mr Landley began, wagging a finger. 'A cow got stuck in the snow. Didn't it get stuck in the snow, Mar...'

'Mr Landley, we believe you!' I shouted. 'Just tell the story and be done with it!'

'...garet? Didn't it?

Mr Parsons twisted his head lost in a fond memory. 'Aye, a cow got stuck in the snow, alright.'

Mr Landley burst into uncontrollable laughter, clapping me on the shoulder again with his dirty hand. 'We got a rope and pulled and pulled, but there was no having it. Even Anthony couldn't move it and he's a natural with animals. We had to whip it on its backside a bit, ho, ho. Think about that! Then it moved.'

'Right,' I said. 'What happened then?'

I couldn't believe what I was asking, but anything for a quieter life.

Mr Landley, Parsons and the earl continued to laugh, the former having to wipe the tears that were streaming down his face in reminiscence. 'Happened, Mr Lavender?' He managed between tears. 'How do you mean, *happened*?'

I looked at Sydney, who stared back. 'I mean, what happened next – to the cow? What happened?'

'The cow?'

'Yes, the bloody cow!'

Mr Landley wiped the remaining tears away. 'Nothing.'

'You mean, that's it? That's the story? A cow got stuck in the snow and you moved it?'

Mr Landley chuckled. 'Yes, an amazing story, eh? Things don't always get so exciting in the country, you know?'

'I bet.'

The earl stood up, animated. 'Brilliant story! Amazing. Bet you've got some interesting stories, Mr Lavender, haven't you?'

'Oh yes!' Mr Landley clapped me on the back again, jerking me forward. 'Tell us all a story.'

'Would you please stop doing that?' I said.

Mr Landley proceeded. 'Mr Lavender's such fun. I bet you have lots of stories. Tell us all a story.'

I looked into the burning coals, thinking of something to shut them up. 'Well, there was this one time that Sydney and I were called into investigate a series of break-ins from a local shop.'

'Break-ins, Mr Lavender?' the earl asked, a frown appearing over his brow.

Mr Landley shuffled closer. 'Oh, this sounds fun, doesn't it, Margaret? Doesn't it sound fun, Margaret?'

'Let him tell the story then,' Stella said.

Emma smiled.

I nodded a quick thanks. 'Yes, a local shop. Funny thing about it was that food was going missing. Not money - food. And there was no damage to the door. The proprietor–'

'Such fun words, Margaret, eh?'

I ignored Mr Landley's interjection. 'The proprietor called us in because he thought he was going mad. Food going missing during the night. Not much, a bag of potatoes here, some carrots there, but it was happening at least twice a week.'

'How mysterious,' the earl said. 'Wonderful!'

Lord Talbot twisted his chair away a few degrees dismissively. 'Yes, missing carrots, how…*fascinating*.'

The earl urged me to continue, as did both Mr Landley and Mr Parsons. 'Well, so here's the thing. We hid in the shop overnight in the back room and waited.'

'Yes, Mr Lavender, what happened?' the earl said, leaning in even more so that I could feel his breath.

Mr Landley squirmed on the chair beside me, and Mr Parsons held a hand over his heart, checking, I assume, that it was still beating.

'Nothing,' I said.

'Ha, ha, wonderful!' Mr Landley shouted in my ear.

Mr Parsons joined in. 'Interesting story.'

I wagged my finger at them. 'Nothing, that is…on the first night. But on the second…BAM!' I punched a fist into my hand. Mr Landley almost fell on the floor in hysterics, the young Landley cried in delight, but when the child in the countess' arms almost stirred, the countess shot me a warning look. Emma stroked her hair, smiling at me.

'What happened?' Miss Parsons asked me, still sitting in the piano chair. 'Did you catch the potato thief?'

The others urged me to continue. 'Yes, we did, didn't we, Sydney?' Suddenly I felt like Mr Landley.

'We did that.'

Miss Parsons sniffed. 'Well done. *So* brave. We're all in safe hands then, if anybody tries to steal some potatoes. Good to know. I'm sure the cook will sleep tonight.'

The earl twisted his fingers, unable to contain his excitement. 'Remarkable, quite remarkable.'

'Well, how about that, Margaret, eh? Isn't that the most amazing story you've ever heard? Something to tell the grandchildren,' Mr Landley enthused.

Mr Parsons agreed.

I held up my hand. 'I haven't finished yet.'

Miss Parsons snorted. 'We can hardly bear the excitement.'

I continued with my point, undeterred. 'It turns out he was picking the locks. He was an expert. An old locksmith fallen on hard times. He was taking food to feed his family. Not much, just enough to keep them going.'

'I do hope he was thrown in prison to rot,' Lord Talbot said. 'Scourge of society.'

'No, he wasn't,' Sydney said. 'We let him off in return for his picking knowledge.'

'You did what?' Lord Talbot said.

Miss Parsons joined in with her indignant outrage. 'You let him go? I withdraw my previous comment. We're not safe if someone comes stealing potatoes.'

'He was feeding his family,' I said, angrily. 'We fed him for his picking knowledge, then later when he was back on his feet, he paid the shopkeeper back.'

Lord Talbot shook his head. 'That's hardly the point. Crime shouldn't be allowed to flourish. It needs to the stamped out at the first instance. You can't be soft on these people. What starts as petty theft leads to all sorts of violence. It's in their blood.'

'Quite right,' Malcolm Wegwipe said.

Miss Parsons agreed.

But the earl stood up and crossed to shake my hand and the dissenters piped down. 'Wonderful story! Quite remarkable.'

Mr Landley came next. 'Never, in all of my life, have I heard such an amazing story.' He stopped shaking my hand to pull out a dirty handkerchief which he blew his nose into loudly. '*That* is the greatest story in the history of mankind. Isn't it, Margaret? Margaret, isn't Mr Lavender's story the greatest story in the history of mankind?'

I laughed. 'I don't know about that, but I do know a thing or two about locks and I know more than a thing or two about liars and criminals. So, if the murderer here thinks they're going to get away with it then they're very much mistaken.' I turned to Malcolm Wegwipe. 'Or my name's not *James*. Bloody. *Lavender.*

CHAPTER TWENTY-EIGHT

We had taken the necessary precautions of retreating to our rooms in groups of three or more wherever possible. The heavy rain had persisted, turning the snow to slush in places, but it still looked deep and hard to get through. A brief inspection of the exits revealed no new footprints in the remaining snow. So no little visitors living in outhouses as was Mr Landley's theory. No, I was still certain the murderer was of our party.

'How do you know it's not one of the servants?' Rose had asked me, on our way up to our rooms.

'Motive, for one. I could easily see how a fellow like Mr Eastwell could have made many enemies; he was a cruel man. To murder him, yes, but to murder his wife in such a brutal manner, no. You could say this lies at the very heart of the mystery. Who would want to kill Mrs Eastwell?'

'But what if Mr Eastwell killed her? Then one

of the servants or anyone else could have killed him?' Rose had said.

'The two-killer theory? That is of course, possible, but then the murder of Mr Eastwell immediately afterwards just doesn't seem to fit.'

'Too much of a coincidence?' Emma had asked, as we'd made our way up the grand steps.

'Exactly. It's possible but...the forging of a suicide note, the administration of what appears to be poison in his flask, his escaping from a locked room – the whole thing had been cleverly and quickly planned. This suggests to me one mind.'

Rose had waited while Emma and Stella had turned out of earshot before she'd whispered, 'With your condition, surely it has to be one of the Talbots or Malcolm Wegwipe as they are the only ones who refused to answer our questions. Nobody else has flagged up as lying.'

'Yes, that's true, but...it doesn't always work out that way.'

'What do you mean?'

I sighed. I hadn't felt like revisiting the loopholes of my condition at this time of night. 'Lord Talbot is the main suspect, but sometimes someone can say something that's a lie, but it comes through as a truth – it's a question of semantics.'

'How?'

I'd drawn her to one side as Malcolm Wegwipe and William Brookes had strolled past us. 'Look, most of the time it works perfectly, but on occasion, not as expected.' I rubbed at my eye.

'But, you're still not explaining *how*.'

'Well. Let's say you shot someone.'

She smiled. 'Lady Talbot?'

'What? Oh, whatever, yes. Say you shot Lady Talbot. If I asked if you killed her, you could say no. In the majority of cases that would read as a lie (if I could read you), but sometimes not, because it could be argued that the person didn't kill them, the gun did.'

'What, really?'

'Yes.'

She crossed her arms. 'That seems a bit strange.'

'Well, sorry, that's just how it seems to work. I did try to explain all this before. What do you want me to do about it?'

'Nothing. Stop being grumpy. So, who's responsible, then?' Rose asked, a little more nervously. 'Could it be anyone here?'

'It's unlikely, but technically, I suppose so, yes. Anybody could have murdered the Eastwells. Anybody.'

❖ ❖ ❖

I couldn't sleep, and I was not being productive of thought. Lying awake and letting ideas drift around in my head was just not possible in my given room. For one thing, the damn figures on the walls were still too off-putting, even in the dark, as I knew they were there. Another reason was the bed. It was still too soft. And of course, I was on high alert for any movement in the corridor.

I'd suggested to Rose that she swap places with Sydney, so she could double up with Stella, but she'd insisted she felt safe enough in her room. She said that her room came equipped with a 'very heavy candlestick' which would be thrust on the top of a stranger's head with great force should they be foolish enough to enter her room. From what I'd seen of Rose, I didn't doubt her for a moment.

Emma and Rose had been working away on the fingerprint analysis task I'd given them, having successfully borrowed most of the items they needed to test against the print I'd found on my chair. Emma had been willing to work into the night on it, but Stella had other ideas and had forcefully suggested she should finish it off in the morning. I hadn't argued.

I briefly closed my eyes but it had no effect. I picked up my pillow, pulled it sideways, and then plumped it back down again. It made little difference. Cursing the bed, I went over the case in my head, running through everything logically. I still favoured the single-killer theory, but nothing was certain. I thumped the pillow in frustration again, releasing a cloud of dust which caused me to sneeze. Then it struck me.

My action had triggered a germ of an idea, something Mr Landley had said. In my mind I tried to discount it, telling myself that it just couldn't be true, that the prospect was just too horrible. I felt panic rising within me, and I had to draw my breath through the still-present dust. However unthinkable the possibility, it seemed to fit.

I closed my eyes and soon it was morning. I was there with Mr Landley and Mr Parsons, our feet hanging over a chair, our toes exposed to the elements. Another one of the earl's games. I wriggled my toes to try to keep them warm but to little avail.

'Really,' I said. 'I must get back to the investigation.'

'Later,' the earl said. 'You can do all that *later*. First, we play wriggly toes!'

Mr Landley turned to face me. 'We play wriggly toes all the time.'

'Great game is wriggly toes!' the earl added.

Mr Parsons concurred.

I tried to move my feet but I couldn't move from the constraints of the iron collar fixed around my ankles.

'Who's going first?' Mr Parsons asked.

'Ah, we roll a die.' The earl shouted for Simon, who brought a large wooden box. He handed it to the earl, who flipped open the lid and took out a large red dice. 'Now, Mr Parsons goes on a one or two. Mr Landley on a three or four. Mr James on a five or six. Ready?'

Mr Landley shook his leg excitedly as the earl rolled the dice. We couldn't see it from our position, trapped as we were. 'It's the number...four!'

Mr Landley cheered.

I tried to protest again but my words were lost in the excitement as the earl picked out something from the box. A large set of shears. 'Time to choose a toe, Mr Landley.'

'Ho, ho. Such fun. This is my favourite part. My big toe, please.' He wriggled his big toe on his right foot.'

The earl nodded and rolled another dice. It spun in the box. 'A five. Yes, you can have your big toe.' Mr Landley cheered as the earl snapped the shears back and forth in front of him in a sharp rasp of metal.

'Can we stop the joke now, please? I'm too busy,' I said.

'Joke, Mr James? It's no joke,' the earl said, as he fed the shears over Mr Landley's wriggling big toe.

'Wriggly toes is a great way to pass the time.' Mr Landley said. 'It's a wonderful little game. I said to Margaret...'

'George, come on,' I said, nervously.

But the earl wasn't listening. He smiled as he leaned all his weight against the shears and snapped them together in a swift fluid motion. They went through the toe effortlessly in a brutal crunch of bone. I screamed in horror as Mr Landley's toe flew off, hitting me in the chest and falling into my lap in a pool of blood and sinew. I screamed again and twisted in my chair. But I was held back by chains that were around my waist. Mr Landley's toe remained in my lap. 'Get it off me! Get it off me!'

'Great game is wriggly toes,' the earl said.

Mr Landley laughed as blood squirted from the hole where his toe had been. 'Wriggly toes is a must for our family.'

'My turn! My turn!' Mr Parsons shouted, hands raised.

I was still screaming, squirming, trying to roll the toe off my lap to no avail.

The earl looked horrified. 'Mr Parsons, we *must* roll the dice, tut, tut.' The earl held the shears in one hand, blood dripping on the floor, and rolled the dice with the other. It rattled in the wooden box. 'Ah, Mr James. It's your turn!'

Mr Landley clasped me on the back. 'Ho, ho, lucky you!'

The earl grasped the shears with both hands and came at me. 'Which toe, Mr James? Which toe?'

I screamed, shouting for Sydney and Rose, then collapsed as I felt the cold metal press over my toes.

I awoke to a loud thud outside in the corridor. My feet were hanging out of the covers. I sat upright, straining. Then I heard it again, a dull thud like something heavy dropping on the floor and then a muffled cry. I hobbled up, reaching for my dressing gown, and stumbled to the door.

I was met with panic and shouts, doors opening, then another far-off noise, and then Rose was there beside me wrapping her dressing gown tight around herself. 'What's going on?'

'I don't know.'

'It's coming from back there.' She pointed to the stairs beyond and we ran on, with others following in our wake. We picked up the pace when we heard another cry.

Mr Landley appeared behind us with a light. 'What's all this then, Mr Lavender? A little game, eh?'

'Hardly.'

He held the lantern aloft and Rose pointed. 'There! Over there.'

A thick rope, attached to the banister edge, taut and straining. More cries from below. We peered over, with the help of Mr Landley's light, and looked down into the faint darkness at a marble floor pierced by slivers of moonlight. Mr Parsons joined us. 'What's going on?'

'A body, there!' Rose pointed, and then the body swung into view on the rope, swinging to and fro. Another victim, another murder. We ran down the stairs towards body number three.

CHAPTER TWENTY-NINE

"'Elp, 'elp!'

It was Malcolm Wegwipe, hanging from the rope upside down. It had caught around his ankle, saving his life, giving him some slack from the noose around his neck. Rose rushed to lift him. 'Help me get him up.'

'Can't we just leave him there?' I said.

Rose gave me one of her looks, then grasped at the loop around his neck. 'Get a knife, quick!'

I patted my empty pockets and looked around in the dim light nonchalantly. 'I haven't got a knife.'

'Find something!'

I wandered around the hall looking for something sharp, as Mr Landley and Mr Parsons joined in the grappling. I conducted a brief stroll. Nothing but paintings hung on the wall on the right. Nothing sharp. I became particularly interested in one that hung just to the left of the fireplace. It depicted a young man on a horse. Neither of them looked very happy. The artist had chosen particularly dark colouring for the background – with murky green trees, a storm-fuelled black sky and grey rocky outcrops. Suggestive. As was the woman seated in the corner. She was hardly part of the picture at all.

'James!'

The sudden urgent shout alerted me to my task. It looked like the three of them were still struggling with Malcolm Wegwipe who was still upside down, not looking particularly happy about it. My attention shifted to something shining on the walls on the left. I ambled over to it. A medieval halberd. I yanked at it snapping a bracket in the process. I carried it back to Wegwipe. 'Move out.'

Rose looked terrified. 'You can't hit him with that!'

'Why not?'

But her sudden movement had further loosened the noose around his neck and he untangled to the floor. 'Aghh, thank you. Thank you.'

'No problem,' I said.

'Oh yes, because *you've* been a big help,' Rose said.

'I have; it was my involvement that loosened the rope.'

She shook her head. 'Never mind.'

I had calculated he wasn't really in any serious danger with the way the noose had wrapped around his ankle. The most likely outcome had been a small tumble to the floor in the manner he'd just demonstrated.

Rose helped a grateful Malcolm Wegwipe to his feet, together with the loonies, as I rested on the halberd.

'Who did this to you?' she asked, but he didn't answer, being too dazed to really hear her.

More and more people were coming down the stairs now. First, the rest of the Parsons and Landleys, followed by Sydney, with Lord Talbot lingering behind.

'You took your time,' I said to Sydney, as I leaned the halberd against the nearest wall.

'What you been doing with that?'

'I was going to whack Malcolm Wegwipe with it.'

'Oh, right. Grand.'

Malcolm Wegwipe himself looked visibly shaken. Apparently, being hung upside down by a rope had that effect. He flicked at his hair, then checked his pockets, looking increasingly concerned. Rose repeated her question.

'I...I have no idea. It was dark.' He felt around in his pocket.

'What is it?' Rose asked.

'I've lost my book. My black book. My notebook with all my things in it.'

'I read a book once.' Mr Landley mused,

looking off into the distance. 'Books are not really my thing, but it was a good one alright, all about farming. Not that you can read about farming in a book.'

'What things?' I asked Wegwipe, watching him closely.

Wegwipe's lips trembled as he spoke. 'My notes about all the…the goings on here…all the quotes.'

'Quotes? You were commenting on how brilliant I was,' I told him.

But our little conversation was interrupted by another scream. I told Wegwipe that I wanted to speak with him urgently first thing in the morning (after a minor lie-in). Then, our party headed back up the stairs, at the top of which we met the earl.

'Mr James, what's happening?'

Mr Landley's bushy face became animated. 'Another treasure hunt.'

'It's got nothing to do with me,' I snapped.

Rose nudged my arm. 'It's coming from the other end of the corridor. Run.'

'Why are we always running towards screams?'

'Shush.'

I almost stumbled as I was urged on by Rose, lit only by Mr Landley's light and the window at the other side of the corridor. Another scream. A woman's.

'It's coming from Lady Talbot's room,' Rose said, still leading the way.

We got to her room. The door was slightly ajar. Rose looked at me, concern etched into her face even though she couldn't stand her. I shrugged, pushing the door open with my foot, as Lord Talbot pushed past me.

'What is it?' he shouted.

Lady Talbot was sitting on the edge of her bed in an apparent state of shock, the bottom of her night dress ripped. 'He…attacked me,' she muttered, head in hands.

Lord Talbot moved towards her. 'Who? Who attacked you?'

When Lady Talbot didn't respond, Lord Talbot asked her again, more forcefully this time. To my surprise, Rose weaved her way towards Lady Talbot, but she brushed her away with a heavy hand.

Then Mr Landley bumbled beside me, bending down to retrieve something on the floor. Mr Parsons took it in his hands.

Lord Talbot urged his wife to answer, and she turned her head pointing at me. 'It was him.'

'Me?' But then I noticed her eyes were not focused on me but on someone behind me. Mr Parsons handed me the object as I turned, following Lady Talbot's gaze. The smooth metal object in my hand was a hipflask, and the person behind me was Sydney.

❖ ❖ ❖

'I want that man arrested,' Lord Talbot said, coming for Sydney, but Mr Landley and Parsons were in the way. 'Right now.'

'This is ridiculous,' I said. 'Sydney hasn't done anything.'

Sydney shook his head, too distressed to speak.

'He wouldn't do that,' Rose said.

Lord Talbot raged with emotion I'd not seen before. 'I want him arrested. He needs to be confined to quarters, immediately.'

The earl beside me looked unsure. 'Well, er…'

Lord Talbot took a step towards him. 'I demand it.'

The earl looked to me, troubled.

'The whole thing's nonsense,' I told him. 'Sydney hasn't done anything. It's a set-up.'

The earl looked down at the hipflask in my hand. Sydney's initials were clearly visible.

Lady Talbot stood up, hysterical, adjusting her night dress. 'He attacked me. He attacked me. It's not safe.'

'Now, now,' the earl began. 'I'm sure it's some misunderstanding.'

'George,' Lord Talbot said, his voice controlled, authoritative. 'I demand that this brute be placed under lock and key.'

The earl dithered, but Lord Talbot pressed him again.

'Well, er, maybe it's for the best. Just for now.' The earl nodded to a footman through into the corridor, who disappeared out of view for a brief moment. 'Just while we sort it out, eh, Mr James?'

I reached for the earl's arm. 'George, this is a set-up. Sydney wouldn't hurt a fly.'

He looked back at Sydney, nodded, still unsure, then bit his lip. 'Still, best be on the safe side, eh?' He motioned with a hand and Sydney was guided towards an empty room by two footmen. Emma, had been watching everything at her door, held back by her mother but she momentarily broke away in anger. 'NO! Stop! Father.'

I remonstrated to the earl, as did Rose, but there was no budging him.

'It's for the best, Mr James.' He sounded solemn, almost broken.

Sydney didn't resist, as he could easily have done; instead, he allowed himself to be taken to the empty room a few doors away. I saw his lost face as the door closed upon him.

'Father! Father!' Emma shouted, almost falling to her knees. Stella had gone towards her but she shrugged her away.

In anger, I turned towards the Talbots. Everyone's attention was on Emma, some offering lost words of consolation, so they failed to catch Lady Talbot's brief smirk and Lord Talbot's triumphant grin.

CHAPTER THIRTY

Emma was inconsolable, but through her distress, I felt her biting anger. It was early morning and I was in their room with Rose.

'Look, the best thing you can do is to finish the fingerprint task,' I told her.

She wiped away a tear with the back of her hand. 'Father wouldn't do a thing like that. He wouldn't have attacked that…that woman.'

'I know. Don't you worry. I'll sort it out.'

She looked at me sharply, her eyes burnt red. 'How?'

Good question. The Talbots had set up Sydney and had planted the hipflask in Lady Talbot's room. The question was, how to prove it?

I gave her my best reassuring smile. 'Just you leave it to me.'

Stella questioned me again regarding the tasks

I'd given Emma. I'd told her that age was not a barrier to intelligence. I handed Emma Sydney's hipflask, but there was no way in hell we were going to get a clean print off it thanks to the mauling Landley and Parsons had given it. Still, it would keep her actively occupied.

'What do you want me to do?' Rose said. 'Help Emma out?'

'No, she knows what she's doing. I want you to track down Simon and look into the rope on the banister. See if he can place it.'

She started to move. 'Right.'

'Wait.'

'What?'

'Don't go on your own.'

'James, I don't need a chaperone.'

'I know, but…best be on the safe side.'

Footmen had been placed in the corridor, monitoring. I shouted one over and asked him to bring up Simon.

'Stella, stay with Emma,' I told her. 'It's very important you don't leave her alone for one moment.'

'I'm hardly going to leave her, am I?'

'No, I suppose not.'

'What about breakfast?' Emma asked.

You could tell she was Sydney's daughter.

'I'll order it up for you. What do you all want?'

I strolled over to Sydney's room after I'd taken their orders, and I knocked on the door, ignoring the two hefty-looking footmen that had been placed on either side. 'Sydney, what do you want for breakfast?'

I heard a bang like a chair falling over and footfalls running towards the door. 'James, I didn't do anything. I've been set-up.'

'I know you have. What do you want for breakfast?'

'I've been thinking…'

'Makes a change.'

'…I left my jacket with my hipflask in it over a chair last night. Think that's how–'

'Great, what do you want for breakfast?'

'What?'

One of the footmen gave me a funny look as I was talking to the door. 'Sydney, I'm not going to ask you again, what do you want for breakfast?'

'Oh, er, boiled eggs.'

'Fine.' I trotted on towards Malcolm Wegwipe's room, which was just a little way down from ours, and knocked on the door loudly.

'Who is it?'

'It's me, *James* Lavender. Get out here, Wegwipe.'

I heard the door unlock and he appeared with dark rings around his eyes.

'Gosh, you look shocking. Come on, I want a word.'

He started to panic. 'Oh, I'd rather talk to you in my room, if it's all the sa–'

'No, no. Whatever you have to say can be said in front of others. You have nothing to hide, remember?'

'About that, yes, but–'

'But nothing, come on.'

He sniffed, flicking back his hair, which looked like it required a good wash. 'But, isn't it best we speak in private, about last night, I mean?'

'Probably yes, but I'm hungry and in need of tea. So get moving.'

❖ ❖ ❖

We were seated in the corner of the breakfast room. Wegwipe was fighting off startled looks from others, though there was only the Parsons lot down at present and William Brookes, who was dunking bread fingers into an egg. I'd ordered my breakfast, insisting that the tea be medium strength.

'Tell me what happened last night. Who did you plan to meet?'

Wegwipe dropped the spoon he had been thumbing. 'What? How did you know I had planned to meet anyone?'

I rubbed my hands together. 'Wegwipe, it was obvious. Your little "theoretical" speech yesterday was aimed at someone in particular. Who?' I stroked my chin and looked in the direction of the kitchen.

He looked at me apprehensively and pulled on his ear. 'Well, I…'

'Look, if you don't tell me everything, you

might find yourself hanging from a rope again, only this time you might not have such luck.' His eyes widened in fright, but then my scones arrived. 'Ah, breakfast!'

The maid placed the tray on the table and began to pour me a perfectly adequate-looking tea. The scones were fat and plump and the little dishes were crammed full of jam and cream. Wegwipe could only stomach a strong coffee.

The maid finished pouring my tea. 'Would there be anything else, sirs?'

'Not for now,' I said. 'I'll shout to you if I need any more – be ready!'

She curtsied and left.

I picked up a scone and crammed it full of jam and cream and prepared to take a large bite. 'Now, tell me all about it.'

❖ ❖ ❖

The earl ran into the now crowded breakfast room. 'I know what we need to cheer us all up, little bums! Let's play little bums!'

It was safe to say he had recovered from last night's shock.

Mr Landley immediately stood up, his chair and some cutlery falling victim to the floor. 'Little bums! *Fantastic* idea. We play little bums all the time.'

Here we go again. It's a wonder how he had time to run the estate.

The little Landley kid jumped up beside him. The toast he was eating flew onto the table, landing in someone's tea. 'Little bums!'

Mrs Landley slapped his arm, but he didn't seem to feel anything at all, lost in the prospect of little bums, whatever the hell that was.

The earl came over to me. 'Are you playing little bums, Mr James?'

'No. I'm busy.'

The earl looked down at the table, which was covered in empty plates and cups. 'Great game is little bums.' He was grinning happily behind his wispy, wizard-like beard.

'I'm sure it is,' I told him. 'But as I say, I'm busy trying to catch a multiple murderer and free my friend from injust–'

'Yes, yes, yes, but you can do all that *later*,' he pleaded.

He was joined by Mr Parsons and Mr Landley, both of them nodding encouragement. Mr Landley began:

'Little bums is a great little game, Mr Lavender, a *wonderful* game. A favourite game of the Queen, I believe.'

Mr Parsons smiled. 'The Queen is said to be fond of little bums.'

'I'm sure she is, but you'll have to excuse me on this occasion.'

They looked crestfallen, but soon began pulling the chairs out into a circle and removing the tables to the corner of the room, leaving mine alone, at least.

Aurea ran into the room, circling her father. 'Little bums. Little bums. Little bums.' He picked her up in his arms as the countess walked in, the thinnest of thin smiles on her pale lips.

They'd soon formed a near-perfect circle in the centre of the room which was fast populated by the Landleys, the Parsons, Malcolm Wegwipe, William Brookes, the countess and Aurea. The earl was stood up at the front with a triangle in his hand. He turned and gave me another pleading look. 'Won't you play, Mr James?'

I heard the little Landley brat mutter:

'The bad man is a sad man.'

I started to reiterate my previous objections when Aurea climbed onto the countess' knee and began to cry. Several people bent over in their chairs to try and placate the little girl.

'What's wrong with her?' Miss Parsons asked.

'She's upset that not everyone's playing.'

Miss Parsons shot me a sly glance. 'Well, some people take great delight in seeing children crying.'

I shook my head with a sigh and stood up.

The young girl cheered. 'Little bums! Little bums!' she shouted, giggling with laughter.

'Sorry,' I said to her. 'But I'm conducting a double murder enquiry and trying to free my associate and friend from social injustice.' I started to walk away and she started to cry again.

The countess stood. 'Mr Lavender, I

completely understand your situation, but couldn't you spare just two minutes of your time? All you have to do is sit for two minutes. It will keep her happy. Just pull your chair up into the circle.'

'I'm sorry, it's not possible.'

The girl continued to cry.

'Please, just two minutes,' the countess urged. 'One minute.' She hugged the girl, who was still crying.

The Landley brat turned to his brother, hand over the side of his mouth. 'The bad man is a mad man.' Then he burst into laughter at his comment.

The little girl ran up to me, holding out her hand, trying to pull me to a chair.

The earl looked on sadly. 'It only takes a minute, Mr James.'

I swore under my breath. 'What do I have to do?'

Mr Landley and the earl cheered.

'All you have to do is sit in your chair,' the earl began. 'And stand, tilting your bum when you think I'm going to hit the triangle. Like this.' The earl demonstrated the correct procedure.

'Right.'

'If you stand too early or too late, you're out.'

'Fine. Just get on with it.'

'Ho, ho,' laughed, Mr Landley. 'That's the spirit - eager now, I see. Margaret, didn't I...'

'Please god, no.'

'...say that–'

The earl dinged the triangle and Mr Landley stopped talking.

I should invest in one.

'Ready?' he declared. 'Let's play....little bums!'

Aurea giggled in excitement as the earl crouched down, triangle held aloft.

William Brookes stood up immediately, followed by Anthony Landley, then a few others. I stood up, but Mr Landley told me to *tilt*, not stand, so I did that for the quiet life. The earl rang the triangle and declared William Brookes out. The game continued.

Malcolm Wegwipe had said that he'd seen her hide the note under the salt. She thought she'd sneaked in unseen, but Wegwipe had seen her. He also admitted that his little 'speech' yesterday was to attract her attention and gain an interview. I lifted myself off my chair slightly, tilting my posterior. The earl rang the triangle some point afterwards and Mrs Parsons was out, to great cries of delight.

'Ho, ho, isn't little bums one of the greatest games of all time?' Mr Landley shouted to me, clapping his hands.

'Indeed.' I had no idea what was going on but it kept them all happy. The game continued.

The note that Wegwipe had found under his door was interesting. It was currently resting in my back pocket. All it said was 'meet now', in the same style of print writing as in the other notes, though it was of course difficult, if not impossible, to tell with such a small writing sample.

Mr Landley cheered, which brought me out of myself.

'Mr Lavender, that was a brilliant move, brilliant!' he said, shaking his head in wonder. 'Margaret, wasn't that a brilliant move? Margaret? Margaret?'

The earl jumped in. 'Yes, yes, I think we have a natural on our hands.'

I hadn't realised I'd done anything, and I had absolutely no idea what was going on, neither did I care, but soon Anthony Landley was walking out to the corner of the room. The earl told us all to sit and the nonsense carried on.

The Talbots hadn't shown up for breakfast, yet. How to rescue Sydney?

'Ho, ho!' Mr Landley shouted.

I jerked up in reaction to his voice and the earl hit the triangle at just the same time. I hoped that meant I was out.

'Amazing, Mr Lavender!' Mr Landley continued. 'What a fine move.'

The earl nodded. 'Utterly amazing.'

Miss Parsons screwed her face at me, then turned away. 'Hm, some people know how to cheat, clearly.'

'Margaret, you're out, I'm afraid,' the earl said. 'After such a perfect move by Mr James.'

Margaret Landley got to her feet, a flash of

appreciation at 'my move', whatever the hell that meant, and then the game continued.

No doubt the Talbots would have to breakfast at some point. There-in lay a possibility. A bragger likes to brag, after all. I felt a pang of cramp in my left leg so I stood up quickly to huge cheers.

'Wonderful move, Mr James!' the earl shouted.

'I said that Mr Lavender would be a fine little bums player, didn't I, Margaret? Margaret, didn't I say Mr Lavender would be a fine little bums player?'

I needed to get away from the nonsense. 'Have we finished?'

'Oh no, Mr James, you're in the final with Aurea and young Frederick.

The Landley brat looked at me then turned around to his brother at the back of the room, then said, in a singsong voice:

'The bad man is a glad man.'

I held up my hands in protest. 'Really, I must go.'

'Nonsense, Mr James, you've made the final!'

'Wonderful, but–'

'It will only take a second,' the countess said, with eyes back on her daughter.

'Fine.' I sat back down.

'Rules for the final,' the earl said. 'Don't forget you have to waft your hands as you tilt.'

'What?' I said.

'Like this.' The earl bent over slightly, arms by

his side and flapped his hands back. His daughter giggled and the earl laughed in return. 'It's what you do when you get to the final.'

I wondered when I would die so I could have some peace.

'Let's just get it over with,' I said.

Mr Landley cheered. 'That's the spirit!'

I sat back down. If I knew how this ridiculous game was played, I could have got myself out on the first go. The Landley brat stuck his tongue out at me in order to put me off and blew a raspberry. Margaret Landley stepped forward and slapped him around the ear and he stopped, mid-rasp.

'Ready?' the earl said, triangle aloft.

It was all quiet, broken only by Mr Parsons talking to Mr Landley:

'I'll bet you Mr Lavender wins.'

'Absolutely.' Mr Landley clapped.

There was a long pause, with the earl frozen, an animated grin behind his thin beard, his eyes darting from side to side. There was a large inhale of breath from someone behind me as the Landley brat almost made a move. I stood to get it over with and was shouted at from all quarters to do the ridiculous hand waft thing, so I did, half-heartedly. And that's when Rose walked in:

'James, what on *earth* are you doing? Have you ordered breakfast?'

Miss Parsons tutted at her. 'They're playing little bums. You're interrupting.'

'Oh no, I forgot to order breakfast, I was just–'

But I was drowned out by the cheers, as the earl dinged the triangle and I was declared the winner. Mr Landley ran towards me, followed by Mr Parsons, both of them clattering me on the shoulders and commiserating the brat and the young girl.

Rose's face seemed to darken. 'James, what about the investigation?'

'Yes, I was just–'

'Ho, ho, Mr Lavender here is a natural at little bums, isn't he, Margaret? Margaret? Margaret, isn't Mr Lavender a natural at little bums?'

The earl strode over, shaking my hand vigorously. 'Mr James, have you ever thought of taking up little bums in the National? You'd stand a good chance of winning.'

I tried to protest and explain to Rose through the nonsense, but Rose was joined by Stella and Emma. Stella didn't look happy either. 'What's going on?'

Rose huffed. 'James is busy playing children's games and he forgot to order breakfast.'

Emma suppressed a half-laugh, but Stella didn't see the funny side of things and continued to rant. 'Sydney's still stuck in the room and you're…'

'Yes, I've got a plan about that.'

'…playing children's games?'

Aurea started to cry and the countess picked her up, trying to console her.

Miss Parsons tutted again. 'You could have let her win.'

I turned around to her, snapping. 'Look, I didn't know what was going on.'

She was going to answer back but Mr Landley beside me had other ideas. 'Ho, ho, very funny. Mr Lavender is always good with his little jokes.'

I tried to drift off as he started up with his usual barrage of *Margarets.* Rose suggested that they order breakfast and she ushered Stella to the table where I'd sat with Wegwipe. 'You've already eaten, I see,' Rose said.

'Yes, yes. It was quite delicious.'

The Landley clan had begun to retreat and I spotted Simon, who had walked down with Rose. The rope had been taken from the stables. Anyone could have wandered in at any point and taken it. I asked him if he'd organised a search of the outhouses.

'Yes, Mr Lavender. Nothing doing. Sorry.'

'Thank you. It was just as I thought. And, er, the little suicide mission?'

Simon's mouth creased slightly. 'No news yet, I'm afraid.'

I thanked him and he removed himself from the room, to carry out his endless list of duties, no doubt.

The girl had stopped crying, thankfully, entertained by the earl who had picked her up on his back and was currently chugging around the room pretending to be a train. Mr Landley, then Mr Parsons, formed carriages behind them and they circled their way around the tables and chairs, making the footmen's lives difficult as they tried to return the room to normal. I joined our table.

'I still can't believe what I've just seen,' Stella said, shaking her head.

'Uncle James, I need to show you the finge–'

I shushed her, holding my finger over my mouth, and she nodded an apology.

Rose ordered breakfast and Sydney's boiled eggs that had quite slipped my mind and turned to me once the maid went. 'Yes, so no go on the rope. How did you get on with Malcolm Wegwipe?'

I was looking over at the earl, who'd put Aurea down, the train having apparently broken down, much to the disappointment of Mr Landley and Mr Parsons, who'd enjoyed their time as train carriages. 'Later.' I told her. 'Anyway, leave the breakfast, we've got something more important to do.'

'What's that?' Rose and Stella said in unison. Emma eyed me curiously.

I ignored them, shouting over to the earl. 'Hey, George.'

'Yes, Mr James?'

'Do you fancy a little game?'

His bright blue eyes illuminated. 'Game, Mr James?'

'Yes. A game. A very fun one.'

'Absolutely!'

Mr Landley and Parsons stood up enthusiastically as always.

'James,' Rose said. 'What's going on now?'

I ignored her. 'Hide and seek, George? How do you fancy a fun little game of *group* hide and seek?'

CHAPTER THIRTY-ONE

Mr Parsons lay under the Christmas tree in the Great Hall, his feet sticking out at one end.

'It's no good,' I told him. 'You need to edge back a bit.'

Beside me were Mr Landley and the earl, our faces squashed against the bristles of the tree.

'I say, this is a great idea, Mr James.'

'Slide back a bit more, Mr Parsons,' I said. 'Your feet will be spotted.'

He mumbled something, but began to shuffle backwards so that his face popped into view. 'Is that better?'

'Rose, can you see his feet?'

Rose was at the other end of the tree.

'No. I can't see them anymore.'

'Great.'

'What now, Mr James?' the earl said, his voice

bright and eager.

'Now. We wait.'

'Oh, this is so much fun,' the earl said.

Mr Landley nodded, which had the unfortunate effect of his large sideburns brushing against my face. 'Yes, it's a remarkable game. It's a wonderful break from farm management, though that's always exciting. You never know exactly how the manure is going to turn out. I must confess, it's been such a brilliant few days, we'll have to do it again next year. I said to M...'

I started to choke, and then Rose told us all to be quiet, that Emma had given the signal from the stairs.

'Remember,' I told them. 'We have to be *absolutely* silent. Not a word.'

'Ho, ho,' the earl said, then placed a finger over his lips as I glared at him.

I looked down at Mr Parsons, face flushed red, trying to suppress a snigger.

'Absolutely silent,' I reminded him.

Mr Landley laughed and I jabbed him in the side.

We seemed to wait in suspense for an age, but it must have only been minutes when we heard footsteps on the stairs. They grew louder and louder, then suddenly stopped. Then a voice, echoing from the bottom of the stairs:

'Ah, *Miss* McCarthy, admiring the Christmas tree I see. How...sweet.'

'Lady Talbot.'

The footsteps advanced and then stopped.

'I must say, you are looking well, Miss McCarthy. That extra weight suits you.'

'Delighted to see you as always, Lady Talbot.'

A few more steps.

'Where's your man, Miss McCarthy? Sorry, he's not your man, is he?'

'No, he's not my man, but he's not too far away...'

Two more steps.

'You know, Miss McCarthy. I always quite admired you.'

'I doubt that.'

'No, it's true. The way you travel around, a single woman, very…brave.'

'You're looking well too, Lady Talbot. You seem to have recovered remarkably well from last night's attack?'

I could feel Mr Landley beside me holding back a sneeze.

There was a pause, then another step. 'Yes, well, the brute's locked up so I'm quite safe now.'

'Oh, please. Sydney didn't attack you at all, did he?'

'You know, Miss McCarthy. When you're a desirable woman such as I, you can't help but attract men, and sometimes, unfortunately, that means stirring the emotions of brutes. One can't help it.'

'Don't talk nonsense. I know it was faked.

Sydney wouldn't do anything of the sort.'

'Yes, well…'

But Lady Talbot's voice trailed off, as more footsteps could be heard, and they were soon joined by someone else.

'Come on, let's go to breakfast.'

Lord Talbot.

'Lord Talbot, how did you set Sydney up? Was it you or her who stole the hipflask?' Rose asked, an edge to her voice.

There was a long pause, and then Lord Talbot said:

'Good morning.'

And the footsteps started to depart.

Then something clattered to the floor.

'Rather careless, Miss McCarthy,' Lady Talbot said.

'Here,' Lord Talbot said.

'Thank you,' Rose replied. 'So now are you going to tell me how you set up Sydney?'

'Good morning.'

And the footsteps departed for good, just as Mr Landley sneezed in my face.

'Damn, they're gone,' Rose said. 'She was about to confess as well, I know it.'

'Never mind,' I said, unable to keep the disappointment out of my voice.

'That was fun,' the earl said, though not as eagerly as before. 'Who won?'

'Erm, Lord and Lady Talbot…for now.' I had to admit.

We stepped out from behind the tree. I got a large scratch just above my left eye for my troubles.

'At least we have this.' Rose was dangling a shiny red bauble from her hand. 'Lord Talbot's print.'

❖ ❖ ❖

Emma was showing me what the problem was. The print on the knife handle was obscured.

I observed it closely. 'That's because the print is on top of another print.'

'That's what I thought.'

'I'm afraid there's nothing to be done. When a print overlaps like that it's just bad luck.'

Sydney, Stella and Emma's room had been turned into something of an experimental laboratory. Stray cutlery, cups and glasses (and now a bauble) lay cluttered on the dressing table, labelled with bits of paper. For some, they had to get more samples from the same person as prints weren't clean enough, so the collection was indeed quite a large one. Stella had grumbled that it was difficult to get ready like this at first, but then softened up when I reminded her it could help to catch a killer.

'Yes, well, we're no closer to that or to getting Sydney out, are we?' she'd said.

I'd told her not yet, but that I was working on it.

Emma had been more enthusiastic. Gone were her tears of frustration from this morning. Now she was only fiercely determined to set things right.

'How about the fingerprint found on my chair?' I said to her.

'It's not matched any of the samples we've taken so far. I think it's just come from a maid.' She peered at the print on the bauble. 'It doesn't look like Lord Talbot's either.'

'Try it anyway. It can't be a maid.'

The room hadn't been cleaned that day with the panic over the missing girl.

She nodded, deftly taking up the bauble with accurate, thin fingers. She dusted it with fine powder from one of the boxes, then began the process of transferring the print to paper.

Behind me, Rose was still unhappy about how Lady Talbot slipped from her hands. 'She would have confessed it, and then we'd have caught her. And I was too forceful with Lord Talbot. I should have played it more casually.'

'Never mind,' I said. 'Keep working on the new print. I won't be a minute.'

'Where are you going?' Rose asked.

'To see Sydney.'

The two footmen gave me a wary glance as I knocked loudly on Sydney's door. 'Sydney, you fat lump.'

'James.' I could hear him hobbling over. 'Are you getting me out?'

'We almost did, but it didn't quite work out. I'm thinking on it.'

'Oh, grand. Thanks for sending the boiled eggs up; they were lovely.'

'No problem. Anyway, when we first visited Mr Eastwell's stable, can you remember what he said exactly when he was talking about raising horses?'

'Was that before you poked him in the eye or after?'

I sighed. 'Before.'

There was the deafening sound of strained thought behind the door. 'About the training marks?'

'Yes.'

'No, not exactly. Is it important?'

'Yes, but it doesn't matter. I think I remember.'

'Grand.'

'Right, see you later. Don't go anywhere.'

'Oh, James.'

'What?'

'Can you order me some tea up? And some biscuits.'

'I'll see what I can do.'

I returned to Sydney and Stella's room. It was immediately apparent that something was amiss

'What's up?' I said.

Emma was beaming proudly. 'It's the print. The one on the chair.'

'Yes?'

'It's a definite match. It's Lord Talbot's.'

❖ ❖ ❖

It was much easier underfoot now. The snow had melted rapidly in the rain and warmer air, turning it into slush and running water. Gone too were the biting winds. I was leading the way towards the Temple of the Four Winds with Rose beside me. Emma had pleaded to come as well, but Stella had firmly ruled it out. Apparently, a little trip to re-visit a corpse was not an 'appropriate task for a child'.

'What are the chances of us finding any further clues on or around the body?' Rose asked me as we walked together.

'Clues that could be used as evidence? Pretty slim, what with the rugby scrum at the crime scene, but one never knows.'

I'd had to fight the loonies off, as they of course had wanted to come on our 'little adventure', as the earl had phrased it. To placate them, I'd told them to write down how long they thought we'd be on a piece of paper and they'd placed it in a large hat, and then they'd sat around staring at it. This had cheered them greatly. Mr Landley had declared it as one of the 'greatest ideas of the last twenty years,' and William Brookes had agreed.

'It's still cold,' Rose said, wrapping her long coat around herself.

'Yes, it is still winter.'

She gave me that look, but I strode on, my bladder heavy. I should have taken care of that before I came out. 'Oh, that reminds me, Sydney requested tea and biscuits.'

'Did you order him some?'

'No.'

'Well, that wasn't very kind of you, was it?'

'I forgot. Busy.'

'Yes, but you just drank several cups of tea, staring into the fire just now. You could have ordered one for poor Sydney.'

'I was musing. You could have ordered him tea.'

'I didn't know he wanted any.'

The statues on the way were now clean and free of snow. A little robin bobbed and fluttered at the base of one, making small forks in the snow.

'Ah, look. Robins are supposed to bring luck,' Rose said.

'Well, yes, but not if you're a worm,' I laughed.

Rose strode over a fallen tree branch. 'Don't you believe in luck?'

I snorted. 'Of course not. I'm not stupid.'

'What? How do you mean?'

I stopped beside her. 'Luck doesn't exist.'

'Yes, it does.'

'No, it doesn't.'

Rose sighed. 'What about the last time we were here? The card game?'

She was referring to a game of cards I'd

had previously with Lord Talbot. I'd won one hundred pounds with a pair of twos.

'It was lucky, yes, but luck as a factor doesn't exist. Only statistical probabilities.'

'What? Oh, forget it.' She continued towards the temple. I followed.

'When you think about it, everything is mathematical.'

'I'd rather not have this conversation. Let's just hurry and get back inside where it's warm.'

'Right, that's fine with me, only you asked. Why ask the question if you don't want the answer?'

When she came to the steps, she hung back a little, wanting me to go in first. Being around the dead was never a pleasant prospect. I climbed the steps, ensuring there was no ice, which there wasn't, and wedged open the heavy door.

'Light the torch in the bracket,' Rose shouted.

But the torch wasn't there. And neither was the body.

❖ ❖ ❖

'Did you have the body moved? I asked the earl, as I handed my outdoor clothing to a footman.

The earl held his pocket watch. 'Twenty-seven minutes, ten seconds.'

Mr Landley cheered and they turned to the hat in the centre of the table. I repeated my question.

He finally replied over the noise. 'Moved the

body, Mr James?'

'Yes, did you have Mr Eastwell's body moved?'

He was distracted again by the loonies reaching for the times in the hat. The Landley brat disrupted events by placing it on his head, which caused strips of paper to fall to the floor. Margaret was in with a timely bash around the ear. This dislodged the hat and sent it to the earl's feet.

'Never mind the hat, did you have the body moved? It's not there.'

'Body, Mr James? Oh, no.'

I asked for Simon to be brought out, and he confirmed the earl's words. The others cheered around me as Frederick was declared the winner of the hat game.

I turned to Rose. 'So we have a missing dead body. That's very interesting. Very interesting indeed.'

❖ ❖ ❖

'Why are you not charging Lord Talbot?' Stella asked me when out of earshot of the others in the drawing room.

I scratched the edge of my nail, my elbow resting on the table. 'Because it's not enough on its own. We have evidence he was in my room, but no actual evidence he handled the knife.'

'Is there nothing we can do about the muddled prints on the knife handle?' Rose whispered.

I'd re-studied them carefully before we set off outside. The two prints obscured each other completely. Absolutely nothing could be done about it.

'Order me some tea, will you, while I think a bit?'

Rose exhaled rather loudly as I considered how to do the impossible. How to extract a fingerprint that had been completely obscured by another. Rose ordered tea and biscuits for Sydney, and a healthy supply for the table.

'Care for a game of cards, Mr Lavender?'

Lord Talbot.

'You've got some cheek, standing th–'

I held Stella back, cutting her off. 'I don't think so,' I said.

He smiled thinly, in that smug way of his. 'I think you'll be interested in the terms.'

'Go on.'

'You give me the opportunity to win my money back from last time, plus a little more, call it…two hundred.'

'And you?'

He made a fake show of considering his wager by pursing his lips and pondering absently. 'How about we drop the charges against your little friend…in the spirit of forgiveness.'

Stella was out of her chair. 'Sydney's done nothing wrong.'

Lord Talbot merely shrugged offhandedly. 'It's a fair deal. How much is the greedy fellow worth?' He smiled again. 'Your call.'

'Don't do it,' Rose said.

Emma agreed. 'We'll think of another way.'

I looked up at Lord Talbot who was now staring at me intensely. I was aware that conversation in the room had ceased completely, with eyes turned my way. 'Only fools gamble, Lord Talbot, and I'm not a fool.'

A small jerk touched his lips. 'Yes, but I hold the upper hand, Mr Lavender. You have little choice.'

'There's always a choice.'

Lady Talbot was soon at his side. 'Ah, *Miss* McCarthy,some men are natural cowards, are they not?'

Rose flushed. 'Do be quiet, Lady Talbot, otherwise someone might get hurt.'

'Oh dear, a physical threat. That Irish blood's never far from the surface, is it?'

The earl bobbled over, standing next to Lady Talbot. 'Now, now, people. How about another game? What about blind man's buff?'

But there was little enthusiasm for the distraction.

'What do you say, Mr Lavender?' Lord Talbot said again. 'Draw poker, call it two hundred on the table for your dim-witted friend?'

Rose leaned over to me, grabbing my arm. 'Don't do it.'

'Uncle, it's a trap.'

Lord Talbot towered over. 'Well, Mr Lavender,

what do you say?'
 Rose whispered. 'No.'
 I looked up at Lord Talbot. 'Let's play.'

CHAPTER THIRTY-TWO

We'd relocated to the turquoise drawing room. On the way there, Rose and Stella had taken turns in calling me all the names under the currently-obscured sun, but I'd told them not to worry. I'd told them that I was the great James Lavender. Yet, this hadn't seemed to reassure them. They'd said something about it not being a good idea gambling Sydney's life away or words to that effect. I'd not really been listening.

I'd asked the earl to send out a search party to look for the missing body. I'd told him where to look. If I was correct in my thinking, the body wouldn't be too far away from the temple. Perhaps in the tree line on either side. Exposure to the elements would wipe any potential clues away, but it was of little consequence.

I'd expected the likes of Mr Landley and Mr Parsons to be jumping up and down, frothing at the lips at the prospect of the card game. In fact, the opposite was true. I'd never seen them so subdued and full of nerves. Most people were the same. Except, that was, for Lady Talbot, who was thrilled at the prospect. David Eastwell seemed to have recovered a little from yesterday. He sat with Miss Parsons, quietly looking on in expectation of the game. Miss Parsons herself had eyes that occasionally sparkled and then dimmed. The only person not watching was the countess, who was sitting in the corner away from it all, her child asleep in her lap. Regardless, I'd allowed myself to be talked into another card game with Lord Talbot. He was a very strong player. My condition would only give me an edge if my opponent tried to bluff, but the last time I'd played him, he'd sat observing the table with cold, calculating eyes, giving nothing away. Maybe this time, with it just being us, he'd talk.

The final chair had been set up and the table was given a final polish when Rose pulled me to one side. 'Don't do it.'

'It's fine, Rose. Honestly.'

'It isn't fine. It's crazy.'

'Yes, but–'

'There are no "buts" you're risking Sydney on the turn of some cards.'

I shook my head and joined the game at the offered chair opposite Lord Talbot.

'Ah, here we are again, Mr Lavender. I told you there'd be a next time.'

The footman who had tucked the chair behind me seated himself at the side of the table and explained the house rules on draw poker. It was a game of skill and luck – or more accurately, skill and probability.

'Cards is a very honourable game, don't you think, Mr Lavender? A gentleman's game.'

The footman dealt out our first hand and then laid the pool cards facedown on the table. It was normal to have five hand cards but, in the variant played here, we only had two and bet on the pool cards.

'I've played many card games, Lord Talbot, but rarely have I seen any honour involved – not where money is concerned. Good hand?'

I had an eight and a four, different suits. A poor hand. Lord Talbot didn't answer. He simply scooped up a handful of chips and threw them into the centre. I folded.

I'd not lost anything, only the minimal stake, but I'd folded immediately, so it looked more dramatic than it was. This was a ploy on my part. I'd fold quickly or slowly, not necessarily in relation to the cards.

Frederick Landley was in my eye-line and sat just behind Lord Talbot to the left. He was swinging his legs, a lolly in and out of his mouth. When he saw my glance, he stuck his purple tongue out at me. A hand clipped his ear from behind, and he continued sucking on his lolly instead.

I folded a second time and a third, and Lady Talbot sniggered, turning to Rose. 'Is he playing the game or just folding?'

Rose made no reply.

On the fourth hand, Lord Talbot folded and I took my minimum stakes back. 'A turn of the winds of chance?' I said.

But he merely smiled, picking up his next cards. We had several more rounds until we got into a moderate exchange of bets. I had two tens, a healthy hand, but not one to push too far.

'Have you got any pictures, there?' I fished.

In response, Lord Talbot counted out the largest amount of chips yet and threw them into the middle of the table.

There were several exclamations around the room. The earl looked pale. Lord Talbot had cast around a quarter of his chip pile in the centre. This was right on the edge of where I would wager.

Lord Talbot looked up from his cards. 'What are you going to do, Mr Lavender?'

'Depends, if you've got a little picture in there.'

A quick smile touched his upper lip. 'Your move.'

I felt the first really nervous tremble. This was a risk, but I decided it was just about worth it, so I matched his bet and we turned the cards over. He had two jacks. I'd lost.

He took the chips without a flinch. Lady Talbot said something derogatory to Rose. David

Eastwell smiled when William Brookes ushered forth a 'capital', but other than that, nobody made a sound. I'd now lost just over thirty per cent of my chip pile, giving Lord Talbot a healthy advantage.

'Oh, that's not good. Is it, Miss McCarthy?' Lady Talbot pretended to ask, but Rose still stood unmoved.

The hands that followed over the next twenty minutes were nothing remarkable, but I'd had more folds than Lord Talbot so my chip pile had gradually reduced further. To make matters worse, now came the time to increase the initial stakes.

'Deal,' Lord Talbot insisted, as the footman had slowed his regular pace.

He did so and I held the Ace of Clubs and the Jack of Hearts. Potentially a very good hand. It was my turn to increase the stakes. I did so by just a few chips so as not to scare off Lord Talbot.

'Interesting,' he said.

'What is?'

'The small raise there. Have a good hand?'

'Have you?'

I saw Mr Landley grab hold of Mr Parsons' jacket, his fingers white.

Mr Parsons brushed his face, then tapped his chest. He looked as nervous as Mr Landley. I glanced at the earl, who held something tightly in his hands. It looked like a paintbrush.

Lord Talbot picked up a large pile of chips and

placed them in the centre. He'd just bet half of my chip pile. I had no choice but to meet his wager, as I couldn't guarantee another potential good hand coming up any time soon.

There were a few cheers, but more groans as I met his bet. We flipped over our cards. He had a pair of eights. If the pool cards hit an ace or a jack, I'd won it. If not, the hand was Lord Talbot's. The footman turned the remaining three cards: a six, a three, and a nine. I'd lost.

Lord Talbot sighed in mock disappointment. 'Oh dear, it looks like that greedy little friend of yours is going to be on his own for a while, but I hear prison food is improving, is it not? Gruel these days, I hear, is almost fit for dogs.'

Stella only just fell short of thumping him, held back by Rose.

Lady Talbot grinned. 'Oh my, it's *sooo* disappointing when you lose, isn't it?'

'Cow!' Rose said.

'Oh, dear me, Miss McCarthy, how…guttural. I'm disappointed in you.'

The earl stepped forward. 'Now, now, let's be nice. Let's be on good terms.'

'Good terms?' Stella said.

Rose wouldn't meet my eyes. Neither would Stella. Emma was still hunched over, trying to be brave.

'Wait!' Lord Talbot said, holding his held hand up towards the dealer. 'I'm a fair man, Mr Lavender.'

'I doubt that.'

'No, no, give credit where credit's due. Let's make another little deal.'

The earl looked troubled.

'What's the deal?' I asked him.

'We turn the top cards over twice. The highest card wins. You have to beat me twice, but if I win one, you've lost. Similar as before.'

'What's the catch?'

'The catch, Mr Lavender?'

'What's in it for you?'

I caught sight of Mr Landley and Mr Parsons. Their faces were as grave as the earl's.

The Landley brat took his diminishing lolly out of his mouth. 'The bad man is a dead man.'

It raised a few sniggers. Until a wallop resounded on the back of his head. Margaret Landley was fast coming up in my estimation.

'Oh, I'm being generous, Mr Lavender, all you have to do is throw in another hundred. Don't forget, if you win you owe nothing and your chubby little friend goes free. If not...' Lord Talbot shrugged. 'He gets daily use of the prison treadmills. Excellent exercise or so I've heard.'

Stella's reaction was hardly ladylike. Emma gasped. It took all of Rose's diplomacy to cool them.

I wiped my hand on my knees. 'Agreed.' The extra hundred would put me in personal debt to Lord Talbot.

Mr Landley shook his head and Mr Parsons

followed. Neither Rose nor Stella both could watch, but Emma looked on.

'Ready?' the dealer asked, himself looking flustered.

'Yes, deal,' I said, leaning back.

Lord Talbot smiled as he received the first card. I took mine. An eight. Hardly great, but not terrible either.

Lord Talbot laced his fingers together and leaned forward on the table. 'Happy?'

I shrugged.

'After three,' he said.

The earl counted to three and we flipped the cards over. Lord Talbot had a seven. I'd won the first hand.

Emma pumped her fist. *'Yesss.'* Which alerted Rose and Stella. Mr Landley stood up cheering. 'Come on, Mr Lavender!'

Mr Parsons cheered beside him.

It was now on one turn of a card. Either I would win and free Sydney, or Sydney would still be facing charges and I'd be in financial debt to Lord Talbot.

Lord Talbot held up a finger to silence his wife, who was about to say something to Rose.

'Just one turn now,' the earl said, addressing Lord Talbot. 'No other deals.'

Lord Talbot nodded. 'Certainly.' He pointed to the dealer, who slid us a card each. Lord Talbot picked his up, guarding it closely to his chest. I rested my fingers on the back of the card, my heart thundering in my chest. I could hardly bring myself to pick it up.

'Come on. Come on,' I whispered.

Emma was scrunched over and both Rose and Stella looked on this time. It was all on this card. I picked it up, my hands clammy with sweat, praying for a high number. I turned it over so that only I could see it and my heart sank. A four. I couldn't hide the disappointment on my face. I heard David Eastwell mutter an 'oh, dear'.

Lady Talbot smiled, but Lord Talbot remained impassive. I could only win if he had a two or a three. A four would mean we would go again, but any higher card would mean he'd won.

'Well, Mr Lavender,' Lord Talbot said, not sounding particularly confident himself. 'Shall we see?'

I nodded, unable to find the right words. I threw down my four and the crowd around me groaned. Emma reeled back. Rose swore and Stella was about to walk away, held back only by the faintest hope Lord Talbot held a two or a three.

Lord Talbot dangled the card in his fingers, and then flipped it over. Ace of Clubs. I'd lost everything.

CHAPTER THIRTY-THREE

'Not so fast,' I said, wagging a finger as I was met by the cries and shouts of all those around me. Stella was already halfway out of the room but turned at my declaration.

'A deal is a deal, Mr Lavender,' Lord Talbot said.

The earl stood over us, wrinkles around his pale blue eyes. 'It's true, I'm afraid, Mr James. The deal was struck.'

Mr Landley rubbed his head, and Mr Parsons looked crestfallen.

Lord Talbot raised his hands. 'Awfully sorry.'

Lady Talbot moved towards her husband, but he brushed her away.

'Not so fast,' I repeated.

The earl rubbed his chin. 'What is it, Mr James?'

Emma eyed me curiously.

'Lord Talbot's card, the Ace of Clubs–'

Miss Parsons laughed. 'Is higher than a four.'

The Landley brat stood on his chair. 'Four-five-six-seVEN-eight-NINE–' He swerved to avoid a hand, then continued. 'Ten-jack-queen-king-A-ACE!'

This time Margaret's hand found its mark and the Landley brat was nearly knocked from his chair.

The earl hadn't been distracted. 'What about the Ace of Clubs, Mr James?'

Lord Talbot's nose twitched, as I addressed the earl. 'Yes, very interesting that card.'

'Stop trying to talk your way out of it,' Miss Parsons said. 'We all heard you make the deal. You can't go back.'

'I'm not going back.'

'That's settled then,' Lord Talbot said, about to collect the chips.

'No. Not so fast,' I said.

'Oh, what is it now, for heaven's sake?' Miss Parsons said, rolling her eyes around dramatically, edging closer to David Eastwell.

The earl still looked puzzled. 'What of it, Mr James?'

I held my forefinger against my lip for a brief moment. 'You know, I had the Ace of Clubs, not that long ago.'

'Fascinating, I'm sure,' Miss Parsons said.

'Hey, why are you getting involved?' Emma said. 'Keep your nose out of it.'

'Well said,' Rose remarked, moving closer to

Emma. 'What about the card, James?'

'I had it not long ago, which is strange, don't you think? Seeing as we've just turned the top cards over. Unless a pack now sports two Ace of Clubs.'

'Just what are you saying?' Lord Talbot said. 'Are you accusing me of *cheating*? That's a very dangerous affair if you are.'

'I'm saying, Lord Talbot, that there can't be two Ace of Clubs in one pack, can there? So, you must be cheating, yes.'

'Nonsense. George, have you heard this? I shall not tolerate such slander.'

The earl looked from Lord Talbot to myself, his lips shaking. 'Mr James, are you clear on what you're saying?'

'Yes. Have the footman check. If he flips the pack over and counts out a dozen cards or so, I expect he'll uncover another Ace of Clubs. This is, of course, impossible.'

Lord Talbot was furious.

'Flip them and see,' I said, nonchalantly.

The earl instructed the footman to turn them over and he did so, flipping the cards so all could clearly see. He counted out fourteen cards and there it was, the Ace of Clubs! There were angry shouts directed at Lord Talbot. Cheating was a disease which would quickly spread through his social circles. The footman picked the card up and placed it on top of Lord Talbot's own ace. The earl picked them both up. Same pack design.

Same card.

'I think you'll find, that means I win,' I said, reaching for a glass of water.

The shouting continued. Lady Talbot walked out of the room, and Lord Talbot stood.

'That's not on, Lord Talbot,' the earl said, gravely. 'Not on, at all.'

'It was just a joke, George.'

The earl didn't look pleased. 'Mr James here is the winner. That means you release his friend, without charge.'

Emma cheered, as did Mr Landley and Mr Parsons, followed by a few others. Stella had to sit down. Only Rose remained impassive. Emma ran around the table, wrapping her arms around me. 'Well done, Uncle James, that was brilliant!'

'Of course, the thing was never in doubt.'

Rose made some dismissive remark.

'Ho, ho, Mr Lavender!' Mr Landley shouted. 'That's remarkable, what do you say, George? Remarkable, eh?'

'Yes, yes, quite remarkable.' But his heart wasn't really in it, and he turned to Lord Talbot. 'That was low. That was very low. What about all the others?'

Lord Talbot raised his hands. 'It was just a little joke, George. That's all.'

But the earl wasn't buying it for a moment. 'No more cards.' The earl turned to a waiting footman. 'Have Mr Sydney released immediately!'

Mr Landley cheered as Emma released my neck from her clutches. I glanced down at the cards on the table. Two identical clubs side by side. 'I have an idea about the murder weapon.' I told her. 'I know how to separate the prints.'

Emma tried to hush me, but I went on excitedly. 'We don't need the flask or any other print, just the knife. Rose, I've figured it out.'

'Figured what out?' the countess asked.

'How to catch the killer.'

The earl stepped beside her. 'You have, Mr James?'

'Naturally.'

'Margaret, did you hear that?' Mr Landley began, 'You can always count on Mr Lavender. What did I say, Margaret? Margar…'

'Come on then,' Rose said. 'Let's head up and work it out.'

'Not yet,' I told her.

The earl shook my hand as Lord Talbot slipped out of the room. 'Wonderful, Mr James! Wonderful!'

But Rose was in my other ear. 'Come on, let's go.'

I tapped her arm as she tried to drag me away. 'Hold on a moment.' I turned to the others. 'I just need to see to an issue of nature, and then do you all want to play a fun game first? We need to have a little fun first, after that.' I pointed at the cards on the table.

'Game, Mr James? Hurray!'

It was safe to say that they were on board with a game, but Rose still looked unhappy. She said something about getting on with solving the murders, but I couldn't quite hear what she was saying over the fuss.

The earl turned to me. 'What game do you have in mind?'

I stood up, straightening my jacket. 'Have you ever played wonky donkey?'

'Wonky donkey?' the earl said. 'That sounds like an amazing game. How do you play it, Mr James?'

'You need to make some antlers, that go on your head. They also need to cover your face. You can make them out of bits of old socks or ties, but you have to make sure your eyes are covered.'

'Like blind man's buff?' the earl asked.

'A bit like that, yes.'

'Ho, ho, did you hear that, Margaret? Margaret, did you hear that?'

'Sounds fantastic,' Mr Parsons said.

'*Yessss,*' the Landley brat said, charging around the room, his hands pointing like a bull. He ran into a footman, who dropped a drink. Margaret chased after him.

I explained the design of the antlers, giving them suggestions on how you can make the donkey hat when Miss Parsons butted in:

'This is the most ridiculous thing I've ever heard. Why are you making antlers for a donkey? Donkeys don't have antlers.'

'Because, wonky donkey sounds better than wonky deer, and it's my game,' I said.

'Quite right, Mr Lavender.' Mr Landley nodded. 'Quite right.'

Rose pulled me to the nearest corner. 'Have you gone quite mad?'

'Look. You've got to trust me. There isn't time to explain.'

Rose didn't reply. She just crossed her arms.

Emma dashed away. 'Father, father!' She wrapped herself around a bemused-looking Sydney, then reluctantly released him when Stella gave him a rare embrace. This was broken by a small round of applause.

They walked over, with Sydney smiling shyly. 'I heard what you did, about the card game. That was very brave of you.'

'Oh, it was nothing.'

'It's so good to be out of there. I was worried for a momen–'

'Yes, yes, stop milking it. I need you for something *very* important.' I fixed him with a steel stare.

Stella tried to intervene to give him a moment to repose himself, but I reminded her that he'd just been sitting around doing nothing as usual.

Sydney stood proud. 'What do you want me to do, James? Anything. Anything at all.'

A flashed him a quick smile. 'I need you to dress up as a donkey.'

CHAPTER THIRTY-FOUR

I was greeted with predictable scenes of chaos as I re-entered the drawing room. The earl, Landleys and Parsons, together with little Aurea, were creating a great deal of mess in making the donkey hat. Mr Parsons was currently wafting his hand, having apparently glued an old sock to himself. Mr Landley was at the centre of preparations with the earl, tugging on the antlers and trying to feed them into the hat the wrong way around. Aurea was on the table knocking over glue pots and paints, while the Landley brat still charged around the room pretending to be a bull with Margaret still trying, and failing, to catch him.

Meanwhile, at the side of the room, Stella was helping Sydney into a huge brown jacket I'd requested from a footman. A large brush lay on the floor beside a frowning Rose. Emma sat beside her, a curious expression on her face as if quietly calculating what the hell I was up to.

The Talbots were seated in the far corner, doing their best to ignore the proceedings but struggling to do so, particularly as the Landley brat kept running past them.

Over in the other corner, Miss Parsons, David Eastwell and Anthony Landley sat close to each other in a seemingly fractured mood, as if some argument or other had broken out amongst them. Malcolm Wegwipe and William Brookes sat just behind them, quietly chatting, though Wegwipe was jotting notes in a new book he had procured from the earl.

'Ah, Mr James,' the earl cried, as soon as he spotted me. 'Can you help with the donkey hat? We seem to be having trouble with one of the antlers.'

Miss Parsons screwed her face at the earl's reference to the donkey antler and muttered something uncomplimentary.

I strode over to the table. 'Of course. What seems to be the problem?'

'The antler is a bit off and the ear won't go on straight.'

'That's fine,' I said, brightly. 'It is wonky donkey, after all.'

Mr Landley chuckled. 'Ha, ha, that's amazing. Of course, it is!'

He then went on to try to get Margaret's attention, but she was still otherwise engaged in the frantic bull race that was, until Lord Talbot's stray foot just happened to stick out at the wrong time as the Landley brat roared past. This sent him sprawling to the floor with Margaret fast upon him.

Mr Landley screamed as he separated the sock from his hand, a chunk of hair taken with it. I scooped up the hat. 'This will do, but we need to relocate to the Great Hall.'

The earl and Mr Landley both beamed excitedly as everyone was encouraged forward, whether they wanted to move or not.

It was naturally a little colder in the Great Hall, with long sweeping draughts easily penetrating thinner clothing. There were a few complaints from the usual quarters, but I replied that they'd soon all warm up during the first round of wonky donkey.

'How do we play, Mr James?' the earl asked, leading me to the centre to explain the rules, the donkey hat trailing by his side.

'It's simple.' I had to suppress a laugh as I turned to face them all, a multitude of faces. Some of them were etched in delight, like Mr Landley; others, perhaps the majority, in fierce annoyance or bewilderment. 'Wonky donkey is a challenging game of skill and reflexes,' I told them, holding back another snigger. 'It's a highly intellectual game.'

Mr Parsons stood firm, looking serious, arms by his side. I continued:

'It takes a great mind to win at wonky donkey.'

Mr Landley nodded, his face also screwed up

and serious.

Miss Parsons huffed. 'Ridiculous.'

I took the donkey hat from the earl and held it before me. 'The person playing the donkey wears this. Sydney here will be the donkey for the first round.' A few people looked his way, then back to me. 'You put the donkey hat on, which covers your eyes, and bend over with the brush pretending to be a donkey.' I took the brush from Sydney, demonstrating the correct stance. 'Then you spin around three times, hence the wonky element, then you charge, shouting, "wonky donkey's coming to get you".'

'Oh my God,' Miss Parsons said. 'I've never heard anything so absurd.'

David Eastwell agreed. 'Childish in the extreme.'

But the earl was not to be deterred. 'Wonderful, wonderful! It sounds a-mazing.'

Mr Landley concurred. 'The best. It sounds like the best game ever, doesn't it, Margaret? Margaret, doesn't it sound like the best game ever?'

The earl scratched his chin. 'How do you win?'

I pursed my lips, thinking. 'If you hit someone with the brush three times, then they become the donkey.'

William Brookes shouted. 'Capital!'

I had to stop the cheers of the usual bunch before I could continue. 'Now,' I said. 'As I say, Sydney here is going to be the first donkey.'

'Why is that man the first donkey?' the Landley brat asked.

'Because…because he's got the jacket on. Now be quiet. So, Sydney here stands in the middle. Give him some space, that's better. Now he's going to start us off, ready?'

Vigorous nods, a wall of tuts and frowns, but we were ready. Rose was refusing to meet my eyes but there was nothing I could do about that.

Sydney placed the donkey hat on, being careful not to knock off the hastily sewn antlers. He bent over with the brush I'd given him, then quickly spun around three times.

'Mind the tree,' I told him, pulling his finger in the direction of the great Christmas tree which still stood impressively under the radiant glow of the cupola, despite the earlier unfortunate vomiting incident. The antlers shook. I stepped back. 'Ready? One, two, three – wonky donkey!'

Sydney spun around immediately with the brush to cries of delight from the Landley brat, the earl, Mr Landley and Mr Parsons. Sydney was off-balance as he spun, the effect of which upturned the wooden edge of the brush which went with an audible crack at the side of the earl's head, hitting him like a hammer blow. There were a few gasps as the earl tottered on his feet, only just rescuing himself from crashing to the floor. 'Ho, ho. That was fun. I guess I've lost a life. Amazing game!' He held his ear to stem the flow of blood. He totted a bit more, but the game carried on.

Sydney spun the other way around this time, shouting out. 'Wonky donkey is coming to get you.' To which the little girl screamed and giggled in delight. The Landley brat pushed his brother in the way of Sydney, and Sydney hit him with the broom flat in his face, this time bristles face on, so the impact was not as dramatic – though it still looked like it registered a sting. Sydney continued. 'Wonky donkey is coming to get you!'

This time, rather than spinning the broom, he rushed straight on, in the immediate direction of the Christmas tree.

'Watch out for the tree!' someone shouted.

But it was too late. Head first, Sydney stumbled into the giant tree, losing his footing when he felt the tree's resistance, his momentum carrying him further forward and he crashed down deep inside it. The brush fell by his side. At first, it looked like the tree would absorb the shock of his great weight, but then it too began to sway and topple. Then there was no stopping it – it arched down, slowly at first, then moved with greater intensity until it came crashing down into the centre of the Great Hall, smashing baubles and sending them flying everywhere. Chaos and pandemonium ensued, screams in between shrill cries and whoops that filled the room. Someone, either Miss Parsons or Lady Talbot, uttered, 'Christmas is ruined forever.' As the tree lifted and then crashed again, scattering yet more baubles all around, Sydney stumbled on all fours, lost in the middle of the tree. Then the outer door opened.

First, the wind invaded, then the swirls of an evening fog disappeared to reveal the frame of a solid figure dressed all in black, in a long, drenched coat that dripped rain water to the floor. The fog cleared some more, and there, in the frame of the doorway bobbled a furious moustache, attached to the equally furious face of Inspector Moss.

'LAVENDER!' it shouted.

Two more faces emerged behind him. The first one was long and thin and struggled for breath. The second one held a moustache which looked like a cheaper copy of the good inspector's. It too was dripping.

'LAVENDER!' Moss shouted again.

'Ah, I see you've received my message, excellent,' I said.

The inspector's eyes darted to the scene of absolute devastation before him. 'What in God's name has happened here?'

'Oh, just a little game,' I said.

He shook his head, water still dripping to the floor as he stepped forward. 'I've heard you have a dead body. Mrs Eastwell. What the hell is going on, Lavender?'

I nodded. 'Yes, we have a body, well two actually, but one of them has gone missing.'

'WHAT?'

I reached down and picked up the donkey hat from the middle of the wreckage. 'Care for a game of wonky donkey?'

'LAVENDAARRRRRR!'

CHAPTER THIRTY-FIVE

It took a while for Inspector Moss to calm down. He'd shouted and raged from the open door for a long time, his famous moustache bobbling along in all directions with the rainwater still dripping from his person to the tiled floor. I think it was fair to say that he wasn't interested in joining our game of wonky donkey. In fact, he'd used some very colourful language to describe quite graphically what I could do with the broom. But, when the sea did eventually settle to only a minor storm, we relocated, once again to the turquoise drawing room, where he began to dry himself by the fire. Walrus and Matthews jostled behind him to find the gaps in his wake. With Moss' outer layers whisked away, he continued to rant over old ground:

'I've come all this way, risking life and limb because I get a scrap of a message from you, Lavender, to find you playing around a Christmas tree with a bloody donkey hat on!'

'To be fair, Sydney was the one with the don–'

'I don't care!'

I rubbed at my arm by the fire as I'd also suffered the inconvenience of the draughts in the Great Hall.

Silence filled the room, and all eyes were transfixed on the inspector. Roughly, with one hand, he snatched up the donkey hat which had been cast on the chair beside him. 'What even is this thing, anyway? Looks nothing like a donkey.'

'Those are the antlers,' I offered.

A large 'V' formed just above the flat of his nose. 'Donkeys don't have antlers.'

Miss Parsons was following the conversation with a joyful glare. 'Exactly.'

The inspector flashed her a look, then turned back to me. 'Go on then, what's happened?'

I swerved to avoid the stray hand of Matthews as he'd nearly hit me pulling it out of a sleeve. He mouthed an apology. 'Well, when Sydney put the hat on, he couldn't see, so–'

'I wasn't talking about the bloody donkey game! I was talking about the bloody murders!' He threw the hat back on the chair.

'Oh, right, yes.'

'Go on then, get on with it.'

I rubbed my other arm. 'Mrs Eastwell was murdered, brutally stabbed in the chest. I sent for you at once – via the good Simon here,' I added as Simon had suddenly appeared by my side, whispering to me that Mr Eastwell's body had been found. He retreated when he'd delivered his message. 'I asked him if he knew anyone capable of reaching you in the terrible conditions, which I gather he did…'

'The chap with the note? Ex-army, wasn't he?'

I shrugged. 'No idea. Anyway, Mr Eastwell was found dead as well. It was made to look like a–'

Inspector Moss's head shot up. 'What? Mr Eastwell's dead?'

'Why, yes.'

'Good heavens!'

'Yes, I know, terrible.'

Moss's dark eyes were back upon me. 'You know what they say? Where there's Lavender, there's trouble.'

Miss Parsons sniggered.

'Do they? I have no idea,' I said.

'Where are the bodies?' Moss asked.

'Mrs Eastwell's is in an outhouse. Mr Eastwell's had just gone for a little walk but has since returned to the Temple of the Four Winds.'

'WHAT? A walk? What are you saying, Lavender? Dead bodies can't walk.'

'This one did, but he's back now.'

He shook his head vigorously, as if dismissing the little walk. 'Any clues? Any suspects?'

'Well, it's funny you should ask. I was just about to deliver a little speech - good timing, eh?'

Bob the Walrus had dried himself sufficiently and had escaped from the proximity of the firing line. Matthews was about to follow him, but

Moss brought him back with a grimace. 'Depends upon what you have to say, but we've a little news of our own, haven't we, Matthews? Go on then, tell them the news.'

Matthews' neck flushed red, as he turned from Moss to the crowd.

The inspector raised a finger. 'Go on, get on with it boy! We've got Lavender's mess to clear up.'

Constable Matthews swallowed, then opened his mouth and closed it again.

The inspector shook his head. 'Stop doing a fish impression. Get on with it!'

Matthews lined himself up in the middle of the fireplace and turned to speak to the crowd. 'Er, we have located the–'

'Can't hear you,' Lord Talbot said, smirking at the young constable's attempts to speak up.

'Sorry. I mean the animal crimes, I mean the–'

'Good heavens man.' This time it was Moss himself that had turned on him. 'Spit it out!'

'Sorry, sir. What I mean is the animal thieves have been caught.'

Puzzled, the earl turned to Mr Landley, speaking to him personally though all could hear him. 'What's the fellow saying?'

Matthews swallowed again, then spoke up, more loudly this time. 'The disappearing animals: Mrs Wobble's sheep, Mrs Brigstock's cow, Mr Eastwell's racehorse…'

The farming element of the crowd cheered

at the news, gifting Constable Matthews a rare smile of relief. People shouted 'who's' and 'how's' to which the inspector had to tell them to pipe down so the constable could explain the details.

'So, with the help of Mr Brown's contacts…' The inspector's quick cough brought Matthews swiftly back on track. 'Yes, we managed to track down a well-known gang of animal rustlers who usually operate just outside of York.' The constable was speaking more comfortably now, though he still looked at Inspector Moss for prompts. He relayed that all the animals had been returned to their rightful homes and the gang had confessed to all the crimes.

'How did they do it?' Malcolm Wegwipe shouted, firmly back in reporter mode.

The constable flushed again. 'Ah, here is where it gets interesting.'

Necks naturally craned further forward.

'There are several possible theories upon how it all happened.'

When the constable said 'theories', he glanced at me, and the inspector lifted his head in derision, but the constable hadn't seen.

Malcolm Wegwipe had his pen poised for action. 'Go on, constable.'

'One theory is that the animals magically disappeared.'

Mr Landley clapped. 'Oh, I like that one.'

'Brilliant!' the earl said.

'Another theory is that one of the gang had a

magic key.'

'A magic key?' Miss Parsons said, twisting her face. 'Whatever next?'

'Yes, a magic key.'

'To every single lock and barn?'

'Yes.'

'Ho, ho, Margaret! Isn't that amazing? A magic key!'

There were a few more shouts and questions which Constable Matthews answered well, then he let the crowd settle. He was in control now. 'But theories are just theories. Really, it will be forever known as the Great Farm Animal Disappearing Mystery of York, 1888.'

This elicited great cries of delight from the regular circles, including Malcolm Wegwipe, who wanted a photograph of Constable Matthews with Mrs Wobble's missing sheep. The constable bowed slightly, his face flushed with pleasure. 'How did I do?' he whispered to me as he stood to one side.

'Very good,' I said, turning to the crowd. 'If I may? I'd like to propose an alternative theory.'

This was also met with great cries of delight from the regular circles, especially the earl, who I'd noticed had managed to sneak a 'special milk' from a passing footman.

I addressed the crowd, turning to my own group. Rose was still failing to meet my eyes. Stella was back to being Stella. Emma was resting her head on a hand, looking tired but still intrigued. Sydney, I noticed, had his back to Stella, but as I turned to start speaking, I noticed a ring of white froth around his lips.

'Fascinating as Constable Matthews' theories are, I would like to suggest that the gang had a little inside help.'

Mr Landley frowned. 'How do you mean?

'What I mean is, that it wasn't a magic key, though keys were involved, neither did any animal magically disappear, no. I propose that an insider, who had skills with animals, access to the keys here at Castle Howard and a great deal of familiarity with the farms, was supplying the gang. That's my theory.'

Silence. Then Malcolm Wegwipe said:

'Naw, that's rubbish. We prefer the constable's theory. Great story, that.'

There were several nods, and 'ayes', from the rest.

I gazed at the inspector.

He'd been resting above the fireplace hogging all of the warmth, listening carefully, but he turned around at my prompting. 'I don't particularly care. It's all settled. That's all I'm concerned with. And if Mr Eastwell is dead, then...' He shrugged.

I shrugged in return. I didn't particularly care either. 'So then, are we to leave it as a mystery?' I was speaking to Moss but the crowd thought I was addressing them and most of them cheered, none louder than Mr Landley and the earl, though Malcolm Wegwipe had a lot to say for himself as well.

'Wonderful, that one. Sell a few papers that will.'

I turned on him. 'I thought truth was at the heart of the *Herald*?'

'Oh, it is, it is,' he said, stammering. 'Absolutely.'

The inspector shook his head. 'Never mind this nonsense, what about the damn murders?'

'Oh yes, we can sort that out if you want?'

'Well, I didn't bloody come here through the snow and rain to look at your donkey hat!'

'True. Should we do it now then?'

'Lavender!'

'What?'

'Get on with it!'

I asked Rose and Emma to accompany me upstairs. Emma leapt up immediately, whereas Rose, I didn't think was going to come at all, but she eventually consented.

I told everyone else to clear the table of glue and paper as we would be, hopefully, needing it for a little demonstration if the fish had bitten. This had the earl, Landley and Parsons all but jumping in the air, which startled Inspector Moss as he was just about to be seated.

We trailed past the army of footmen who were trying (unsuccessfully) to right the tree.

'Uncle, how are you going to separate the fingerprints? Do you know how Lord Talbot did it? How he poisoned Mr Eastwell, I mean.'

I paused at the top of the stairs. 'All in good time.'

Rose walked on ahead.

'What's wrong with her?' I said.

Emma suppressed a laugh, shaking her head and following on behind.

Rose got the door first, having got the key from Stella, but she didn't need it, as the door swung inwards as soon as she'd laid a hand on the doorknob. 'Oh, my God!'

'What is it?' Emma shouted, running towards her, entering the room.

I strolled on behind, eventually making my way inside.

'Look!' Rose shouted. 'Just look what's happened now. Just look. This is all your fault. Happy now?'

The dressing table had been ransacked, the fingerprints destroyed and the murder weapon was missing.

CHAPTER THIRTY-SIX

Rose was doing an accurate impression of Inspector Moss, minus the moustache, only her particular barrage seemed tinged with hurt. 'This is all your fault.'

'You already said that.'

She made a funny noise, almost a squeal. 'Why are you so infuriating?'

'I'm not.'

'Yes, you are. If we'd come up here when I said, none of this would have happened.' Her hand trailed to the space above the dresser, with its ripped-up pieces of paper containing the fingerprints they had taken and the empty space where the knife had been.

Emma sat on the edge of the bed, head in her hands.

'Well?' Rose said. 'What do you have to say for yourself?'

'Who? Me?'

'Yes, you!' She rubbed the back of her neck. 'This is your fault. If you weren't too busy trying to please your little fan club then...'

'Fan club? What do you mean, my little fan club?' I sat on the bed beside Emma, rubbing her arm, which caused her to flinch.

'Fan club. Your little donkey fan club.'

'Oh, you mean, wonky donkey?'

'Of course, I mean...' She turned away as if she no longer wanted to look at me.

Emma uncovered her eyes and turned to me. 'What are we going to do now? Everything's ruined.'

'No, it's not.'

'Of course, it is. Look at it! The kitchen knife's been stolen.'

'Excellent.'

Rose turned slowly. 'James?'

'How are we going to separate the fingerprints, now?' Emma asked.

'We can't.'

Rose turned a little more. 'Care to explain?'

'Of course.' I got up from the bed, closed the door and sat back down. 'You can't separate prints when they are together like that. It's impossible.'

'But, you just said you could,' Emma said. 'After the card game.'

'I did.' I rubbed at the side of my mouth, watching them both closer, enjoying the clouds of confusion which began to clear.

'You set this up,' Rose said. 'You wanted Lord Talbot to come up here. Why?'

'To get a new print!' Emma said. 'To trick him.'

'Of course.'

'The donkey game was a distraction?' Rose asked.

'Naturally. And Sydney did an excellent job of knocking over the Christmas tree.'

'Uncle!'

'Well, it worked, didn't it? Now, you take the fingerprint materials downstairs, just leave me a little to do the one on the doorknob, and I'll meet you there.'

'But, the fingerprint kit's been taken,' Emma said.

'No, it hasn't. It's under the bed.'

'What? How?' Emma asked.

'I put it there, of course. Now, stop wasting time, get to it, come on. Chop, chop.'

❖ ❖ ❖

'What's going on here?' was Inspector Moss' greeting as I made my way back into the drawing room, amid a flurry of chatter and expectation. Rose and Emma were busy setting up the fingerprinting on the central table, ignoring the stares of those around them. Most people were seated, (non-alcoholic) drinks in hand, though Lord Talbot preferred to stand in the corner of the room, watching proceedings with only a sideways glance, as if murder were beneath him.

'A little game of fingerprints,' I said, as I made my way to the front alongside the good inspector.

'What nonsense is this?' the inspector asked.

'Science.'

'Science? Is this more of your make-believe?'

'Not at all, inspector.' I turned to face the crowd, all of whom had now transferred their enthusiasm my way. I held up the finger of my right hand and started to wiggle it at them. 'Fingerprints.'

Mr Landley cast a puzzled expression to the earl who grinned.

'Fingerprints,' I said, again. 'Are the future of criminal investigation.'

The earl looked at his own still, wriggling it around. 'Fingerprints, Mr James?'

'Let me explain.'

'You'd better,' the inspector said.

Emma indicated that they were ready. I continued, my finger held to the crowd. 'Look at the end of your finger. What do you see?'

'Earwax,' Mr Landley said.

There were a few muffled huffs of laughter.

'Well, wipe the earwax off your finger and what do you see?' I said, rhetorically. 'You see individual swirls and patterns, but did you know that every single human fingerprint is unique?'

'Nonsense,' Miss Parsons said, turning her

hand back over.

'It's true.'

Mr Landley started to give one of his 'Margaret, Margaret' exclamations, but the wonderful inspector silenced him with a grunt and a glare.

'Right. So, as fingerprints are unique, they can help us prove a person touched a metal or shiny item, say a…murder weapon.'

'Sounds a bit far-fetched to me,' Mrs Parsons said, but nobody really took any notice.

'Observe.' I walked over to Emma. She placed the metal tin before me and I dabbed my finger into the black powder before rolling it on a small piece of paper which I held in the air like a playing card. 'This is my fingerprint. Utterly unique to me. Now, who wants a go?'

'Me! Me!' shouted Aurea, running to the table. 'I want to play.'

The countess held out a hand to stop her but relented when I said that it was fine. Emma and Rose helped her with it and then gave her some pencils to draw around it, and she was seated behind the countess, lost in her scribblings.

'Now,' I said. 'Let everyone take a print as I proceed.'

Miss Parsons made a yawning motion with her hand to which Anthony Landley laughed

'Lavender, get on with it,' Inspector Moss said, again.

He could be quite an impatient fellow.

'Two murders,' I said. 'One, Mrs Eastwell,

brutally stabbed. Another, Mr Eastwell, poisoned.'

'He killed himself, in grief,' Miss Parsons said.

'He did not.'

'How do you know?'

'If he killed himself, then who tried to kill Wegwipe? I know he's annoying, but still...'

He looked up from his notebook, frowning.

'Please, miss,' Inspector Moss began. 'Don't interrupt, otherwise we'll be here all day. Carry on, Lavender.'

'Right, so. Two deaths. Two additional attempted murders.'

Inspector Moss' moustache took on a new bounce. '*Two* attempted murders now? What on earth's been going on? Who?'

I pointed at Mrs Parsons. 'A hand upon the back. On the stairs.'

A few people turned to her, as if they'd forgotten this little detail, lost, as we had been, in all the nonsense.

'Yes,' she said, a slight hesitation in her voice. 'About that, I may have just imagined the hand.'

The inspector put his head in his own hands. 'Lavender, are you going to clear this mess up?'

'Of course.'

The earl and the countess had freely given their fingerprints during the exchanges, leaving no excuses for the others not to follow their lead.

'Let's start at the beginning,' I said. 'We arrive here, Christmas Eve in the worst of worst ever snow blizzards. We're trapped together, which can often exacerbate emotions, but even without that, it was immediately apparent that there was quite a bit of tension in the room…to put it mildly. Certain people did not get on.'

'Mr Eastwell and Mr Talbot,' Mr Landley said, which was what everyone was thinking.

Lord Talbot sniffed.

'More rivals,' I said. 'The Landleys and the Parsons, rivals in work.' Mr Landley started to protest, but I stopped him. 'But, I have seen from my own eyes, that there is no animosity between them…at least in terms of the heads of the family.'

I turned to Sydney, looking his way for the first time. It was clear, from his screwed-up little gnome face, that he and Stella must have 'had words'. What about I wasn't sure, but perhaps the special milk had something to do with it.

'Rivalry,' I continued, 'exists from a young age as a natural condition. You see it even in very young children. You see it in the workplace. Rivalry exists–'

'Lavender!' Inspector Moss shouted.

'Right, get a move on. Motive. Who had the motive for the killings?' People started looking at each other without turning their heads. I dipped my hand into my top pocket. 'This was found under the table on the stairs where the vase had stood.'

Inspector Moss squinted. 'What is it?'

'A button,' Malcolm Wegwipe answered.

'Whose?'

'His,' Miss Parsons said.

'What? Lavender?'

'Yes, it is mine. Question is, who put it there?' I gave them all my familiar glance. 'Puzzling, yes?' I continued as the good inspector's moustache started preparing for an enormous wobble. 'It puzzled me at first, but then I worked it out. It must have fallen off during the treasure hunt. During that…unfortunate event, I collided with Mr Eastwell. It must have fallen off then.'

'Mr Eastwell planted it?' Inspector Moss asked.

'No. I do not think so. Next, we have the murder of Mrs Eastwell herself, stabbed with a kitchen knife that anybody could have taken. This was also found in my room.'

'It's not looking good for the detective,' Miss Parsons said to her mother, loud enough so that all could hear.

'How the hell did it come to be in your room?' Inspector Moss said.

'I'm getting to that. Now, the murder occurred whilst we were searching for the missing girl.'

'Some of us were searching…' Miss Parsons muttered, but Inspector Moss silenced her sharply.

'Sydney,' I said. 'Can you tell them the condition of Mrs Eastwell's bed?"

'Her bed?' Constable Matthews said I think without meaning to speak out loud.

'It had blood along the side and it was wet at the bottom.'

'Precisely, an important point.'

'Lavender! What's the wet got to do with anything, and who tried to frame you?' Inspector Moss asked.

I nodded, slowly. 'Lord Talbot, care to help him with any of those questions?'

Everybody twisted around to face him as he continued to lean against the wall. 'I do hope you're not accusing me of murder, Mr Lavender? Or of wetting the bed.'

Mr Parsons sniggered at his last comment and Mr Landley joined in with a few words of wisdom about bed wetting.

I took a step towards Lord Talbot. 'It was you who planted the button under the table. You were in Mr Eastwell's group for the treasure hunt. You saw it happen. And this…' I took out a folded piece of paper, one which I had saved before wonky donkey. 'This was found on a chair in my room.'

'What is it?' Inspector Moss asked.

I handed him the fingerprint. 'Care to match it with the one Rose has just taken from him?'

He studied them closely, side by side.

'Like two little clubs, aren't they?' I said, grinning at Lord Talbot.

'They're identical,' Moss revealed.

There were cries and shouts which died down until the only thing that could be heard was the regular scratching of Wegwipe's pen.

'I do hope you're not accusing me of murder,' Lord Talbot repeated. 'That would not be good for you.'

I spun around to Lord Talbot. 'You cannot take the moral high ground. There was water on the bed which came from the snow outside. You were of the mad chicken party frantically hunting around in the snow. You had the kitchen knife. You planted it in my room. You planted the button under the table. You hated Mr Eastwell. You had a grudge against me, but no, you did not kill her, or Mr Eastwell.' There were more ripples of conversation which soon dissipated. 'Motive. Hating Mr Eastwell was not a sufficient motive for stabbing his wife, though tampering with evidence, and planting it on me, is a crime.'

Of course, I could have used this little ploy if I'd lost the card game with Lord Talbot. I wasn't really going to risk everything.

Lord Talbot shifted his weight from the wall, leaning back against it.

Inspector Moss turned towards him. 'We do not take lightly with meddling in such a way, man.'

'It's not up to me, inspector. It's entirely up to you, but perhaps a sizable donation to the single mother's charity is called for?' I turned to Rose who half-closed one eye.

'I'll think on it, Lavender,' Inspector Moss said. 'So, if Lord Talbot didn't kill her, who did?'

'Exactly,' Malcolm Wegwipe said.

Others mirrored his words.

'From the start of the very first day. I felt that, beyond all the nonsense, all the little balls...'

'Ball in the hole,' Mr Landley corrected.

'All the fun and games and the noise, that I was in the presence of evil.'

The silence was only broken by Wegwipe. 'I like that line.'

I continued. 'Mr Landley gave me an idea when–'

'Yes!' Mr Landley clenched his first. 'Always happy to help. Margaret, didn't I...'

Thankfully the good inspector cut him short, allowing me to carry on. 'To get the cow out of the snow they had to whip it on its behind.'

'Not too hard,' Mr Parsons said. 'We didn't do it to be cruel.'

'No, but that was enough to provide me with an interesting idea. Sydney, can you remember what Mr Eastwell said to us yet about the training marks on his horse?'

Sydney scratched his head. 'Well, I've been thinking about that since you asked. He said something like discipline is the way to raise man and beast.'

'That's the one. We immediately recoiled at the way he'd treated his racehorse.'

'That's no way to treat an animal,' Mr Landley said. 'No way at all. Is it, Margaret? Margaret, isn't it no way to treat an animal...'

'No way to treat an animal at all,' Mr Parsons said, a dark cloud over his face.

'…Margaret, isn't it, no way to treat an animal?' Inspector Moss looked sick.

'That was our reaction, wasn't it, Sydney?'

'Yes, it was.'

'But, there's the other way to look at it, as well, isn't there?'

'What do you mean?' Inspector Moss said.

'Such harsh discipline as a way to raise *man* and beast. As Mr Landley also suggested during our interview the Eastwell family were too strict, they didn't play games. Oh, no. It was certainly a strict upbringing. Young Master Eastwell, care to tell us about that?'

A chill descended upon the room.

David's lip jerked but no sound came forth. 'Yes, Father was…quite cruel.'

'Yes,' I said. 'Reminds me of the picture at the bottom of the stairs. You know, the one with the angry boy and the horse, the mother in the corner not really part of the scene. Oh, I think he was more than, quite cruel, wasn't he? And what about your mother? Did she stand by and let it all happen?'

Miss Parsons took a sharp intake of breath. 'Are you accusing him of murder?'

'Surely not?' her mother said.

'Yes. Yes, I am.'

The room erupted.

'But, he's just a child,' the countess said.

'Crazy,' Miss Parsons shouted. 'Absolutely crazy.'

I let the protests die down, one by one. 'He's not a child. He's seventeen and it's not crazy.' I went to my pocket. 'This is the print I've just taken from the Browns door handle. It's where the kitchen knife was being tested. This print is the same one that was on the knife.' There were yet more cries. I held the paper up, showing everyone a pressed mark. 'Why did you have to kill your mother, David?'

CHAPTER THIRTY-SEVEN

David shot up, the chair scraping harshly behind him. 'She knew what a monster he was. Everyone did, but nobody did anything about it, nobody! She watched as he beat me with that riding crop of his. The staff did, yet they did nothing. She deserved to die and so did he.'

'So you admit it?' Inspector Moss said.

'Yes, yes. I did it and I enjoyed watching them suffer.'

People got to their feet. Miss Parsons reeled, moving away from him as if she was going to be his next victim. The earl, to his credit, took a step forward, as did Sydney, so David Eastwell was going nowhere.

'Why, David, why?' the countess said, unable to shake herself from the horror of what she was hearing. 'Why go to such, such horrible lengths?'

He shrugged casually. 'They deserved it.'

'How did you do it?' Inspector Moss asked.

'Why don't you ask him? He seems to think he knows everything.'

Inspector Moss turned one eye to me. 'Lavender?'

'I do know everything,' I said to David. 'Stop me if I'm wrong.' Then I turned to the rest of them, some of whom had sat down again, though they gave David a wide berth 'So, the girl goes missing, lost in her harmless game. This provided the perfect opportunity for chaos, which was even more perfect to him than the treasure hunt vase attempt. So, he goes out like everyone else looking for the girl, blending into the crowd, but he sneaks back inside. I'm guessing he stole a kitchen knife earlier in the day; no one would notice just one missing kitchen knife. Maybe he'd hidden it in a room, or somewhere close by.'

'The plant pot, in the hall.'

'Thank you. He collects the knife, and, probably hiding it behind his back, goes into his parents' room. Mrs Parsons is long gone by this point.' Mrs Parsons' cheeks began to flame. 'The less said about that, the better...So, David creeps into the room. His father had suffered a blow to the head and had been given a restful tonic to help him sleep. I'm guessing now that Mrs Eastwell was also asleep or just drifting off, having been taking care of her husband.'

'She was asleep.'

'Thank you. She had to be, for David wouldn't risk her waking her husband even through the sleeping draft. At this point, he leans over the bed, wetting it in the process from the snow on his coat and trousers, and stabs his mother in the chest.'

'Oh, how utterly appalling,' the countess said, turning to her daughter, who thankfully wasn't taking anything in, being still occupied with her drawing.

'Horrific,' the earl agreed.

Wegwipe was gleefully writing. 'Shocking.'

'What then?' Inspector Moss asked.

'Then, careful not to wake him, he lets the blood drip around his father, on his hands and shirt. He then swiftly falls back, planting the knife in Lord Talbot's room, washes his own hands, and makes his way back outside.'

'Wouldn't he get more blood about his person?' Inspector Moss said.

'That's what the rag was used for, to help shield himself.' I explained about the rag covered in blood found on the scene.

'And I'm gathering he placed the knife in Lord Talbot's room to implicate him?'

'Yes, and no.'

'Lavender?'

'My guess is that he wished to make it look like a feeble attempt to implicate Lord Talbot. That people would easily see through it and his father would hang.' I looked up to David Eastwell for clarity.

'Yes, but if that failed and Lord Talbot did swing, then, so what?'

'Fair enough. However, that didn't quite work out, as we've already discussed, as Lord Talbot then planted the knife in my room. So, that's when you had to come up with your hastily-done mock suicide.'

'Yes.'

'I must congratulate you on your little acting performance before all that.'

'Acting performance?' Rose asked.

'Yes,' I continued. 'As you then came back into the house after re-joining the search for a while, only to pretend to discover your mother killed.'

'Yes, I thought I'd find father, but he must have woken up and was wandering somewhere.'

'Yes, he'd woken up after his bump on the head, after the sleeping draft, covered in blood. He was in a clear state of genuine shock when we all saw him shortly afterwards. He must have wandered around the top corridor and then gone back into the room with blood still on his hands. His shock was real, but yours wasn't.'

'No.'

'And you made the countess and the earl here believe their child had been murdered, didn't you?'

The countess froze.

David laughed. 'I was just having a bit of fun.'

The countess lunged at him, but the inspector,

who was standing close to her, held her back. 'Now, now. Try to calm yourself.'

'I should have known it then. That nothing in your eyes. That bit wasn't an act. Like Rufus the bull, as Mr Parsons reminded us. No empathy.'

It took a while for everyone to regain composure, and then the inspector told me to continue.

'We conducted our interview in which you answer truthfully – you did return to the room and find your mother dead.' I looked over at Rose. 'So, everything came across as genuine in your interview. Your acting too was still top-notch.'

'Yes, I learned to act from a young age to avoid a beating. Never show fear in front of father. Pretend it didn't hurt when it did. Pretend not to show pain to the servants, that sort of thing. One gets good at acting.'

'I doubt you're going to elicit any sympathy. The next thing was to take care of your father. I take it you prepared a little escape bag for him? Only, his flask was laced with poison, arsenic. Where did you get it?'

'Strong rat poison. From the sheds.'

'Oh, yes, of course. The gardening shed.'

'How did you get in the room we locked your father in?' the earl asked.

'I stole the master key. I know where the keys are kept.'

'Yes,' I said. 'Hardly difficult.'

'So, then what happened?' Inspector Moss

asked.

'It would not be difficult to convince Eastwell to flee the house considering the state he was in. Daavid hands him the bag and directs him to sneak out of the downstairs window, telling him to take refuge in the Temple of the Four Winds. Maybe he said he'd arrange someone to get him out.'

'I said I had a deal with a footman. Lies of course.'

'There you go. Mr Eastwell has a smoke. Then a drink from the flask, and that's the end of him.'

'But what about the suicide note?' Wegwipe said.

'And the note on the table?' Mrs Parsons asked.

'I'm coming to those. So, there we are around the table on Christmas Day. The young Master Eastwell cannot rely on chance; we must find the body. So, he plants the note on the table.'

'But, he didn't go anywhere near the table,' the countess said. 'I was close by all the time.'

'True, but he didn't plant the note himself. Miss Parsons did.'

Mrs Parsons stood up, shouting. 'Utter nonsense.'

'It's true, isn't it, Wegwipe?'

Wegwipe blushed but assented.

Miss Parsons retreated into her chair. 'I thought it was a joke. He'd said he'd found a puzzle on the floor. I didn't have anything else to do with it.'

Rose glared at her, as did Emma. The inspector turned back to me. 'Well?'

'It's true, Miss Parsons didn't know what she was doing.'

'Thank you,' she said.

'She's just stupid.'

'What? Hey,' she protested mildly.

'You also must have told him about what I said to you specifically about finding clues, during the interviews. David must have worried there were clues still on the body so he moved his father's corpse from the scene.'

'Surely not?' the inspector said.

David merely nodded. 'I'm stronger than I look. A life of unfair punishment.'

'But the act of moving the body trying to obscure clues merely created another clue. I knew the message was getting back to the killer. It was Miss Parsons I said that to. You see, there is no escape,' I said. 'The note found on Mr Eastwell was also planted by David in the wild scram when we found the body.'

David smiled. 'Yes, I encouraged people to get excited and push forward creating a scene. Good job, Mr Landley.'

Mr Landley screwed up his face. 'Rotten egg.'

'Rotten egg, indeed,' Mr Parsons added.

I continued. 'Just a point. A suicide note is rarely printed in hand. Then trying to silence Wegwipe for something you thought he saw was far too rash.'

Malcolm touched his neck. 'Quite.'

'Indeed,' William Brookes said, opposite him.

It suddenly dawned on me. The sickness I'd suffered that went over the Christmas tree. It had possibly come as a reaction from my condition after we'd interviewed David. My first thought of an evil presence in the room on the first day perhaps was part of it too. I was looking at Mr Eastwell, but his son was just behind.

I'd noticed Inspector Moss puzzling over the fingerprint I'd given him. 'Anything wrong, inspector?'

'Yes, these fingerprints don't look the same to me.'

He'd been comparing the second print I'd given him from the door handle with David Eastwell's fresh print.

'Of course, they don't. That print isn't David's.'

'No?'

'No. It's mine.'

CHAPTER THIRTY-EIGHT

David's face twisted in rage. 'What? You said the print was mine.'

I smiled. 'Yes, I did say that, did I not?'

'Liar!'

'Lavender?' Moss still held the fingerprints in his hand, still puzzling. 'Care to explain?'

'You can't separate prints. That's impossible. However, young David here happened to overhear me saying that they could after the card game. Then during Sydney's unfortunate accident during wonky donkey, David raided the room looking to destroy the evidence. Clearly, he wasn't going to put a print on the door handle as he knew about fingerprints, but I planted a little seed of doubt. Prints don't matter if you confess in front of everybody, do they?'

David continued to rage. 'You tricked me.'

'Indeed. What did you overhear?' It took a

while for David to calm down, but when he did, he spoke in a matter-of-fact way. 'I overheard you talking about the fingerprints early on.' He looked over at Malcolm Wegwipe. 'He wasn't the only one listening at doors.'

'Go on,' I encouraged.

'I thought I was safe when I just exposed my father's body to the elements, but then when you said you could separate the prints on the knife I had to act quickly. So when the tree fell over during that ridiculous game, I broke into the Browns' room to destroy the evidence. I didn't think I'd left a print on the handle but...I obviously fell into your trap.'

'Hee, hee, Mr James does it again.' The earl strode forward, shaking my hands. 'Remarkable!'

He was soon joined by Landley and Parsons who echoed my brilliance. Mr Landley shook my hands vigorously. 'Well done, Mr Lavender. Well done!'

I turned to Sydney and Rose. Rose turned away, but Sydney was grinning as usual, the argument between himself and Stella clearly forgotten.

Inspector Moss didn't linger long. David had been secured, and between himself and Constable Matthews, was taken away via Walrus, who'd been provided with fresh horses. Moss said that he'd send a team out to collect the bodies, and somehow, he'd managed to find a glass of brandy to tilt before his departure.

Malcolm Wegwipe had also somehow managed to talk himself into the journey, saying that he wanted to help, and if that also meant he could get home to write up some urgent stories for the *Herald*, then that just happened to be a bonus.

'You've done it again, Lavender,' Moss had said. 'By God man, I've no idea how, but it gets me out of trouble with the commissioner.'

I'd shaken his hand. 'My pleasure, I'm always happy to help the constabulary. Happy to lend a much-needed brain.'

His moustache had shot me a final wobble, but its owner shook my hand hard in return.

With David Eastwell taken away, and the joint moustaches of Moss and Walrus whisked away too, naturally the mood had lightened. Glasses of special milk and special apple juice had been passed around among the remaining guests who celebrated with lightness, aside from the Talbots and Miss Parsons who sulked in the corner and took to their rooms well before the night had ended.

Emma had cornered me at the side of the fire and asked me about what really had happened in the animal case. Rose turned her head at that but was still only half-talking to me. I waited until Simon was within earshot before I went on to explain.

'So, you don't buy into the constable's great disappearing theory, then?'

Emma laughed, putting a hand to her mouth.

'Oh, no.'

'Good. I gave you much more credit than that.'

I glanced over to the crowd as the earl cheered loudly. Both he and Sydney were taking it in turns in a tamer version of wonky donkey, passing the hat between themselves and spinning it around. Aurea was jumping up trying to take it from their heads and they roared when she took it off them which resulted in great cries of delight.

I turned back to our conversation. 'Rose, care to share your theory?'

She flinched her nose. 'No, you go ahead.'

'So, we know the gang has confessed to the thefts, but they didn't take the animals directly. Someone else did that and then passed the animals over.'

'Right, Uncle, but who?'

'Someone who has access to the properties and access to the keys here at Castle Howard.' Simon flinched at that. 'And more importantly, motive to do damage to the Landleys.'

'The Parsons?' Emma said.

'Exactly. Rose?'

Rose cleared her throat. 'So who? Mr Parsons, Mrs Parsons or Miss Parsons? Surely, the only one that fits is Mr Parsons. I can't see the other pair getting their hands dirty in a barn, but just look at him.'

Mr Parsons was currently on Mr Landleys back with the donkey hat on, with Aurea chasing after them.

'Wonky donkey!' the earl shouted. 'Wonky donkey needs some more special milk!'

'Confusing,' Emma said. 'It could all be an act but...'

Rose shook her head. 'I don't think so either.'

I tapped Emma's arm. 'Let me help you both out.' Rose tutted slightly, but I carried on undeterred. 'What you need to do is think a bit more widely. You're thinking a bit too literally.'

Emma frowned. 'How do you mean?'

'Instead of thinking in a straight line, try thinking in a triangle.'

'Well, that clears it up,' Rose said.

'Stop being miserable,' I said. 'It's Christmas!'

Emma put a hand over her mouth.

The fuss around wonky donkey was eventually replaced by a new enthusiasm for blindfold charades. Why every other game had to be upgraded to its blindfold version I had no idea, but blindfold charades it was to be. The earl took up the sport first with his usual enthusiasm for nonsense. By this time, however, the group consisted of the usuals, minus the Parsons who had since retreated to their beds. Mr Parsons had wanted to stay and play, but his wife had insisted upon their retirement. Thankfully, it wasn't long before eyes began to close (aside from the earl and Mr Landley, who were as animated as ever) and we all equally retired for the night for a well-deserved period of repose.

CHAPTER THIRY-NINE

The next morning, we said our goodbyes. First, Mr Parsons shook my hand. 'I don't think I've ever enjoyed myself so much. It's even better than the Kirby affair.'

Sydney was standing beside me. 'What's the–'

But I put my hand out to stop him. 'Oh yes, the Kirby affair. Great fun that, wasn't it?'

Mr Parsons beamed. 'It was that.'

Then Mr Landley stood before me, smiling away. 'Mr Lavender!' He smacked his lips in my face. 'It's been an absolute pleasure. As always. You're the life and soul of the party. Here you go. I haven't forgotten.'

I looked in my hands – a tube of ointment.

'Just remember, Mr Lavender, right up. Right up.' He made a suggestive motion with his finger and clenched fist.

I eventually managed to get rid of him and

then the earl and the countess lined up, thanking me, as well as Sydney, Rose, Emma and Stella, shaking our hands in turn. 'Mr James, quite remarkable how you solved it all. Remarkable. Even better was wonky donkey. The greatest game of all time.'

With all the rest of the goodbyes said, we travelled on our way to the Castle Howard platform through great rivers of slush and snow. Emma had once again opted to travel with myself and Rose, and she was sitting in the middle of us both. She turned to me as soon as a footman closed the last carriage door and we trotted off with a final wave.

'I've been thinking,' Emma said.

'Good. It's quite a productive habit. If truth be told.' I let my father's walking cane rest against my knee, freeing my hands. 'What about?'

'The triangle.'

'Ah.'

'Well.' Emma twisted forward. 'I think the triangle you were referring to relates to Anthony Landley, Miss Parsons and David Eastwell. Am I correct?'

'Yes. Yes, you are.'

'It was obvious that Anthony cared for Miss Parsons and Miss Parsons cared for David Eastwell, but their feelings weren't…what do you call it?'

'Reciprocated?' I offered.

'Yes, that's the word. So, I think it could

have something to do with this, but I don't know what, exactly, but I think Miss Parsons is definitely guilty somehow.'

'Rose?' I prompted.

Rose turned her attention from the window to our conversation. She had still been a little distant, certainly not her usual self, but she was at least communicating now. Women are strange creatures indeed, often angry for no good reason at all. I've come to realise that the best way forward is usually to ignore it, and it often self-righted in the end. She tapped her finger on the seat beside her. 'I agree with Emma. Did Miss Parsons hire the rustlers?'

'No, I do not think so.'

'But she's involved?'

'Certainly.'

Rose's nose twitched in that usual way. 'David Eastwell, then? Vindictive individual that he is, though I don't see how he profits by it.'

I shook my head. 'Not David Eastwell.'

'Mrs Parsons, then? The Parsons seek to profit by it, after all.'

I continued shaking my head. 'You're just guessing now.'

Rose let out a sigh of frustration.

'Is it Simon?' Emma asked. 'That's why you waited for Simon to be in earshot yesterday. Has Simon been paid? And obviously, he has access to all the keys.'

'Nope. I wanted Simon to hear. I had a little

conversation with him while you two were messing about playing blindfold charades.'

'Go on then, Mr Brilliant,' Rose said. 'Why don't you explain? We can tell you're dying to.'

My top lip twitched of its own accord. I turned to look at them both. 'Miss Parsons.'

'What?' Rose shouted. 'You just said it wasn't Miss Parsons, now you say it is.'

I shook my head. 'Miss Parsons.'

'Uncle James, you'd better explain, or I think Rose might thump you.'

I cracked my knuckles, leaning forward ever so slightly, but the Castle Howard train platform loomed into view. 'I'll tell you on the train.'

'Oh, God,' Rose began. 'Do you always have to be so annoying?'

'That's just Uncle James.'

Seated in our carriage, now joined by Sydney and Stella, we continued our conversation, Emma having filled them in on our discussion.

'Right,' I said. 'So, locked barns, disappearing animals, magic keys. It's all very straightforward.' When none of them bit, I continued. 'We know the gang is responsible for taking the animals away, but who got them out of the barns and stables?'

'The magic key?' Sydney said, grinning.

'No.'

'Who then?' Emma asked.

'It's obvious.'

'Who?' Emma shouted.

'Anthony Landley did.'

'What?'

Rose leaned forward 'Anthony? It can't be. Why would he sabotage his own father's reputation? Wait, yes. Yes, that makes sense.'

'I don't understand,' Emma said.

Rose filled her in. 'Miss Parsons manipulated Anthony. She wrapped him around her finger, anybody could see that, even James.' She eyed me sulkily. 'That's right, isn't it?'

'Indeed.'

'But how did he get into the locked barn? How did he get into the stable?' Emma asked.

Sydney nodded, wisely. 'Magic key.'

'Be quiet. Anthony Landley was good with animals. He'd been with his father for years; the animals were used to him. He regularly accompanied his father on the rounds. Also, remember Mr Landley's stupid story about the stuck cow? It was Anthony who helped manage to move it He has a natural way with animals. He also had access to the keys, being a regular at Castle Howard. It wouldn't have been difficult to steal them temporarily before anybody noticed. He also walked out of the room when myself and Sydney first visited Mr Landley. Guilty conscience?'

Rose frowned. 'But what about Mrs Wobble's barn? There wasn't a key to the padlock at Castle Howard. No spare key at all.'

I smiled. 'That's true, but there was a house

key. Anthony was able to steal the house key and get the padlock key from the kitchen. The dog, Killer, was familiar with Anthony. Anthony would know he wouldn't bark.'

'But, would he do that?' It was Stella who had spoken. A rare treat.

'Yes,' I said. 'Didn't you see how Miss Parsons was flashing those expensive diamond earrings about? Costly those. A gift from Anthony, I bet.'

'She was the one behind it all,' Rose said. 'Trying to bring down the Landleys to help her father and impress David Eastwell. But now she gets away with it.'

'I wouldn't say that,' I said. 'Not if my little word with Simon bears fruit, and I think it will.'

They settled into a quieter melee of questions, but by that time, we were almost back in York. For once, the platform was quiet, with no rugby scrums, what with the period and the conditions which were still pretty harsh, if not outright hostile. Emma's jubilant nature had shrunk and now she was visibly upset to be back, like a sudden return from an eventful holiday. Rose kept glancing at her sympathetically. I asked her what was wrong to which the reply 'nothing' was the automatic response.

All of a sudden, Sydney ran across the road almost ending up under the back wheel of a carriage.

'Jesus, Sydney. What's wrong?' I said. 'Have you found a pie?'

He shook his head. 'Paper,' he shouted across to us as we stood over Lendal bridge, gazing down at the little, tied-up boats bobbing away on the water. He came jogging back, panting.

'Sydney Brown,' his dear wife remonstrated. 'You nearly got yourself killed.'

'Here, look at this.' He opened the paper, struggling in the slight wind over the bridge. 'It's the article from Wegwipe.' He flashed me the paper:

CASTLE HOWARD'S CRAZED CHRISTMAS KILLER – THE EASTWELLS MURDERED BY THEIR SON!

David Eastwell has been arrested on suspicion of double murder, as James Lavender McCarthy has...

'What the hell?' I nearly fell over the bridge. 'Are you serious? Bloody McCarthy, now?'

'Yep, listen.' Sydney read out loud. "...once again wrestled with evil with his team of assistants–"'

This time it was Rose who interrupted him. 'Well, he's not wrong there.'

Emma looked at her closely.

Sydney continued: '"David brutally stabbed his mother while poisoning his father, but James Lavender McCarthy–'

'Sydney, I haven't got time for this nonsense.'

'No, let me finish.'

'No.'

'But what about the "Missing Animal Mystery"?' he pleaded.

'Absolutely not.'

'Constable Matthews is mentioned. And there's a photograph of him stood next to Mrs Wobble's sheep!'

'Put it away!'

Sydney sulked but folded the paper, and we walked along over the bridge as Stella wanted to head home too. Emma still looked gloomy.

'What's wrong?' I asked.

Rose made some funny motions with her eyes.

'What's wrong?' I repeated.

Emma's lip quivered. 'Nothing, er, thank you. I…I know it wasn't exactly as planned, but I did enjoy it.' She rubbed at her eyes. 'I don't mean to make light of the people dying, just…' She shook her head and we marched on.

I nodded. 'Then why are you sad?'

'Oh, James, don't you know anything?' Rose said, reaching out and rubbing Emma's arm.

Emma sniffed. 'It's fine.'

'What is it?'

Rose turned to me sharply. 'What are *you* doing tomorrow?'

I smiled. 'Eating apple tarts and reading. I've got a lot of catching up to do, you know? I can't wait.'

'Exactly.'

We turned a corner.

'What do you mean?' I said.

Rose shook her head, still looking at Emma.

'Stop a moment,' I said. We stood outside the

museum gardens close to the prison. A robin hopped down from a tree branch but, took one look at Sydney and dived away. 'Does it have anything to do with going back to really dull and boring work tomorrow?'

Emma turned away, her attention fixed on the monastery walls.

'If it is,' I said. 'Then maybe this will help.' I took the letter out of my pocket and handed it over.

She ripped it open with the ferocity of Sydney's aggressive nature, read it at a glance and crushed me with a hug, tears fully flowing. 'Oh, Uncle James. Thank you. Thank you.'

It was a contract of employment.

'It's just part-time, mind,' I said, looking at Stella to reassure her, though I had discussed it with her previously. 'Just a little office help.' I winked at Sydney, who grinned back.

She carried on crushing me. 'Thank you. Oh, thank you.'

I hugged her back, briefly. 'Of course, if I'm crushed to death then there'll be no business...'

She pulled back, laughing through her tears. 'Sorry.'

Rose helped wipe her eyes with a handkerchief, and then Sydney escorted them home after she'd ushered forth several goodbyes. I strolled around to the minster with Rose, the silence loud between us.

'So, why don't you tell me what's wrong?' I

asked.

She took a while before answering. 'Is there any point?'

'Probably not, but you never know.' I smiled.

She didn't. 'I know that I'm only an apprentice and my input doesn't matter.'

'Of course, it matters. I value you greatly.'

'Ha.' She looked away, then turned back to me. 'You don't tell me anything. You don't consult me – like with the ridiculous game…'

'Wonky donkey? It's not ridiculous. It's the greatest game of all time. The earl said so.'

She laughed briefly. 'I'm not consulted though, but I am a woman, after all.'

'It's not that I don't consult you, and the fact that you're a woman has nothing to do with it…it's just that I have my methods, and sometimes there is no time. Ah, anyway, Sydney's back.'

'Yes, well, thank you. I must go.'

'No. Wait. I have another little present for you. I arranged it at great expense – it cost me some apple tart time.'

'What?'

'Come.' I led her along by the minister with Sydney now beside us. We turned into the minster courtyard. The pie seller who refused to tell what meat was in his pies was back.

'Can I interest you in a delicious pie? Sirs? Madam?'

Sydney sprang up beside me. 'James, look, it's

that pie man with the special crust.'

'Absolutely not,' I told him.

Sydney tugged on my sleeve. 'Come on. Remember about the crust?'

'A secret recipe, been in my family generations,' the seller said proudly.

Sydney turned to Rose. 'Do you want a pie?'

'There's dog meat in them,' I told her.

Rose looked disgusted. 'That's the surprise? You want to buy me a pie with dog in it?'

'Hey, the meat's unspecified,' the pie seller shouted, but Rose wasn't listening.

'I can't believe you, James. I just can't believe you. This is your surprise. If this is some final insult or a joke, it's just not funny.'

'No, no. Of course not. That's not the surprise.'

'What is it ? A York Minster pinafore?'

'No.'

'No?'

'No.'

She seemed to calm and I led her by the elbow and we all swerved past the pie seller towards home, with just Sydney craning his neck longingly.

'Look.' I pointed.

The fading winter sunlight shone above our little agency, and I smiled at the contrasting expressions that reflected on their faces. One, ever-grinning in boyish joy, the other in complete and utter shock. For, the gold lettering in the window now read: 'Lavender, Brown and

McCarthy'.

AUTHOR'S NOTES

All the characters featured in this story are entirely fictional apart from George and Rosaline Howard (9th Earl/Countess of Carlisle) and their child, Aurea Howard (1884-1972). However, I have largely invented their personalities for the purpose of the story. The earl studied art at Trinity College, Cambridge and was an excellent artist who has many works in public and private galleries including the National Portrait Gallery, the Tate, the British Library and the York Art Gallery.

The earl didn't actually inherit the title until March 1889, when the 8th Earl of Carlisle, William George, died and passed it on to his nephew. For the purpose of this story and the first book, *Lavender and Brown – The York Mysteries*, however, I needed to bring this forward a year so I could include the parallels to the Jack the Ripper murders (as described in the first book), while still having the energy of the 9th Earl for the scenes at Castle Howard estate.

Rosalind Howard (1845-1921), was a promoter of women's political rights and a temperance movement activist. It appears that after an early period of devotion, the couple lived largely apart due in part to differing political leanings and personal differences. She was so fiercely opposed to the consumption of alcohol that she refused to speak to her daughter, Dorothy, after her marriage to Francis Henley, a brewer. She had strained relations with most of her children and friends and suffered ill health throughout her life.

Aurea Howard (1884-1972) was the youngest of eleven children. She married Denyss Chamberlaine Wace in 1923, but the marriage was annulled in 1926. (Wace died in a cafe in 1944 during a German bombing raid.) She later married Major Thomas MacLeod OBE in 1928, and this marriage lasted until his death in 1963.

Fingerprint analysis was in its infancy in 1888. However, it was soon to become central to crime investigation. In 1880 Dr Henry Faulds published an article in 'Nature' exploring the idea of fingerprinting, which was to be expanded in 1892 by Sir Francis Galton (cousin to Charles Darwin) who explored a system of fingerprint identification. In 1901, Sir Edward Henry helped further the use of fingerprint analysis which was then used throughout England. As someone on top of current events in crime detection and interesting theories, James Lavender, I felt, would absolutely be ahead of the curve in looking for the very latest in theory and technology in his pursuit of crime detection. At the very least, it would supply him with something interesting to read while sat outside Boaters enjoying one of Adam's cakes.

All the public houses mentioned in the story are real and would have been functioning to the best of my knowledge at the time the story is set.

Boaters is fictional, though a café now stands in the place where Boaters is described.

James Lavender's rented property is based on two properties on High Petergate. One of them is available as a holiday let, and the other is an old cafe which currently stands empty.

ACKNOWLEDGEMENTS

Thanks for Emma for an amazing cover design once again. Special thanks once again to Megan C for proofreading and editing so well. Sally Davidson for the massive job of editing in the first instance - a bottle of special apple juice is heading your way! Thanks once again for my family for reading the early drafts and offering vital feedback, especially my wife who gets to read the same pages over and over again at all of its various stages!

ABOUT THE AUTHOR

John Neely

Thank you for reading Lavender and Brown! This series has been hard work, but also very enjoyable. I am an independent author living in Sheffield who, as well as reading and plotting for Lavender and Brown, likes sitting in the sun with a cold beer. If you would like to contact me, then I would love to hear from you and your thoughts on the series. You can do so via the Lavender and Brown website - lavenderandbrown.com.

As an indie author, I have no publishing or marketing team. It's just me! I rely on word of mouth from good people like you to spread the craziness of Lavender and Brown. Please take the time to rate or review on Amazon and Goodreads. It really helps.

Thank you.

BOOKS BY THIS AUTHOR

Lavender And Brown – The York Mysteries

Welcome to the crazy world of Lavender and Brown!

Meet James Lavender:

Being able to tell when people are lying must be the ideal gift for the private detective. Well, not if your name is James Lavender – lazy, self-entitled, impossible to deal with; and they're not even his worst qualities!

Meet Sydney Brown:

James' beleaguered pie-and-pint-loving business partner. He's the only person in the world who knows James' secret. He's honest, trustworthy, and thick-skinned – well, he has to be!

Meet Rose McCarthy:

A beautiful actress and pushy apprentice figure who walks into their detective agency requesting a job. James is not going to stand for that, is he?

Meet Mrs Wilkins:

James Lavender's poor housekeeper. Don't worry, she gives as much as she takes. Whether it's throwing mops or shoes at her uncaring employer. She always wins in the end.

The plot?
Oh, didn't you hear? The Lavender and Brown detective agency stands on the edge of bankruptcy. Surely, the small matter of a missing gardener's not going to prevent that, is it?

Set in the year 1888 in the historic city of York. It's a satisfying whodunnit mystery series, featuring a host of riotous characters and farcical comic situations. Let the chaos begin!

Lavender And Brown – York Shorts

The perfect introduction to the crazy world of Lavender and Brown. The chaotic mystery comedy series set in York in 1888.

The Midnight Potato Thief

Follow James Lavender and Sydney Brown on their very first case – in The Midnight Potato Thief! Someone is stealing potatoes (and other food products) in the middle of the night and leaving little notes. No, it's not exactly what James expected when setting up a detective business at all, but can they solve the mystery?

The York Treasure Hunt

Join James Lavender and Sydney Brown as they race against time to track down the loot against the devious criminal, Bill Weatherall. You can play along too. Simply find the interactive map of York from 1852 and join them on their adventures.

Mrs Digby's Cat

Oh, dear. Things have not been progressing very well for James Lavender and Sydney Brown when they are left looking for crazy lady's cat. And what about the card game? Surely, nothing can go wrong on that front with James' ability to spot lies, can it?

Printed in Great Britain
by Amazon